Elihu Burritt

Ten-Minute Talks on All Sorts of Topics

Elihu Burritt

Ten-Minute Talks on All Sorts of Topics

ISBN/EAN: 9783337848903

Printed in Europe, USA, Canada, Australia, Japan

Cover: Foto ©Andreas Hilbeck / pixelio.de

More available books at **www.hansebooks.com**

TEN–MINUTE TALKS

ON

ALL SORTS OF TOPICS.

By ELIHU BURRITT.

WITH

AUTOBIOGRAPHY OF THE AUTHOR.

BOSTON:
LEE AND SHEPARD, PUBLISHERS.
NEW YORK:
LEE, SHEPARD AND DILLINGHAM.
1874.

PREFACE.

A few words of preface or explanation may be proper and expected in regard to the character and object of this volume. Almost a generation has passed since the last book of the author was issued in this country. None of the dozen volumes which he wrote in England in this interval have been republished here, or have had any considerable circulation in the United States. About twenty-five years ago a small volume, containing some of his earliest writings, and called "Sparks from the Anvil," was received with much favor by the public, and had a pretty wide reading. The book herewith given to the public contains a selection of short papers on a larger variety of topics, and written mostly in England for a little monthly edited by the author, together with several articles contributed to the press in this country since his return from Europe. He has thought that some of the readers of his earliest productions might be interested in seeing his later views and sentiments on similar and other questions. As his first book, published in this country twenty-five years ago, must have been long out of print or out of circulation, he has been all the more encouraged to put forth this volume, which will make its readers acquainted with the spirit, object, and variety of his later productions. Only two or three of them on the same topic are here given, but if the reception of this series should warrant it, a second will probably be issued.

As the author has been connected with movements that have brought him before the public at home and abroad in past years, and as many incorrect statements in regard to his life and labors have been published in periodicals and in biographical works, he has felt it a duty he owed to the public to present the leading facts in his personal history, as if written by a third person who was well acquainted with them. If they shall be of any use to young men starting in the world under similar circumstances, it will repay him well for the reluctance he overcame in presenting such personal matters to the public.

If this volume, therefore, shall be favorably received for the sentiments, opinions, and facts it puts forth on a considerable variety of topics, the author will be specially gratified to be thus readmitted into the goodly fellowship of American writers.

E. B.

New Britain, Conn., Oct. 21, 1873.

CONTENTS.

———◦◦◦———

SOCIAL AND ARTISTIC SCIENCE.

INDUSTRIAL AND FINANCIAL QUESTIONS.

POLITICAL QUESTIONS.

NATIONAL AND INTERNATIONAL QUESTIONS.

AUTOBIOGRAPHY.

TEN-MINUTE TALKS.

AUTOBIOGRAPHY OF THE AUTHOR.

Elihu Burritt, the third of that name, was born in New Britain, Connecticut, December 8, 1810, and was the youngest son in a family of ten children, numbering five sons and five daughters. The first of the name, or the remotest traceable ancestor of the American branch of the family, was William Burritt, who came from Glamorganshire, and settled down in Stratford, Connecticut, and died there in 1651. At the beginning of the American Revolution his descendants took different sides. One branch left New England and went to Canada, with other loyalists, and fought for the British crown; the other families threw themselves with equal devotion into the American struggle for independence. Elihu Burritt, the grandfather, at forty-five, and Elihu, the father of the subject of this notice, at sixteen years of age, shouldered muskets in that long war. For thirty years and more after the close of the Revolutionary War, the little, hard-soiled townships of New England were peopled by small farmers, owning from ten to one hundred and fifty acres.

9

The few mechanics among them — the carpenters, black-smiths, and shoemakers — were also farmers during the summer months. Indeed, in those months every man and boy was wielding plough, hoe, sickle, or scythe, in-cluding the minister, who generally owned and tilled the best farm in the parish. The father of Elihu Burritt was one of these farmer mechanics, plying the shoemaker's hammer and awl during winter weeks and rainy days, and the hoe and sickle in summer. His son adopted and followed a wider diversity of occupation, and could say at fifty that no man in America had handled more tools in manual labor than himself. Soon after the death of his father, in 1828, he apprenticed himself to a blacksmith in New Britain, and followed that occupa-tion for several years. Having lost a winter's school-ing at sixteen, in consequence of the long illness of his father, he resolved to make up the loss at twenty-one, by attending for a quarter the boarding-school his elder brother, Elijah Hinsdale Burritt, had established in his native village. As every day he was absent from the anvil cost him a dollar in the loss of wages, his earnest desire for more learning was quickened by the expense of each day's acquisition. He gave himself almost en-tirely to mathematics, for which he had a natural taste, aspiring only to the ability of being an accurate surveyor. Before leaving the anvil for this quarter's study, he was in the habit of practising on problems of mental arith-metic, which he extemporized and solved while blowing the bellows. They were rather quaint in their terms, but quite effective as an exercise. One was, How many barley-corns, at three to the inch, will it take to go

around the earth at the equator? All these figures he
had to carry in his head while heating and hammering
an iron. From this he was wont to go on to higher and
quainter problems; as, for example, How many yards
of cloth, three feet in width, cut into strips an inch wide,
and allowing half an inch at each end for the lap, would
it require to reach from the centre of the sun to the centre of the earth, and how much would it all cost at a
shilling a yard? He would not allow himself to make
a single figure with chalk or charcoal in working out this
problem, and he would carry home to his brother all the
multiplications in his head, and give them off to him and
his assistant, who took them down on their slates, and
verified and proved each separate calculation, and found
the final result to be correct. It was these mental exercises, and the encouragement he received from his
brother, a mathematician and astronomer of much eminence, that induced him to give up three months, at
twenty-one, to a quarter's study. During this term he
devoted himself almost entirely to mathematics, giving a
few half hours and corner moments to Latin and French.
At the end of the term he returned to the anvil, and endeavored to perform double labor for six months, in
order to make up the time lost, pecuniarily, in study.
In this period, however, he found he could pursue the
study of languages more conveniently than that of mathematics, as he could carry a small Greek Grammar in his
hat, and con over τυπτω, τυπτεις, τυπτει, &c., while at
work. In the mean time he gave his evening, noon,
and morning hours to Latin and French, and began to
conceive a lively interest in the study of languages,

partially stimulated by the family relations and resem-
blances between them.

Without any very definite hope or expectation as to
the practical advantage of such studies, he resolved to
risk another three months in pursuing them.   So, at the
beginning of the following winter, he went to New Haven merely to reside and study in the atmosphere of
Yale College ; thinking that that alone, without teachers,
would impart an ability which he could not acquire at
home.   Besides, being then naturally timid, and also
half ashamed to ask instruction in the rudiments of
Greek and Hebrew at twenty-two years of age, he determined to work his way without consulting any college
professor or tutor.   So, the first morning in New Haven
he sat down to Homer's Iliad, without note or comment,
and with a Greek Lexicon with Latin definitions.   He
had not, as yet, read a line in the book, and he resolved
if he could make out two by hard study through the whole
day, he would never ask help of any man thereafter in
mastering the Greek language.   By the middle of the afternoon he won a victory which made him feel strong and
proud, and which greatly affected his subsequent life and
pursuits.   He mastered the first fifteen lines of the book,
and committed the originals to memory, and walked out
among the classic trees of the Elm City, and looked up
at the colleges, which once had half awed him, with a
kind of defiant feeling.   He now divided the hours of
each day between Greek and other languages, including
Latin, French, Spanish, Italian, German, and Hebrew,
giving to Homer about half the time.

Having given the winter to these studies, he returned

to New Britain with a quickened relish for such pursuits
and a desire to turn them to practical account. In this
he succeeded so far as to obtain the preceptorship of an
academy in a neighboring town, in which he taught for
a year the languages and other branches he had acquired.
This change from a life of manual labor, with close application to study, seriously affected his health ; so, at the
end of the year's teaching, he accepted the occupation
of a commercial traveller for a manufacturer in New
Britain, and followed it for a considerable time. He
now, at the wish of his relatives, concluded to settle
down to a permanent residence and business in his native
village. In the wide choice and change of occupation
for which New England men are inclined and accustomed,
he set up a grocery and provision store, unfortunately
just before the great commercial crash of 1837, which
swept over the whole country, and paralyzed business,
and even property of all kinds. He was involved in the
general break-down, and experienced a misfortune which,
for the time, was grievous to him, but without which he
would have left no history worth writing or reading.
Having lost his little all of property by this misfortune,
he resolved to start again in life from a new stand-point,
or scene of labor. He consequently started on foot and
walked all the way to Boston, hoping not only to find
employment at his old occupation, but also increased facilities for pursuing those studies which his recent and
unfortunate business enterprise had interrupted. Not
finding what he sought in Boston, he turned his steps to
Worcester, where he realized his wishes to a very satisfactory extent. He not only obtained ready employment

at the anvil, but also access to the large and rare library of the Antiquarian Society, containing a great variety of books in different languages. He now divided the hours of the day very systematically between labor and study, recording in a daily journal the occupation of each. When the work at his trade became slack, or when, by extra labor at piece-work, he could spend more hours at the library, he was able to give more time to his study of the languages. Here he found and translated all the Icelandic Sagas relating to the discovery of North America; also the epistles written by the Samaritans of Nablous to savants of Oxford. Among other books to which he had free access were a Celto-Breton Dictionary and Grammar, to which he applied himself with great interest. And without knowing where in the Dictionary to look for the words he needed, he addressed himself to the work of writing a letter, in that unique language, to the Royal Antiquarian Society of France, thanking them for the means of becoming acquainted with the original tongue of Brittany. In the course of a few months, a large volume, bearing the seal of that society, was delivered to him at the anvil, containing his letter in Celto-Breton, with an introduction by M. Audren de Kerdrel, testifying to its correctness of composition. The original letter is deposited in the Museum of Rennes, in Brittany, and is the first and only one written in America in the Celto-Breton language. It bears the date of August 12, 1838.

Having made himself more or less acquainted with all the languages of Europe, and several of Asia, including Hebrew, Syriac, Chaldaic, Samaritan, and Ethiopic, he felt desirous of turning these studies to some practical account. He accordingly addressed a letter to William Lincoln, Esq., Worcester, who had been very friendly to him, alluding to his tastes and pursuits, and asking him if there was not some German work which he might translate, for which he might derive some compensation. A few days afterwards, he was dumfounded and almost overwhelmed with confusion on seeing his letter to Mr. Lincoln published in full in a Boston newspaper. Mr. Lincoln had sent it to Governor Everett, who had read it in the course of a speech he had made before a Mechanics' Institute ; and the author felt as if smitten with a great shame by the sudden notoriety which this unexpected publicity put upon him. His first idea was, not to go back to his lodgings to take a garment, but to change his name, and abscond to some back town in the country, and hide himself from the kind of fame he apprehended. But after a few days he found himself less embarrassed than he anticipated by this premature publicity, though he received many kind expressions of friendly interest from different and distant quarters. Governor Everett invited him to dine with him in Boston, and offered him, on the part of several wealthy and generous citizens, all the advantages which Harvard University could afford. These, however, he declined, with grateful appreciation of the offer, preferring, both for his health and other considerations, to continue his studies in connection with manual labor.

The following winter, 1841, he was invited to appear before the public as a lecturer, perhaps mostly out of a mere curiosity to see and hear " the Learned Blacksmith," as he had come to be called. He accordingly wrote up a lecture, trying to prove that *Nascitur, non fit,* was false ; that there was no native genius, but that all attainments were the result of persistent will and application. He drew this argument from his own experience, as certainly his taste for languages had come from no inborn predilection, tendency, or ability, but had been purely and simply a contracted or acquired appetite. In this lecture he employed, as an illustration of intellectual achievements under pressure of strong motives, the story of the boy climbing the Natural Bridge in Virginia, a description which has been widely read, and which deeply impressed the audiences he addressed in New York, Philadelphia, Baltimore, Richmond, and other cities and towns north and south. In the course of one season he delivered this lecture about sixty times, and he had reason to believe it was useful to many young men starting in life in circumstances similar to his own. At the end of the lecture season he returned to the anvil in Worcester, and prosecuted his studies and manual labors in the old way, managing to write a new lecture in the interval for the following winter.

Before he appeared in public as a lecturer, he had tried his hand for a year at editing a little monthly magazine, which he called " The Literary Geminæ," half of which was made up of selections in French, and the other half was filled with articles and translations from his own pen. Its circulation was too limited to sustain its expense, so that it was discontinued at the end of the year. But new subjects of interest now supervened to change the whole course of his thoughts, life, and labor. The

Anti-Slavery movement had now assumed an aspect and an impulse that began to agitate the public mind and political parties. The subject of this notice began to feel that there was an earnest, honest, living speech to be uttered for human right, justice, and freedom, as well as dead languages to be studied mostly for literary recreation. About the same time, his mind became suddenly and deeply interested in a new field of philanthropic thought and effort. Indeed, apparently a slight incident shaped the course which led to all his labors in Europe. He had sat down to write a kind of scientific lecture on The Anatomy of the Earth, trying to show the analogies between it and the anatomy of the human body; how near akin in functions to our veins, muscles, blood, and bones, were the rivers, seas, mountains, and arable soils of the globe we inhabit. Before he had written three pages, he became deeply impressed by the arrangements of nature for producing such different climates, soils, and articles of sustenance and luxury in countries lying precisely under the same sun, and within the same parallels of latitude around the globe. He was especially struck at the remarkable difference between Great Britain and Labrador, lying within the same belt, and washed by the same sea. It seemed the clearest and strongest proof that this arrangement of nature was designed to bind nation to nation, lying even in the same latitudes, by the difference and the necessity of each other's productions; that it contained a natural bond of peace and good neighborhood between them. He was so much impressed by this evident provision of nature, that he gave up the treatment of the subject which he had

2

planned, and made a real, radical peace lecture of it.
The place and occasion of its first delivery were interesting and unique. A Baptist society or church had just
bought at auction the celebrated Tremont Theatre in
Boston, and they decided to have a course of lectures
delivered on "the boards" before the building was al-
tered for a place of worship. "The Learned Blacksmith" was invited to deliver this course, and he made
his first appearance on the stage of a theatre with his
new lecture on peace. He had never read a page of the
writings of Worcester or Ladd on the subject, nor had
he had any conversation or acquaintance with any of the
advocates of the cause. But several of these were present in the large audience, and, at the end of the lecture,
came forward and expressed much satisfaction at the
views presented, and at the acquisition to their ranks of
a new and unexpected co-worker ; who, for the next thirty
years, gave himself to the advocacy of the cause so dear
to them.

On returning to Worcester, Mr. Burritt decided to
forego and suspend studies which had been to him more
the luxuries than the necessaries of a useful life. He
accordingly started a weekly paper, called "The Christian Citizen," devoted to the Anti-Slavery cause, Peace,
Temperance, Self-cultivation, &c. The circulation was
not large, but scattered through all the northern states,
and it acquired a pretty large circle of sympathetic readers. It was the first newspaper in America that devoted
a considerable portion of its space to the advocacy of the
cause of peace ; and it awakened an interest in it in the
minds of hundreds who had not before given thought to

the subject. The editor's own mind became more and more deeply engaged in the cause, and, to bring it before the public more widely, he set on foot a little operation, which he called "The Olive Leaf Mission." He wrote a short article, of about the length of a third of a column of a common newspaper, and printed it on a small slip of paper, surmounted by a dove with an olive leaf in its bill. He sent out at first a dozen copies of this olive leaf to as many papers, on trial, and was delighted to see it inserted in nearly half of them. He was thus encouraged to increase the number from month to month, until he at last sent out a thousand to as many papers all over the Union, two hundred of which gave them insertion. While he was carrying on this operation through the press, the "Oregon Question" came up, and assumed a very serious aspect, threatening an actual rupture between the United States and England. A few earnest men in Manchester, alarmed at the tendency and animus of the controversy, endeavored to arrest both by a special and unprecedented effort. They resolved that the newspapers and political speakers in the two countries should not hold the issues of peace and war entirely in their own hands. One of their number, Joseph Crosfield, a meek, earnest, clear-minded Quaker of Manchester, originated the expedient adopted. It afterwards took the name of "Friendly International Addresses;" or manuscript letters from English towns, signed by its leading inhabitants, and addressed to the citizens of American towns, expressing an earnest desire for an amicable settlement of the controversy, and entreating their co-operation in bringing it about. These friendly addresses from

England were forwarded to Mr. Burritt, and by him to their respective destinations. He also had copies of them made into Olive Leaves, and sent' to all the newspapers in the United States. Two of them he took in person to Philadelphia and Washington. The latter address was from Edinburgh, and bore the names of Dr. Chalmers, Professor Wilson, and other distinguished men of that city. This he showed to Mr. Calhoun, who read the address, and looked at the signatures with much interest. He cordially approved of the expression of such sentiments in direct communications between the people of one country and the citizens of another, on questions of such vital importance to both, and he promised to do what he could to effect an amicable arrangement of the existing difficulty.

In consequence of his co-operation in this movement, and of his correspondence with the English friends who originated it, Mr. Burritt sailed for England in May, 1846, on the steamer that carried out the news of the settlement of the Oregon Question. He proposed to be absent only three months, with the intention of making a foot-tour through the kingdom. But the openings for labor in the peace cause that presented themselves on his arrival, induced him to prolong his sojourn in England three years; during which, with the help of a devoted associate in Worcester, he still carried on " The Christian Citizen " in that town. A few weeks after he first met his English friends in Manchester and Birmingham, with their entire sympathy and support, he developed the basis of an international association, called " The League of Universal Brotherhood," designed not only to work for the abolition of war, but also for the promotion of friendly and fraternal feelings and relations between different countries. The signing of the following pledge constituted any man or woman a member of the association : —

"Believing all war to be inconsistent with the spirit of Christianity and destructive of the best interests of mankind, I do hereby pledge myself never to enlist or enter into any army or navy, or to yield any voluntary support or sanction to any war, by whomsoever or for whatsoever proposed, declared, or waged. And I do hereby associate myself with all persons, of whatever country, color, or condition, who have signed, or shall hereafter sign, this pledge, in a League of Universal Brotherhood, whose object shall be, to employ all legitimate and moral means for the abolition of all war, and all the spirit and manifestations of war throughout the world; for the abolition of all restrictions upon international correspondence and friendly intercourse, and of whatever else tends to make enemies of nations, or prevents their fusion into one peaceful brotherhood; for the abolition of all institutions and customs which do not recognize and respect the image of God and a human brother in every man, of whatever clime, color, or condition of humanity."

This basis of association presented a broad foundation for philanthropic labor, embracing objects and operations far beyond those contemplated by Peace Societies proper. To bring these before the public, Mr. Burritt gave up his proposed tour on foot through England, and went up and down the country addressing public meetings and social circles on the subject. Through the most generous aid of Joseph Sturge, of Birmingham, he commenced the publication of "The Bond of Brotherhood" in that town as an exponent of the spirit, principles, and objects of the new association. These commended themselves to a great number of influential persons in all parts of Great Britain. In less than a year several thousand in the United Kingdom had signed the pledge, and an equal number in the United States. The association was formally organized in London, in May, 1847, and took its place among the benevolent societies of the day, and began to work outward to the circumference of its basis of action. One of the first operations it set on foot was one for the abolition of all restrictions upon international correspondence and friendly intercourse. International postage was then almost a crushing restriction upon such intercourse, especially between the hundreds of thousands of Irish and English immigrants in America and their poorer relatives and friends in the mother country. In September, 1847, Mr. Burritt first developed the proposition of a Universal Ocean Penny Postage ; that is, that the single service of transporting a letter across the sea in any direction, or to any distance, should be performed for one penny, or two cents, this charge to be added to the inland rate on each side. Thus the whole charge proposed on a single letter between any town in Great Britain and any town in the United States was to be three pence, or six cents. A very lively and general interest was manifested in this proposition among all classes. In the course of two winters, Mr. Burritt addressed one hundred and fifty public meetings on the subject from Penzance to Aberdeen, and from Cork to Belfast. Hundreds of petitions were presented to Parliament in behalf of the reform, and the movement in its favor was recognized as a popular agitation.

In the winter of 1847 Mr. Burritt visited Ireland, to explore the depth and distress of the Potato Famine, and to describe it, as an American eye-witness, to the people of the United States. He spent four days in Skibbereen, the most distressed district, going from cabin to cabin, and seeing sights of misery and despair that were harrowing and heart-rending. These he described in a small pamphlet entitled "Four Days in Skibbereen," which was published and circulated in England, and also sent, through "The Christian Citizen" at Worcester, to a thousand newspapers in America. This, with an appeal written on the spot, in hearing of the wailings of the famished creatures that surrounded the little inn at night, may have tended to increase the contributions of food and clothing sent from the United States.

A few days after the deposition and flight of Louis Philippe from France, Mr. Burritt went over to Paris to endeavor to prepare the way for a conference of the friends of Peace from different countries in that capital. No meeting of the kind had ever been held on the continent, and as the new *régime* in France had raised, as their banner, "Liberty, Equality, and Fraternity," the opportunity seemed favorable for inaugurating such a movement. After a few weeks' sojourn and conference with men most likely to co-operate in Paris, he returned to England, and visited most of the large towns, with the view of securing delegates to the proposed convention. A considerable number of influential men promised to attend it, if it should be held, and everything for a while promised favorably. But the "Three Days of June" intervened with their deeds of violence and blood. This calamitous event barred the way to the proposed meeting in Paris, so that it was held instead in Brussels, in September, 1848. Here it succeeded beyond the most sanguine expectations of its friends. The Belgian government and authorities did everything that could be asked of them, and more too, to facilitate and recognize the meeting. There were about one hundred and fifty delegates present from Great Britain, many from France, Germany, Holland, and other countries. The sessions lasted three days, and all the discussions and proceedings were conducted and characterized with the best spirit and harmony. An earnest address to the Governments and Peoples of Christendom was adopted and signed by the president and vice-presidents, and presented personally by them, as a deputation, to Lord John Russell, then Prime Minister of England. This address was not only forwarded to all the governments of Europe, but was published in many of the continental journals. The meeting at Brussels, which the English delegates only ventured to call a *conference*, was recognized and denominated a PEACE CONGRESS by both the continental and English press, and it constituted a new and important event in the history of the cause, and gave to it a new impulse and character.

The friends of Peace in England, greatly increased in number, courage, and faith by the demonstration in Brussels, now set on foot more vigorous operations. The League of Universal Brotherhood united with the London

Peace Society in a special effort to press upon the consideration of and adoption by the English Parliament of a motion to be brought forward by Richard Cobden for Stipulated Arbitration, or for special treaties between all the governments of Christendom, by which they should bind themselves to refer to arbitration any question which they could not settle by ordinary negotiation. Rev. Henry Richard, the able and eloquent secretary of the London Peace Society, and Mr. Burritt, as representing the League of Universal Brotherhood, travelled together up and down the kingdom, addressing public meetings in behalf of Mr. Cobden's motion. Other advocates of the cause did the same. A great number of petitions were presented to the House of Commons, and other influences brought to bear upon it in favor of the measure. This was brought forward by Mr. Cobden, before a full house, in a most effective speech, followed by a very animated and important discussion. More than seventy members voted with Mr. Cobden, and this debate and division, at the end of so many public meetings, impressed the idea of Stipulated Arbitration deeply upon the mind of the nation, and in a perceptible degree upon all the governments and peoples of Christendom.

When the movement for Stipulated Arbitration had been brought to this issue, Mr. Richard and Mr. Burritt went upon the Continent to prepare for the Peace Congress which it had been resolved to hold in Paris, in 1849. The way was now clear and free for convening such an assembly. Some of the most able men of France not only gave their adhesion and sympathy, but their generous and active co-operation, to the undertaking. An international committee of arrangements was formed to develope and settle the agenda of the congress, composed of such men as Frederic Bastiat, Victor Hugo, Emile de Girardin, M. de Cormenin, Joseph Garnier, Auguste Visschers, President of the Peace Congress in Brussels, Richard Cobden, and other English members. The French government did all in its power to facilitate the congress and give to it the stamp of its approbation. It admitted the whole English and American delegation without examination of their luggage at the custom-house, and without any other passports than their tickets as members of the congress. It gave them free access, on the presentation of these tickets, to all the Galleries of Paintings, Libraries, and Public Buildings in Paris. As a finishing token of its respect, it directed the fountains of Versailles and St. Cloud to be played for their special entertainment — an honor which hitherto had been paid only to foreign sovereigns visiting Paris. M. de Tocqueville, the Minister of Foreign Affairs, invited all the delegates to his official residence, and showed them the most sympathetic attentions and interest in their philanthropic object. Before the opening of the congress, he had invited Messrs. Richard and Burritt to breakfast with him *en famille*, and had manifested an earnest good-will to the cause they were laboring to promote.

The Peace Congress of 1849, in Paris, was the most remarkable assembly that had ever taken place on the continent of Europe, not only for its objects, but for its personal composition. The English delegation numbered about seven hundred, and were conveyed across the

Channel by two steamers specially chartered for the purpose. They not only represented but headed nearly all
the benevolent societies and movements in Great Britain.
Indeed, Richard Cobden told M. de Tocqueville that if
the two steamers sank with them in the Channel, all the
philanthropic enterprises in the United Kingdom would
be stopped for a year. There were a goodly number of
delegates from the United States, including Hon. Amasa
Walker, of Massachusetts, Hon. Charles Durkee, of Wisconsin, President Mahan, of Oberlin College, President
Allen, of Bowdoin College, and other men of ability.
Nearly all the European countries were represented by
men full of sympathy with the movement. Victor Hugo
was chosen president, and, supported on each side by vice-
presidents of different nations, arose and opened the proceedings with probably the most eloquent and brilliant
speech he ever uttered on any occasion. Emile de
Girardin, Abbé Deguerry, Curé de la Madeleine, the
Cocquerels, father and son, spoke with remarkable power
and effect, as representing the French members; Richard
Cobden, Rev. John Burnet, Henry Vincent, and other
English delegates delivered speeches of the happiest
inspiration; Amasa Walker, President Mahan, Charles
Durkee, and others well represented and expressed
American views and sentiments; and delegates from
Belgium, Holland, and Germany spoke with great earnest-
ness and ability. The congress was continued for three
days, and the interest in its proceedings constantly increased up to the last moment. The closing speech of
Victor Hugo was eloquent and beautiful beyond description. Emile de Girardin said of it, that it did not termi-

nate, but *eternized* the congress. The next day the government gave the great entertainment at Versailles, which was varied by a very pleasant incident. The English members gave the American delegates a public breakfast in the celebrated Tennis Hall, or Salle de Paumes, at Versailles, so connected with the great French Revolution. Richard Cobden presided, and testified to the appreciation, on the part of the English members, of the zeal for the cause of peace shown by their American brethren in crossing the ocean to attend the congress. A French Testament, with a few words of pleasant remembrance signed by himself as chairman of the meeting, was presented to each of them, and which will be doubtless treasured in their families as an interesting souvenir of the occasion.

As at Brussels, an address to the governments and peoples of Christendom was drawn up by Victor Hugo, Richard Cobden, and other members of the Committee on Resolutions. This was presented to Louis Napoleon, then President of the French Republic, by Hugo, Girardin, Cobden, Visschers, and other national representatives. It urged Stipulated Arbitration, Proportionate and Simultaneous Disarmament, and a Congress of Nations, as three measures for abolishing War and organizing Peace between nations. These propositions were pressed upon him very ably and earnestly by the deputation, and they seem to have produced a deep impression upon his mind; for within the last few years he has proposed one or two of these measures to the governments of Europe for the settlement of serious questions, and for the diminution of armaments in time of peace. Several young Frenchmen, who attended the congress as mere boys, were greatly impressed, and when they came to manhood, they organized The League of Universal Peace in Paris, which has become a powerful organization, and the centre and source of other societies for the same object on the Continent. It was at the annual meeting of this League of Peace that the celebrated Father Hyacinthe delivered one of his most eloquent addresses, which has obtained such wide circulation as a model of rhetoric, good sentiment, and logic.

The next Peace Congress was appointed to be held at Frankfort-on-the-Main, and it was determined to make it worthy to follow the great meeting in Paris. Mr. Burritt, having prolonged his sojourn in Europe from three months to three years, returned to the United States with Professor Walker, Hamilton Hill, and other members of the American delegation. On passing through Manchester, he received the following testimonial in reference to his labors for the cause of peace and universal brotherhood, as stated in the Examiner and Times, of that city. It was beautifully engrossed, and enclosed in an elegant mahogany case, and signed in behalf of the meeting by George Wilson, Esq., Chairman of the Anti-Corn Law League.

"At a meeting of the friends of peace, held in the League Rooms, Manchester, October 5, 1849, it was moved by John Bright, Esq., M. P., seconded by Sir Elkanah Armitage, and resolved, unanimously, That the heartfelt thanks of this meeting are due to Elihu Burritt, whose great intellectual powers and high moral faculties, regulated and directed by a deep sense of religious duty, have been devoted, regardless of his own case,

and health, and worldly prospects, to promote the principles of
peace; and whose eloquent utterance, by speech and pen, has
placed before the nations of the earth, in attractive beauty, the
doctrine that war is repugnant to the spirit of the gospel, and
destructive to the best interests of mankind : That its thanks are
especially due for his recent indefatigable and successful labors
to bring together, in the capital of a warlike and powerful nation, a great congress, at which arbitration, instead of war, in the
settlement of disputes between nations, was recommended with
a force of truth and eloquence which could not fail to carry conviction to the millions hitherto looking for no wiser nor better
arbitrament than sanguinary conflict : That, regarding the influence he may continue to exercise in promoting peace on earth
and good will towards men, as the great promised result of
the Christian dispensation, this meeting rejoices that he is now
about to enjoy, in his native land, and among his early friends,
some relaxation from his exhausting labors, and expresses its
ardent hope that he may soon be enabled, re-invigorated in
health, and endued with fresh energy, to resume the good work
in a field of world-wide usefulness to which he has set his
mind."

On arriving in America, Mr. Burritt was welcomed by
the citizens of New Britain with a testimonial of respect
and esteem which he prized above all other public expressions of regard that he ever received.   An assembly
that filled the new Town Hall to overflowing, including
a large number of distinguished persons from Hartford
and other towns, came together to give him this welcome
and token of sympathy and approbation as to his labors
at home and abroad.   The venerable Professor E. A.
Andrews presented to him, on their behalf, the following
address, which was seconded by Hon. J. M. Niles, Dr.
Bushnell, and other gentlemen from Hartford : —

"MR. BURRITT: Your fellow-citizens here assembled have authorized me, as their representative, to express to you their most cordial welcome on your return once more to your native village, and to the scenes and companions of your early life. You will see, sir, in the circle which surrounds you, not a few of those who here commenced life with you, whose childhood was inured to similar toils, who shared in the same active sports, and who daily resorted to the same humble school-room, where your literary ardor, which ever since those days has burned so brightly, was first enkindled. In the name of each of these, and of all your old associates and early friends here present, and, above all, in the name of your fair friends who in such numbers grace this large assemblage, and by whose hands these rooms have been so beautifully adorned for this occasion, I bid you, sir, a hearty welcome, after long absence, to your native land, and to those scenes endeared to you by the memory of kindred and of home. These all, in common with distinguished friends here present from other towns, men to whom our state looks for counsel, and on whom its freemen ever delight to bestow their highest honors, rejoice in this opportunity of manifesting their respect for one who, by eminent success in the pursuit of knowledge, in circumstances of unusual difficulty, has reflected so much honor on his native land. Arduous indeed is that student's path, who, trusting to his own unaided efforts, firmly resolves to win for himself that wreath of fame which, like the crown of Israel's first king, is bestowed on those alone who tower in stature far above the surrounding multitude. Such a path, sir, we have seen you tread; and, with mingled emotions of joy and pride, we now congratulate you upon a success so complete that it may well satisfy the loftiest ambition. We especially rejoice that a literary reputation so well earned is now fully known and recognized, not in our own country only, but equally so in foreign lands.

"But, sir, we would not, in our admiration of intellectual cultivation, forget the still more important culture of the heart. We have witnessed with the highest satisfaction that, while eagerly devoted to the pursuit of knowledge, and while ministering to your own necessities by laboring daily with your own hands, you have cheerfully devoted your. powers and attainments to the task of elevating the social and moral condition of mankind. To do this, and to do it wisely, is the greatest problem of this and of every age — a problem to be solved in no other manner than by following the teachings of unerring Wisdom. Amidst the conflicting views of mankind in relation to the proper means for the attainment of this great end, we can still rest in the assured confidence that the long night of error will at last draw to its close, and the dawn of that better day will beam upon the nations. To co-operate with the plans of Infinite Wisdom in hastening forward this consummation is the proper mission of man. The day, we trust, may even now be near, when organized systems of oppression and violence will vanish away; when the feebler shall find in the more powerful, not oppressors, but friends and protectors; and when the controversies of nations — if such controversies shall then exist — shall be settled, not by violence, but by the eternal principles of justice.

"We are gratified, sir, that your efforts have been directed, with such flattering success, to the means for removing from the minds of men a belief in the necessity of a final appeal to arms in adjusting national disputes. In this enterprise the wise and good of all nations will bid you God speed; and surely the blessing of the Prince of Peace will rest on those who, in imitation of his example, seek to promote 'peace on earth.'

". . . Once more, sir, in the name of my fellow-citizens, and, may I be permitted to add, in my own name also, I bid you a hearty welcome to your native town. We regret that your visit is so brief, but hope that, short as it is, it will serve to impress the conviction still more deeply upon your heart, that whatever honors await you abroad, in the society of the learned and noble of other lands, you can nowhere be regarded with more sincere affection than by the people of this village, and by the circle of the friends by whom you are now surrounded."

Mr. Burritt's response to this and other testimonial addresses may be found in his " Lectures and Speeches."

After a few weeks in Worcester, during which he associated Mr. J. B. Syme, from Edinburgh, with his co-editor, Thomas Drew, in conducting " The Christian Citizen," Mr. Burritt commenced a tour through most of the states of the Union with the view of securing delegates to the Peace Congress at Frankfort. Many of these were appointed at public meetings, and a goodly number engaged to cross the ocean to take part in the proceedings of that new Parliament of the People. In the following May, 1850, he returned to England, and went with Mr. Richard upon the Continent to prepare for the forthcoming congress. They visited nearly all the principal towns in Germany, including Hamburg, Berlin, Dresden, Munich, and Stutgart, and had interviews with many of the most distinguished men in Germany, and obtained their promise of co-operation, or adhesion to the objects of the movement. Among others, they saw the venerable Alexander Von Humboldt, Professor Liebig, Tholuck, Hengstenberg, and other eminent men.

The congress at Frankfort was all its most sanguine friends could have hoped. It was more representative of European countries than the one at Paris. It required two special steamers to convey the English delegates up the Rhine. There were delegates from all the German states, and some from Italy. France was well represented by Emile de Girardin, M. de Cormenin, Joseph Garnier, and others, who had taken part in the Paris congress. Auguste Visschers, President of the Brussels congress, was present and full of earnest activity and zeal. The American delegation was large and influential, including Professor Hitchcock, Rev. E. Chapin, Rev. Dr. Bullard, Rev. E. B. Hull, Rev. Mr. Pennington, and others from different states. Richard Cobden was not only a leading spirit on the platform, but was present several days before the sessions commenced, as a member of the Committee of Organization, and gave his invaluable aid to the preparation of the Resolutions to be presented, discussed, and adopted, which were the most difficult, important, and responsible of all the proceedings. The German members of the committee were most hearty in their co-operation, and the whole population of Frankfort manifested a lively interest in the new and strange Parliament that was to be held in the city of German Emperors. Its place of assembly was specially appropriate. It was the great and venerable St. Paul's Church, in which the Parliament of New Germany assembled in 1848, in the unsuccessful attempt to reconstruct the great Fatherland on a new basis of Union, Freedom, and Fraternity. Herr Jaup, of Darmstadt, was chosen President, Professor Liebig, Richard Cobden, M. de Girardin, Auguste Visschers, and Professor Hitchcock, were some of the Vice-Presidents. The congress lasted three days, and all the proceedings were marked with a harmonious and earnest spirit. The same measures as at Paris were discussed and approved, and an address adopted to the governments and peoples of Christendom, pressing upon their attention these plans for " organizing peace," to use Lamartine's expression.

An incident of peculiar interest occurred at the last session of the congress. A war had already broken out between Schleswig-Holstein and Denmark, upon a question in which all Germany, especially Prussia, was involved. A number of influential men in Berlin desired the congress to express an opinion on the merits of the question, and telegraphed to that effect, asking that a hearing might be given to a commissioner that had been despatched to Frankfort for that purpose. This was Dr. Bodenstedt, a very learned and able man, and earnest partisan of the Schleswig-Holstein cause. But the congress could not entertain the proposition, as it was precluded by one of its fundamental rules from meddling with any local or current question of controversy. But after consultation with Dr. Bodenstedt, it was thought allowable and proper that three members of the congress should go in a voluntary or individual capacity to the belligerent parties, and try to induce them to refer the controversy to arbitration. Consequently, on the return of the English and American delegates from Frankfort, Joseph Sturge, Frederic Wheeler, and Elihu Burritt left them at Cologne, and proceeded to Berlin, where they met Dr. Bodenstedt and his friends, and procured letters of introduction and other directions for their mission. They then proceeded immediately to Kiel, and had an interview with the members of the provisional government, and laid before them the object of their visit. They were well received, and letters were given them to the military authorities of Rendsburg, the headquarters of the army, which was preparing for another battle with the Danes. They repaired to that fortress, and had a long interview with the civil and military chiefs, and submitted to them the simple proposition whether, at that stage of hostilities, they would consent to refer the difficulty to arbitration if the Danish government would do the same. Having fought so long, and feeling able and determined to win their cause by arms, they hesitated as to the form of their consent to the proposition, lest it might indicate weakness; but the deputation put it so conditionally on the corresponding action of the Danes, that they fully acceded to the proposed basis of settlement.

Having obtained the consent of the Schleswig-Holsteiners to refer the question to arbitration, the deputation next proceeded to Copenhagen, and had several interviews with the Danish ministers. Here a difficulty of another nature had to be met and overcome. To submit the question to arbitration was, to a certain or sensible degree, to recognize the Schleswig-Holsteiners as an independent people, on the same national footing as the Danes themselves. The deputation addressed themselves to this difficulty with great earnestness and assiduity. There is no question that the simple eloquence of Joseph Sturge's goodness of heart, and the plea he made with tears moistening and illuminating the beautiful radiance of his benevolent face, impressed the Danish minister more deeply than any mere diplomatic communication could have done. At any rate, the peculiar difficulty involved in the proposed reference was waived, and the Danish government consented to the preliminary steps to arbitration. The foreign minister nominated a distinguished civilian to be put in correspondence with some one chosen to the same position by the Schleswig-Holstein authorities; and the deputation left Copenhagen, feeling that one stage towards the settlement of an aggravated question had been accomplished. They again proceeded to Kiel, and announced the result of their mission to Denmark, and a gentleman of great ability and judgment was appointed to be the medium of communication with the gentleman appointed by the Danes. Messrs. Sturge and Wheeler now returned to England, leaving Mr. Burritt to conduct the correspondence necessary to the gradual induction of direct negotiation between the two parties to the dispute. He remained three months in Hamburg for this purpose, and had considerable correspondence with the Danish authorities on the subject. But just as the negotiations seemed on the point of effecting a settlement by arbitration, the Austrians marched into Schleswig-Holstein, and sprung a judgment upon the case, and closed it summarily. The effort, however, to settle the question by arbitration, even when the parties were at open war, evidently made a favorable impression upon the public mind, and it would probably have succeeded had it not been interrupted by forcible interference.

While Mr. Burritt was in Hamburg, he originated a quiet scheme of operations for bringing the spirit, principles, and objects of the Peace movement before the masses of the people of the Continent of Europe. This was the revival or application of the Olive Leaf system which he had set on foot in the United States. He first arranged with a newspaper of large circulation in Paris, to insert, once a month, about a column and a half of matter, made up of short articles and paragraphs from such writers as Erasmus, Robert Hall, Dr. Chalmers,

Cobden, Channing, Worcester, Ladd, and other distinguished authorities. This was called "An Olive Leaf for the People." The French paper charged one hundred francs for each Olive Leaf inserted; but for this sum it not only printed but circulated all over France thirty thousand copies monthly, and that, too, with the virtual commendation, as well as responsibility, of the editor, effecting a work of enlightenment which could not have been accomplished for five hundred dollars through the medium of tracts, even if their distribution had been allowed. The plan worked so well in France, that Mr. Burritt entered into arrangements with the leading journals in Germany and other continental countries for the monthly publication of an Olive Leaf of the same character. The conductors of these journals were willing to make liberal terms for the insertion, partly out of sympathy with the matter, and partly because it was put among the selections made by the editor, and did not occupy any space given to paid advertisements. The average price of each insertion in these German, Dutch, Danish, and Italian journals was about six dollars. To make this operation the more effective, it was desirable and necessary that it should be conducted very quietly; that its very origin and support should be virtually concealed from the readers of the Olive Leaves, that they might receive them as from their own ·editors, and not know that their insertion was paid for. On returning to England in the spring of 1851, the League of Universal Brotherhood, of which Mr. Edmund Fry, a most indefatigable worker, had become the secretary, resumed its independent field of labor, embracing two special operations. The first was the agitation for an Ocean Penny Postage, the other, "The Olive Leaf Mission," as just described. Up to this time the ladies of Great Britain had never been especially enlisted in any department of the Peace movement. The Olive Leaf Mission seemed to present a very appropriate and effective enterprise for them. Consequently it was resolved to commend it to their adoption by a special effort. Mr. Burritt, therefore, in visiting all the principal towns in England, Scotland, and Ireland, for the purpose of addressing meetings in behalf of Ocean Penny Postage, generally met, in the afternoon of the same day, a company of ladies of all denominations, at a private house, and explained to them the Olive Leaf Mission, and how easily and quietly they might operate through it upon the public mind in foreign countries. In almost every case, after such an explanation, the ladies formed themselves into an association, which was called an "Olive Leaf Society," which met once a month, corresponded with similar societies, and raised a certain amount to pay for the insertion of the Olive Leaves in Continental journals. In the course of two years, over one hundred of these ladies' societies were organized, as the result of these interviews and explanations, and they sustained the whole expense of the mission, which was about two thousand dollars a year. The Olive Leaves were translated into seven different languages, and published monthly, in more than forty different journals, from Copenhagen to Vienna, and from Madrid to Stockholm. Thus several millions of minds in all those countries were kept continuously under the dropping of ideas, facts, and doctrines which fell upon them as quietly as the dews of heaven.

The Peace Congress of 1851 was held in Exeter Hall, London, during the Great Exhibition, under the most auspicious impulses and tendencies of the universal mind of Christendom. Peace and the brotherhood of nations seemed to be the watchwords of popular hope and faith. These pleasant words of greeting festooned the streets of London, and, as it were, gilded the Crystal Palace itself. As it was expected, the assembly in Exeter Hall was the largest and most influential Peace Congress that had been held. There were full two thousand present, and about two hundred ministers of different denominations sat upon the platform. The venerable Sir David Brewster, LL. D. presided, and opened the proceedings with a most impressive speech. Richard Cobden and other eminent Englishmen spoke with great power. France, Germany, and Belgium were ably represented by members whose speeches were earnest and effective. Rev. Dr. Beckwith, Secretary of the American Peace Society, and Mr. Burritt, made the principal speeches as delegates from the United States. A beautiful spirit of fraternal unanimity pervaded the proceedings of the congress, and no one who took part in them will be likely to forget the occasion as long as he lives.

The following year, 1852, was marked by an event which made it desirable, and even necessary, that the Peace Congress should again be held in England. This event was the *coup d'état*, which suddenly transformed the French Republic into the Second Empire. The friends of Peace, therefore, met at Manchester; but though it was a very satisfactory meeting, and well attended, it was far more English or national in its composition than the previous congresses had been. The sudden and violent act of Louis Napoleon produced a profound and angry sensation in England and other countries. It aroused a wide-spread and energetic indignation in the English press and Parliament, and seemed to excite and inflame the old hereditary suspicion and prejudice towards the French nation as well as government. The French press was held back by severe restriction; but if full liberty for recrimination had been allowed it, the two nations would have been in imminent danger of drifting into war. As it was, that danger was very serious. Leading English journals and public men wrote and spoke with that unrestricted expression of sentiment so characteristic of the English mind and habits. The League of Universal Brotherhood resolved to try the plan of friendly international addresses, as a counteracting influence against this rising tide of hostile sentiment. Through their instrumentality, over fifty of the largest towns in Great Britain sent manuscript letters or addresses to as many different towns in France, disclaiming all sympathy with the unfriendly sentiments expressed by public journals and speakers, and conveying to their French brethren their hearty good-will and assurances of esteem and inviting their earnest co-operation in preserving and strengthening amicable relations between the two countries. London, Edinburgh, Glasgow, and Dublin addressed such communications to Paris, Manchester to Marseilles, Liverpool to Lyons, Birmingham to Bordeaux,

Bristol to Brest, Leeds to Lisle, Sheffield to Strasburg, &c. Most of these addresses were signed by the mayors and other authorities of the towns, and by a large number of their principal citizens. The one from Glasgow bore four thousand names, including the city authorities, members of Parliament, the heads of the University, and other influential persons. Mr. Burritt was the bearer of these addresses, and travelled over most of France to present them in person to the proper authorities. He also made copies of every address for all the journals of the town, and waited upon their editors to obtain insertion of them, which was always accompanied with a favorable introduction. Thus the whole French nation were made acquainted with the real sentiment of the English people towards them, which English newspapers and political speeches had greatly misrepresented. The effect or result of this movement cannot be ascertained, but it so happened within a year that England and France were united, as they never had been before, in a great and perilous enterprise, and were seen marching shoulder to shoulder in the Crimean War.

The Peace Congress of 1853 was held in Edinburgh, and was marked with several special characteristics. One of these was the presence of John Bright, who had never before attended one of these great meetings. Here he sat beside his old *confrère* in reforms, Richard Cobden, and the two men spoke for peace with their old inspiration in the Anti-Corn-Law agitation. Another incident of peculiar interest was the presence on the platform of the veteran and celebrated admiral, Sir Charles Napier, who made a vigorous speech, claiming himself to be as good an advocate of peace as the best of them, although he would put down war by war. Cobden's answer to his arguments was a masterly effort of reasoning power. Dr. Guthrie, and other eminent men of Edinburgh, took a part in the proceedings, and the meeting was regarded as one of the most successful of the series.

Immediately after the Edinburgh Congress, Mr. Burritt returned to the United States, and gave himself entirely to the Ocean Penny Postage agitation. He addressed public meetings on the subject in many of the considerable towns, and also had the opportunity of laying it before members of the legislatures of Massachusetts, Maine, and Rhode Island. A committee was formed in Boston to sustain and guide the movement, of which Dr. S. G. Howe was chairman. Having addressed many public meetings on the question in different states, Mr. Burritt spent three months in Washington, seeking to enlist members of Congress in behalf of the reform. The chairman of the postal committee, Senator Rush, was quite favorable to it; and at his request Mr. Burritt drew up a report for the committee to adopt, presenting the main facts and arguments to be urged upon the attention of Congress. Hon. Charles Sumner agreed to bring forward the proposition, and Senators Douglas, Cass, and others on the Democratic side of the house, promised to support it. The Nebraska Bill, however, blocked the way from week to week, and as the postponement was likely to be prolonged, Mr. Burritt made a tour through Southern and Western States to enlist an interest in those sections. He visited Richmond, Petersburg, Wilmington, Charleston, Augusta, Macon, Milledgeville, and other southern cities, in several of which he presented the subject at public meetings, and personally canvassed for signatures to petitions to Congress in behalf of the reform in all of them. And it is an interesting fact, that the first and only petitions from Charleston and other southern centres for an object of national interest were presented by Senators Mason, Badger, Butler, and Toombs, for Ocean Penny Postage. From Chicago, on his return journey, Mr. Burritt passed through Canada, and obtained petitions to the British Parliament in Toronto, London, Hamilton, and other towns.

In August, 1854, Mr. Burritt returned to England, and confined his labors principally to the Ocean Penny Postage question, still conducting the Olive Leaf Mission on the Continent. The League of Brotherhood now concentrated its efforts upon these two movements. Under its auspices an Ocean Penny Postage bazaar was held in Manchester, which supplied funds for more extended operations. A wide-spread and active interest was awakened in the subject, which resulted in a deputation of more than two hundred influential men to Lord Aberdeen, to urge upon the government the most forcible considerations in favor of the reform. The venerable Sir John Burgoyne, and many influential members of Parliament, and leading men from all parts of the kingdom, formed the deputation. In the mean time, a large number of petitions were presented daily in the House of Commons, where Right Hon. T. M. Gibson had undertaken to bring forward the proposition, and Hon. C. B. Adderley, from the conservative side of the house, was to second the motion. Mr. Burritt went to Holland and Prussia, and had interviews with cabinet ministers of those countries, with the view of obtaining their co-operation, at least to this extent — that if England and the United States reduced the ocean rate to a penny, they should engage to reduce their inland charge on letters crossing the sea to one penny. Under the pressure of all this public interest in the question, the English government reduced its postal charges to India, Australia, Canada, and to all its other colonies, to six pence for a single letter, and to four pence to France. This was full one half of what was sought in the agitation, and as the government intimated a willingness to go farther after trying the experiment, the movement was virtually closed, as the main argument on which it rested had been met. A long delay attended the second instalment, so that an Ocean Penny Postage between England and the United States and other countries was not fully realized until 1870.

A war had now broken out and was raging between the Allied Powers and Russia. The Peace movement, in its special operations, was arrested. The antagonism between Slavery and Freedom in America was becoming more and more threatening to the peace of the nation. Mr. Burritt, with the hope of doing a little towards the pacific and equitable solution of this perilous question, assumed, while in London, the editorship of a small monthly periodical in Philadelphia, called "The Citizen of the World," published by G. W. Taylor. In this he advocated the proposition of Compensated Emancipation, to be defrayed by the whole nation out of the proceeds of the Public Lands, to be devoted exclusively to this purpose. After a year's sojourn in England, he returned to America, and gave himself for several winters to the advocacy of this plan of abolishing slavery; residing in summer, and working on a small farm he had purchased, in New Britain. Here also he started a weekly paper, called "The North and South," which had a considerable circulation in both sections, and which he devoted mainly to the proposed measure. In the course of his advocacy, he addressed public meetings in almost every considerable town and village from Castine in Maine to Iowa City, travelling nearly ten thousand miles for this purpose in one winter. In all these meetings he put the proposition to vote, and on an average, full two thirds of all present raised their hands in its favor. Having presented the subject in this way to the public, and there being as yet no organized association to support the movement, he endeavored to get up a national convention for that object. He therefore sent out a form of call for such a convention, which received the signatures of nearly a thousand influential men from all the Free States, and from some of the Southern also. The convention was held in Cleveland, Ohio, in August, 1856, when a goodly number of delegates assembled from various parts of the country. Dr. Mark Hopkins, of Williams College, Mass., was chosen President. Gerrit Smith and other earnest anti-slavery men took part in the proceedings. Resolutions in favor of the scheme were adopted, and a society called The National Compensated Emancipation Society was organized, with the venerable Dr. Eliphalet Nott as President, Dr. Hopkins, Governor Fairchild, of Vermont, and other influential men of different states, were chosen Vice-Presidents, and Mr. Burritt Secretary. Gerrit Smith gave one hundred dollars, and J. D. Williams, of Ithaca, fifty dollars on the spot to start the society; and a few weeks afterwards, Mr. Burritt went to New York to open an office and act as Secretary of the new association. In this capacity he labored to get up state conventions in favor of Compensated Emancipation, and these were held successively in several different states. He also plied the newspapers with short articles and paragraphs on the subject, and a very promising and increasing interest began to manifest itself in this peaceful and fraternal way of removing the great incubus and evil pressing so heavily and dangerously on the nation's life and character. Some of the papers in the Southern States published several of these short articles, especially one giving the amount which each state would receive for the emancipation of its slaves. Several of these southern journals began to discuss the proposition in a way that was best calculated to commend it to the consideration of the southern mind; for they based their objections to it, as if intentionally, on the weakest grounds, or on premises of their own adoption. One of the first of these was, that the Northern States never could be brought to put their hands in their own pockets to such an extent, or to give up their portion of the public domain to the extinction of slavery; that they would insist upon saving their pockets and their consciences by putting the whole burden of the system and its abolition upon the South; that their only plan was to kill Slavery by hedging it within an area which would become too small for it to breathe and live in, and where

it must die of plethora ; that the slaves would impoverish
the land as they increased in number, and both would
become worthless in some not very remote future ; that
the system would thus be stifled under a general bankruptcy of the whole South.

Mr. Burritt labored long and hard to impress upon the
northern mind the conviction that the whole nation could
not afford to let Slavery die under the financial ruins or
general bankruptcy of the South ; that we stood in a
moral relation to the system which would not justify us
in waiting for its extinction by this slow, stifling process
of " restriction ; " that the whole nation ought to bear
the burden of its removal ; that it would better " pay "
the whole nation to bear it on its strong, broad shoulders,
than to let the entire burden crush the South under the
general breakdown which was anticipated for that section.
He endeavored to demonstrate that the nation had the
means in its public lands to buy slavery out of existence,
without taking a dollar from the pockets of the people
of the Free States ; that these lands, if well husbanded,
would yield enough to pay two hundred and fifty dollars
per head for all the slaves in the Union, young and old,
halt and blind ; and also to produce a surplus of at least
three hundred millions of dollars for the good of the
slaves, as a kind of " freedom suit," after their emancipation ; that the spirit of this great joint act of justice and
duty would unite North and South with bonds of fellowship which had never existed between them.   He pressed
upon the public mind, as far as he could, the consideration that the nation could not more gratefully recognize
the gift of such a continent, before God and humanity,

than by consecrating that portion of its domain between the Mississippi and the Pacific to the emancipation of all the slaves within its borders. He urged that this vast domain, if not thus devoted to a great national object, would be alienated by private speculation ; that railroad monopolies and other corporations and rings of capitalists would grab up the whole area, piece by piece, by a corrupting process that would impoverish the political morality of the government and nation.

The scheme proposed began to be favorably considered and discussed. Many petitions to Congress were presented by members of both houses, including Messrs. Seward, Sumner, and others in the Senate. But just as it had reached that stage at which congressional action was about to recognize it as a legitimate proposition, " John Brown's Raid " suddenly closed the door against all overtures or efforts for the peaceful extinction of slavery. Its extinction by compensation would have recognized the moral complicity of the whole nation in planting and perpetuating it on this continent. It would have been an act of repentance, and the meetest work for repentance the nation could perform. But it was too late. It was too heavy and red to go out in tears. Too late ! it had to go out in blood, and the whole nation opened the million sluices of its best life to deepen and widen the costly flood. If, before these sluice-gates were opened to these red streams, so hot with passion, one *bona fide* offer had been made by the North to share with the South the task, cost, and duty of lifting slavery off from the bosom of the nation, perhaps thousands who gave up their first-born and youngest-born to death might have looked into that river of blood with more ease and comfort at their hearts. Although the earth has drunk that red river out of human sight, it still runs fresh and full, without the waste of a drop, before the eyes of God; and the patriot, as well as Christian, might well wish that He could recognize in the stream the shadow of an honest effort on the part of the North to lift the great sin and curse without waiting for such a deluge to sweep them away.

The proposition to which Mr. Burritt had given so many years of labor, by speech and pen, was now forever barred by the flaming two-edged sword of civil war. It had been to him one of the most hopeful labors of his life; one so full of good promise to the nation that he gave to it a kind of enthusiasm which he had felt in no other undertaking. Up to this time he had never stopped to earn money or to acquire property; and at fifty years of age he was without other resources than what he could find in a small stony farm in New Britain, tilled by his own hands. During the summer he wrote most of his editorials, in his shirt-sleeves, on the head of a lime cask in his barn, pen and hoe alternating through the day. When soliciting signatures to the call for the Cleveland Convention, he mowed an acre on a Fourth of July, and wrote about twenty letters in his barn the same day, his farm being nearly a mile from the village. A few kind Quaker ladies of New Bedford sent him money enough to pay the postage of a thousand letters; and the whole sum contributed by the friends of this peaceful scheme of Compensated Emancipation amounted to about two hundred dollars. At the organization of a National Society at the Cleveland Convention, he was chosen Secretary, and was encouraged more by his faith in the cause, than by any patent facts, to open an office in the Bible House, New York, for the new association, at the rent of nearly three hundred dollars a year. Here he labored night and day to interest the public mind, and to obtain the adhesion of influential men and journals to the cause. He sent out thousands of circulars and printed statements, developing the scheme, and soliciting co-operation in making it successful. But these documents and the rent of the office absorbed all the money which Gérrit Smith and J. D. Williams had contributed at Cleveland to start the society, and they did not bring twenty dollars into the treasury. Unwilling to charge a single meal or a night's lodging upon these small funds of the society, Mr. Burritt had to subject himself to the interesting experience of many a reformer, and tried to live on sixteen cents a day for food. This he effected by using cheap cold water from the pump and a small loaf of brown bread for breakfast and tea, and a twelve-cent cut of meat for dinner. Still there was a wide interest awakening in the cause, though it did not take that pecuniary direction necessary to support a movement involving considerable expense. But "Old John Brown was marching on," and at Harper's Ferry he put his foot on "Compensated Emancipation" and stopped its march forever.

Mr. Burritt now settled down upon his little farm, without any regret that he had given so much time and labor to avert a catastrophe which so many thousands, North and South, had predicted and apprehended with good reason.   After such a long strain of mental exercise and excitement, it was a luxury to him to pull off coat and vest and harden his sinews again to robust outdoor work.   No farmer ever entered into his occupation with more zest, or more enjoyed the effort to make two spires of grass grow where one did not before.   He also exerted himself to awaken a new and deeper interest in farming in the town, where manufacturing had absorbed more of the energy and ambition of the inhabitants. Through his efforts in this direction an Agricultural Club was formed, of which he was appointed secretary, and which for twelve years has met regularly in the winter months to discuss agricultural matters.

Early in 1863 Mr. Burritt again visited England, not with the expectation of reviving the movements he had originated there, but rather to see old friends and co-workers and revive the pleasant memories of former years.   He spent that winter in lecturing upon subjects of general interest in various parts of the kingdom, and in the following summer he set out on a foot tour from London to John o'Groat's.   His chief object was an agricultural one — to visit the largest and best farms in England and Scotland, and to take notes of all he saw, which might interest and benefit the New Britain Agricultural Club, if their value extended no farther.   With this view he visited Alderman Mechi's celebrated Tiptree Hall establishment, Babraham, the estate of the late Jonas Webb, the distinguished stock-raiser, Chrishall Grange, the largest farm in England, cultivated by Samuel Jonas; also the establishment of Anthony Cruikshank, the great short-horn breeder in Scotland, and a great many smaller farms. He reached John o' Groat's on the 28th of September, having made a zigzag walk, sometimes diverging twenty or thirty miles from a straight course, in order to see different farming establishments or sections of country. On his return he made his notes and observations into a large volume, entitled "A Walk from London to John o' Groat's," containing photographic portraits of the distinguished agriculturists before mentioned. He sent copies of this work to the New Britain Club for circulation among its members. The book was published by Messrs. Sampson, Low, & Co., London, and had a good circulation, in two editions, in England. On the 1st of June, 1864, Mr. Burritt started on a foot-tour from London to Land's End, to complete the traverse of the island. On this journey, also, he diverged in various directions from the straight line, once nearly forty miles, to see the largest flock of sheep in England. From Land's End he returned by the western sea-coast, up the valley of the Wye, thence through Herefordshire, Worcestershire, Oxfordshire, and Berkshire, back to London. During the following winter he lectured in a large number of towns, between Truro, in Cornwall, and Inverness, in Scotland, besides preparing for the press his second book of travels — "A Walk from London to Land's End and Back," which also went to two editions in a few months.

In the spring of 1865 Mr. Burritt was appointed Consular Agent for the United States at Birmingham, without any solicitation on his part, and accepted the post with some hesitation, and even reluctance, fearing it would be a bar to all literary labor. But after a while he found he could manage to write for the press even in the office, with the clerk at the same table, and subject to interruptions every half hour in the day. As it was one of the duties of American consuls to collect and communicate to the Department at Washington facts relating to the industrial pursuits and productions of their consulates, he visited the various manufacturing towns and villages in the Birmingham district, and published a large volume, called "Walks in the Black Country and its Green Border Lands." This also went to the second edition in a few months, and was regarded the first and only popular history of Birmingham and the surrounding district which had ever appeared. On receiving a copy for the Department, Secretary Seward wrote to the author, expressing much satisfaction in regard to the character and value of the book. The next year Mr. Burritt wrote a book called "The Mission of Great Sufferings;" he also collected his previous writings, and published them in several volumes. At the close of 1866 his most intimate English friend and co-worker, Edmund Fry, died suddenly on the platform in London, while addressing a public meeting on the Peace question. Mr. Fry had been secretary of The League of Universal Brotherhood until its amalgamation with the London Peace Society, and had conducted The Board of Brotherhood for many years. Mr. Burritt now assumed the entire editorship of the periodical, to which he had been a regular contributor while in the United States. He undertook also to fill it with the productions of his own pen, and the supplying of sixteen large pages monthly made no slight literary task. At the end of the year he changed the name it had borne from 1846 to " Fireside Words," with the view of making it more of a general or literary character. He devoted a department of it to the young, in which he proposed to give familiar, simple, " Fireside Lessons in Forty Languages," which cost him much labor to prepare. In addition to these literary and official labors, he accepted invitations to lecture in most of the towns and villages of The Black Country, which service he always performed gratuitously, for the pleasure of making acquaintance with the people of the district, and of helping on their institutions for intellectual improvement.

On the election of General Grant to the Presidency, nearly all the United States Consuls in Great Britain were removed to make room for more worthy or more importunate claimants for the situations. Mr. Burritt, of course, was one of the superseded; which, however, he had but little pecuniary reason to regret, for Congress had cut down the annual allowance of the Birmingham consulate to fifteen hundred dollars a year, although the business of the office amounted to about five million dollars per annum, and cost, for office rent, clerk-hire, and other expenses, over one thousand dollars a year to carry it on, thus leaving the Consular Agent hardly five hundred dollars for his services and support. And, what was a singular circumstance, the more business done for the United States government, the less was the compensation of the Agent, as his inevitable expenses were larger, while his allowance was not increased. Mr. Burritt had represented this circumstance to the Department, who generously rectified the matter in favor of his successor, erecting the Birmingham Agency into an independent consulate, with a full salary to the incumbent. On leaving the post, Mr. Burritt received several gratifying testimonals of esteem from the inhabitants of towns in the district for the interest he had manifested in their institutions. The most prized of these expressions of good-will was the presentation of a set of Knight's Illustrated Shakespeare, comprising eight splendid volumes, by the people of the parish of Harborne, a suburb of Birmingham, where Mr. Burritt resided during the four years of his consulate. The following is the address presented by the vicar of the parish at a large public meeting of persons belonging mostly to his congregation : —

"HARBORNE, May 26, 1869.

" *To* ELIHU BURRITT, ESQ., *Consul and Representative of the United States of America, Birmingham.*

"Respected and dear Sir : We have heard with the most unfeigned regret that your residence amongst us is about to terminate. During your four years of sojourn in the parish of Harborne, we have ever found in you a kind and sincere friend, and a warm and generous supporter of every good and philanthropic work. We are only expressing our hearts' true feeling in saying that we very deeply deplore your anticipated departure, and shall ever remember with the liveliest emotions your oft-repeated acts of courteous kindness. Your aim has always been to forward the interests of the parish from which you are now, on the termination of your mission, about to separate. We are sure the affectionate regard of the parishioners generally will follow you to your new sphere of labor and usefulness ; and it is our prayer and heartiest wish that your life may long be spared to pursue your honorable career, so that by your writings, not less than by your example, many may receive lasting good. We take leave of you, dear sir, assured that you will not forget Harborne and its people, on whose hearts your name will long remain engraved. We ask you to accept the accompanying volumes, with this numerously signed address, which we think will, in your estimation, be the most assuring token of our deep regard and affectionate remembrance of yourself, and respectful appreciation of your character."

To this address Mr. Burritt replied as follows : —

" Mr. Chairman, Ladies and Gentlemen: I am so deeply affected with surprise and other mingled emotions at this most unexpected expression of your good-will, that I do not know what to say, or what to say first. The language of the heart is simple, and my words must be few and simple. With my heart running over with grateful thoughts, I thank you for this rich token of your kindness. To say, ' I thank you,' is a very short and simple expression; but I assure you it means not only my thanks this evening, but thanks that shall last as long as my life, for this precious testimonial of your regard. I say it honestly, that I shall carry the memory of Harborne with me to my last day on earth. The four happiest years of my life I have lived here; for all my other years I had been a kind of wanderer. I had been engaged in public movements that took me about the world in different directions, and left me no time to settle down in any fixed residence. But here in Harborne I found the first home of my own that I ever possessed, a home in which my happiest memories will live as long as I can remember any of the experiences of past life. Here I found a home-like people and a home-like church, in which I could sit down with them in social sympathy and silent communion through all the quiet Sabbaths of the year, and feel myself one of the congregation, and as much at home with them as if I had been born in Harborne, and baptized in its parish church. It has been to me a rich privilege and enjoyment to say *we* with you in all that pertains to the best interests of the parish, just as if

I had cast in my lot with you for the rest of my days. The beautiful music of your Sabbath bells has been a song of joy to me, and it will come to me in my dearest memories and dreams of Harborne like a whisper from heaven. I accept this splendid gift of your good-will with all the more grateful pleasure, as a token, also, that I shall not be forgotten by you when I am gone from your midst. I wish most earnestly to be remembered by you all; and I hope, if my life is spared, to remind you occasionally that my spirit is still a resident of Harborne, though in person I am far away. I should like to have all the children of these schools remember that a man of my name once resided here, who felt a lively interest in them, and loved to see their happy faces in these rooms and at church; and if I ever write any more books for children, it will be a delight to me to send the first copies to them. The little legacy of my life I shall leave in the books I have written, and it will give me pleasure to think that there will be one library in Harborne in which they may all be found, by those who may wish to see what thoughts I have endeavored to put forth during my residence among you and before it commenced. In conclusion, this anniversary is one of deep and affecting interest to me. Four years ago I came into these rooms for the first time with my dear niece, now present, as strangers to you all. We had not expected to be recognized as residents of Harborne, for we had been here only a few days; but we shall never forget the warm and generous welcome you gave us on that occasion. Indeed, we were almost overwhelmed with such a hearty manifestation of your kindness to us. Ever since that happy evening in our experience, we have lived in the atmosphere of the same kindness and good-will; and I desire on her part and on the part of her sister, as well as my own, to thank you most heartily for all your kindness and good wishes on our behalf. These make a good bye which they will remember with grateful sensibility on their voyage across the ocean, in their native land and their mother's home. Both these dear companions, who have made and shared the happiness of our Harborne home, will carry with them, as long as they live, a most pleasant memory of your esteem and good-will from the first to the last day of our residence among you; and if we should be spared to settle down together again in our American home, we shall often talk over the happy years we have spent here. So far as we can do it in thought, we shall often sit down together in the same church pew we have so long occupied, and fancy we are listening to the same voice from the pulpit, and to the same sweet voices from the choir, and imagine we are surrounded by the same familiar faces. We shall connect Harborne with our own native village by a tie of lasting personal interest. I hope the name we gave our delightful home here will be retained by successive occupants, so that 'New Britain Villa' will be left with you as a pledge of mutual remembrance, as a kind of clasp between the village of our birth and the village of our adoption. Once more I thank you from our united hearts for this splendid, this precious testimonial of your regard. I would thank you again and again for your kindest of words and wishes. I thank you for your generous expressions towards the country to which we belong, and which, to an infinitesimal degree, we have represented among you. I hope the day may come when the same sentiments will be felt and expressed between our two great nations as you have cherished towards us and we towards you, and which we have interchanged this evening. It will be the crowning remembrance of my life that I have labored to bring about this state of feeling between England and America. And now may Heaven bless you all, both here and in the world to come."

Mr. Burritt remained in Birmingham several months, after leaving the consulate, in order to set on foot an enterprise which he thought would be of great benefit to a great number of persons both in England and the United States. This had for its object to lessen the hazards of emigrants to America, by obtaining homes or employment for them there before they left England, to which they might go direct, and not drift about and lose time and money in seeking situations after their arrival. For this purpose he established an International Land and Labor Agency in Birmingham, which so commended itself to the confidence of the public in both countries, that the newspapers in each gave it gratuitously all the publicity it needed to make its spirit, principles, and objects widely known and approved. In less than three months after its first opening, more than a thousand farms, from Maine to California, were committed to it for sale to English purchasers, varying from five hundred dollars to fifty thousand dollars; and some of the first sold to such purchasers were farms in New England. As the Agency was founded on a philanthropic basis, and had no bias or interest in one section above another, the information it supplied, in regard to the climate, soil, productions, advantages and drawbacks, of different states was regarded as very trustworthy and correct; and soon young English farmers, and men of other occupations, acted upon it, and went out, under the auspices of the Agency, to New England, the Middle States, Virginia, North Carolina, Tennessee, and other parts of the country. The Agency also undertook to supply American families with English servant girls, who soon came into great request in different sections of the Union; it also found employment there for English farm laborers and men of all occupations. While laboring to open and establish this Agency, Mr. Burritt took a lively and practical interest in a new literary enterprise started at the same time in Birmingham. This was " The Midland Illustrated News," which, to a certain degree, was to compete with the " London Illustrated News," with its

vast means and circulation. He contributed a paper to
the new periodical nearly every week for many months,
out of desire to see it succeed as a Birmingham enterprise and interest.

When Mr. Burritt settled down to four years' residence
in Birmingham, he had been continuously engaged for
twenty years in labors connected with the Anti-Slavery,
Peace, Ocean Penny Postage, Compensated Emancipation, and other reformatory movements. Through all
this period he had totally abstracted himself from those
literary pursuits and recreations of which he had become
so fond before he was led into the field of philanthropic
effort by the incident already noticed. For it had been
impossible for him to pursue these favorite studies under
the strain of mental labor and excitement which these
enterprises involved. So, when the official appointment
he accepted had withdrawn him to a kind of settled
private life, and given him time and opportunity to revive the studies he had so long suspended, he found that
he had dropped out of his memory six different alpha-
bets, to say nothing of the words and literature of the
languages to which they belonged. But he was very
glad to find that these were not entirely lost, but that he
was able to recover them easily, and to pursue the old
course of study with quickened relish and ability. It
had been the dream of his later life to spend a year in
old Oxford, to breathe its classic atmosphere and to enjoy its venerable associations, to live and move and have
a temporary being in the culture of its centuries of learning. But, instead of a year, he was only able to spend
six weeks in that grand old city of palaced learning;

still, in this short space he realized all he anticipated in regard to its incomparable privileges, elevating
companionships, student and social life. The acquaintance he made here with Max Müller, Dr. Bosworth,
Thorold Rogers, and other professors and dignitaries of
the University, was one of the most enjoyable and profitable acquisitions of his life. With a strong desire to
connect some literary work with his short residence in
Oxford as its birth and dating place, he reconstructed the
Psalms of David into twelve different lines of reflection, or twelve Meditations followed by twelve Prayers,
such as the meditations would naturally suggest. This
little devotional work, dated at Oxford, was published
by Samuel Bagster & Sons, London, and by Anson D.
Randolph & Co., New York.

Charles Dickens died suddenly a few days before Mr.
Burritt returned to America; and feeling that the spontaneous and instantaneous sentiment of the world at such
a death would be the best monument that could be erected
to the great author, he sent a note to the London Times,
proposing to collect in a volume the articles that should express that sentiment in the journals and other periodicals
of different countries, and requesting their publishers to
send him copies for this purpose. A great number came
to him from all parts of the world, in all the languages
of Christendom. From these he collected ample matter
for a large volume, translating much of it from the
French, German, Italian, Danish, Dutch, and Swedish
languages. Though the best illustration of beautiful
diction, noble and generous sentiment, which a hundred
eminent writers and clergymen of different countries

could produce, none of the publishers of Dickens's works, who had made so much money out of their editions, were willing to bring out this memorial volume, lest it might not pay them the usual profit on their business speculations. Still, Mr. Burritt, who had never asked or expected any pecuniary compensation for this work, never regretted having performed it; for it gave him the satisfaction of feeling that no other living man had so read the mind of the civilized world on the life and character of Charles Dickens, as he had done in these " Voices of the Nations " over his grave. The " Household Monument," which he had hoped to see erected in hundreds of homes of the admirers of the distinguished author on both sides of the Atlantic, is now preserved and appreciated only in his own, and he deems it worth all the labor he bestowed upon it as such a personal possession.

Mr. Burritt returned to America in 1870, after a sojourn of over seven years in England, during which time he had brought out nearly a dozen volumes in that country on different subjects. It was a delight for him to be again at home in his native town, among kith and kin, the friends and neighbors of his youth, after having spent the most part of twenty-five years in his four different campaigns of labor abroad. He received their old kind welcome from the people of New Britain, who had cut his name broad and deep in the frontlet of an elegant and massive school building in process of construction, on his arrival. He now entered upon the enjoyment of a quiet literary life, while taking part in all the pleasant duties of a citizen of his native town. The compilation of David's Psalms into Meditations and Prayers had interested him much in the study of the Scriptures, and he spent several months in preparing a volume of " Subject-Readings " from the Bible, comprising all it said on each of the subjects selected, as Faith, Hope, Prayer, Patience, Love, Peace, Temperance, Industry, &c. In doing this, he often turned over all the leaves of the Bible, from Genesis to Revelation, to find a verse or reference bearing on the subject, not willing to trust to any Concordance. This compilation is still unpublished, and if it should never be published, the labor performed on it will well repay him in the knowledge of the Scriptures he acquired in thus searching them through and through in the work. He next compiled a little volume entitled " The Children of the Bible," containing all the Old and New Testaments say of and to children, by precept and example. Having accomplished these little works of compilation, he sat down to a subject which had much occupied his reflections for thirty years, and wrote a volume in an assumed style, which must always conceal its authorship, and on one of the most serious subjects that can exercise a human mind. This was brought out in London, in 1872, and has elicited many notices in England and America, without suggesting any clue to the author, who sent it out into the religious world to stand or fall on its own intrinsic merits, without the influence of a name for or against it.

Having finished these literary undertakings, Mr. Burritt now entered upon a work which he had had in his mind ever since he used to visit the Antiquarian Library at Worcester, in 1838. He had thought that the books professedly written for young students, in the languages, were written for their teachers instead, who were to act as interpreters between the author and learner, as if he did not like to have a common pupil come directly between the wind and his dignity as an erudite grammarian. Especially in the study of Sanskrit, he was impressed with the lack of simplified expositions of the peculiarities of that language, which are so difficult for beginners, of any age, to master. Having encountered these peculiar difficulties, which bar the entrance into that and other Oriental languages, he sat down to compile just such a book as he most needed in studying them. This volume is to be entitled "Social Walks and Talks with Young Students among the Languages." The first of the series embraces simplified grammars and reading exercises in Sanskrit, Hindustanee, Persian, and Turkish, put in such plain and easy forms of exposition as will assist the young beginner over the threshold of those languages with less effort and delay than he would otherwise be subjected to. Should this volume be published, it will be the first rudimental work on these languages ever issued in America.

While engaged in this philological work, the consummation of the Washington Treaty opened up a new page and promise for the cause of organized and universal peace. It was unlike any other treaty between two nations, for it not only arranged for a High Court of Arbitration for the settlement of a very aggravated difficulty between the United States and Great Britain, but it preceded that tribunal with a kind of preliminary Congress at Washington, which developed new rules for the guidance of the arbitrators, and supplied a very important part of an international code. Thus the convention of the High Joint Commissioners at Washington, and the Tribunal of Arbitration at Geneva, were, by far, the nearest approximation to that Congress and High Court of Nations which the friends of Peace had been pressing upon the governments and peoples of Christendom for forty years. Mr. Burritt, for more than twenty-five of this period, had labored to impress this proposition upon the public mind, both in America and Europe. At the Peace Congresses at Brussels, Paris, Frankfort, and London, he had made this proposition, first developed by William Ladd, the sole subject of his speeches. The arrangement for settling the " Alabama difficulty" adopted and carried out this long-advocated scheme to a most promising extent and success. The friends of Peace in America and England felt that a golden opportunity now presented itself for advancing their great cause to a stage which had so long occupied their thoughts and hopes. A series of public meetings in all the large cities, beginning at Boston and ending at Washington, was set on foot by the American Peace Society. Mr. Burritt joined heartily with Rev. J. B. Miles, Secretary of that society, in attending these meetings, and spoke at over thirty of them, bearing all his own expenses in the journeys they involved.

These meetings were designed to impress upon the public mind the vast importance of the Washington Treaty, and the new rules of International Law, and the High Court of Arbitration it had provided, not only for the settlement of the Alabama difficulty, but for the peaceful solution of all similar questions of controversy between nations. Mr. Burritt employed his pen as devotedly as his tongue in behalf of this " new departure ; " and when the fictitious and insincerely tentative " consequential claims " were foisted into " our case," he denounced them in the severest language that the leading public journals would admit. As soon as the Geneva Tribunal had made its award, the American Peace Society determined to do what it could to convene a great International Congress, in America or Europe, for the purpose of putting the top-stone to that temple of peace which now seemed ready for such a crowning. A call or note of invitation to such a congress was issued, signed by Ex-President Woolsey, Reverdy Johnson, and a long list of eminent men. It was arranged that Mr. Burritt should accompany Mr. Miles to Europe, to confer with leading minds there on the subject, and secure their presence and co-operation at the proposed congress ; but, in consequence of an injury received on a railroad journey just before the time fixed for their departure, he was unable to go on the mission, and Mr. Miles went alone, and met with remarkable success. Before he left, at a full consultation, Mr. Burritt urged a variation from the old Peace Congresses, held twenty years before in Europe. He proposed that the one now to be convened should consist of two entirely distinct bodies, meeting at different halls in the same city ; that one should be a senate of jurists, consisting of forty or fifty of the most eminent authorities and writers on international law in Christendom ; that their express work should be to review all the precedents and authorities extant, add, construct, and reconstruct, and elaborate, clause by clause, an International Code, clothed with all the moral force which their individual, representative, and collective character could give to it, and which no government in Christendom would be likely to ignore or reject. Then the second body should be a great popular assembly, perhaps numbering a thousand, of all professions, — philanthropists, economists, ministers, editors, &c., — who should discuss every aspect, point, and principle embraced in the condition and policy of organized and permanent peace. Mr. Miles submitted this proposition to the distinguished men whom he conferred with in Europe, who expressed their approbation of it, as the best way for obtaining that practical result from the congress which would be of such value to all nations.

The foregoing sketch is given to the public to forestall and prevent any posthumous exaggerations or mistakes which might otherwise appear in some future biography, should the life here referred to be deemed worthy of a notice at its close. All its principal facts and features are here given in the simplest narrative, and if they should be of any worth to any young man setting out in life under similar circumstances, the author will not have lived in vain.

INCIDENTS AND OBSERVATIONS.

69

BREATHING A LIVING SOUL INTO DEAD WORDS.

"CAN these dry bones live?" asked the seer of old, on seeing a valley strewn with them. "Can these dry bones live? Did they ever live?" many a reader has asked of himself, on looking over a book-valley filled with lifeless, disjointed words. Yes, many sentences of commonplace words and thin and weak ideas, which, in cold, inanimate type, seem dead to the reader, have thrilled and stirred hundreds to the deepest emotion when listening to them as they fell burning from the tongue. Words are the veins, but not the vital fluid, of mental life. As in the case of the dry bones the prophet saw, a living spirit must pass over and through them before they glow, and breathe, and throb with life. Spoken words are often delivered upon the mind of the listener with a temporary force and impression which the written cannot produce upon the reader. In the first place, listening to a public speaker is a congregate exercise, and he can play upon the sympathy of a hundred minds drinking in the same thoughts at the same moment. Even if they were all blind, and could not see each other's faces as they listened, they would be conscious of the tide of feeling that the speaker was raising in the invisible assembly. Thus he has a peculiar advantage over the writer in this simple sentiment of sympathy in a compact congregation of hearers; for, in ninety-nine cases in a hundred, the author's words fall upon the mind of an isolated reader without any accessory charm or force that the tongue can give or ear receive. Then, if the preacher or orator has an impressive or well-modulated voice, he can give to his words a power which type cannot reproduce, or save from evanescence. But the great, capital advantage he has over the writer, though transient, is in the projectile force of feeling he can throw into his words through his voice, eyes, face, and action. Many a speaker, by the very mesmerism of his own heart-power, has raised dead words from the ground and made them electrify a great audience with their startling life. I have seen this effect produced under a great variety of circumstances, and with the simplest words. I once attended a negro church service in Virginia, where a large chapel was filled with slaves of every age. One of their fellow-members had died the week before, and a colored brother on the platform was "improving the occasion." He had gradually brought the congregation to a certain level of emotion by his simple and pathetic tribute of affectionate regard for the deceased. When he had raised them to a sympathetic point, from which they would have easily subsided to a calmer feeling without new explosive force on his part, he turned himself half round from the audience and uttered the simple words — "Jimmy lies dere in he grabe." Could those maimed words live? a classical scholar might ask. Yes, they did live, with a vitality and power that might well have astonished the prophet who saw the dry bones stir with animation. They filled the walls of the house as with a mighty rushing wind of human emotion, with sobs of sympathy and ejaculations of intense feeling. Half the audience rose to their feet, and several men and women waved their arms, with uprolled eyes, as if swimming up to heaven in their ecstasy. "Jimmy lies dere in he grabe!" were the simple words through which he produced this effect. They were the veins through which he transfused three hundred human hearts with the vital fluid of the feeling which filled his own to this passionate outburst. How cold they look in type! Who would read them with any interest above the general sentiment which the bare statement is calculated to inspire? They come to the reader's mind in their bald and isolated meaning, abstracted from every accessory or surrounding circumstance that affected their utterance. No printed words could convey an idea of that outburst of feeling which forced itself into that simple exclamation, of the tremor of his voice, of the expression of his countenance, as the white tears ran down his black face. He stepped to the left edge of the platform as he half turned from the audience. He bent his form and placed a hand on each knee; he stretched out his neck as if to look over the sharp edge of the grave; for a silent moment he trembled from head to foot, in every joint and in every hair of his head; then, in a voice tremulous with a melting pathos, as if his tears were dropping upon the dead face of their departed friend, he sobbed out, "Jimmy lies dere in he grabe!" Never did I hear before six words uttered with such a projectile force of feeling, or that produced such an effect upon an audience.

Another instance I will notice to illustrate the effect

which mere heart-power in the speaker may give, even
to words that may have no intellectual meaning to an
audience.   The Peace Congress in Paris, in 1849, was
perhaps the first public meeting in France in which
French, English, Americans, Germans, Spaniards, and
Italians ever assembled together to discuss principles and
topics in which they felt a common interest.   Those of
us especially who had labored for months to bring about
this great re-union were much exercised with doubt as
to the result of assembling within the same walls, and on
the same platform, hearers and speakers who did not
understand each other's language.   This doubt was increased by the apprehension of one or two French
members of the Committee of Arrangements, that many
of their countrymen, after listening for a few minutes to
an English speech they could not understand, would
arise and leave the house out of sheer weariness of mind.
Richard Cobden was the only English-speaking member
who could address the assembly in French.   So, when
our first orator arose to speak, we watched from the
platform the faces of the French auditors with lively
concern.   It was the Rev. John Burnet, of London, a
man of much genius and power as a speaker, with a flow
and a glow of rich Irish wit and. accent, which always
made him a great favorite at home.   He had not proceeded a minute before we could perceive the action of
the subtile force of sympathy upon the French portion
of the assembly.   Although not one in ten could understand the meaning of his words in print, they came to
them from his lips with a force of feeling that affected
them deeply.   And when, in the middle of his speech,

he brought out a noble sentiment towards their nation, the whole English and American portion of the audience arose and gave three great cheers, that made the roof tremble. From that moment to the end of the last session the electric current of sympathy between speaker and hearer was complete, even without intelligible language as a conductor. On the second day, when an eloquent, impassioned English popular orator was in his peroration, he threw a fervor and force of feeling into a climax sentence which perfectly electrified the French audience. The whole gallery of them, at a great distance from the platform, arose, and scores of ladies waved their handkerchiefs in the enthusiasm of their delight and admiration, though probably not one in twenty could understand a word of English. I was sitting by the side of a French member of the Committee on the platform, whom I had met from day to day, and knew to be unable to read or understand English. He was swaying and tremulous with emotion, and the tears were coursing down his cheeks " like rain-drops from eaves of reeds." I asked him, in a whisper of surprise, if he understood the speaker. " Non, mais je le comprends ici " (" No, but I understand him here "), said he, laying his hand upon his heart. Here was a striking illustration of the heart-power that may be thrown into common words, for those that produced this wonderful effect would not move any thoughtful reader when cold and laid out in type.

Still, notwithstanding the advantage the orator or speaker possesses in being able to breathe a living soul into dry words, to give them, as it were, his own eyes, face, voice, and action, the writer often wields a higher power, because it is everlasting and unchanging. Men have written, who, from their lightning-tipped pens, have thrown into a few simple words a current of electric feeling which has shot through forty centuries and a hundred human generations, thrilling the sympathies of men of almost every race, tongue, and age. There is the cry of tender and manly distress which Esau uttered at the knees of his old blind father, when he lifted up his voice and wept, and said, in broken articulation, " Bless me also, O my father ! " All the intervening centuries, and all the moral mutations affecting humanity, have not attenuated the pulse of those words. Whoever wrote them threw into them a projectile force of feeling that will thrill the last reader that peruses them on earth. Judah's plea for Benjamin before Joseph, in Egypt, young David's words to Saul on going forth to meet Goliah, and his lament over Absalom, have an in-breathed life and power which will last as long as human language.

Even what may be called artificial feeling has given written words a power that has moved millions for more than two thousand years. All the theatres built and filled in Greece, Rome, France, England, and America, originated in this inbreathing power, which actors, trained high in emotional education, could throw into sentences penned by some quiet writer, perhaps, in his garret or kitchen. How these great tragedians have walked through the book-valleys of dry words and breathed them into thrilling life ! "What is he to Hecuba, or Hecuba to him?" What? why all that Hecuba was to herself in the wildest storm-bursts of her grief. His tears, though counterfeit, were as wet as hers. His heart played the bitter discords of woe upon its torn or twisted strings as sadly as hers. His voice broke with the sobbing cadences of sorrow as touchingly as hers. His face and form quivered with all the agonies of her despair. If she had stood up before the audience in all the affecting personality of her experience, she could not have acted out her distress and grief with more life and power.

It is true these trained actors of feeling avail themselves of other accessories than their emotional or elocutionary faculties. They enhance the force and effect of their impersonations by various kinds of scenic auxiliaries to give them all the vividness of real life. But many of them, without any of the trappings of the stage, have breathed a power into simple and familiar words which has made the hearts of listeners almost stand still in the intensity of their sympathy. I conclude with one illustration of this faculty.

The Lord's Prayer contains sixty-five simple words, and no other threescore-and-five have ever been together on so many human lips. For a thousand years they have been the household, the cradle words of Christendom. Children innumerable, in both hemispheres, have been taught to say them in their first lessons in articulate speech. They have been the prayer of all ages and conditions; uttered by mitred bishops in grand cathedrals, and lisped by poor men's children, with closed eyes, in cots of straw at night. The feet of forty generations, as it were, have passed over them, until, to some indifferent minds, their life may seem to have been trodden out of them. Indeed, one often hears them from the pulpit as if they were worn out by repetition. A few pretentiously-educated minds may even ask their secret thoughts, " Can these dry words live?" Yes, they have been made to live with overpowering vitality.

Edwin Booth, the celebrated tragedian, was a man who threw into his impersonations an amount of heart and soul which his originals could scarcely have equalled. He did Richard III. to the life and more. He had made human passions, emotions, and experiences his life's study. He could not only act, but *feel* rage, love, despair, hate, ambition, fury, hope, and revenge with a depth and force that half amazed his auditors. He could transmute himself into the hero of his impersonation, and he could breathe a power into other men's written words which perhaps was never surpassed. And, what is rather remarkable, when he was inclined to give illustratious of this faculty to private circles of friends, he nearly always selected some passages from Job, David, or Isaiah, or other holy men of old. When an aspiring young professor of Harvard University went to him by night to ask a little advice or instruction in qualifying himself for an orator, the veteran tragedian opened the Bible and read a few verses from Isaiah in a way that made the Cambridge scholar tremble with awe, as if the prophet had risen from the dead and were uttering his sublime visions in his ears. He was then residing in Baltimore, and a pious, urbane old gentleman of the city, hearing of his wonderful power of elocution, one day invited him to dinner; although strongly deprecating the stage and all theatrical performances. A large company sat down to the table, and on returning to the drawing-room, one of them requested Booth, as a special favor to them all, to repeat the Lord's Prayer. He signified his willingness to gratify them, and all eyes were fixed upon him. He slowly and reverentially arose from his chair, trembling with the burden of two great conceptions. He had to realize the character, attributes, and presence of the Almighty Being he was to address. He was to transform himself into a poor, sinning, stumbling, benighted, needy suppliant, offering homage, asking bread, pardon, light, and guidance. Says one of the company present, " It was wonderful to watch the play of emotions that convulsed his countenance. He became deathly pale, and his eyes, turned tremblingly upwards, were wet with tears. As yet he had not spoken. The silence could be felt ; it had become absolutely painful, until at last the spell was broken as if by an electric shock, as his rich-toned voice, from white lips, syllabled forth ' Our Father which art in heaven,' &c., with a pathos and fervid solemnity that thrilled all hearts. He finished ; the silence continued ; not a voice was heard nor a muscle moved in his rapt audience, until, from a remote corner of the room, a subdued sob was heard, and the old gentleman (the host) stepped forward, with streaming eyes and tottering frame, and seized Booth by the hand. ' Sir,' said he, in broken accents, ' you have afforded me a pleasure for which my whole future life will feel grateful. I am an old man, and every day from boyhood to the present time I thought I had repeated the Lord's Prayer ; but I never heard it before, never !' ' You are right,' replied Booth : ' to read that prayer as it should be read caused me the severest study and labor for thirty years, and I am far from being satisfied with my rendering of that wonderful production. Hardly one person in ten thousand comprehends how much beauty, tenderness, and grandeur can be condensed in a space so small, and in words so simple. That prayer itself sufficiently illustrates the truth of the Bible, and stamps upon it the seal of divinity.' So great was the effect produced," says our informant, " that conversation was sustained but a short time longer, in subdued monosyllables, and almost entirely ceased ; and soon after, at an early hour, the company broke up and retired to their several homes, with sad faces and full hearts."

" Can these words live ? " Let any man who thinks, and almost says, that they have lost their life by repetition, ask any one of the company that listened to Edwin Booth on that evening to say what is his opinion on the question. But some conscientious persons may possibly object that the effect he produced was dramatic ; that he only gave to the words the force of artificial or acted feeling. Suppose this be granted : if artificial or counterfeit feeling could produce such effect, what impression ought not *genuine* emotion in the utterance of that simple and beautiful prayer to produce on an audience ?

THE GREAT CHESHIRE POLITICAL CHEESE.

How few English or American readers can see or hear the name *Cheshire*, without thinking of the rich and golden cheese associated with it! The mind, at the mere mention of the word, darts off to those great doubloons of the dairy which so distinguish the famous pastoral county of England. So indissoluble is the association, that the eldest daughter of the county in America, Cheshire in Connecticut, a little Puritan town, felt, in taking and wearing the name, that, next to the religious faith of its English mother, it ought to do honor to her reputation as a cheese-making community. And this it did. The Connecticut Cheshire was hardly a dozen years old when it became noted as a dairy town, and turned out cheeses which would have done credit to Old England's Cheshire. Nor was this all, nor the best. So fully and faithfully did the early settlers of the place cherish this relationship and association, that when a small colony of them pushed their way up into the hilly interior of Massachusetts, they not only called the town they planted and peopled there Cheshire, but they made it more famous still for cheese. One, the joint production of all the dairies in the town, was the greatest prodigy, probably, that was ever recorded in the history of milk and its manufacture ; especially taking the motive into consideration.

Early in the present century, to use a popular saying, " politics ran high " in America. The nation was hardly

6

a dozen years old as an independent state. Its most
vital institutions were in process of erection. There was
a sharp division of opinion between the chief architects.
One set were for building all the states into a rigid quadrangle, with the national capitol in the centre overshadowing and dominating them all. These were the " Federal-
ists." The Jeffersonian builders were for lowering the
capitol by a story, and for giving the individual states
more local independence and more unrestricted sunlight
of liberty. These were called "Democrats;" and the
contest between the two parties waxed exceedingly fierce.
From the first a religious element was thrown into it,
and made it glow with the hottest combustion of theolo-
gical odium. Thomas Jefferson, the great democratic
leader, was charged with being an infidel of the French
revolutionary school. Never did the " No Popery "
tocsin stir a Protestant community to deeper emotion
than did this war-cry against democrats and democracy
in the New England States. The Puritan pulpits thundered against them and their chief with all the large
liberty of pulpit thunderbolts. Only elect Thomas
Jefferson President of the United States, and there
would be an *auto-da-fe* of all their Bibles, hymn-books,
and sermons; the altars of New England would be demolished, and all their religious institutions would be
swept away by an inrushing and irresistible flood of
French infidelity.

In the little town of Cheshire, nestling among the
middle hills of Massachusetts, a counter voice of great
power was lifted from its pulpit against this flood of
obloquy and denunciation that rolled and roared against

Jefferson and democracy. One of the most remarkable men that ever filled a pulpit stood up in this, and beat back the fierce onset of this odium against the great political chief he honored with unbounded trust and admiration. This was Elder John Leland, one of the most extraordinary preachers produced by those stirring times. He was a plain, blunt man, of keen common sense, trained for action by a combination of extraordinary circumstances to that extent, that he could hardly be called a self-made man. His whole reading and thinking were concentrated upon two great books — the Bible and Human Nature. He knew by heart every chapter and verse of these two vital volumes of instruction. The rude and rough energy of his mind, which his religious faith did not soften, made him a kind of Boanerges in the New England village in which he was born. But these characteristics assumed a more pronounced type under the peculiar discipline to which he was subsequently subjected. He commenced preaching in Virginia while still a very young man; and it was to him the pursuit of usefulness under difficulties, which few ministers in civilized, and few missionaries in uncivilized countries, ever met and overcame. Society in Virginia and the other slave states at the time was morally in a kind of inchoate form, and "the poor whites" were more ignorant and demoralized than at a later period of their condition. To gather up a congregation of such a motley character, especially in the rural and thinly-settled districts, and to fix their attention upon religious truth or serious subjects of reflection, was a most arduous undertaking. At first, the young men, he said, would gather together in the large, square pews in the corners of the church and commence playing cards, being screened from general observation by the high, wooden boarding of their pews. To get their ears he had to resort to very eccentric anecdotes and illustrations, in which he managed to convey some religious instruction. What was at first a necessity became at last a habit; and his pulpit stories, and his odd, but impressive manner of telling them, soon attracted large congregations, and made him famous as a preacher throughout the state. He was a very sedate man, and his grave countenance never relaxed or changed expression when he was relating anecdotes that melted his audience into tears, or half convulsed them with suppressed laughter. Still he never fell into such wild oddities of manner or matter as distinguished the unique and inapproachable Lorenzo Dow; but, with all his eccentricities, he maintained to the last a consistent Christian character and deportment. Indeed, he said, towards the close of his life, that he never smiled but once in the pulpit, and the occasion was enough to justify a slight departure from the rigid rule of gravity. He was preaching on a very warm Sabbath in Virginia. The church was situated on a large green, and the great door, which was directly opposite the pulpit, was thrown wide open to admit the air. " I saw," said he, " a man come staggering along and take a seat on the steps directly in front of me. He soon fell asleep, and commenced nodding. A large goat that was feeding on the green took it for a challenge, drew back, and prepared himself; then, coming up with great force, he struck the poor man in the head and knocked him almost into the church. I then had to stop, for it broke the thread of my argument, and I could but smile, while I was recovering my equilibrium, and the poor drunkard was scrambling out of the way of his antagonist." Surely few clergymen could have blamed him for that temporary smile under the circumstances.

Such was the preacher who made intimate acquaintance with Thomas Jefferson while he was in Virginia. The great father of American democracy reciprocated the elder's esteem, and unfolded to him his public life, and all the principles and opinions on which he sought to base the structure and institutions of the young republic. Leland returned to New England, and settled down as pastor for life in Cheshire, Massachusetts. Soon after he commenced his ministry there, the country was shaken from north to south, and east to west, with the most vehement agitation that it has ever experienced. Jeffersonian Democracy or Hamiltonian Federalism was the question and issue depending upon the struggle. Leland threw himself into it with all the energy of his political convictions and mental life. He gave the Federal preachers a Roland for their Oliver, and more too. His pulpit shook with the thunder of his rough and ready eloquence. Never did a mesmerist so shape and control the will of a subject as he did the mind of his whole congregation and parish. The influence of his opinions and eloquence reached far out beyond the limits of the town, and impressed thousands. Cheshire, to a man, followed his lead and followed his convictions long after he ceased to lead or live. For several generations they were born and they died Democrats of the Jeffersonian school. No presidential election in America, before or since, ever evoked or represented more antagonism. The religious element was the most irrepressible and implacable of them all. The whole religious community, in New England especially, had recoiled from the principles and sentiments of the French revolutionists. Most of the New England ministers led, or sought to lead, their congregations against the enemy that was coming in like a flood. If the term may be allowed, they sandwiched the name of Jefferson between Voltaire and Tom Paine. Democrats and infidels became equal and interchangeable terms of opprobrium. But the Puritan politicians were outvoted, and Thomas Jefferson was elected President of the United States by a large and most jubilant majority.

No man had done more to bring about this result than Elder John Leland, of the little hill town of Cheshire, in Massachusetts. Besides influencing thousands of outsiders in the same direction, he had brought up his whole congregation and parish to vote for the father of American Democracy. He now resolved to set the seal of Cheshire to the election in a way to make the nation know there was such a town in the Republican Israel. He had only to propose the method to command the unanimous approbation and indorsement of his people. And he did propose it from the pulpit to a full congregation on the Sabbath. With a few earnest words he invited every man and woman who owned a cow, to bring every quart of milk given on a certain day, or all the curd it would make, to a great cider-mill belonging to their brave townsman, Captain John Brown, who was the first man to detect and denounce the treachery of Benedict Arnold, in the Revolution. No Federal cow was allowed to contribute a drop of milk to the offering, lest it should leaven the whole lump with a distateful savor. It was the most glorious day the sun ever shone upon before or since in Cheshire. Its brightest beams seemed to bless the day's work. With their best Sunday clothes, under their white tow frocks, came the men and boys of the town, down from the hills and up from the valleys, with their contingents to the great offering in pails and tubs. Mothers, wives, and all the rosy maidens of those rural homes, came in their white aprons and best calico dresses, to the sound of the church bell that called young and old, and rich and poor, to the great co-operative fabrication. In farm wagons, in Sunday wagons, and all kinds of four-wheeled and two-wheeled vehicles, they wended their way to the general rendezvous — all exuberant with the spirit of the occasion. It was not only a great, glad gathering of all the people of the town, but half of their yoked oxen and family horses ; and these stepped off in the march with the animation of a holiday.

An enormous hoop had been prepared and placed upon the bed of the cider-press, which had been well purified for the work, and covered with a false bottom of the purest material. The hoop, resting on this, formed a huge cheese-box, or segment of a cistern, and was placed immediately under the three powerful wooden screws which turned up in the massive head-block above. A committee of arrangement met the contributors as they arrived, and conducted them to the great, white, shallow vat, into which they poured their contingents of curd, from the large tubs of the well-to-do dairyman to the

six-quart pail of the poor owner of a single cow. When
the last contribution was given in, a select committee of
the most experienced dairy matrons of the town addressed
themselves to the nice and delicate task of mixing, flavor-
ing, and tinting such a mass of curd as was never brought
to press before or since. But the farmers' wives of Cheshire were equal to the responsibility and duty of their
office. All was now ready for the *coup de grace* of the
operation. The signal was given. The ponderous screws
twisted themselves out from the huge beam overhead with
even thread and line. And now the whey ran around the
circular channels of the broad bed in little foamy, bubbling
rivers. The machinery worked to a charm. The stoutest
young farmers manned the long levers. The screws
creaked, and posts and beam responded to the pressure
with a sound between puff and groan. It was a complete success. The young men, in their shirt sleeves,
with flushed and moistened faces, rested at the levers, for
they had moved them to the last inch of their force. All
the congregation, with the children in the middle, stood
in a compact circle around the great press. The June
sun brightened their faces with its most genial beams,
and brought into the happiest illumination the thoughts
that beat in their hearts. Then Elder Leland, standing
upon a block of wood, and with his deep-lined face over-
looking the whole assembly, spread out his great, toil-
hardened hands, and looking steadfastly, with open eyes,
heavenward, as if to see the pathway of his thanksgiving to God, and the return blessing on its descent, offered
up the gladness and gratitude of his flock for the one
earnest mind that had inspired them to that day's deed,

and invoked the divine favor upon it and the nation's leader for whom it was designed. Then followed a service as unique and impressive as any company of the Scotch Covenanters ever performed in their open-air conventicles in the Highland glens. "Let us further worship God," he said, "in a hymn suitable to the occasion." What the hymn was, whether it was really composed for the ceremony, could now hardly be ascertained. But, as was then the custom, the elder lined it off with his grave, sonorous voice; that is, he read two lines at a time, which the congregation sung; then he gave out two more, thus cutting up the tune into equal bits with good breathing spaces between them. The tune was Mear, which was so common in New England worship that wherever and whenever public prayer was wont to be made, in church, school-house, or private dwelling, this was sure to be sung. It is a sober, staid, but brave tune, fitted for a slow march on the up-hill road of Christian life and duty, as the good people of New England found it in their experience.

Now, here was a scene worthy of the most graphic and perceptive pencil of the artist; and no English artist could do it to the life, unless he had actually seen with his own eyes, or could photograph in his own fancy, the dress, looks, and *pose* of that village congregation singing that hymn around the great cheese-press of Cheshire. The outer circle of ox-carts, farm and Sunday wagons, the great red cattle that ruminated with half-shut eyes in the sun, and the horses tied in long ranks to the fences — all this background of the picture might well inspire and employ the painter's best genius. The occasion was not a sportful holiday. Nothing could more vividly and fully express the vigor of political life in the heart of a town's population. The youngest boys and girls that stood around that cheese-press knew the whole meaning of the demonstration, and had known it for six months and more. The earnest political discussion had run from the church-steps to the hearth-stone of every house, however humble, up and down those hills and valleys. The boys at their winter school had taken sides to sharpen the warfare, although they all went with the elder and their parents in opinion. They shortened the appellations of the two political parties, and resolved themselves into *Dems.* and *Feds.*, though the most high-spirited boys were very loath to take the obnoxious name of *Feds.*, even as a make-believe. For two or three winter months at school, they had erected snow forts, and mounted upon their white walls the opponent flags of the two parties. From these they had sallied out into pitched battle. Many a young *Fed.* and *Dem.* had been brought down, or had the breath beaten out of his body in the cross fire of snow-balls, some of which had been dipped in water and frozen to ice in the preceding night. Amid shouts and jeers, and garments rolled in snow, the village youngsters had fought these political battles from day to day and week to week ; and now they stood around the press with their parents and elder brothers, with as clear a perception and with as deep an interest as the best-read politicians of the town could have and feel in the demonstration. Such was the congregation in the midst of which Elder John Leland stood up and dedicated to the great political chief, Thomas Jefferson, President of the United States,

the greatest cheese ever put to press in the New World or
the Old. He then dismissed his flock with the benediction, with as solemn an air as if they had been laying
the foundation of a church ; and they all filed away to
their homes as decorously and thoughtfully as if they had
attended religious service.

When the cheese was well dried and ready for use, it
weighed *sixteen hundred pounds.* It could not be safely
conveyed on wheels to its destination. About the middle of the following winter, when there was a good
depth of snow all over the country, the great Cheshire
was placed on a sleigh, and Elder Leland was commissioned to take the reins and drive it all the way to
Washington. The distance was full five hundred miles,
requiring a journey of three weeks. The news of this
political testimonial had spread far and wide, and the
elder was hailed with varying acclamations in the towns
through which he passed, especially in those where he
put up for the night. The Federals squibbed him, of
course, with their satirical witticisms ; but they caught a
Tartar in the elder, who was more than a match for them
in that line of humor. Arriving at Washington, he proceeded immediately to the White House, and presented
his people's gift to President Jefferson, in a speech which
the elder only could make. He gave him some of the
details of the battle they had fought for his election and
reputation ; how they had defended him from the odium
and malicious slanders of the Puritans, and how they all,
old and young, gloried in his triumph. He presented the
cheese to him as a token of their profound respect, as
their seal-manual to the popular ratification of his elec-

tion. It was the unanimous and co-operative production of all the people of Cheshire. Every family and every Democratic cow in the town had contributed to it.

The President responded with deep and earnest feeling to this remarkable gift, coming from the heart of a New England population; receiving it as a token of his fidelity to the equal and inalienable rights of individual men and states. This portion of his speech has been preserved: "I will cause this auspicious event to be placed upon the records of our nation, and it will ever shine amid its glorious archives. I shall ever esteem it among the most happy incidents of my life. And now, my much respected, reverend friend, I will, by the consent and in the presence of my most honored council, have this cheese cut, and you will take back with you a portion of it, with my hearty thanks, and present it to your people, that they may all have a taste. Tell them never to falter in the principles they have so nobly defended. They have successfully come to the rescue of our beloved country in the time of her great peril. I wish them health and prosperity, and may milk in great abundance never cease to flow to the latest posterity."

The steward of the President passed a long, glittering knife through the cheese, and cut out a deep and golden wedge in the presence of Mr. Jefferson, the heads of the department, foreign ministers, and many other eminent personages. It was of a most beautiful annatto color, a little variegated in appearance, owing to the great variety of curds composing it; and as it was served up to the company with bread, all complimented it for its richness, flavor, and tint; and it was considered the most perfect specimen of cheese ever exhibited at the White House. The elder was introduced to all the members of the distinguished party, who warmly testified their admiration of such a token of regard to the chief magistrate of the nation from him and his people.

Having thus accomplished his interesting mission, Elder Leland set out on his return journey to Massachusetts. The great cheese and its reception had already become noised abroad, and he made a kind of triumphal march all the way back to Cheshire. On arriving there, there was another meeting, hardly second in attendance and interest to that around Captain Brown's cider-mill in the summer. The elder recounted to his parishioners all the incidents of his reception, and presented to them the thanks of the President. Then they all partook of the great yellow wedge of their cheese, which they ate with double relish as the President's gift to them, as well as theirs to him. Thus the little hill town of Cheshire ratified, signed, and sealed the election of Thomas Jefferson, who has been called justly the Father of American Democracy. It was a seal worthy the intelligence, patriotism, and industry of a New England dairy town, and one which its successive generations will speak of with just pride and congratulations.

A RURAL EVANGELICAL ALLIANCE.

I ONCE spent a Sunday in a rural village in Shropshire, where I saw the best illustration of an evangelical alliance, on a small scale, that I had ever witnessed. It was a small district, embosomed among the hills, and planted with clusters of thatched cottages, in threes, fours, and fives, the youngest looking a century old. A few houses of a better sort stood half hidden and half revealed, scattered along the sunny hill-sides, or nestling in clumps of trees in the valley. Here was a genuine rural community, as completely English as it was a hundred years ago. Here you might enjoy to the full the reality of your earliest dreams of an English country village of the olden time. It was delightful to one who loved such dreams to think that, in face of all the sweeping and transforming work of " modern improvements," such a community could be found, unruffled in its existence by the noisy march of eager civilization. The quietude of seven Sundays in a week seemed to rest upon it. Even the busiest industries of the working days did not break its Sabbath stillness, any more than the chirp of crickets or the caw of rooks could have done.

The whole parish probably numbered about fifty tenant farmers, and perhaps four times that number of farm laborers. A clergyman, doctor, and two or three school teachers made up the professional class. The community was too small, poor, and quiet to support a lawyer. To go out from London, or any other large town, to spend a Sabbath in such a parish, was to witness and enjoy the most salient and interesting contrasts in society; and it was one of the richest treats I ever shared. The community was too small for the play of denominational zeal or self-seeking. United, they could only stand with some effort; divided into sects, each would be a willow stick in strength. Still, few as they were, they could not all be of one religious faith or form of doctrine and worship. Doubtless all the denominations in England were represented in the beliefs and predilections of the rural villagers. But they were obliged to concede and compromise in the matter of these denominational opinions and forms, in order to have any social worship at all. For there were only three small places for such worship in the parish. Two of these were unique little buildings of the Established Church, each capable of seating from sixty to eighty persons. The other was a Wesleyan chapel, which would hold a hundred.

The clergyman, as a minister of the Established Church is called, preached in one of his little churches in the morning, and in the other in the afternoon, as they were a mile and a half apart. He had watched over and ministered to these two little folds for twenty-seven years, and he had done it with a single-hearted faith, devotion, and earnestness that had never waned or weakened. The two " livings " together yielded him but a little more than five hundred dollars a year; but he had a good and comfortable parsonage and a few acres of land rent free. Here, in the quietude of this rural home and rural round of duties, he had kept his mind in full and fresh communion with the world of thought outside, with its learning and literature, and had surrounded himself with a large library, which they had filled. No educated man in London could have mingled in these intellectual fellowships or enjoyed them with greater relish. Here he had educated his own children to a high standard of attainment in classics, mathematics, and other college studies, and he had also been a teacher to many of the village children.

The Sabbath sun arose over the hills, and filled all the quiet valley with its smile and light. My host, the most considerable and intelligent farmer of the parish, was a Wesleyan; and when I asked him about the order of the day, I found it was to exemplify a very pleasant evangelical alliance. We were to go to the Wesleyan chapel in the morning, and interchange with the Episcopal church the rest of the day. So the rector went off to his most distant field in the forenoon, and we went down into the valley, by winding footpaths through meadows, across brooks, and along green hedges, to the little chapel. By similar paths, converging to it from all directions, came men with sun-bronzed faces and hobnailed shoes, and housewives and girls and boys, showing the ruddy life of out-door work and exercise. When they entered, and walked up the bare wooden aisles to their seats, the house felt their tread to its very rafters. As their preacher was engaged elsewhere, the service consisted of a prayer-meeting, led by my host. It was characterized by all that glow and fervor of spirit and utterance which distinguish the denomination in all countries, and give their social prayers such unction and power of contagious sympathy as to draw out loud responses to their fervid sentiments from the goodly fellowship of worshippers. An incident had occurred a short time before which now quickened their supplications with a personal interest. Two sons of my host had just sailed for America, to make a home in West Tennessee for the whole family. They were only eighteen and nineteen years of age, but were well-educated and pious young men, most affectionately remembered by the whole communion of the chapel. It was affecting to see a row of those sunburnt men kneeling, as it were, behind a breastwork of heavy hobnailed shoes, praying with such emotion for the protection and well-being of these young men. They were mentioned in every supplication, and every man who did it on his knees prayed as if they were his own and only sons.

At three o'clock the service in the little parish church, almost opposite the residence of my host, was to commence. Its little bell, hung from a beam resting on two posts at the gable, began to call out the villagers with the smart but small voice of a large dinner-bell. They heard it up the hill-sides and down in the valley, and came at its invitation by footpaths through the fields and by narrow, crooked lanes, hedged head-high with blooming hawthorn. As we were so near the church, we were to start when we saw the clergyman pass. In a few minutes he made his appearance in a companionship which showed the best elements of a true evangelical alliance, after the gospel pattern. He had been a man of medium height; but from some infirmity in his later years he was bent short at the breast, almost at a sharp angle. On one

7

side of him walked his graceful and highly-cultivated daughter, deeply read in Greek and all scholarly learning, but gentle, and meek, and quiet, with better graces. On the other side of the pastor walked a first-rate specimen of an English farm laborer. He stood full six feet in his heavy, hobnailed shoes, which must, however, have added a full inch to his stature. He had on his head the round felt hat peculiar to his class. But its proud distinction he wore in the white smock-frock which it does one's eyes good to see, if he has ever delighted in stories of English rural life. It would be difficult for an American who has not actually seen it to get a good and proper idea of this unique garment. It is altogether a different thing from the old tow frocks worn by some of our farmers fifty years ago, although resembling them in shape. It is as much the uniform of the English farm laborer as is the red coat that of the English soldier; and he wears it as proudly to church and on all public occasions. It is not only for use on week days, but for ornament on Sundays. It is literally ornamented to the highest conceptions of rustic genius in its make-up. At breast and back it shows the most elaborate embroidery of the rustic needle. Indeed, I have seen some of them (evidently kept for public appearance) that seemed to bear in their ornamentation a full month's work of such a needle. When put on white as snow, of a Sunday morning, Joe Dobbin walks to church with as much self-consciousness as any New York belle in Stewart's best. Then this long, embroidered robe covers, if not a multitude of worse defects, at least defects in the clothes it conceals, which the wearer would not like to be seen at church.

It was interesting to see this evangelical triad walking to the sanctuary side by side, representing the refined and rough elements and forces of society. We followed them, and saw and realized in the little church such a pleasant fellowship of creeds and worshippers as I never witnessed before. My Wesleyan host was one of the wardens of the church, and the Wesleyan schoolmaster the pastor's clerk, to lead the readings after him and the responses. He was a stoutish man, with a square, bald head, thickly hedged at the sides with iron-gray hair. The austerities of a Calvinistic creed, or the equally serious cares and perplexities of a schoolmaster's life, had given a stern, unsunny expression to his face and voice; but he gently helped the pastor on with his black gown, and smoothed down its crumpled folds tenderly. He then took the clerk's desk, bowed his head in silent invocation, as if " to the manner born," and afterwards went through all the service with a reverent voice and clerkly emphasis. When the sermon began, he took a seat in a pew by the side of the pastor's daughter; and they sang psalms and hymns together out of the same book, he leading the tunes. Half the congregation, if such a small company could be so called, was composed of Wesleyans and other Dissenters. But all entered into the services, repeated the creeds, and uttered the responses as heartily as if it were their own mother and only church. The pastor looked upon them all as his own flock, and no shepherd ever watched over his sheep with more interest. Indeed, for twenty-seven years he had kept a Sunday checkbook, as well as week-day diary; and in this he had put down the number and persons present at every service, for all this long period. The attendance in this one place of worship had averaged about forty persons, young and old, for this space of time.

In the evening the little evangelical alliance met in the Wesleyan chapel, which was well filled. Their local preacher, a wheelwright from a neighboring village, was now in the pulpit. If his thoughts did not suggest study by the midnight oil, his large, rough hands showed hard week-day toil from sun to sun. His heart was full of gospel truth, and he poured it out in a volume of voice which made the building respond to his own emotion. He had the H difficulty strong upon him, and spoke of the final consummation of all earthly things, when the " helements hof hair" should be on fire, with remarkable force and fervor. But the superfluous H did not impair the meaning of his words, nor lessen their effect upon the audience. I noticed that the vicar's learned and accomplished daughter, who presided at the melodeon, listened to the sermon with meek and reverent attention. She again sat by the Wesleyan schoolmaster, and played and sang by his side as sweetly and devotionally as she did in the afternoon in her father's pew. When the service ended, it was pleasant to see Churchmen, Wesleyans, and other Dissenters walking home from the sanctuary in a goodly fellowship that lasted through the week, from Sabbath to Sabbath.

Nor was it only on the Sabbath that they met in religious worship. On every Friday evening there was a service in my host's large kitchen hall, as completely

English, of the olden time, as one could be. It was to a farmer's retainers what the banqueting hall of the old feudal baron was to his hospitality. It was a long room, paved with brick, and hung overhead with sides of brown bacon, hams, and dried herbs, with a long black gun, of Queen Bess's stamp, lying in the middle, on wooden brackets. One side of the room was bright and glorious with the great jewelry of an English kitchen — shining pans and dishes of tin and copper, of wonderful disk and depth. At one end, and absorbing nearly its whole breadth, was the old-fashioned fireplace, with its seated depths into the chimney, that would hold a whole family inside the mantel. Up and down the centre ran the great table, around which many generations had gathered to their meals. It was one entire slab of English oak, full four feet wide and twenty long, and just as black, and smooth, and polished as ebony.

Such was the place of week-night prayer, at which this little evangelical alliance met and spent an hour in Christian fellowship. The vicar was always present, and led the devotions; and what was written in their hearts they uttered in supplication and thanksgiving, without printed book or creed. It was well worth a long journey into the country to spend a Sunday in such a community, to witness " how good and how pleasant it is for brethren to dwell together in unity."

A QUAKER MEETING IN LONDON.

A LEAF FROM MY PRIVATE JOURNAL.

FRIDAY, May 21, 1852. — This was a day of deep interest. Went in the morning to the meeting for public worship in the Devonshire House, which was filled to its utmost capacity with Friends from every part of the kingdom. As a spectacle, no human congregation can surpass it in impressive physiognomy. The immaculate purity of the women's dresses, as they sat, a multitude of shining ones, arising in long, quiet ranks from the floor to the gallery on one side of the house, and the grave mountain of sedate and thoughtful men on the other, presented an aspect more suggestive of the assemblies of the New Jerusalem than of any earthly congregation. In a few minutes the last comers had found seats; and then a deep devotional silence settled down upon the great assembly like an overshadowing presence from heaven. The still, upbreathing prayer of a thousand hearts seemed to ascend like incense, and the communion of the Holy Spirit to descend like a dove, whose wing-beats touched to sweeter serenity those faces so calm with the divine benediction.

The deep silence of this unspoken devotion grew more and more intense, as if the whole assembly were listening to voices which their spirits alone could hear, and which a breath would drown. Then one arose, in the middle of the house, with tremulous meekness, to unburden the heart of a few brief message-words which it feared to withhold, lest it should sin against the inspiration that made them burn within it. Then, from another part of the house, arose the quavering words of prayer, few, but full of the earnest emotion and humble utterance of faith and supplication. Then moments of deeper silence followed, as if all the faculties of the mind and all the senses of physical being had descended into the soul's inner temple, to wait there for the voice of the Spirit of God. How impressive was the heart-worship of those silent moments! There was something solemn beyond description in the presence of a thousand persons of all ages so immovable that they scarcely seemed to breathe.

The " Minister's Gallery " was occupied by a long rank of the fathers and mothers of the society, from all parts of the United Kingdom, who seemed to preside over the great communion like shepherds sitting down before their quiet flocks by the still waters of salvation. In the centre sat a man and woman, a little past the meridian of life, and apparently strangers. The former had an American look, which was quite perceptible even from the opposite end of the building; and when he slowly arose out of the deep silence, his first words confirmed that impression. They were words fitly spoken and solemn, but uttered with such a nasal intonation as I never heard before, even in New England. At first, and for a few moments, I doubted whether this aggravated peculiarity would not lessen the salutary effect of his exhortation upon the minds of the listening assembly. But as his words began to flow and warm with increasing unction, they cleared up, little by little, from this nasal cadence, and rounded into more oral enunciation. Little by little they grew stronger and fuller with the power of truth, and the truth made them free and flowing. His whole person, so impassive and emotionless at first, now entered into the enunciation of his thoughts with constantly increasing animation, and his address grew more and more impressive to the last. He spoke for nearly an hour, and when he sat down and buried his spare figure under his broad-brimmed hat, and the congregation settled down into the profound quiet of serene meditation, I doubted whether it would be broken again by the voice of another exhortation.

But after the lapse of a few minutes, the woman who sat by the side of the American minister — and she was his wife — might be perceived in a state of half-suppressed emotion, as if demurring to the inward monition of the spirit that bade her arise and speak to such an assembly. It might well have seemed formidable to the nature of a meek and delicate woman. She appeared to struggle involuntarily with the conviction of duty, and to incline her person slightly towards her husband, as if her heart leaned for strength on the sympathy of his, as well as on the wisdom she awaited from above. Then she arose, calm, meek, and graceful. Her first words dropped with the sweetest cadence upon the still congregation, and were heard in every part of the house, though they were uttered in a voice seemingly but a little above a whisper. Each succeeding sentence warbled into new beauty and fulness of silvery intonation. The burden of her spirit was the life of religion in the heart, as contrasted with its mere language on the tongue ; or, what it was to be truly and fully a disciple of Jesus Christ. Having meekly stated the subject which had occupied her meditations, and which she felt constrained to revive in the hearing of the congregation before her, she said, " And now, in my simple way, and in the brief words that may be given me, let me enter with you into the examination of this question."

At the first word of this sentence, she loosened the fastenings of her bonnet, and, at the last one, handed it down to her husband with an indescribable grace. There was something very impressive in the act, as well as in the manner in which it was performed — as if she uncovered her head involuntarily in reverence to that vision of divine truth unsealed to her waiting eyes. And in her eyes it seemed to beam with a serene and heavenly light, and to burn in her heart with holy inspiration ; to touch her lips and every gentle motion of her person with a beautiful, eloquent, and solemn expression, as her words fell in the sweet music of her voice upon the rapt assembly. Like a stream welling and warbling out of Mount Hermon, and winding its way to the sea, flowed the melodious current of her message ; now meandering among the half-opened flowers of unrhymed poetry ; now through the green pastures of savlation where the Good Shepherd was bearing in his bosom the tender lambs of his flock. Then it took the force of lofty diction, and fell in a volume of silvery eloquence, but slow, solemn, and searching, down the rocks and ravines of Sinai ; then out, like a little river of music, into the wilderness where the prodigal son, with the husks of his poverty clutched in his lean hands, sat in tearful meditation on his father's home and his father's love.

More than a thousand persons seemed to hold their breath, as they listened to that meek, delicate woman, whose lips were touched to an utterance almost divine. I never saw an assembly so subdued into motionless meditation. And the solemn, impressive silence deepened to a stillness more profound when she ceased to speak. In the midst of these thoughtful moments she knelt in prayer. At the first word of her supplication, the whole congregation arose. The men who had worn their hats while she spoke to them, reverently uncovered their heads as she knelt down to speak to God. Her clear, sweet voice trembled with the burden of her petition, on which her spirit seemed to ascend into the holy of holies, and to plead there, with Jacob's faith, for a blessing upon all encircled within that immediate presence. When she arose from her knees, the great congregation sat down, as it were, under the shadow of that prayer, in meditation more deep and devotional. This lasted a few minutes, when two of the fathers of the society, sitting in the centre of the ministers' gallery, turned and shook hands with each other, and were followed by other couples in each direction, as a kind of mutual benediction, as well as a signal that the meeting was terminated. At this simple sign the whole congregation arose, and quietly left the house.

· THE ENGLISH DAY.

THERE has been no day in the life of the American nation marked by such peculiar interest as the " English Day," at the great Peace Jubilee at Boston. It was not the grand music that made it surpass, in several most happy characteristics, the other days of the long banquet of the world's best melodies, though this in itself lifted the great multitude to a height as rapturous as any to which they were borne by any after-flood of symphony. There were histories, memories, associations, and co-incidences that gave to the music of those hours a power and effect which twenty thousand trained voices and instruments could not alone produce upon the vast assembly. There were profounder meanings than these alone could express, to be translated into the silent language of the heart by all who witnessed that scene with the attentive faculties of reflection. For it was a scene of sublime representation, as well as the most mul-titudinous concert of human voices ever heard on earth. A great history was enacted as a variation in the loftiest songs that human and metal lips could raise. At this gathering of the nations, two stood face to face in a re-lationship that can never bind two others together by ties so strong and many, by memories so mutual, proud, and precious. The mother and daughter stood there, looking into each other's faces, with the history of a hun-dred years between them, — a century, lacking but a lit-tle, between them and the last of the years when the same parental roof-tree covered them both. One could feel that the common memories that reached across the narrow space between, and dwelt upon those years of childhood and motherhood in their common home, made not a " mournful," but a happy and tender " rustle " in the hearts of every thoughtful American and Englishman under that vast roofage. This sentiment gave to the thousands of voices that hailed the opening moment of this scene the inspiration of a sympathy that seemed to thrill the building itself.

It was a moment that only those present could feel and remember in its full inspiration. The first day of the pentecost of music had put the choral mountain of singers, and all the varied singing and instruments of melody, into their best tune for these English hours. The Jubilee had opened with that grandest of all songs that ever lifted the praise of human hearts and lips into the ears of God — OLD HUNDRED. Never on earth before was it sung with such heart and power, and never, perhaps, until it is sung anew by the sacramental hosts in heaven, will it be so sung again. The effect was indescribable. No figures nor parallels of speech could give one who did not hear it any idea of the impression it made upon the thousands who sang and the thousands who listened. All the doxologies of the two Englands, Old and New, for a hundred years, seemed to respond with their soft and solemn echoes, and mingled with the flood of molten voices that rolled up and down the choral mountain, ascending, widening, deepening, and strengthening, until its waves of symphony beat against the lofty roofage of the edifice, and made the pendent flags of all nations keep time in fluttering sympathy with the inspiration. If Old Hundred may well be called the *Marseillaise* for the hosts of the Christian world to sing on their march " to the battles of the Lord against the mighty," " Nearer, my God, to Thee," was a song equally happy to close the first day's feast of music ; and if music alone could lift a human congregation nearer to God, then none ever assembled on earth could have been raised higher than the multitude who listened to that favorite hymn, in which all, from one end of the building to the other, mingled their voices.

This first day of the feast was one virtually of rehearsal and preparation for singers and listeners, tuning their lips, ears, and hearts for the morrows that were to follow. Twenty thousand voices, that had given their sweetest music to the Sabbath devotions of hundreds of New England churches, had poured their best notes, for the first time, into one swelling flood of melody ; and the flood had upborne them to an inspiration of heart and tongue which had never thrilled the same number of human singers before. Such was the preparation for the English Day. There was not a man nor woman in the sides of that choral mountain who did not know and appreciate the affinities, histories, and memories that were to make the English Day differ from all that were to follow it at the festival. When, therefore, the file-leader of the British Grenadier Band emerged from under the great organ, heading " the thin, red line " that slowly threaded the mountainous orchestra to its base before the great multitude, there was a scene, as well as acclamation, which it would have done the hearts of the two great nations good to have witnessed and heard with their millions. The thousands who saw and heard for them grasped the whole significance of the scene and the moment, to the full meaning and inspiration of all the histories, memories, and associations they brought to life. England, and her queen, and her historical centuries, and all our proud inheritance in them, stood there before us in that red line of men, in tall bear-skin caps, facing the palpitating, fluttering mountain of singers. The cheering multitude behind them rolled back the flood of acclamation that rose and swelled from floor to roof, and made the vast building tremulous with the emotion of thirty thousand human hearts, all stirred to the same sentiment of welcome and delight. There they stood in a line so immovable that they looked like a row of red statuary, not a hair of their bear-skin caps, nor a border or hem of their coats stirring in the midst of the agitated human sea that impended over them and surrounded them on every side.

Of course there were minutes of multitudinous cheering, with thirty thousand men and women on their feet, with waving of handkerchiefs, which preceded the first note from that "thin red line." There was space in these intervening minutes for the thoughts of other and many years; for the incidents, coincidents, and associations of the scene and hour. This British band of musicians had marched into Boston on the very day, almost a century gone, when their countrymen marched, in their red, brave lines, up the slopes of Bunker Hill, reddened by the first conflict that sundered the English speaking race in the twain of separate nations. This very hour, the same space between, hundreds of English soldiers, who fell on that day, were being laid in a thin, red line, in a soldier's grave. They fought and fell in the very uniform worn by their grandchildren before us. They had charged up those embattled heights in the same tall bear-skin caps. The thoughtful minutes were full of memories and associations that reached into the histories of the whole family of nations, and which the scene brought home to our reflections with the freshness of yesterday's events. This day, fifty-seven years ago, the fathers of this red-coated band before us marched away from the field of Waterloo, at the head of the British army, filling the air of heaven with their grandest strains of victory. And here now stood their sons, in the same uniform and stalwart, solid stature, before us, awaiting a lull in the tempest of cheers to pour forth the mellow music of human brotherhood. Here were the rival bands of France and Germany to listen with the great multitude to the British overture, and to respond with their best music, each in the day set apart to its nation.

It needed but a minute for a mind awake to the inspiration of the scene to bring all these historical incidents and associations to a vivid focus of view and reflection. Out of the midst of these, in living presence, the band-leader now gave the signal. As if all those instruments had but one breath, their voices poured out a flood of music, so pure, and sweet, and full, that even to call it silvery would suggest a metallic cadence which would not do it justice. Indeed, to common ears it would seem impossible that brass, silver, or gold could be trained to such music of tongue that the natural accent of neither could be recognized in the highest tides of their symphony. At their loftiest reach, bugles, cornets, clarinets, and every other instrument, blended in such a soft volume of utterance that it sounded almost with a plaintive cadence, and this quality was well fitted to feast a lively imagination with pleasant fancies. As the tall grenadiers stood at the base of that choral mountain, facing its towering heights of spell-bound thousands, they seemed to be rehearsing the experiences of the common mother country since the day when her eldest daughter went out to set up a home of her own. They seemed to be telling a mother's story to such a daughter, not proudly, but gently and tenderly, with a mother's voice, as soft as ever with her first affection. It sounded like a story here and there wet with a falling tear, and tremulous with a sigh at some sad memory that mingled with the thought of intervening years. Then, as if the whole choral host had been touched to deepest sympathy with the sentiment of the story, they arose suddenly to their feet to respond to it. Their response seemed a spontaneous and instantaneous utterance of that sympathy. Its words seemed to come to their lips as naturally as the smile to their eyes at the first outburst of those enrapturing strains. At such a moment they could not, nor a soul in the great multitude, have thought of any other responding words than " GOD SAVE THE QUEEN."

Never since queens began to reign on earth was the English National Anthem sung by so many human tongues and hearts under one roof. Nowhere under the British sceptre, though the linked continents and islands that own its sway shall belt the great globe itself, will that anthem be so sung again. Here, in sight of Bunker

Hill, and on the very anniversary of that memorable day in our common history, the granddaughter of George the Third received the grandest choral ovation that ever honored a human sovereign on earth. Twenty-five thousand American hearts, and nearly as many of their voices, mingled in the uprising flood, as the one " voice of many waters." All the vast instrumentalities that human skill could train to musical utterance seemed touched with spontaneous inspiration. The great organ, played by tiller rods as long as a steamship's keel, put in the emphasis of its mighty bass, and scores of brass cannon, whose swift keys were touched by electric nerves, like the wires of a piano, beat time with the accents of their deep and mellow thunder. Up and down the mountain orchestra and out upon the human sea rolled the ground swell of the anthem. Anon Gilmore, the Napoleon of the Jubilee, leaned over on one foot and smote with his wand at this side and that of the vocal mountain, like another Moses at Horeb, and a deepening torrent of melody gushed out into the careering flood. How many thousands in that sublime moment wished that Queen Victoria had been present in person, to hear how American lips and hearts could sing that anthem !

But the climax of ecstasy had not yet been reached. Seemingly as spontaneous as " God save the Queen" had been the response to the overture of the Grenadier Band, we all knew that it was so put down in the programme. As natural and fitting as it was, its expectation modified the pleasing effect of accidental spontaneity. But what followed was as unexpected as a choral song from the clouds. Hardly had the ebb and flow of the

8

National Anthem subsided into their expiring ripple,
when a sudden wave of the leader's wand over that " thin,
red line " brought out THE STAR-SPANGLED BANNER in
all the proud glory that the best musical instruments in
the wide world could give to it. It was a Roland for an
Oliver in the happiest sense of brotherhood. If " God
save the Queen " was never sung with such a concert of
heart and voice in England as here under Bunker Hill,
it was equally true that " The Star-spangled Banner "
was never played with such power and effect on the
American continent as it was by the British Grenadier
Band, as a response to their national anthem. No similes
nor illustrations could convey in words an idea of the
scene and sentiment of that moment. The incident was
as sudden as lightning, and thrilled the vast audience like
electricity. All arose to their feet, and their delight
deepened into a veritable ecstasy as the grand strains of
our national hymn filled the vast building with such a
glory of music. Twenty thousand handkerchiefs were
waving to and fro like so many white doves waltzing
on the wing. Deeper, richer, and grander arose the
strains of those incomparable instruments, which seemed
to breathe with spontaneous inspiration, and the very
building itself appeared to palpitate with the human
emotion that deepened at every note. Never since human hymns were sung did one follow the other with
such effect upon listening thousands. It was the happiest incident of all the festal days of the Jubilee. No
moment in the history of the two nations could have
made the incident more felicitous, beautiful, and touching. While the astute discussions of wordy diplomacy

were arraying the two governments in dispute, the two great peoples embraced each other in these two songs with a sense of brotherhood they never felt before. They recognized "the consequential claims" of the old kith and kin, of the old histories and memories which were their glorious and proud inheritance, as indivisible as one human life. This was the sentiment that led and lifted the tide of emotion to its most rapturous height; and when the last strain died away murmuring against its end, the great triumph of the Jubilee was felt and owned by every soul present. The English Day was alone well worth the structure of the Coliseum, and all that it had cost of faith, hope, genius, and effort, to convene under its roof twenty thousand singers, and the best musical instruments and capacities of the world.

IT'S LIKE PARTING WITH MY OWN LIFE.

A MAN and his wife, of middle age, called at our office for some assistance in getting a passage back to America. They were English born, but had resided in the United States many years; when, having gathered together a little property, they had come to England to visit some relatives much poorer than themselves, though rich in good will. Unwilling to be guests of honest poverty, they invested their little fortune in a small business, with the hope of paying their way, without burdening their relatives or wasting their own means. But their enterprise was a failure, and they lost all their savings, and were left without means to get back to America. In this dilemma they applied to us for aid. They had a beautiful Pomeranian dog with them, a bright, sprightly, affectionate creature, which never had the fear of poverty or hunger before its eyes. We suggested that, even if any benevolent persons should pay their passage home in an emigrant ship, the captain or owners would not allow the dog to accompany them, and that it would not be proper for them to solicit help while in possession of such a dog. They had not thought of this before, and both were surprised and distressed at the idea of parting with their pet. It was born at the time of President Lincoln's assassination, and they had brought it to England with them as a living memento of that martyr-patriot; and the woman took it up into her arms, and caressed it as if her own infant child. There was a sharp and long struggle between necessity and affection. It could hardly have been more painful if it were the question of leaving their only born behind them in a strange land. Both sobbed aloud and wept like children. We offered to give them a sovereign for it, and promised to treat it tenderly, saying they must give it up to some one. The woman finally consented, in a flood of grief, to give it over to us, and tried to bring her husband to the same mind. He was a hardy-looking man, with long, crispy, black hair, and " face like the tan." He was dressed like the fireman on board of a steamer, or half engineer and half sailor. But he could not stand it. He burst into tears, and rushed out of the room to hide his face. His wife entreated him back, and tried to reason with him. The dog made several leaps to get up into his arms, and looked at him with eyes seemingly full of the tenderest of human emotions. The poor man looked down upon him for a few moments with a doting fondness which was truly affecting; then, dashing out of the door, he cried out, " I can't do it! It's like taking away my own life!" His wife followed him, weeping, saying that if she could bring him over to the parting they would call again in course of the day. But we never saw them again.

———•◦•———

A MODEL FARMER'S HARVEST-HOME.

THE size and surroundings of a regular old-fashioned farmer's fireside shows the companionships and sympathies that lived and breathed in the society that gathered around it in the olden times. That kitchen hearth-stone, depend upon it, was not made so broad and deep for the farmer's wife and children. They constituted hardly half the circle that sat around the red fire-light on a winter's eve. The sun-browned men and boys of the plough, sickle, scythe, mattock, and flail, who tilled his fields and ricked and threshed his harvests, ate his home-made bread and drank his home-brewed beer by that fireside, and shared with him and his family the merry and musical illumination of the yule-log. Those were the days when capital and labor, when employer and *employé*, lived in close companionship and much goodly sympathy. But little by little they have receded from

each other socially and in common sentiment.   There are
a thousand old farm-houses in England with kitchen
fireplaces large and deep enough, in frontage and sidings,
for a good-sized family, and men and boys to till a holding of five hundred acres ; but, in nine cases out of ten,
probably, the laborers have been evicted from that
hearth-circle by the new customs of fastidious civilization, or have emigrated voluntarily to the frontiers of the
farm, or even to distant villages.   As capital and labor
have thus gradually seceded from each other locally, they
have equally seceded in sympathy, until, in many cases,
a most unhappy state of feeling exists between the
employer and his men ; one party trying to get as much
labor as possible from the other for the least money, and
the other bent upon getting the most money for the least
labor.   Once in a while this feeling explodes in the con-
flagration of the harvests which underpaid or ill-used
laborers have reaped and ricked for a stingy-hearted
farmer.

Now, all this is wrong and unnatural, and more so
between farmers and their laborers, in a certain sense,
than between large manufacturers and the operatives
they employ, who must be housed in the whole of a
small village.   Any custom, new or old, that can be
adopted to bring back this old social feeling and companionship is a boon and a blessing to the country.   We
notice, with much pleasure, the Harvest Festivals that
are becoming more and more frequent in agricultural
districts.   These are very good in their way, and the
more of them the better.   But they cannot bring the
farmer and his own men together in the old happy spirit

of the Harvest Home in his ample kitchen. We had read of these social and festive gatherings from our youth up, but were never present until a few weeks ago, when we were invited to one by a large and well-educated farmer in the neighborhood of Lichfield. Here it was carried out to perfection in act, sentiment, and enjoyment. It was to us a scene of the liveliest interest, illustrating the spirit of our dream of the social life of the olden time. And, what gave zest to the feast, it was not a compensation for a year's fast of friendly intercourse and sympathy on the part of the host towards his men ; it was the crowning expression of his good will and care for them through the past months of labor. Having made himself a model farmer's home, surrounded and embellished with what a cultivated country gentleman could desire, he had attached all his men to him by his generous thought and care for their comfort. While making grottoes, ferneries, and fountains for the enjoyment of himself and his own family and friends, he was laying out recreation grounds for his laborers hard by, where they might play at skittles or other healthy games after their work for the day was done. It was as pleasant a sight as any social life we ever read of could produce, to see him at one end of the long table and his foreman at the other, and the space on each side filled with all the men and boys he had employed on his farm. We should like to have had the whole scene photographed to the life of all its features, — the faces with all the hot harvest red upon them ; the surroundings and overhangings of the large kitchen ; the deep sides of pendent bacon over the table, and great hams hung at intervals between them; the side walls garnished with kitchen ware of polished copper and tin; the grand old fireplace with its social histories legible to the mind's eye, and the happy light of thorough enjoyment which seemed to beam from and upon every countenance. It was a sight that did one good to look at and remember in the toil and endeavor of business life. Then the spread of good things the table presented was both the picture and original of large-hearted and broad-handed hospitality, giving all a quickened appetite by its sight and savor. "The Roast Beef of Old England" was here, not only in song, but in substance, grand and luscious. It was represented by a round that weighed forty-five pounds before it was put to the fire, and never could such a bulk of English beef have been roasted to more even and thorough perfection. Few men, we fear, ever arose to say grace over such a feast in a farmer's kitchen. What a knife was that he passed through the savory round! It was as long as a sword, and thin as the blade of a band-saw. It was a harvest home in the most literal and minute sense, — harvest brought into the house and upon the very table, as well as festooned above it — bouquets of golden wheat and barley ears alternating with field and garden flowers and fruits. If the labor that produced the banquet was a prayer, the eating of it was a praise and thanksgiving. What eyes looked upon the feast, what appetites set to its enjoyment!

When the great round of beef and the other concomitants of the feast had been cut down half way to the table, and there was a hush in the ring and clatter of knives, forks, spoons, and plates, the social dessert was

introduced by the host in a short speech of welcome to
the special or extra guests that were present, including
his brother from Birmingham, a gentleman from Lichfield,
Edward Capern, the Rural Postman Poet, and ourself.
Each of us was honored with a toast, which was received
by the men and boys in the heartiest manner, all standing upon their feet, with the home-brewed in their hands,
while they sang a verse or two of an old table song,
ending something like this, so far as we could catch
the words : —

> " For he is a jolly good fellow,
>   And so say all of us ;
>   Hip ! hip ! hip ! hurrah !
>   For he is a jolly good fellow," &c.

Every man and boy sang this refrain with rollicking
enthusiasm. We noticed that several of the faces on
both sides of the table were rough with the furrows of
fifty or sixty years, but every furrow was full of a young
heart's light.

The guests responded to the toasts in short speeches,
which were most heartily received. Capern, in addition
to one or two full of genial humor, sang one of his own
songs, the whole company coming down in the chorus
with right good will and voice. Then came the toast of
the evening. Our host arose, and proposed the health of
his foreman at the other end of the table in a short
speech, which ought to be printed and circulated among
all the farmers of the kingdom. He spoke of the way
he had gone in and out with the men of the farm ; how
wakeful was his eye and watchful was his care for his

master's interests, while he was equally solicitous and
active for their comfort, as a friend, companion, and
fellow-worker. Then he said how much pleased he had
been through the year, not only with their work, but
with the spirit in which they had done it. It was his
delight to see the face of every one of his men sunny
and cheerful, and nothing troubled him more than a
sulky or discontented look in the field. For himself, it
was his earnest wish and thought to make their life and
labor as happy as possible to themselves, as well as
profitable to himself; and his wife, their mistress, was
one with him in this desire and effort. He spoke in a
feeling manner of their devotion to his interests during
the past harvest; how that he had often expressed a wish
that they would rest for a while in some of the hottest
hours, fearing they would be overpowered with the heat,
but that they had gone on with their work without
flagging, and even were often in the field at three in the
morning drawing wheat or barley.

The foreman arose, and spoke for himself and the men
in a little speech, full of good sense and feeling; and the
whole company, including our host, sang with exuberant
heart and voice, "For he's a jolly good fellow," &c.
Being called upon several times to say a few words, we
dwelt upon the spirit of the feast, as the best illustration
we had seen of the good feeling and pleasant companionship that should exist especially between a farmer and
his men. They should all feel that they were rowing
in the same boat, and should all pull together as if making for the same shore. We told them of the hardy
whalers of New Bedford; how they made a joint-stock

enterprise of every voyage, in which the owners of the ship had a certain number of shares, the captain and mate, and every man of the crew, even to the cabin-boy, having each a specified proportion of the stock. Thus they all said *we* and *our* at every furrow they ploughed with the keel, and every stroke of the oar. Every barrel of oil they took they all looked upon as *ours*, and at home it was divided between them according to the rate to each agreed upon before they first set sail on the voyage. Every farm should be carried on in the spirit, if not to the letter, of this arrangement; so that every man and boy employed upon it should say *we* and *our* in regard to every day's labor, to every sheaf of wheat, pig, lamb, or chicken on the establishment; or make the employer's interest, wish, and will their own, feeling that they would share proportionately in the prosperity and pleasure they thus jointly produced.

This idea of *we* seemed to please the men, and they gave us the "Jolly good fellow," &c., with great gusto, in response to our speech. A little before twelve the host and guests retired, leaving the men at the table for a little while to themselves. But in a few minutes he was called for to give them a parting song; so he went back to the table and sang them their favorite piece, then shook hands with them all round, and rejoined us in the dining-room, when he gave us many incidents and facts illustrating the pleasant feeling existing between himself and all the hands employed on his farm. For ourself, we never sat down to a social banquet with a greater relish of enjoyment. It realized to the full all we had fancied of the social life of the olden time.

THE CONNECTICUT RIVER.

THE seers and saints of old speak of " the strength of
the hills " as if they were the special gifts of the Creator
to his favored people for their defence. The history of
later nations has shown us that they have found more
in the strength of the hills than defences against the attacks of outside enemies ; that they have drawn from
them a moral vigor of character, keenness and activity
of intellect, and a love of country which has produced
the most enduring and elevated patriotism. But if its
mountains and hills are the bone and muscle of the earth,
its rivers are its blood, even in the sense of a moral
vitality to its human races. No parts or elements of a
country are so historical as its rivers, or reflect so faithfully the character of its people. All the upland streams
and rills of their experience seem to run down into their
main rivers, and these to take the hue of their moral and
political life.

America has its historical rivers, which mirror the life
and character of its different communities just as truthfully and perceptibly. The Mississippi, the Missouri,
the Ohio, and the James are marked each by its historical characteristics. Each not only seems to record, but
to resemble, the character of the people settled upon its
banks. The two most historical rivers in North America,
in the fullness and variety of these senses, are the Connecticut and the St. Lawrence. To the New Englander
and Old Englander no other rivers in America embrace

so much of varied record and interest as these two beautifully-bound and illustrated volumes.

The Connecticut is the central representative river of New England in almost every sense and aspect of reflection. It runs forever full of the bright, pure waters from New England mountains and hills. Here you find New England at home, in the full play of her life and character. Here she is at work, with all her infinite and matchless industries, that never pause nor rest, week in, week out, the year around. Here are her representative communities, her sample towns, villages, factories, farms, schools, and the houses and cottages of men representing all classes of her people. The long, blue river runs through them and her history, like a self-registering gauge, every mile of it marked by some distinctive feature. Here are two centuries in presence and comparison, with their contrasting experiences, which the mind almost unconsciously sets one against the other on the way. For, to make the journey of either river without this exercise of reflection would be travelling through a country with one eye shut.

The Connecticut bears the record of such noble heroisms as the Rhine, with all its mountain castles of old baronial robbers, never equalled. No expedition that ever sailed up or down that river could compare for sublime courage and faith with Captain John Mason's fleet of two sloops, that sailed down the Connecticut from Hartford, against the powerful Pequots, with all the ablebodied men of the English settlements on board. What deed of patriotic daring and devotion in the history of our English race should rank higher in the glory of human acts than that of this little forlorn hope, when its leaders, in the face of the fortified foe, sent back a part of their handful of men to protect the defenceless homes they had left behind ! Not that they were too many, like Gideon's band, to meet the enemy's host, but because those log-cabin hamlets at Hartford, Windsor, and Wethersfield, which held their hearts' treasures, had been left with too few armed men to defend them.

Every mile of the river above Hartford has its association with the first perils, hardships, and heroism of the pioneers of the English colony. This was the Mississippi of New England, on her slow, brave march across the continent. This was her great and unexplored West, the *terra incognita*, which she feared to let her oldest children explore and possess. More than once her Colonial Assembly voted against this perilous enterprise. Here it was that Pastor Hooker with his flock came out from their long, painful travel through the dark, rough wilderness, and looked down from these green slopes upon the blue river and the winding meads of the valley. Every one of these white, green-shaded towns, on either side as we ascend, has its vivid associations with those first years of peril, heroic daring, suffering, and patience. Each has its own *sagas*, its own legends and traditions, like those that entertain the winter firesides of Iceland — stories of hair-breadth escapes, of hand-to-hand struggles with the Indians, bears, wolves, panthers, and other aborigines of the forests and mountains. Here is Bloody Brook, with its record of massacre by the tomahawk, which filled all the homes in New England with mourn-ing and lamentation. Onward a little farther are Turner's Falls, where the swift and unsparing vengeance of the English colonist fell upon the sleeping bands of their fierce enemy. Here is old Deerfield, reposing in the peaceful quiet of its ancient elms, with its very name associated with one of the most stirring events in a century of Indian warfare. A few years ago the house of its first minister, which the Indians tried to burn over his head, was still standing ; and its oak door, hacked with tomahawks and perforated with bullets, is treasured here as the most precious heir-loom of the village's history.

This is a mere glimpse at the historical background that reflects an additional feature of interest upon the natural scenery of the Connecticut. This scenery in itself is as picturesque and pleasing as any American river can show. If it is not so bold and grand as that of the Hudson through the Highlands, its pictures of beauty are hung in a softer light and longer gallery, with no blank or barren spaces between them. No river between the two oceans, from sea to source, presents a greater variety of landscapes, or in happier alternation and *pose*. The artists of the Royal Academy might learn something from nature here in the art and taste of hanging pictures. Of course, they cannot rival nature in having a mirror for the floor of their gallery to reflect the masterpieces on its walls. For its whole length the river presents its scenery in this double aspect.

It was a happy circumstance for us that we had the best light possible to bring out these salient features to their best perspective. The sky was overcast with thin clouds, through the folds of which the July sun, between the showers, poured, itself unseen, a flood of golden light, like a gladdening smile, now upon this wooded gorge, then upon that bald mountain-top, and its green slopes down. As a veiled artist looking at his own pictures with a pride and admiration that illumine them, so the sun, all through the showery day, beamed and gleamed, invisible, upon a succession of infinitely-varied landscapes, now on this, now on that side of the river, as if to show to human eyes what its own loved best. Nature's statuary, painting, and music alternated in the happiest succession on the right and left the whole length of the valley. Mountains with fir-haired crowns, and bare, gray faces, looked smiling at the green pastured hills on the other side. Landscapes that laid their heads on the heaving bosom of the purple clouds, rounded into view and out of it at every turn. And here and there the little mountain rivers and streams lent to the beauty of the scene the music of their white cascades in all the varied cadences of their tenor and treble.

For nearly a hundred miles of its winding course, the Connecticut hems the opposite shores of Vermont and New Hampshire with a broad seam of silver, which each state wears as a fringe of light to its green and graceful border. Then the river, narrowed to a fordable stream, bends away towards its source from the railway route, which follows the Passumpsic branch, crossing and recrossing, and playing hide-and-seek with it through the upper towns and villages of Vermont. The scenery to the last, though formed of the same elements and painted with the same foreground and background colors, is varied at every mile by landscapes and views which attract and delight the eye as much as if each were the only one of the kind to be seen on the journey.

I have said that New England will be found at home on the Connecticut in all the features, faculties, and senses of her home life and character. She is at home on it in all these qualities, as if living, acting, and moving before her own mirror. Here you may see reflected her industrial communities and activities, the endless fertilities of her inventive genius, her manufacturing establishments and educational institutions alternating with each other, and both blending with a hardy and thrifty agriculture, in the varied scenery of human industry which fills all the valleys with the beauty and joy of golden harvests, and softens the rugged faces of a hundred mountains with meadow and pasture for thousands of sheep and cattle. Here is Hartford, at the head of navigation for sloops and schooners, with small, if any, capacities for foreign commerce, and with small variety of manufactures. It is one of the smaller cities even of New England, and with no natural resources for faster growth. But not a city in the wide world, of the same population, can compare with it for the possession and employment of capital in banks and other moneyed institutions. Here is Springfield, sitting quietly under its venerable elms at the junction of four railways, with green arbors built out by nature from the crescent hills to command the best views of the river. Here it is, with " The Arsenal," and " The House with Seven Gables," which New England genius has made immortal structures. Here, a few miles above, is Chicopee, known abroad as the cognomen of Ames in mechanical reputation. Then comes the river Holyoke, where the whole volume of the Connecticut has been, as it were, *Niagarized* for countless spindles and machinery of every faculty and motion. The mountain Holyoke, with its famous Mary Lyon's School, looks down from its educational heights upon these busy industries, and Easthampton and Amherst, with their institutions of New England learning, side by side with all these mechanical activities, recognize and share in them the intellectual fellowships of practical life. Here is Northampton, shaded by the living elms that Edwards planted and solemnized by the theology he preached — an English town in the characteristics of its social life. Hadley, Deerfield, and Greenfield are agricultural towns, each with the record of two centuries, which would make for it an interesting volume of incident and experience.

Crossing the line of Massachusetts, the river shows on either side some of the best sample towns of Vermont and New Hampshire. Vermont is virtually the oldest daughter of Connecticut, and we pass through its Windsors, Wethersfields, Hartlands, and Hartfords, almost in the same order of succession as in the mother state. These Green Mountain villages show "the strength of the hills" as a source of mental and industrial vigor to their communities. These, the greenest in America, produce and present most strikingly this characteristic. They are vast beehives of ingenious industry all the year through, with their cells as full of its honey in midwinter as in midsummer. The highest a sheep can climb sends it down with the wealth of its wool, as a bee laden at upland flowers; and green slopes, that wheels cannot

mount, flow, as it were, with the milk of grazing herds.
Their rushing, dashing streams are all set to the music
of machinery, whose wheels beat time to the accents of
their flow. Each little river turns daily the pines of the
nearest mountain into the framework, flooring, and covering of a two-story house for distant districts void of
such timber. To feed the busy mills with it all the year
round is the work of the long winter months, when the
white Mountains resound and respond to each other
with the sound of the axe from morning till night. As
the snow begins to soften at the approach of spring,
another busy industry is interpolated as an interesting
and profitable occupation. These snow-bound hills, as
stark and stiff as if girdled with the frigid zone, begin to
compete with the tropics, and to rival the products of the
warmest climates. They pit their hardy maples against
the cane-fields of Cuba and Louisiana, and challenge
them to produce a sweeter sugar than their pellucid juices
supply.

These mountains are as fertile in the production of
mental as of manual industries. They set the machinery
of thought into ingenious action to overcome what some
may call the inauspicious circumstances of climate and
soil. It would illustrate this fertility to take the census
of the inventions of minds that received their first bent
and stimulus among these snow-bound hills. A single
instance will suffice to show this characteristic. Our
landlord at the White River Junction, who carries on
two or three large hotels in the White Mountains, and
several farms and mills in Vermont, said that three boys,
who lived with him successively on his homestead, be-

came inventors of machinery of immense value to the country. The first invented a self-acting jenny; the second, a self-operating mule, which saves sixty per cent. of the manual labor once required for the same work; while the third produced a portable knitting-machine as labor-saving as the sewing-machine. Within a few miles of this point the sculptor Powers was born, and other men who have made their mark in the world. All these varied and blended characteristics make the scenery of the Connecticut peculiarly interesting to the observant traveller.

THE ST. LAWRENCE AND QUEBEC.

JOHN QUINCY ADAMS, in a short speech to the Canadians at Niagara Falls, said that Nature had too few of such master-works to give one of them entire to a single nation; so she had divided this between two, in equal shares. But, for five thousand miles, from one side of the continent to the other, one may notice this happy arrangement of division. Having ascended the Connecticut valley to the Canadian line, we come to the beautiful Lake Memphremagog, which, in a quiet summer day, might well merit the name given by the Indians to another lake in the same region, "*the smile of the Great Spirit.*" And this is only one hasp in the azure jewelry which Nature has furnished for covering and beautifying the seams between the two territories from the Atlantic to the Pacific. The rainbow over the Niagara spans the central gateway opening upon each. The St. Lawrence, the Great Lakes, and rivers and waters of the farther west, flowing diversely into two oceans, make, but hide, the boundaries of the two national divisions; just as a common blood, language, religion and law blend, while they bound, the life, character, and destiny of the two great families of the English-speaking race.

Lake Memphremagog is a body of water between thirty and forty miles in length, and from two to five in breadth, with its bosom studded with islands beautifully embossed. The scenery from the great hotel at its head is like that of the Rhine from the Hotel Bellevue at Bonn. Some of the mountains that soften into blue as they tower up in the distance stand higher on their base than the Rhenish peaks. One of these, the Owl's Head, measures the height of three thousand feet above the level of the lake. One of the largest hotels in the United States entertains the visitors at this quiet and delightful summer retreat, and a large two-story steamer gives all who wish it an excursion of forty or fifty miles daily.

On crossing the line into Canada, a New England traveller observes that Vermont and New Hampshire lap over upon East Canada for a considerable distance, and he notices for a while no marked distinction in the scenery of industry and thrifty life and occupation. Hundreds from these states have settled in the province and mingled with its population, retaining their character and habits, and impressing them upon the whole community. As we proceed northward, we pass through sections where the influence of the old French element becomes distinctly marked. We are soon on the wide and dark battleground of the axe, where it is winning its slow conquests over these northern forests which have withstood the march of civilization for two hundred years. Here we come into the region of log cabins, huts, and houses, and one is almost surprised to find them so near the New England border. It is interesting to see in them the outposts of civilized life, occupied by the hardy skirmishers it deploys upon the wilderness to clear the way for the grand march of populous towns and villages.

Here a field as large as Waterloo shows the marks of the unsparing steel and fire. The defeated pines that stood up to the battle, like serried ranks of grenadiers, now lie upon each other, broken and blackened skeletons. The field adjoining is the scene of a sharp and decisive engagement five years ago ; and the plough is beginning to do its smoothing work, and to furrow it for its first crops of grain. Another field, nearer to the woodman's cabin camp, is the scene of his first encounter with the forest. Ten years ago he smote it stoutly with steel and fire, and now it is a green and level meadow ready for the scythe. Every year he marches upon the flank of the forest, and wins a new field with the axe. He follows slowly and patiently with the plough. His wheat harvests deploy year by year, and push back the wilderness. His log cabin grows with their growth. It becomes a goodly house, the home of a large and industrious family, and the centre of a growing and thrifty village.

In a few hours a long range of blue mountains indicated the course and nearness of the St. Lawrence, and we were soon in sight of that mighty river and of the Gibraltar of America. Both more than equalled our anticipation and conception. The traveller who has ever seen the Bay of Naples and the oldest and strongest cities of Europe, must be peculiarly impressed by the first sight and second sight of Quebec.

There is not another such city in either hemisphere, when viewed in all its surroundings and aspects; nor is there such another river to build such a city on. An American, who has only read of fortified towns in the Old World, is filled by this at first sight with wonder and astonishment. "Is this really the American continent?" he will most likely ask himself, as he looks up from the opposite shore to the steep mountainous bluff, crowned and girded with fortress upon fort, and fort upon battery, from base to the topmost height. The city that belts the foreshortened mountain, below and above the old gray wall that divides it, seems at first view to have been translated whole from the Old World. It makes a harmonious and natural setting for the lofty fortress, and conforms itself to bastions, breastworks, and batteries, filling all the irregular spaces left for civil life and habitation from the river upward.

The citadel is the best stand-point for the aspects of nature which distinguish this prospect above any other on the continent. Certainly, for natural scenery, embracing in one vista all the elements that combine to make a magnificent and charming view, no place can exceed this. The eastward view from Stirling Castle does not equal it. Arthur's Seat nor Edinburgh Castle commands such a grand sweep of prospect, embracing such varieties and combinations of features and aspects. The characteristics of Scotch scenery from Marmion's stand-point are reproduced here on a larger scale. Here, expanding in the view, is something more than " the shores of Fife, Preston Bay, and Berwick Law." Burntisland and all the other islands that float on the bosom of the gallant Forth, " like emeralds chased in gold," are overmatched on the broader bosom of this mighty river by islands of nobler round and equal setting. The nearest, the Isle of Orleans, is the first jewel of the river, which embraces it with an arm of equal girth on either side. It rounds up to a graceful eminence, crested with woods and fertile fields, and sloping gently to the water's edge for the whole circuit of thirty miles. On the right, just across the river, a young Quebec is mounting a rocky bluff of almost equal height, crowned with three immense forts to match the old city in " martial show." On the left, white villages, strung on one street, and marked off by tin-spired churches, extend down the northern shore. Over these and all the green, sloping expanse between, the eye may follow the undulating heights of the Laurentian range, and find in them all that Scott describes.

> " And westward far, in purer blaze,
> On Ochill mountains fell the rays,
> And as each heathy top they kissed,
> It gleamed a purple amethyst."

But what is " the gallant Forth " or " Father Thames," the Rhine or the Nile, to the St. Lawrence? or the river of any continent to compare with it for its commercial capacities, its affiliations and connections?

Let us descend into the public garden, and from one of the seats under the shadow of the twin-faced monument erected to the joint memory of Wolfe and Mont-calm, look off upon the scene below. The river spreads out before us a perfect cross. The St. Charles on one side, and the broad arm of the great river put out on the other around the Isle of Orleans, make a transverse at right angles with the main or direct current. Looking northward, between the masts of the great timber ships at anchor, you see the smoke and red funnel of an ocean steamer approaching. It comes up slowly and softly, with hardly a ripple at its bow to its pier under the cita-del, that looks down upon it from the lofty height as upon a mere river yacht in size.

Yet that steamer registers three thousand tons, and is only one of nearly thirty that stop at this port on their way to and fro across the ocean. These suggest, but do not measure, the capacities of this river. Let us apply a standard that may help us to a better conception of them. Suppose that Sandy Hook were the Straits of Belle-Isle, and the Hudson were the St. Lawrence in length and volume. Then, to be at an equidistance with Quebec from the sea, New York should be at Buffalo, and Albany at Detroit; and this last point would not be the head, but the scant half-way mark, of the navigation of the river. This will help us to realize its capacity. Keeping this measurement in view, remember that Mont-real is not half way even in the navigable length of the river. From that port, though nearly one thousand miles from the ocean, the navigation of the St. Law-rence extends fourteen hundred miles. The continu-ity of its navigation from Duluth, on Lake Superior, to the Straits of Belle-Isle, nearly twenty-four hundred miles, is complete. In the vital relationship that Nature intended, the St. Lawrence is the jugular vein of all those great American lakes and of the rivers that feed them. Commercially, it sustains, or was created to sustain, this relation and function to the best half of the continent, as may be seen from another point of view.

Let us look at the relation which the St. Lawrence establishes between Europe and that section of this continent most necessary to European countries. In all but the article of cotton, this section produces what they most want from America; especially what England most lacks and needs. It is the great grain, provision, and timber-producing region. The most fertile corn-growing states east of the Rocky Mountains abut upon the great lakes, of which the St. Lawrence is the only ship-way to the ocean. The best pine lands on the continent border upon this vast contiguity of waters. There is no river in America that has so many rapid tributaries, to furnish mill-sites and water power as the St. Lawrence. Then, from its mouth to the head of Lake Superior, the mineral resources of the same region are proportionate to its agricultural productions and capacities. Its mines of iron, copper, lead, and zinc are almost countless and inexhaustible.

Then, in addition to all these elements of commerce, look at the character of the populations who people the vast region bordering upon the waters that find their only navigable pathway to the sea through the St. Lawrence. Let the eye pass over these lake and river states, taking in Minnesota, Wisconsin, Illinois, Michigan, Ohio, Northern New York, and the two Canadas. See how native American, English, Scotch, Irish, French, German, and Scandinavian — the best industrial elements in the world — make up the population of this immense region, all uniting, in the peace and harmony of free institutions, to develope its endless resources.

Thus there is no river on the American continent that approaches the commercial importance and value of the St. Lawrence to England, and Europe generally. Its capacity and value are in the very infancy of their development; but in a few years they will show the world what they are and may be. It is only just beginning to be utilized in the sense applied by John Quincy Adams to the Falls of Niagara — as a river provided by Nature for two nations to share alike as their common roadway to the ocean. As such a road, both have the same interest to free it from all obstructions to the passage of their sea-going ships. Both, separately or jointly, can do this. Jointly, what could they not do? If a Suez Canal were needed around Niagara Falls, or around any other rapids of the river, the two countries might make it the most profitable work of international partnership ever accomplished. What a fitting memorial of the great consummation of the Washington Treaty such a joint work would be! What would better grace the " new departure " of the two nations taken at Geneva, than the sight of files of ocean steamers floating their flags from the head of Lake Superior down the St. Lawrence to the sea! Looking across to the three immense forts which the Mother Country is constructing with her own money on the opposite ridge above Point Levis, one cannot but regret that she did not give it to the widening and deepening of the Welland Canal, or to a work of like utility, in which her own people might share equally with the Canadians, without lessening the benefit the latter might derive from it. In a word, there is no river in India, or in any other region of the globe under the British crown, of such commercial value to England as the St. Lawrence.

———◦◦◦———

BIRTHPLACE OF RIP VAN WINKLE.

COMMUNITIES, large and small, in various ages of the world, have contended for the honor of giving birthplace to men of fame — especially to great authors. But some of these writers, by the inbreathing power of their genius, have created fictitious personages of more vigorous and lasting vitality than even their illustrious progenitors. A thousand of common readers or listeners are well acquainted with the name of Sancho Panza where one has ever heard of Cervantes. Sindbad and Robinson Crusoe are hearth-side words to half the children in England and America; but how few of them could tell who wrote the story of those incomparable heroes to the young? How many well-read people could say off-hand what was the Christian name of the author of that most admirable of all fictitious characters, "Uncle Toby"? Now, all who have been delighted, guided, strengthened, or lighted by the lives and sentiments of these fictitious personages, must be nearly as much interested in visiting the houses in which they were born as in visiting the birthplaces of the authors of their being. Who would not go a long way to see the room in which Falstaff or Hamlet was born, and cradled, and brought up to the full stature of his manhood?

Now, Rip Van Winkle is a celebrity whose name and character are pretty well known in all countries that have any literature of their own. And Rip was born in Birmingham, and was the eldest of a considerable family, begotten and reared in that town by Geoffry Crayon, Esq., *né* Washington Irving. The house is still a goodly, white-faced building, standing two stories and a half in height, with a modest front door and portico; but it is taken in from the sight and noise of all the streets — being enclosed in the great brick quadrangle of Wiley's Gold Pen Factory, of which it forms a kind of interior transept. It seems to be an accidental felicity in its surroundings that it is so paled with gold pens and entertained with the music of their manufacture. A man of exuberant fancy might be pardoned by common sense for at least seeing in this coincidence a happy, if a mere mechanical, tribute to such a fluent, graceful, and genial writer.

A few days ago I visited this birthplace of Rip Van Winkle with the venerable Henry Van Wart, Esq., who married the sister of Washington Irving, and who is now nearly eighty-five years of age. Although the distance was considerable, he walked it with me at a young man's pace; and, on the way, told me many things about his distinguished brother-in-law that were never put in print — going back to his very babyhood. It was a pleasant incident of his infancy that, soon after he was christened with the name of Washington, that man of beloved and pure renown was passing up Broadway, New York, attended by a numerous procession of all ranks, ages, and occupations. The nurse of his little namesake, with the child in her arms, pushed her way through the crowd that lined the sidewalks, and was standing within a few feet of the general as he passed. He noticed the little bead-eyed, crowing youngster that was kicking out its puggy toes, bouncing and biting its thumbs, and trying to shout "hurrah!" with the rest. He paused a moment to give the baby as kind and sunny a smile as a childless man could give to "somebody's child." At that moment the nurse held out her charge towards him, and said, "Please, sir, its name is Washington, and it was called after you." The general instantly stepped out of the line, laid his hand upon the head of little Irving, and invoked a blessing upon his life, and passed on — little thinking that the baby-life which he had thus blessed would become so illustrious in after years at home and abroad.

Washington Irving had opened his literary career very young and very brilliantly in the production of Knickerbocker's History of New York, and in several smaller essays of his genius, when he was induced by his elder brother, and other relations or friends, to enter upon a commercial life in Liverpool. He was about as poorly fitted, by lack of mental affinity and business habits, for such a life, as any young man of his age could well be. The time, too, was as unfortunate for the success of the undertaking as they could have hit upon in the choice of half a century. It was near the close of the last great French War, and by the time that the new and hopeful firm had launched out beyond their depth in the flood that was to lead on to fortune, the great collapse and crash came, and their house came to the ground, like hundreds of others all over the kingdom. Washington fell deeper than his brothers — for he fell from a greater height of hope. They lost only money — as ten thousand others had done in the wide overthrow, and lost it as honestly as the best of them — but he lost more, and what money could not express or restore. A heavy, dark cloud settled down upon his genius. It seemed like a total eclipse, behind which his mind could emit but thin and feeble annular scintillations. It shut off from his mental reach that hopeful, enthusiastic life he lived at home in America. All his capacities and prospects as an author were blighted, apparently forever. He had lost all that inspiration and glow of intellectual activity which once stimulated and rewarded his ambition to excel as a writer.

In this state of mental obscuration, weakness, and despondency, Washington Irving went to Birmingham, to spend a few months in this very house, then the home of his brother-in-law, Henry Van Wart, also the friend and companion of his early youth in Tarrytown, on the Hudson. Everything that could be said or done to recover his mind from this eclipse was said and done in his sister's house by all the members of the family circle. He tried, and they tried their best to break the spell upon him ; and when he was in his happiest frolics with his little nephews and nieces, and his face was all aglow with the radiance of his affection for the children, the bonds seemed to relax, and his mind to emerge from the Doubting Castle which

had held him so fast in its darkness. Then he would
retire to his room, and, with pen in hand, see if his
strength had returned; but it was in vain; the spell was
still upon him. His mind gave no sign of his old genius;
not a thought touched by its inspiration would flow at
the command of that feathered wand which once summoned beautiful conceptions and images from the vasty
deep of a fluent imagination.

This condition had lasted for several months, when,
one soft and lovely evening in June, Mr. Van Wart, in
their usual walk, made a special effort to encourage him
to shake off this nightmare from his spirits — to induce
him to believe that he could do it by sheer force of will.
But every argument, incitement, and encouragement was
in vain. He said he had put his mind under every
possible influence that was calculated to emancipate it
from the bondage, but without any success. He had
visited the choicest places to commune with Nature, but
got no relief. He had laid himself down on his back by
the hour on the soft and sunny slopes of the green hills,
and looked up into the gentle June clouds at play upon
the broad prairies of the blue sky, and tried, O, how
hard! to mount them with his thoughts, and soar away
upon their tinted wings into some far-off region of fancy,
where his mind should break away from the long fascination of despair, and be itself once more in the freedom
and glory of its first ambition. He had followed with
his eye and ear the happy lark, as it lifted itself up on
its morning song into the blue of heaven, as if it bore
the sweetest of human joys, to the home of the angels,
and he wished it could carry up to them on its wings a

whisper from his soul for help from its bondage. Then
he had sauntered by the meadow brooks, and listened to
the music they made to the meditating cows that lay
upon their daisy-freckled banks. He had listened, with
attentive but enfeebled faculties, by burns and braes, in
groves full of song-birds, and in all places that would
once have stirred his mind to the poetic pulse of thought
and feeling; but it had all been in vain. When he took
up his pen, on returning from this communion with
Nature, that deadening spell was upon him still, and
he feared that he never should be able to shake it off
and resume his literary life, which had commenced so
promisingly.

There was no use arguing against this sentiment and
presentiment of mental weakness and obscuration; but
Mr. Van Wart adopted a happier expedient. As it were,
he took Irving's arm on a walk that outflanked the
darkness of the eclipse. He took him around it back to
the days and walks of their youth on the Hudson, and
touched those memories within him which the mind of
manhood and of old age holds freshest and dearest,
whatever clouds or floods may come between. He took
him to those places which were the play-grounds of their
childhood, and of the happy years between it and the
first of life's bright summer. Sleepy Hollow was their
favorite resort — for its people were as unique and odd
in their ways and looks as the strange valley itself. In
fact, it was the abode of the queerest characters that
were ever gathered together within the same space.
Such quaint Dutchmen, in speech, dress, and habits, could
not be found elsewhere in the whole country. Their

10

sayings and doings had given the two young men rich practice in recitative. The Hollow was full of live stories when they were young. It was just the place to take Irving to in order to bring the sun of his youth to bear upon his darkness. His brother-in-law recalled to him the laughable incidents they had themselves witnessed there; the oddest characters of the valley, the ridiculous legends and customs, habits, and sayings, and idioms that a grave man even could not hear described without laughing the tears into his eyes.

Irving laughed, internally, from the crown of his head to the sole of his foot; and the walls of his Doubting Castle crumbled and fell. The sun was still behind the clouds, and it now pierced and scattered them, and shone in upon him with all the warmth and light of his brightest and happiest days. He retired to his room while it was yet dusk. He put pen to paper, and thoughts came with a rush, faster than he could write them — all the faster, seemingly, for being fettered so long by the ice of his long mental despondency. All night long he plied his pen as it never moved before. Sleepy Hollow, with all its eccentric life and legends, stood revealed before him as he wrote. Its shapes and souvenirs all merged into one character, and on that he painted into the short hours of the slumbering household. At every one of them that image, quaint and olden, showed a new feature under his touch. The June sun, at its earliest rising, looked in through the shutters, and saw him where he sat at its last rays the evening before. When the family were all astir, and breakfast awaited their gathering at the table, he entered the room radiant with the old light of his genius and intellect. He came with his hands full of the sheets he had written while they were all asleep. He said it had all come back to him; Sleepy Hollow had awakened him from his long, dull, desponding slumber; and then he read the first chapters of "Rip Van Winkle," the character that came to him in the visions of the night, after the conversation of the previous evening.

It was interesting to see the breakfast room in which Irving read, from the still wet sheets, the story of Rip Van Winkle, and to stand in that room with the host of the author of that distinguished celebrity, who could remember and describe the very expression of his guest, the new radiance of hope and gladness that set his face aglow, as he came through that door with his manuscript in his hand. Nor was it a temporary return of his genius; it flowed more spontaneously than ever, and Rip Van Winkle was not its only offspring in that house. The Sketch Book was born in the same room, though it received some of its development in other localities. Then there were scores of unwritten novelettes which he read off from his mind to his little nephews and nieces, who gathered around his sofa of an evening to hear them. He would compose fascinating stories about fairies for them, and read them off just as if they were in print. When he was in the midst of the improvised tale the whole family would softly approach and form an outer circle behind the children, and listen with their interest to the story.

Take it all in all, we doubt if any other house in Birmingham could possess more interest to a well-read visitor than the birthplace of Rip Van Winkle, which we have here attempted to present to the reader as it was presented to us.

THE COMMENCEMENT CARNIVAL AT OXFORD.

MANY Americans have witnessed the carnival at Rome, and have been astonished at what they saw and heard. It has amazed them that the whole population of a great city, rich and poor, educated and ignorant, could give themselves up to such silly and noisy vagaries. But the carnival at Rome does not equal the Oxford Commencement in strange incongruities; for the great masses of the Eternal City are frivolous and characterless, amused with the lowest forms of vulgar fun. The higher classes, who share the grotesque anarchy of the hour with them, do it to increase the popular enjoyment. But the Commencement hour at Oxford is produced by a far different set of actors, and for the enjoyment or amazement of a far different set of spectators. In these characteristics there is nothing elsewhere in the wide world to compare with it. Fewer Americans have witnessed it than its vulgar competitor at Rome. But all reading men have heard of it, and perhaps many of them hope to see it some day. I once realized this hope, and saw what I had never seen described to the life, and what I shall not attempt to describe myself so as to convey anything more than an approximate idea of the scene.

I deemed myself highly favored in procuring a ticket of admission many days beforehand, through one of the venerable professors of the university. A citizen of our young country, who is susceptible of historical impressions, feels them vividly in this old, gray commonwealth of colleges. They make for him a more awe-inspiring presence than Napoleon assigned to the Pyramids of Egypt. Their time-eaten walls, showing their deep wrinkles through the fondling ivy, seem permeated with a thousand years of the world's best learning. Grand histories and grander lives of great men have left their footprints around these august fountains of erudition. One might think that this deep and solemn presence of glorious ages, dead but speaking, would make even young men walk softly under it, or quiet the flow of boisterous mirth to a harmless current. Of all the buildings in which such an influence might be expected to operate in this way, the University Theatre would seem to have the pre-eminence. This is the very Mars' Hill of Oxford — the arena where its athletes and pretorian bands of Minerva have contended for prizes which were as guerdons of immortality to ambitious competitors.

I was early at the door of this famous edifice, but not so early as a hundred others, from all parts of the kingdom, half of whom were probably graduates, coming up to pay their tributes of affection and admiration to Alma Mater. Every moment for half an hour at the entrance swelled the gathering crowd to at least a thousand men, all pressing towards the door. When it at last opened, there was the regular English rush, like the dash of a storming party against a fortified gate or bastion. In less than a minute, seemingly, the crowd occupied every foot of standing space of the paved pit or arena of the theatre. The circular seats that arose to the gallery proper from within a few steps of this level, were

already nearly filled with the beauty and grace of the
realm, representing hundreds of its best families. Many
of them were the mothers or sisters of the young athletes,
or other aspirants for the honors the day was to decide
or bestow. This surrounding cloud of witnesses, illumined and tinted with all that could give lustre and love-
liness to beauty, grew more and more compact until its
variegated crest and fringe belted the entire space between the arena and gallery, with the exception of a
small section in the centre reserved for the great dons
of the different colleges or halls. A few minutes of almost embarrassing waiting followed. Speaking geo-
graphically or *hedo*graphically only, heaven and earth
were brought very closely together, or the black, swaying crowd of men on the pit floor, and the rustling, fluttering mountain, tinted with every hue, that arose by
gentle acclivity along three sides of the building. The
two clouds seemed to act and react upon each other in
this close and unmodified presence. For ten minutes a
thousand men had nothing else to do than look into the
faces of nearly as many ladies, all in the bloom of English beauty and fashion, who, in turn, were shut up to the
scenery of manly life that filled the arena below. The
electricity of a reciprocal interest might be imagined
from the contact of so many eyes all aglow with the light
of the hour.

Did any one ever hear the crack of a dozen thunder-
claps, and the rush and roar of a black tempest out of
clear sky? Then it was nearest like what we saw and
heard as suddenly in this grand old theatre at the moment I have described. The door of the upper gallery

burst open, and the under-graduate " gods " rushed in like the storming force on the Redan. The fierce and impetuous host was led by a red-haired hero, in a long and armless toga of seedy black, flowing out from his shoulders like the dun banner of a buccaneer or brigand. With hair streaming in the same direction, and eyes full of fire, he rushed down the gallery, shouting, " Order ! order ! " as if the circular mountain of a thousand ladies, and the thousand quiet gentlemen at its base, were engaged in a Kilkenny contest. He led the storming force, and no thousand men ever dashed into the breach of a beleaguered city with louder vociferation. The whole reading world knows how Oxford muscle is trained for boat-racing, and what feats it performs in this line of exercise. But the feats of lung-power achieved in this grand old theatre by the under-graduates surpass anything accomplished on the Thames at the great boat-race. It is well known and acknowledged that no crowd of men in the world can discharge such a volley of cheers as the same number of Englishmen. Nowhere else can you hear such thundering cataracts of the human voice. Foreign sovereigns visiting England are struck with astonishment at this prodigious outpour. Who heard it in London when a million gave an English cheer to the gentle, blue-eyed Alexandra will never forget it. The Persian Shah will remember it above all the incidents and pageants of his receptions. One listening to the roar and crash of voices in the Oxford theatre on this occasion might imagine that it was the training-school in which this great lung-power of the entire nation was developed to such unparalleled volume and vociferation.

There could not have been more than a thousand undergraduate tongues engaged in the explosion. But it was absolutely terrific. These young men, doubtless, belonged to the best families in the kingdom ; enjoying and acquiring all the refinements the best social education could impart. Here was, perhaps, the most highly educated and cultivated company of ladies and gentlemen that any object could bring together, to witness and admire their acquisitions and deportment. Not one of those young gownsmen in the gallery would have opened his mouth to one of those elegantly-dressed ladies without modulating his voice to its most polished accents. But now his tongue, and a thousand like it, were unbridled to the wildest liberty. Their crash, claps, and rattling volleys were astounding. The mothers, sisters, and friends-apparent of nearer relation, looked up with manifest astonishment at actors in this carnival whom they recognized.

In a few minutes these voice-volleys assumed a new force and direction. The obstreperous gods of the gallery, in their wildest liberty, are very fastidious, and brook nothing common or unclean in the crowd of spectators. Their eager eyes quickly detect any trifling variation in the regulation dress, and pour down upon the victim's head a crushing avalanche of indignation. Such a victim they soon discovered standing very near me — a plucky young Englishman in salt-and-pepper pants. Instantly the batteries of the gallery opened upon him. The hot hail of indignation fell down upon him in hissing volleys. I never before realized what the finger of scorn could mean. Here were a thousand pointed at the victim from three sides of the gallery; and every one of them seemed to crack and snap with an electric discharge of scorn. The thunder was equal to the lightning, and no tempest in the natural world was ever fuller of both. The whole assembly of spectators followed the direction of these surcharged fingers, and recognized the fated object with increasing sympathy or interest. He stood in stout defiance against the attack for a long time. Being very near, I watched his face to see if the lightning had struck him. Occasionally a streak of crimson ran down his cheeks; but he stood firm, as if determined to brave it out till the storm was exhausted. One of the file-leaders of the gallery, seemingly astonished at this obstinacy, and taking it to be ignorance of the cause of the attack, took off his black gown and waved it at the man, as if to show him that he had come in without the regulation garment. But in doing this he showed his own salt-and-red-pepper pants, which nullified the force of his expostulation. For several minutes the battle raged with increasing fury. The bombarded man stood proud, firm, and defiant. At last, as nothing could be done until the tempest ceased, a policeman made his way to the object of all this wrath, and conducted him out of the building; and his exit was marked by rounds of cheers that would have done sufficient honor to the fall of Sebastopol.

Hardly a minute elapsed after this incident before another filled the house with still more emphatic uproar. The masters of the twenty-one colleges, headed by the Vice-Chancellor of the University, and followed by a procession of distinguished scholars, now entered the

south door, and moved up through the crowd to what
might be called the throne-end of the hall.   With them
came the proctors and other dignitaries, brought more
directly into disciplinary relation to the students.   Now
for the moment of high carnival.   Every under-graduate
tongue is free.   All the repressions of a year are removed ;
all the pent-up feelings may have their outburst ; and
they did with marvellous force.   They poured down upon
the procession of dons in crimson robes such a fall of
bursting groans and hissing rockets of derision as seemed
to stun their march.   What particular masters or proctors were meant and hit by these shells of indignation
may possibly have been known to themselves, though
the conscience must have taken the place of the ear to
reach this conclusion.   But all this belonged to the carnival.   The grand dignitaries of the university walked
this gantlet with perfect equanimity, and ascended to
their seats with suave and smiling dignity, just as if
the whole scene were a part of the regular programme.
As bands play at great dinners between and during the
courses, so the gallery-gods seasoned the exercises at their
sweet will and taste, cheering and hissing *ad libitum*.
First in order was the conferring of titles and honors on
eminent scholars, in short speeches in Latin.   Cheers or
groans from above responded without fear or favor, or
regard to any distinction which a great reputation had
won.   Cheers for " The young ladies ; " for " Engaged
ladies ; " for " Married ladies," alternated with cheers or
non placet voices responding to the honors conferred.
When a distinguished Edinburgh professor's name was
announced for an LL. D., one of the gods shouted, " Who

is he? What has he done?" The same cross-fire was kept up during the essays and orations of the graduates. Midway in the utterance of a Latin sentence, "Three cheers for the lady in blue!" or some other outburst, would drown the speaker's voice.

Taking it all in all, considering the place, the actors, spectators, and influences which one might think should affect its character, the Oxford Commencement or Commemoration must surpass the carnival at Rome in many stranger incongruities.

GLIMPSES BY THE WAYSIDE
OF HISTORY.

RISE AND PROGRESS OF "WE," OR OF THE NATIONAL SENTIMENT.

WHATEVER was the length of each of the six days of the creation, whether each was equal to our week, month, year, or century, the whole period the six represented had elapsed before there was a human *We* living and moving upon the earth. We say a *human We*, for there was another, an almighty and eternal *We*, breathing forth the vast and varied creations of its omnipotence. The Creator had formed and fashioned the material world up to every feature and function of its present structure. He had set the sun, and moon, and stars in their places; He had divided and distributed the waters, the mountains, hills, valleys, and plains, and perfected all the planetary machinery and movements for the alternation of seasons and th ediversification of climates, soils, mineral and agricultural productions; He had stocked the seas, rivers, and streams with fish, and the fields and forest with beasts and birds, of every variety known to them now; He had caused the green herb and the green tree, of every kind of shade, flower, and fruit, to *grow* out of the ground, to delight the sight and taste of the after-created being who was to possess and enjoy them all; and not only herbs, and plants, and shrubs, but trees, bearing fruit of their kind, had *grown* up to full maturity from the ground, and had filled Eden with their flower and flavor before the garden

159

had received its keeper; He had done all this before He revealed the great *Wehead* of the Universe; before He said, "Let Us make man in Our image." All the preceding creations, animate and inanimate, were each single and simple in its individuality, in its being and object. One Power spoke them into existence, with the utterance of one omnipotent personality. But Adam was to be, not only the first and fountain-head of all human societies, but to be a trinity in himself, in the endowment and exercise of three distinct natures. Hence there seems a reason, that a finite mind may grasp, why the Creator, when He came to breathe into His crowning work a living, sentient soul, should say, "Let Us make man;" as if to impart to him a being resembling the personal constitution of the Godhead.

But He who made him, and gave him a physical, intellectual, and moral nature, endowed with their triune sense, emotion, and action, said that it was not good for man to be alone when thus constituted. He had proved this condition by actual experience. The Scripture history gives no intimation as to the length of this probation of solitude. There was a time, we cannot know how long, when Adam was *alone.* The trees of Eden were full of birds of every plumage and voice, and they sang to his listening ears the best songs of their delight. Every beast that now walks the earth, walked in his sight, and offered him its best companionship; but he was still *alone;* he could not say *We* with one likest himself of them all. Even if he had been created with the physical nature only that he wore, he could not have had a fellow-feeling with the most sagacious and domestic animal that he met in his walks; he could not have said, looked, or felt *We* with the horse, dog, or ape.

If it may be said with reverence, his Creator could sympathize with his solitude in the sentiment or remembrance of a personal experience. In many prayers and spiritual songs that have moved the hearts and lips of Christian men and women, the idea is put forth, that there was a time when God himself was *alone;* that there was a time when He, too, said of Himself what He said to the first man, that it was not good for Him to be alone; not good for the glory of His grace and for the permeation of the universe with the light and life of His love. So He created, for His own companionship and service, angels and ministering spirits of various rank and duty. He now created for Adam a companionship as well fitted to him as a help-meet and ministering spirit. It was a human being, of the same flesh and blood; and the first husband gave to the first wife on earth a name which no other wife could or ever did bear, for its sublime and beautiful meaning. He had given her at first sight a genus-name, simply signifying her species, sex, and relation to himself. It meant but a little more than a human female. At what particular point in their mutual experience he gave her the other name she was to bear and be known by through time and eternity, we cannot know. Perhaps it was at the birth of their first child, that, seeing in a new vision her relationship to a race of human beings that was to cover the earth, he called her *Eve.* No language, living or dead, can supply a word of more wide and beautiful significance than that Hebrew monosyllable. No one not well versed in He-

11

brew can grasp the whole of that significance, and not one in a hundred can express it in English. Moses did not fully unfold it in the reason he assigned to Adam in thus naming his wife, nor have any Greek, Latin, or English translations made the meaning of the term more clear and comprehensive. Eve, in Adam's mind and in Adam's word, meant the *Living One*, just as Jehovah means the *The Being One*, in all the tenses of existence. When her first-born lay on her bosom, and when he gazed upon the lovely beauty of her young motherhood, and called her *Eve*, he saw in her, not the *living one* only, but the life-producing life of all that were to live on earth.

Thus Adam and Eve were the first human We that walked the earth and breathed the odor of its first flowers in wedded life. The happy pair were the first to say of the joys of that life, *our* love, *our* home, *our* children, *our* hopes, *our* lot in the here and hereafter. From that primeval We radiate all the concentric circles of human society yet formed ; and the last and largest in the history of the race will have its genesis in the same source. We may find an instructive and interesting subject of reflection in tracing the progress and development of these expanding circles and spheres of its sentiment, action, and organization. The second circle in its expansion was the first human family. Here the Scripture account gives us but scant material for conjecture, as to the number of children included in that first family circle. Cain and Abel had evidently come to what we should call middle manhood, before the blood of the first murder stained the earth. It would seem that each had chosen, and pursued for some time, a special occupation for himself, as a permanent business for life. Cain went forth, and went a long way, from the scene of his great sin ; from the companionship of that home he had darkened and alienated by his deed. He formed in his self-banishment the second family circle of which we have any mention. The memory of his crime, and his ever-present sense of guilt, doubtless, not only exiled himself, but his family, from all intercourse with his father's house. His mother gave birth to another son, whom she called Seth, or a *substitute* for the murdered Abel. In him we have the record of the third human family that now began to multiply themselves simultaneously within a certain district of country, probably separated from each other by long distances, on account of their pastoral occupation. The spirit and bludgeon of Cain soon came into active exercise, apparently not so much in the act of war between clans, as in violence and bloodshed between individuals. Indeed, up to the day that Noah entered the Ark, we have no intimation in the Scripture narrative that either a nation, or even a clan, of any considerable population, had been formed. The social principle appears to have been of feeble attraction, operating very slowly upon the scattered families given to a nomadic life. The only permanent habitation we read of was the city which Cain built, very likely for defence against the avengers of his brother's blood, which, like Banquo's ghost, reddened before his eyes in frequent and fearful apparitions of his guilt. It is very doubtful if any one clan or community, numbering a hundred persons, had planted themselves in one permanent city of habitation before the Flood, so as to have what we call, in homely phrase, a *town* feeling, or enough of it to say *we* and *our* with the common sentiment and in the common interest of a municipal population.

With regard to the whole population of the human race at the time of the Flood, we have but few and uncertain data for estimation. We have only the basis for an approximately correct calculation, in the space of time allotted to them for multiplying and replenishing the earth. This period is assumed to have been about fifteen hundred years. At what ratio did they increase within this space? This we can only estimate by the data deduced from comparisons with familiar facts in the subsequent history of mankind. In the first place, then, the Scripture narrative does not intimate that mankind increased more rapidly before than after the Flood. Only one case of antediluvian polygamy is recorded; and if polygamy were common, we know that in countries in which that system exists there are, in the general average, no more wives nor children, in a given population, than where only one wife is allowed. Nor does the great age of the antediluvians seem to have made any perceptible difference in this matter. To be sure, only the male heirs of the family name and estate are mentioned; but there is no reason to suppose that either Adam or Methuselah had more children than Jacob or David. Noah had no daughters at all, and only three sons. Then a most fearful state of demoralization, violence, and bloodshed prevailed among the antediluvians, which must have decimated the population, and made its increase very feeble and slow. Taking these facts into consideration, their population, at the time of the Flood, did not probably exceed twenty-five hundred persons. It is almost certain that no confederation, nor community, that could be called a nation, had been organized; that no national sentiment nor strong local feeling had been developed among them. They were doubtless divided into small nomadic pastoral tribes and predatory bands, living on the plunder of men and beasts, with a few walled or stockaded villages built for safety. They sunk so deep in the most degraded demoralization and wickedness, that only one righteous man could be found among them all. Indeed, one can hardly conceive that even the ordinary family affections existed among them; so that, in very deed, Noah and his small family were the only circle of human beings that could and did say *we* in its true meaning, when the door of the ark was closed upon them. As it beat about, rudderless and pilotless, over the waters, they not only formed in themselves the only source for the perpetuation of mankind, but they constituted the only *we*, the only society, saved from the wreck of the drowned world. To follow the gradual development of that society-germ through its successive concentric circles of expansion, will form an interesting subject of further study and reflection.

THE "WE" OF THE EARLIEST NATION.

In pursuing the " Rise and Progress of We," no better, and, indeed, no other, history of the earliest nations can be found than the Scripture narrative supplies. We shall, therefore, rely entirely upon the data which the Bible contains, in touching upon passages of that history.

When Noah went forth from the ark, his small family constituted the only human *We* left alive on the earth to people it with its various races. However the posterity of Adam may have diverged into different clans before the Flood, they had all converged into his little circle of eight persons. No man of the antediluvian world was better fitted than himself, not by righteousness of life merely, but by intellectual enlightenment and practical experience, to head the human race in this narrow gap of its existence. Not a thought worth anything to man was drowned in the Deluge. Not an art, not an occupation was lost. On the contrary, before the fountains of the great deep were broken up, or the windows of heaven were opened, Noah had acquired and employed an amount of mechanical science and skill exceeding all the outside world possessed at that moment. He had had a divine Teacher, and followed rules which no human being of that day could impart in building the ark. There was more art, genius, thought, and perhaps even labor, put into that structure, than into all the other antediluvian edifices raised upon the earth. Considering the tent, pastoral, or nomadic life of those times, we may reasonably believe that there was more timber framed into the ark than had ever been used in the dwellings of mankind up to the day that the patriarch went into it with his family. And when he left it, anchored but not wrecked, on Mount Ararat, he left in it more of mechanical skill and architectural thought and genius than was drowned by the waters of the Flood.

Here, then, we have a new point of departure for the human race. At fifteen hundred years from the first man, we find, where Noah left the ark, the line of their continuation "like footsteps hidden by a brook, but seen on either side." The great rudderless and mastless hull, aground on the mountain's crown, was not only the masterpiece, but all the pieces of the old world's art in one. What all the wild and domestic animals he preserved were worth for the perpetuation and improvement of their species, it was worth as a storehouse of models for the race of man now starting anew on the high road of progress and civilization. The modes and models for framing timber into permanent houses, and in vessels for sea and river, that towering hulk supplied. In Noah and his three sons was a store-mind, full of the mechanical skill, and genius, and taste for ship-building and house-building. Let us see how soon, and in what way, they employed or taught that skill and genius. And we will follow closely the Scripture account, diverging neither to the right nor left hand from the narrative until we come abreast of some well-defined current of what is called profane history.

First after the Flood we have a list of the seed-germs of the nations that were to fill the earth. And the fact is worthy of notice, that Ham, whose posterity Noah is thought to have cursed on awaking from his wine, is the central and most important figure in the triad of patriarchs who were thus to people the world with their descendants. It would seem as if the inspired record bore *designed* testimony and reproof against Noah for uttering such wish and words against an innocent son for what was, doubtless, an act of tender reverence, not only to his father, but to his two elder brothers, who were only entitled by age, and the duty attaching to it, to take or prescribe the proper steps in so painful and distressing emergency. However the defenders of African slavery may have regarded the seeming imprecation uttered by the patriarch while his mind and moral sense were still confused and perverted by the influence of strong drink, nothing is clearer than that God, so far from making the children of Ham inferior in position to the children of his two elder brethren, gave them a higher placing in the world as centres of population and power. Nimrod, a kind of Alexander the Great in his time, was Ham's grandson, " and the beginning of his kingdom was Babel," and only the beginning ; for he went on building other cities. Asshur, probably his first-born son, "went forth out of that land and built Nineveh," and other cities called large in the Scripture history. While Ham's eldest son was thus founding the great kingdoms of Assyria on the Euphrates, his second son, Mizraim, was establishing a realm of greater renown in Egypt on the Nile ; while the youngest, Canaan, was founding the most maritime nation of the old world on the shores of the Mediterranean, with Tyre and Sidon for their capitals or chief ports. Thus these three sons of Ham — Cush, Mizraim, and Canaan — were planted at the three points of an equilateral triangle, which included the richest and most important countries of Asia and Africa; and they filled the included space with a great history, as well as with great kingdoms. The descendants of Japhet peopled "the isles of the Gentiles," Javan seemingly taking possession of the Grecian Archipelago. The posterity of Shem occupied regions not so well defined, and were probably more pastoral and migratory than the children of the other two brothers. Indeed, the Scripture history ascribes the leading position in civilization to the sons and grandsons of Ham and to their immediate descendants. They were the first builders of permanent cities after the Flood, and cities, too, of renown, such as Babylon, Nineveh, and Resen, in Assyria; "populous Noe" in Egypt; and Sidon and Damascus, and other important centres of population and business, in Phœnicia or Palestine.

But before these homogeneous families of mankind diverged into their several countries of habitation, it may be interesting to trace the progress of the social sentiment among them. That sentiment had been intensified in the small family circle that drifted about in the ark in the long and tempestuous months of the Deluge. They had learned by this most impressive experience to say *we* in a sense which no other human family had attached to that term. And when they came forth at last to walk and breathe the green earth, and to look the blue and quiet heavens in the face, they not only retained that feeling, but inspired their children with it. It seemed

to grow with their growth and strengthen with their
strength ; and when they numbered a certain population,
they made it the central principle and ruling motive of
their political economy.   As they travelled westward in
a body, they came to a district of the continent that
seemed to them well adapted in every way for carrying
out that economy.   Warned by the experiences of the
antediluvian world, by the dangers and demoralization
of a vagrant, wandering life in lawless clans or bands,
they resolved here and now to organize and locate themselves as one compact nation.   Without one dissenting
voice all their various families now said *we*, and entered
into all the intimate fellowship of the sentiment.   Now
the national feeling took strong hold upon their minds ;
and no people in the world ever seemed to aspire with
more ambition to a national being and a national name.
See how this feeling came out in striking forms of expression : " Let *us* build *us* a city and a tower — let *us*
make *us* a name, lest *we* be scattered abroad upon the
face of the whole earth."   How significant is this appeal
addressed to the social sentiment within them !   How
remarkably the motives are put in these expressions !   It
was not only, nor first, the city or the tower, but the
name that was to hold them together, and prevent their
being scattered abroad, as were the barbarous families
before the Flood ; a name that should cover all their
aggregate being with its appellation ; which they and
their out-widening posterity should wear forever as an
honor, and a glory, and a protection ; which should be
the proud and common inheritance of the poorest man's
child among them all ; and which should give him the

feeling of wealth and dignity in the hardest lot of poverty or trial. It was a unanimous sentiment, and they all set at work under its inspiration to build the outworks of the national being which they coveted. Doubtless Noah himself gave direction and impulse to this feeling. With all the thrilling memories of his experience fresh and strong in his mind; with only one of the nine centuries of his life intervening between that hour and the day when he saw the old world drowned in the Flood for its unspeakable wickedness; and believing, as he had good reason to believe, that its inhabitants sank into those depths of depravity in a large degree in consequence of their vagrant, unsettled life, — he must have had an intense desire that his posterity should avoid the rock on which the antediluvians split and perished; that they should settle down in one permanent habitation; pursue the occupations fitted to a permanent residence; become a united and unanimous nation, subject to well-defined and permanent laws; in a word, that they should be brought under the action of all those influences which produce a high civilization. As their common head and lawgiver, even as a mere political leader, it is almost absolutely certain that he must have felt and believed all this. But there were higher motives that moved his mind. He was the spiritual father of the whole community who thus began to build them a city, a tower, and a name on the plain of Shinar. He was their prophet or priest as well as king. No mere man that lived before or after him ever was honored of God with such a mission and ministry. He stood in the most affecting and touching relation to his grandchildren that surrounded him. Out

of the great and awful sermon of the Flood he was to
speak to them of righteousness, temperance, and a judgment to come.   To fulfil this great and solemn duty, he
must have not only desired, but directed, that they should
thus settle down together in a permanent city of habitation, where he could spread over them his patriarchal
influence during the last centuries of his life.   And such
a patriarch's voice and wish must have been a law of
action to all his descendants.   It is impossible to conceive of a deeper veneration than they must have felt
and manifested for such a man, who had so walked with
God on the dark mountains of the roaring Flood; who
had held, as it were, to his bosom the whole remnant of
the human race.   Then his three sons, now at the prime
of their manhood, were with him, each like an Aaron,
to impress the counsels of their aged father upon their
children and their children's children.

Such was the " We " of Babel.   It was not only the
largest, but virtually the first, ever formed on earth on the
basis of a municipal community.   It included all the
families of at least five generations from Noah; and he
and his three sons resided among and presided over them.
We have no data whereby to estimate their entire population.   Although the patriarch had only three sons and
sixteen grandsons, his descendants in the next three
generations would have increased by what might be called
geometrical progression; so that in Peleg's day, or at the
dispersion of the community, it probably numbered
several hundreds.   There is an interesting meaning
attaching to the Hebrew word *Peleg*, which one well
versed in that language can only appreciate in its full

and special significance. It does not mean division in a chopping-up sense, but a division into threads. We are inclined to think our word *fillet* is derived from it, for only a dot turns the Hebrew F into P. One instance will serve to show its general application. In the 1st Psalm it is said of the righteous man, that " he shall be like a tree planted by the rivers of water ; " but literally, " by the *water pelegs*, or continuous streams, as water-courses." And this was the way in which the little commonwealth of Babel was divided. And this was evidently the object of their dispersion or colonization in different sections of the continent. They had served a sufficient apprenticeship to municipal institutions in their mud-walled city. They had learned the first principles and processes of law and order. They had enjoyed all that Noah and his three sons could impart to them of counsel and observation, drawn from their experience on the other side of the Flood. All that these venerable patriarchs could tell them of God and his dealings with the race of man, they had heard. They were now to leave this first school of human government, and carry out its lessons in widely-separated and independent communities, each of which should ultimately expand into a nation. At the time of their division, each community, or nation-germ, was equal to every other, and equal to the one that remained in Babel, in every element and faculty of civilization. The moral, mental, and mechanical outfit was doubtless the same in one as the other.

And now the day and the occasion came for the pupil families of this first government-school to graduate, to go forth and beget and educate nations. It is still a matter of question with many what was really the first or ostensible cause of this severance. A majority of those who have read the narrative thoughtfully seem to have come to the conclusion that the language of the Babel community was literally changed, and new and strange ones created instantaneously; that where they had all spoken Noah's mother-tongue, a large number of them now had their memory so confused or obliterated, that they forgot the words so familiar to their lips and ears, and could no longer pronounce or understand them when pronounced the same as ever by those who still understood and used them. Now, we are inclined to think that it was a more serious division than this of languages that led to their dispersion. For if they had still been of the same mind to dwell together in unity, they would soon and easily have overcome the difficulty of speech, as one section of them would have doubtless retained their mother-tongue, and have been able to teach it to the rest, if the other portions of the community had really forgotten it. Then, if their languages had actually been divided, the differences between them could not have been wider than they were in Abraham's day, who journeyed about in many Asiatic countries, and even sojourned for a while in Egypt; yet he always seemed to understand the language of the people with whom he dwelt, and they to understand his. It may be ascribed to a sentimental predilection, but we must prefer to believe that Adam, Noah, Abraham, David, and Isaiah spoke the same grand old tongue, and that no radical break in it was made on the line between them. As Noah lived nearly seventy years after Abraham was born, and as the "father of the faithful" probably had seen that venerable patriarch, and perhaps had listened to religious instruction from his lips, we may reasonably believe the language of the two holy men was literally and grammatically one and the same.

We are therefore inclined to the belief that a less innocent and more serious division than literal and grammatical changes, miraculously introduced into their language, was the cause of the breaking up of the first little nation organized at Babel. Doubtless it was the speech of the heart, not of the lips, that was divided and confused. Cross-ambitions, cross-purposes, and the ill tempers of jealousy, envy, and suspicion, created diversities of language which were more obstinate than any differences which the literal structure of human speech could produce. A hundred Babels in the world's history have passed through similar experience. With as strong a determination and interest to build them a city, a tower, and a name, as a compact, unanimous commonwealth, after a while a confusion of language, a division of counsels, supervened ; then one or two branches of the great family went forth to found a nation. Political and religious persecutions have produced many of these dispersions, both in ancient and modern times. Lack of land and lack of labor have played their part in planting the surface of the earth with these seed-germs of great kingdoms and commonwealths. The very wrath of man has thus been turned to account by Providence in keeping humanity from stagnation, and in peopling the continents and islands of the globe. Truly, " as an eagle stirreth up her nest, fluttereth over her young, spreadeth abroad her wings, taketh them, beareth them on her wings," so Providence has led forth the different branches of the human race from its first centres of habitation. Babel was the first nest thus stirred up; and the young communities nursed in it were borne forth to their mission on those mighty, outspread wings, which protect as well as transplant the great communities of mankind.

Having thus noticed the sentiment and structure of the first national We organized in the history of the world, we will hereafter follow the course of that sentiment through some of its subsequent ramifications and results.

THE "WE" OF THE HEBREW NATION.

It would probably be deemed a reasonable estimate to put the population of the human race at five hundred at the dispersion from Babel. Although Noah's own family was small, and his grandsons were only sixteen in number, the descendants of the latter must have made a considerable community by Peleg's time, in which the division took place. We have no intimation in the sacred history as to the names or number of the bands that went forth in different directions to form themselves into independent communities; nor do we know what branch remained in the city. It would be natural to suppose that Noah and his three sons would have staid by their homes and altars within the walls they had caused to be built for the permanent residence of themselves and their posterity.

With the exception of an incidental mention here and there, the Scripture narrative thenceforward leaves nearly all these various branches, and confines itself to the history of one family, and to what may be called the central line of that; for it but slightly alludes to several offshoots which expanded into large populations.

In Abraham and his posterity not only were all the nations to be blessed, but to have the first records of their history. At the distance of two hundred years from the dispersion, he found numerous clans or tribes everywhere on his westward journeyings. These must have been smaller than the clans of ancient Scotland; indeed, the whole of Palestine seems to have been full of them, every village having its king. In Egypt the patriarch found a larger kingdom already established, with a monarch upon the throne, surrounded by princes who paid him the usual Oriental homage. This was about three hundred years after the flood; and assuming the whole population of the earth to have sprung from the eight persons preserved in the ark, it probably numbered half a million of souls in the day of this the first Pharaoh mentioned in Scripture. Doubtless Egypt, from its fertility, had already drawn to the banks of the Nile twenty or thirty thousand inhabitants, who constituted the largest community under one king that had been established up to that date. Egypt must have doubled its population by the time that Abraham's grandson Jacob went down into it from Canaan with the nucleus of the Hebrew nation in his own large family of seventy persons. But though perhaps the most populous kingdom in the world at the time, it was not then, and never has

12

been since, a nation in a popular sense. It had a splendid royalty and a religion full of pomp, gorgeous circumstance, and show ; but all who could and did say *we*, and *our*, and *us* were the ruling dynasty, its blood-relatives and favorite noblemen. Not only were the children of Israel enslaved, but the whole Egyptian population were serfed and owned, together with their lands, by the king. The Scripture history tells us how they thus became crown property, under the premiership of Joseph. From that day to this, what may be called a national sentiment has never existed in that country. The masses of the people have had no more to do with their own than with the structure of a foreign government. They never had any part or lot in it, except as blind and dumb subjects to its rule. Occasionally, in the fitful phantasies of despotism, there would come an interval when its rule lay lighter upon their shoulders, when a more sagacious and generous sovereign would come to the throne and wield a softer sceptre ; but Egypt never had a people that felt their peoplehood, that ever felt the genuine and manly pulse of a national being or sentiment.

In such a country, under such a government, and surrounded by such a degraded population of native serfs, the children of Israel lived, groaned, and grew for generations. Under the weight of an oppression which would have crushed other tribes of men, they multiplied, until, in the end, they probably outnumbered the Egyptians themselves. For five generations the Scripture account of their condition and experience is suspended. We know not what manifestations of His being and will the God of Abraham, Isaac, and Jacob made to them in their house of bondage during this period. But the iron bonds of oppression must have held them together, as well as all the traditions of their forefathers, and the religious faith or rites which they were likely to retain. If they were not a nation, they were a race, and all its history had been handed down from generation to generation. Two linked memories could reach Jacob. The grandfather of Naasou, the prince of Judah, under Moses, ought to have seen that venerable patriarch. Thus almost every possible influence contributed to keep them a separate people, in sentiment and fact, while they sojourned in Egypt. Besides, the Egyptians regarded them and their occupations with the strongest aversion or religious antipathy, so that no blending of the two races could have taken place. When the hour of their deliverance came, and they marched forth from the land of bondage under Moses, not one of them seems to have been left behind. Even before the Red Sea parted to make them a pathway, they formed "a peculiar people" in respect to a national sentiment, the like of which no other, before or since, ever manifested or felt.

Then came the long and trying discipline which was to fit them for the great mission in the world to which they were called. The arms of the Almighty were indeed thrown around them, night and day, with wonderful manifestation, to intensify their nationality, to detach and isolate them from all the other populations of the earth, and to ward off all influences that tended to merge them with the peoples who surrounded them either as friends or enemies. During their long bondage in Egypt, they must have been greatly demoralized by the fantastic superstitions and idolatries of that country. The revelations of the only true God were doubtless few and far between, and all public worship or recognition of Him suppressed. From this long, leaden sleep of religious life they were aroused by the startling wonders wrought by the divine presence and power through Moses. Thenceforward those grand manifestations preceded and followed them in their long march to Canaan. The uplifted waters, walled up on both sides of the dry roadway through the Red Sea, when they had crossed its beds, fell back not only upon Pharaoh and his host, but also upon Pharaoh's deities and all the rude idolatries of the heathen. The cloud by day and the pillar of fire by night that led and lighted them through the wilderness, the wonders of Horeb and Sinai, and the daily manifestations of the divine power and presence, were parts of the discipline through which they were to be raised up to be " a peculiar people," a consecrated people, set apart, and set on high, to bless all nations with their spiritual life and light.

But the demoralizing influences of Egypt had so permeated and corrupted their moral nature that they turned their eyes back towards that pagan land with eager longing at almost every stage of their journey. The moment the divine presence was not overshadowing them in some special and powerful manifestation, their minds turned again to the quadruped deities of Egypt. After quaking with awe at the thunders and lightnings of Sinai, they made a golden calf after the Egyptian pattern, and worshipped it at the very base of the burning mountain, because Moses delayed his coming from its holy heights with the tables of God's law written by His own fingers. Even in the very sight of the promised land they threatened to choose another captain to lead them back to the Nile. The generation that formed their character in that house of bondage and gross idolatry could not be raised even by such a discipline to the peoplehood of the nation that God had determined to plant in Canaan. So the children uncorrupted by these influences, and mostly born on the march, were chosen to the mission which their fathers were incompetent to fulfil. And, born as they were under the very cloud and pillar of fire; educated under such a divine discipline; under the unbroken and vivid impression and sense of God's power and presence, — even they could not stand before the seductions of heathen influence when they arrived in Canaan. The wars they waged with the aboriginal clans of the country consolidated and held them together for a time by the strongest necessity of union. But when they had effected the subjugation of these native tribes, the national feeling, the sentiment of consecration as a peculiar people, began to lose its vitality. Whenever this sentiment had waned to a certain weakness, they lapsed into the service of strange gods and strange people. Then a leader was raised up to rescue them from this moral degradation and servitude, and restore them to the sense and status of a united nation. Through this long period they merged and emerged several times; now seemingly blended or lost in surrounding populations, now brought forth again by the outstretched hand of an Almighty Power. For two or three centuries, and even to the middle of David's reign, they had no capital, nor central seat of government, nor much of the structure of a confederate nation. During most of this space of time they acted as independent tribes, sometimes singly, and again by twos and threes, and at wide intervals as an entire confederacy. For twenty or thirty years at a time they had no ruler or leader, temporal or spiritual. Then a kind of second Moses or Joshua was raised to break their captivity, and to bring them back to the worship of the God of Israel. It was hard standing for them in the midst of such surroundings. The cloud by day and the pillar by night had been withdrawn. The divine manifestations that almost daily visited their forefathers in the wilderness came now but rarely. They had but little more than vague or varying traditions of those experiences. All that Moses had received and written was accessible only to but few, if not hidden from all for long periods. The Levites and priests were merged with the people, or went over with them to pagan worship. The peoples on their right hand and left, especially on the Mediterranean, were more advanced than themselves in the arts and sciences of the old world's civilization, and their mythology and gorgeous religious systems took hold of the Israelites with fascinating attraction ; and they repeatedly went after these " other gods," and served as serfs the people that made and worshipped them.

After a succession of temporary dictators, or judges, who ruled the people according to their own mind and will, we come to a new point of departure in the history of the Hebrew nation. For two or three centuries they had been a loose confederacy of tribes, with no permanent head or capital. They had often been divided and conquered as a result of this condition. Several times they had fought with each other, and one of their tribes had been almost entirely exterminated in one of these domestic struggles. They now resolved to consolidate themselves, and become a united, compact nation, instead of an uncertain group of clans, ruled by a priest who, though a holy man himself, often transferred his priesthood and power to wicked and profligate sons, as in the case of Eli, and even Samuel himself, whose sons " turned aside after lucre, and took bribes and perverted judgment." The people put their motives for changing their government before the venerable hierarch in these words : " We will have a king over us, that we also may be like all the nations, and that our king may judge us, and go out before us and fight our battles." From this time forth they became a nation, like those around them in political structure. For the first time the twelve tribes felt the inspiration and bond of a *national* sentiment. Up to this date the mere *race* feeling had predominated among them. Saul commenced his reign with small means for establishing a kingdom. The Philistines had not only disarmed the Israelites, but prevented their re-arming themselves by carrying off all their smiths. " So it came to pass in the day of battle that there was neither sword nor spear found in the hand of any of the people that were with Saul and Jonathan." He had no capital in which to erect his throne, and which the tribes recognized as a common centre. They had been demoralized by subjugation to different powers for several generations. He had a great work before him, and, with all his faults, he accomplished it with remarkable energy and success. He beat back all the enemies of Israel on every side and to a great distance, and raised the people of his realm to the stature, power, and sentiment of a recognized nation.

After an interval of civil war between the two houses, David ascended the throne of Israel, and doubled its power and prestige. He subdued peoples that Saul only discomfited, and defeated and half destroyed nations which his predecessor never encountered. He planted garrisons far beyond the boundaries of his own realm, and even held Damascus, the strong city and capital of the Syrians. He was, beyond all the line of Hebrew kings, a man of war, and carried the power and dread of Hebrew arms and name over regions they never reached before or since. Never before or since did a king wield such a sword and pen simultaneously, or sing and fight with such inspiration. While hunted like a partridge in the mountains, or hunting down the enemies and oppressors of Israel at the head of invincible armies, his heart breathed out prayers that fitted every necessity, emotion, longing, and experience of every human soul that should desire to offer up petition or thanksgiving to God in any land, language, or age, up to the last year of time. His power of organization was marvellous. No sooner was he fairly enthroned over all the Hebrew tribes, than he set his hand and heart to the work of erecting them into the great central nation of the world, which should command the admiration and homage of mankind. He would found a capital which "for situation should be the joy of the whole earth." He would erect a temple for the Hebrew religion which should eclipse for its grandeur everything the world had seen or conceived. The house, dedicated to the worship of the Hebrews' God, and the worship itself, should throw all the heathen temples and rites into the shade, and not only prevent his own people from straying off after strange gods, but attract strangers from distant lands to his royal city. This splendid object was constantly before him in all his bloody campaigns. For this he despoiled surrounding nations that had made Israel to serve and sin for centuries. For this he filled the city he built with treasures and stores without tale. In the eighth year of his reign the site of his new capital was a fortified mountain of Judea, still held in force by one of the aboriginal tribes of Canaan. The Jebusites made a stout and long resistance, and for a long time he only got possession of a part of their inheritance, which he called Mount Zion. Thence he fought his way to the whole, and Jerusalem, the glory of his kingdom and the joy of his song, arose grand and beautiful to the whole world, ready for its crowning structure, the Temple of Israel's God. The plan of this edifice was just like one of David's prayers, when his heart was full of joy and hope. It was an inspiration of beauty in its minutest detail. His mind seemed to see the great and splendid whole as in a vision, and every function and feature that could give effect to the worship that was to be celebrated within its walls. He portioned out gold " even to every candlestick by weight," and had in his eye the place and pattern of the smallest ornament. Before a blow was struck or a stone laid, he organized such a choir of vocal and instrumental musicians as the world had never seen, to be in training for the sacred songs of Zion.

But when all was ready for the signal; when the vast treasures and spoils of many nations were brought forth for the work; when the armies of masons, carpenters, and artificers of every craft were awaiting the word of command, and the plan of the temple lay unfolded to its last and finest feature, — there was found too much blood on the hands that David uplifted to God for His blessing on the grand undertaking. He was bidden to hand it over to Solomon, whose very name was more fitting to the House of God. The veteran monarch transferred the charge in language as grand as the act itself. And Solomon just crowned the kingdom his father built. The united reigns were a continuity of one *régime*, commencing with David's first foothold on Mount Zion, and culminating with the sublime scene enacted at the Dedication of "Solomon's Temple." Fifty years of the two reigns made the great epoch of Hebrew history; and this period measured the whole length of the nation's real life. Within this space of time the twelve tribes were not only united, but unanimous under one head: their clan feeling expanded to the generous sentiment of a great people. All the circumstances that could develop this sentiment were acting upon them. They saw, in the span of one generation, their scattered populations, so often reduced to the rule of their heathen neighbors, without a permanent capital for their government, or a temple for their religion, now raised to the status and reputation of the foremost power in the world. The pomp and splendor of Solomon's court; the grandeur of their temple, doubtless the noblest building hitherto erected on earth; the gorgeous rites of their religious worship; their great choir of "sweet singers" and players on newly-invented instruments, — these, and a hundred other realizations, far exceeding the early ambitions of the children of Israel, filled the measure of their happy experience. They said *we* and *our* in regard to this experience, and to the glorious future opening upon them, with a patriotic pride and fervor of feeling they never felt before. This sentiment must have warmed to a new glow in Solomon's auspicious reign, when foreign kings and queens visited his court, and paid him the tribute of their homage and admiration, not only for his personal wisdom, wealth, and splendor, but for the beauty and grandeur of a city and temple which made Jerusalem to the contemporary Eastern world what Rome and its St. Peter's are now to Europe architecturally.

But, a few years after this consummation was attained, the fabric of the Hebrew nation was sundered in twain. An insolent act or expression of a young would-be despot broke in pieces the grand structure that had just reached and presented its splendid proportions before the world. The joint work of David the warrior and Solomon the statesman was undone by that act. Both had taxed the twelve tribes to their utmost capacity of endurance in order to build up a grand capital and a grander temple for the kingdom. Both had swept a vast region of territory outside of the realm, and despoiled numerous cities and populations to this end. It was natural and inevitable that the ten tribes, at a time when the clan feeling was still susceptible of jealousy, should feel that Judah and

Jerusalem were getting the lion's share of Hebrew glory
and power.   Under these circumstances, the petition they
addressed to Rehoboam was as moderate and just as any
ever presented to an absolute sovereign : " Thy father
made our yoke grievous ; now, therefore, ease thou somewhat the grievous servitude of thy father, and his heavy
yoke that he put upon us, and we will serve thee."   But
the young king, following the evil counsels of his young
and reckless courtiers, returned a reply which the history
of royal autocrats and despots can hardly parallel for its
stinging insolence : " My little finger shall be thicker
than my father's loins ; for whereas my father put a
heavy yoke upon you, I will put more to your yoke : my
father chastised you with whips, but I will chastise you
with scorpions."   There is no reason to wonder at what
followed : " The people answered the king, saying, What
portion have we in David? and we have none inheritance
in the son of Jesse : every man to his tent, O Israel ;
and now, David, see to thine house.   So all Israel went
to their tents."

Thus ended the life and being of the Hebrew nation
as one consolidated, united people.   The chasm between
the two sections was never bridged, and they never more
came together under one head.   After a long period of
separate existence, often at bloody war with each other,
and both departing more and more from the faith and
worship of the God of their fathers, they were carried
off bodily into the Babylonian captivity.   There, speaking the same language, holding the same memories and
traditions of their history as a united nation under David
and Solomon, they may have hung their harps upon the

same willows, and mourned together the sin and folly which had led to their subjugation and exile.

A short time prior and subsequent to this bitter end, inspired prophets arose, gifted to see in dim vision, and to describe in language to correspond with such vision, the advent of a God's "Anointed," or a *Messiah*, who should restore the kingdom to Israel, and make it glorious and everlasting. This prediction of a coming future, when all that had been lost should be regained, took hold of the Jewish mind with all the force of the strongest faith. It comforted them in exile by "the rivers of Babylon," and by all the other rivers of their captivity. To this ideal it seemed to go, and no farther — that the promised Messiah should ascend the throne of David, and raise the Hebrew nation to the greatness and glory it had under that father and founder of the Jewish monarchy. Other populations might be subject to his rule, as tributaries, as hewers of wood and drawers of water, as there were under Solomon; but the Hebrews only should be the people of the realm. This evidently was the largest and only *We* they expected or wished to see established in Palestine. For this realization of the prophecies they longed and looked as those that watch for the morning. Up to the birth of Christ this expectation bounded and contained all their hopes. They could see and wish nothing beyond it. Not one of the fishermen of Galilee that followed Him and listened daily to His teachings, not even the favored disciple who leaned upon His bosom, could raise his eyes to look beyond this small scope of earthly power. After all He had said and done to reveal the character of His reign, they still held fast to the old idea of their countrymen, that His kingdom was to be of this world; that it was to be the kingdom of David restored and established forever under His sceptre. When they were " scattered like sheep without a shepherd " from His cross, and wandered about in couples, murmuring over their crushed hopes, they said to the inquiring stranger, " We trusted that it had been He which should have redeemed Israel." Even after the baptism of the Pentecost, when the Spirit of God seemed to transform them into new men, and to give them a vision of Christ's kingdom which they had never caught before, the old idea clung to their souls in another form. Even if it were not to be an earthly, but a spiritual rule, it should embrace only Israel. The outside barbarians, or Gentiles, such as Greeks, Romans, Syrians, and the like, should have no part nor lot in it. The Jews should not have to say *we* with such aliens, or to admit them as fellow and equal subjects of the sceptre of the " Anointed," the Messiah, promised to Israel. Peter, the very van-leader of the apostleship, made a stout resistance to such a thought, and even contended with the Lord in the vision, against preaching His gospel of grace to these outsiders. Read his explanation and apology to his fellow-apostles for such an innovation. See with what astonishment they all opened their eyes and lifted up their hands at the idea and fact: " Then hath God also to the Gentiles granted repentance unto life ! "

Such, then, was the *We* of the Hebrew nation. Such, in the mind of that people, was the national being to which they aspired; for which they waited, hoped, and prayed through long centuries of subjugation and exile. Never did an idea take hold of a race of men with such force. For two thousand years the wandering and persecuted Israelites, scattered among the nations, have held to this one great thought. The Christ to whom all the kingdoms of the world, worth the name, now bow the knee of their faith and homage, they insist is not their Messiah. Jesus of Nazareth may rule and mould all the empires, kingdoms, and republics of Christendom, and the brazen tongues of all its million Sabbath bells may add theirs to all its human voices in adoration of His name and power, but until a being of flesh and blood shall come to localize himself in Judea, and restore the throne and realm of David, and bring back the scattered tribes of Israel to a temporal rule and state, they will recognize and honor no other Messiah. Truly they are a peculiar people, and never so peculiar as at this moment, in the tenacity with which they cling to this interpretation of the prophecies in face of evidence which floods the world with its light. When "the fullness of the Gentiles shall come in," their eyes will be opened, as Peter's were in the vision, to see what a *We* the empire of "The Anointed" was to constitute and embrace.

We will next glance at the commonwealth of Greece, and notice some of the characteristics of the *We* they founded.

THE NATIONAL "WE" OF GREECE.

GREECE once so covered the world with its disk of light and glory, that, reversing the order and action of the sun's annular eclipse, the ring that surrounded it was the outer darkness, while itself was the lustre of humanity. Indeed, we should not know that there was such a dark circumference, nor what beings peopled it, were it not for the light of Greece. Jerusalem and Athens were the two fountain-heads of human history for the first forty centuries, one of the sacred, the other of the secular annals of mankind. Greece not only made grand and brilliant histories of her own, but wrote all that is worth remembering of the life, and being, and doing of all other nations, excepting the Hebrew. Rome lit her great torch of civilization at the lamp of Greece; and later-born nations have gone to her for oil, and found that it would burn bright and clear even in the colder latitudes of their being. Outside the Bible, what a Mohammedan fanatic said of the Koran might be said by a Grecian sage — that all that had been written of mankind that was not in Greek literature was superfluous, and might be destroyed without loss to the world. What do we of to-day know of the history of ancient Assyria, Persia, Media, Egypt, Asia Minor, and Scythia, except through Greek historians or their Roman copyists? Who are the Latin orators, historians, poets, philosophers, painters, sculptors, and architects, who were not pupils of the great masters of Greece? What would have been Cicero without a Demothenes, or Virgil without a Homer, for a predecessor and teacher? Then in religion, as well as literature, compare the gods and goddesses of Grecian mythology with the quadrupedal, centipedal, volant, and reptile deities of Egypt. Compare their worship and its rituals with the cruel and disgusting abominations of more eastern idolatry. Compare their ethical and intellectual philosophy with the fantastic conceptions of the Hindoo mind ; their Solon, Socrates, and Aristotle with any men that Persia or Media ever produced. In patriotism, what antecedent or subsequent histories of mankind can give more illustrious examples than that of Leonidas and his Spartan band at Thermopylæ? What one nation of antiquity ever produced axioms of purer morality, or of richer wisdom, or proverbs that are more likely to go down to the last generations of men? After all that has been written and said of the impress that Greece made upon the world, of her place in history and humanity, few, even Gladstone himself, have reached the full fact of her shaping and determining power, first upon the Roman empire, then through Rome upon the later nations.

Still it is a fact, which juvenile wisdom has comprehended, that there are " spots in the sun." The naked eye may detect them ; but, seen through a powerful medium, these spots become huge craters and lagoons of opaque matter. To get at many facts in her real life and character, one must look at Greece through a smoked glass, especially when he contemplates her at the full-orbed splendor of her glory. In examining and presenting a few of these facts, we would not dim nor depreciate a single ray

13

of that lustre. We only adduce them to illustrate the rise and progress of " We," showing the growth and manifestation of a national sentiment at different stages of the world's history.

The country which came to be called Greece, at some unknown period after its first discovery and settlement, must have been for more than a century on the extremest frontier of civilization, and even humanity. It was peopled by the descendants of Noah's grandson, Javan, a name which would not likely be spelt nearer the Hebrew in Greek than *Iona*. And that was the general name given to the people of the country by the nations from which they originally went. The isles of the sea inhabited by the posterity of Javan, must have been the Ionian Islands, for Moses could have heard of no other in his day. Island populations in all ages and regions have been thus necessarily the most benighted and barbarous in their aboriginal condition. All the explorers and navigators of the last two centuries attest to this fact, and the missionaries who have labored to elevate these islanders have found to their sorrow how slowly they change their character. But neither Columbus, Cabot, or Cook ever discovered human beings so utterly degraded and brutish as were the aboriginal inhabitants of the Grecian isles and mainland. To say that they planted themselves on the extremest frontier of civilization would be putting their condition far short of the fact. Considering the character of the times, they were as far from civilization as the Esquimaux Indians were from Iceland in the ninth century. In habits, disposition, and modes of life, they resembled the beasts of prey, their fellow-inhabitants. According to their own historians, they lived like beasts, in holes, caverns, and the hollows of trees. They fed on acorns, nuts, natural fruits, and herbs. But even when they had no other homes but these holes to fight for, they developed those characteristics which marked every subsequent age of their history. They fought with each other, first by individuals, then by families. It was a long time before they could fight in packs like wolves; and they learned these small lessons of union under the pressure of sharp necessity. By uniting their strength they found that their piracy paid better, and won more spoil for each individual, than if he fought or stole with his single hands. And this union of forces was as valuable and necessary for defence as aggression; for of course the victims of their violence and thefts learned how to unite themselves also to repel and return the murderous assaults upon their lives and property, if they possessed anything worthy the name of property. This principle seems to have run through all their leagues, councils, and confederations, until they lost even the semblance of national life. So slow was the progress of their elevation, and from such a low level did they arise, that they almost paid divine honors to the first philosopher they produced or captured, who taught them to build huts, and clothe themselves in skins. No people known to ancient history remained so long and deep in utter barbarism; perhaps because none was so long isolated or barred outside the line or reach of civilization. While the Persians, Phœnicians, Jews, Egyptians, and Midianites were at the zenith of their enlightenment, the Greeks were about where the

North American Indians were found when the English began to plant colonies on that continent. Indeed, they had not progressed so far as those Indians towards the structure of a nation or of a national sentiment. When Solomon was in all his glory, and the Hebrew nation in all its unity and greatness, the Greeks were divided into more clans than the Indians in the six New England States, and were no more advanced than they in the useful or civilized arts.

But, with all their barbarism, and almost continually at war with each other, when other peoples were out of their reach, the policy of union made considerable progress, especially when it was necessary for some piratical expedition on a larger scale than usual. This was the case in connection with their famous expedition against Troy, which Homer's genius celebrated, and, perhaps, in a great measure created. Outside of this grand epic, we have but a meagre and vague history of this event. It shows how long after the expedition he wrote, and under what new influences and for what new readers he wrote, that he put a woman at the bottom of the affair. But at a time when they sold their children and bought their wives, what was Helen to them, or they to Helen? Undoubtedly their descent upon Asia Minor was the foray of pirates, pure and simple, and all the romance that stirred them to or in it was the cupidity of plunder. Troy, doubtless, was the first as well as the richest city they had ever seen. Possibly it contained more wealth than the whole of Greece at the time. The fleet of little vessels, which Homer magnified into ships, but which the Iroquois Indians would have called war-canoes, was commanded and manned by the largest number of Greek chiefs, sailors and soldiers, that had ever been leagued together in one enterprise.

Here, then, we have a stage in the history of Greece, at which the numerous little communities which peopled the country present the temporary coherence, force, and sentiment of a nation. It was a very important point for them to reach, when the prospect of the spoils of a large and civilized town could thus unite them and hold them together through such a long experience of hardship, danger, bravery, and suffering. Clans or tribes, which had preyed upon each other in Greece all the way back to the time when each only represented a single family, now fought side by side with equal courage under the walls of Troy. At the close of each battle in a foreign land and with a foreign foe, they must have yielded more and more to the sentiment of a common country, a common race, and a common language; perhaps to feel that a permanent union as a nation would be preferable to their old condition. Then there was another influence more important still that resulted from their union in this enterprise. It brought all the leading and the brightest minds of Greece not only into the first, but into a long and most intimate contact with the civilization of Asia Minor. In this respect and in this way, it did more for their enlightenment and the elevation of their country, than the crusades did for the rude but energetic nations of Western Europe. Indeed, in a reverse order, it did for them what the rule and occupation of the Moors in Spain did for that country, and, through it, for France, England, and other lands. If the Moors did not go to

Greece, the Greeks went to them, and staid with them long enough to learn some of the rudimental arts and habits of civilization. Whatever obscurity involves Homer, his time and his story; whatever proportion of his heroic epic was the pure and simple creation of his poetical imagination, the siege and capture of Troy must be accepted as real facts of history. Even the unwritten lore of tradition, on which he may have depended for the groundwork of his Iliad, could not have emanated from sheer fiction.

With the expedition against Troy commences really the authentic history of Greece. And, what is somewhat remarkable, ever after this event the Greeks tended eastward in their movements, pressing back upon Asia. With this their first broadside contact with civilization, probably their language began to take those characteristics which made it, at a later age, the grandest of human tongues. So, from this event we may date the history of the Greeks as a people, if not as a nation.

Homer has made such illustrious heroes of the Greek chieftains or clan-leaders who besieged and captured Troy, and has surrounded the enterprise and achievement with such a gorgeous mist of glory, that it is difficult to reduce the event to the actual dimensions of fact. But this may be assumed as unquestionable, that the first time the different Grecian tribes ever united in a common cause, or with a common sentiment, was in this famous foray upon Ilium. It is quite probable that they had never built or thought of building a city until they had taken and destroyed Troy. When they appeared before its walls they were mere barbarians; and Homer

might as well have written his Iliad in Choctaw as in the
language spoken by Agamemnon or Achilles. Perhaps
neither of those heroes would have been able to read a
single verse which the great poet gave to their exploits.
The best spoils they brought back from the sacked and
ruined city were the ideas impressed upon their strong
and savage minds by their long contact and conflict with
the highest civilization of Asia Minor. Nearly all the
populations between the Euxine and the Mediterranean
on the Asiatic side of the Bosphorus rallied to the defence of the Trojans. Thus every band of men the
Greeks encountered was far more advanced than themselves in all the arts of civilized society. Indeed, for many
centuries their laws and customs were framed and en-
forced with the express object to keep them from the enlightenment, occupations, and usages of the old nations of
Asia; to perpetuate and foster in them the wild, unta-
mable energy of barbarian freebooters. The implacable
ferocity with which they massacred the population of the
captured city, sparing neither age nor sex, was as natural
to their revengeful natures as were acts of the same ma-
lignity to the painted savages of New England in their
assaults upon the English colonists. But the animus
with which they levelled to the dust the noblest edifices,
which had been the admiration of Western Asia, showed
that they warred against such monuments of art as
against enemies to their own character and habits. But
while they were battering or burning them down, the influence they dreaded took hold of their minds with resist-
less fascination.

The leaders who returned to Europe after their ten

years' war in Asia were not the men that left their country on the expedition. They had resisted the influence
to which they had been subjected, but it was too strong
for them. They unconsciously yielded to its shaping on
whatever side it acted upon their character. They began to build cities, and temples, and monuments after the
models they destroyed in Troy. They began to resolve
themselves into larger communities, each with a central
population and a recognized government. Athens took
the lead in civilization, and attracted teachers and scholars
from Egypt and other enlightened countries. Out of the
spoils brought back from Asia by the Greek crusaders
the elements of the Greek language were constructed
into a speech that grew in power from century to century,
until it became the grand, central, mediating tongue of
the nations. Homer raised it to this culmination of glory
by his immortal epics. All the learned men of the world
began to study and develop it, and to enrich it with their
best thoughts. The scholars of Egypt, headed by the
Ptolemies, the orators, poets, and historians of Rome,
and Jewish rabbies, and even Paul himself, honored it,
and used it as the only classical language in the world.
The Greeks, in all their long internecine wars, were
proud of it, and boasted of it as their common inheritance. Indeed, it embraced them all in the circumference of the only *Our* that they ever formed and kept
unbroken. In the most brilliant periods of their civilization there were too many little *selfs* to make a great *We*.
Thus Greece never became a nation, nor ever felt the
inspiration and energy of a great national sentiment.
The only time that they approached this condition was

when they were hooped together, as it were, by Xerxes and his prodigious force. Still they were forever forming temporary alliances, leagues, and councils. They introduced a term into their language to describe these arrangements, which the word *allies* does not define. Their " *summachoi* " meant nothing more nor less than *partner-fighters.* Their leagues were little more than a number of Grecian states clubbed together to fight the rest and share the spoils of the war. What Athens and Lacedemon were to each other so were the smaller cities arrayed against each other, twos by twos or fours by fours. No all-embracing sentiment of patriotism could ever overcome, supersede, or absorb their miserly, suicidal feeling of small selfishness. The rest of the world does not furnish a parallel to the petty jealousies, ambitions, leaguing, and counter-leaguing that divided and devastated Greece. With all the splendor and glory of their civilization ; with all their long and thickset array of the most brilliant men, as statesmen, philosophers, orators, poets, and historians, who have inspired the ages with the life of their immortal thoughts, at no recorded moment in their history did the best of them, either Aristides, Demosthenes, or Solon himself, ever seem to grasp the thought of uniting all the different populations of a territory about as large as Scotland in one compact, well-centred, harmonious nation. They resisted every tendency to such a union, and every policy that seemed to lead to it, as if it would extinguish all the vitality and value of their local entities. Even in the most despairing straits, when an overwhelming foreign invasion was pouring in a million of armed men to subjugate the Grecian states, several of

them not only stood out against a union for defence, but
even went over to the powerful enemy to assist him in
the reduction of the rest.   This was the case with the
Ionians when the forces of Xerxes were overrunning land
and sea.   When Athens and other cities were laid in
ashes, and the Athenians and their allies were drawing
up their ships in order of battle in the Straits of Salamis
for a struggle that was to decide the fate of the whole
Grecian race, they found the Ionians arrayed with the
Persian fleet against them.   Whether it was to gratify a
private animosity against some particular Grecian state
which they burned to see destroyed in the general con-
flagration, or whether they were hired with Xerxes' gold
to fight against their countrymen, history does not enable
us to determine.   But Themistocles, the Athenian com-
mander, succeeded in reaching them with an influence
which constrained them to withdraw from the battle just
in time to give the victory to the Greeks.

These implacable jealousies and animosities were both
the defensive and aggressive weapons which foreign powers and domestic usurpers could always wield against
Greece, and keep it in a state of hostile disintegration.
And the saddest circumstance of all, foreign powers were
counselled to use these weapons instead of their own
by illustrious Greeks themselves who had been exiled
from Athens or Lacedemon.   Alcibiades, alternately
idolized and exiled by the Athenians, now leading their
armies and navies, now plotting against them in the
councils of their most inveterate enemies, gave lessons
to the Persian monarch in the science of dividing and
conquering the Grecian states by keeping them at war

with each other. " Always help the weakest party," was the axiom in which he embodied his advice to the Persians. Justinus, who gives the best *résumé* of Grecian history of any Latin author, thus sums up the policy of Alcibiades : *Nam regem Persarum, dissentientibus Græcis, arbitrum pacis ac belli fore ; et quos suis non posset, ipsorum armis victurum* — " For the king of the Persians, while the Greeks are quarrelling among themselves, will become the arbiter of peace and war, and conquer with their own arms those he could not with his." The Persians adopted this counsel of the most brilliant and versatile demagogue that Greece ever produced for its demoralization, though no one nation ever produced a greater number or variety of them. Indeed, the character has been recognized so completely Grecian that it has stuck exclusively to the Greek language ever since its origin, and has never been transferred to any other. *Demagogue* has been taken in, and adopted by them all, pure and simple. Even the Germans, with all their bold originality in elaborating synonymes and isonymes, cannot make one out of their honest language which would so fully define such a character as that of Alcibiades, and of hundreds of other eloquent, ambitious, impetuous, unpatriotic *selfs* that preceded and succeeded him in Athens, as that significant term, which has come to be understood by the masses in all civilized countries. There were always such characters from Athens, Lacedemon, and other Grecian capitals, flying for refuge against popular indignation to foreign courts, and scheming and plotting with the enemies of their country to gratify their private revenge ; compassing the destruction or the subjugation of a state to foreign rule because it had rejected their own domination.

What the Persians learned to practise, Philip knew how to carry out on a larger scale. "Divide and conquer," was a policy by which he wrought out the great ends of his ambition ; and even when these ends were manifest, and union could alone thwart them, division was never more easy to be organized between the states that succumbed to his rule. In some cases one was willing to perish if it could involve another in its own destruction. No quarter of a century of history can be cut out even of the annals of the most barbarous nations, so filled with perfidy and every form of demoralization as the twenty-five years of Philip's sway. It is a page that is heart-sickening to read for its records of all that is revolting and hateful in the character of individuals and the conduct of states. Still, if Philip, with hands of iron despotism, had been able to construct a nation out of the states he subjugated, or even kept them from wasting each other with their miserable intestine wars, a modern world might have pardoned his policy of conquest and the tyranny of his rule. But at the very zenith of Grecian intellect, when its orators, poets, and philosophers commanded the admiration of the world, and filled it with their axioms of wisdom and morality, they lacked the quiet and steady virtue of patriotism : they never could say, form, or feel *We* on a large scale : no city of them all would consent to be less than the capital of a nation. No pressure from without or motive from within could solve these little jealous and ambitious *selfs*, or expand or unite them in one great commonwealth, or in one great common sentiment. What was common to the states was common to the individuals that composed them. They set up and put down in sudden and quick succession every possible form of local government. Despotisms, democracies, aristocracies, monarchies, Thirty Tyrants and Four Hundred Tyrants alternated at Athens. Had not the ambition of the Greeks been divided upon a dozen different centres, one might have thought that it would have expanded under Alexander the Great to embrace a large empire like the Assyrian or Roman. But when such an empire seemed nearing its realization, and Grecian rule about to be established over the whole known world, Athens, even in the full glory of its intellect and genius, could not lift itself high enough above its own petty self to grasp the idea and feel the ambition which Alexander's conquests might otherwise have inspired. Better be first in Attica than second in the space and populations of two continents.

Any one who reads the history of Greece, as we have already remarked, through a smoked glass, or without being blinded by the brilliancy that is apt to dazzle or divert the vision, will feel a species of relief when he sees the eagles of Rome planted at Athens and Lacedemon, and all the other capitals and centres of the country. Whether he likes the Roman rule or not, he feels that it will do what the English rule has done in Ireland, and the Russian in Poland — keep the people from fighting with each other, and hold them fast under a solid sway.

Thus the Greeks were the mightiest race, but the smallest nation, of the old world that occupied a large place and played a great part in history. No one can put too high an estimate on the illuminating and transforming influence of their mind upon all the other populations of the earth. But at the noontide of their intellectual glory, when they were wont to call every other people barbarians, they were incapable of forming and maintaining a great and unanimous commonwealth. Their patriotism was intense, but it burned only at small points, like the wick of a candle. Leonidas would die with his Spartans at the gap of Thermopylæ to stay the invasion of the Persians by an hour, but it is probable that he would have let them in without contest sooner than have seen Lacedemon second to Athens, or Athens the capital of consolidated Greece. Owing to this radical and incurable defect in their character, they never formed, in fact or feeling, so great a *We* as the two Hebrew tribes of Judah and Benjamin constituted in a small portion of Palestine.

THE ROMAN IMPERIAL "WE."

WHEN the student of Grecian history and character followed that brilliant and unhappy people through the wretched annals of their civil wars, mutual animosities, and antagonistic ambitions, he must hail the Roman eagle, spreading its strong pinions over the scene, with a feeling of relief. The retrospect is sad. A race of illustrious statesmen, heroes, orators, and poets, with the best educated populations of the world, after the probation of centuries, have made an utter failure in the effort or pretension of erecting a coherent, patriotic nation. One now turns to that rough, rising power in the then far west of Europe, to see what it will be and do; whether it will achieve a better success than the people of Greece, whom it has just subjugated. Soon he recognizes a fundamental difference in the character of the two races. In the first place, he sees a great centre of irresistible attractive force formed at the heart of the new realm; and he feels that Rome will not break upon the rock on which Greece split. She has no Athens and Sparta to forbid or fracture the structure of a great nation by their rival ambitions. The centripetal attraction of " the eternal city " overpowers the contrary forces, and sends the pulses of patriotism through the growing empire. Then the rugged discipline of necessity hardens the bone and muscle of the Roman people, and trains them to wrestle with success for the first and greatest place in the world. Their first foes are not Trojans or Persians, but barbarians ruder than themselves at the outset of their career. Their growth in civilization is slow, but steady and strong. They gradually develop that solidity and firmness of character which distinguish them from the Greeks and other races of men. Rome lights her lamp at Athens, but it is filled with her own oil instead of phosphorus. If it burns less brilliantly, its light is steadier and evener. She hangs up that lamp over her Seven Hills, and its rays reach farther than any one ever lighted before.

The national sentiment of the Romans grows with the growth of their dominion. Their capital is a grand moorage for their patriotism. Its centripetal attraction reaches outward farther and farther. No city in the world ever drew like it; not even Jerusalem, as a political centre, though it was the all in all of Judea. Assyria had its Babylon and Nineveh at the same time; Greece had its Athens, Sparta, Thebes, and Philippi; but the Roman empire, in the best age of its strength and glory, had only Rome, and it possessed more moral and political force as a capital than any other city the world ever saw, or ever will see hereafter, Paris, perhaps, excepted. In glancing at the history of ancient and modern nations, we have only proposed, as it were, to feel the pulse of their patriotism, or to notice the strength and warmth of their national sentiment, and the spontaneity of cohesion and union in their respective populations. With the exception of the Jews, the Romans were the only great people that had ever felt the inspiration of real patriotism. And yet they founded an empire by force, and then held its diversified populations to itself by many liens of common interest and respect. Indeed, the very word " patriotism," as well as the idea it expresses, is of Roman origin. It meant something more and better than the mere love of country for its glory and power. Those three words of universal and everlasting renown, " *Romanus civis sum,*" were never uttered with a fuller sense of their significance than in the distant dependencies or colonies of the empire. Roman citizenship became the right and boast of multitudes who never spoke a word of Latin to the day of their death. It was a dignity which the nation was at all times ready to vindicate before or against the world; and he who wore it, even in common life, stood erect among men, proudly conscious of the prerogative. In whatever latitude he lived, to whatever land or language he was born, this prerogative was a lien that attached him to the throne of the Cæsars, and to the Roman capital, and to the Roman name. It reached across the desert, sea, and island, and was as strong at the British Eboracum as at the chief city of Judea. It was not a mere sentimental value or boast. It entitled to the steady and strong protection of law and justice ; it inspired the feeling in every man who possessed it, that behind him there was a mighty power for his defence that could and would shake the world to avenge his wrongs.

No man born in Italy itself, or in any part of the colonial empire of Rome, ever said *" Ronanus civis sum "* with a fuller sense of the right and dignity those words expressed, than Saul of Tarsus. Nor was it as a mere subterfuge that he appealed to that right, or interposed it between himself and his bigoted and infuriated countrymen. His whole bearing through his apostleship showed that he valued the dignity as much as the right attaching to his Roman citizenship. And yet he declared, and almost boasted, that he was a Hebrew of the Hebrews, and, as touching the old Jewish faith and worship, a Pharisee, and even had surpassed them in his persecution of the Christian Church. Nor was he less a Jew in national sentiment when he put himself under the Roman ægis, and claimed the protection of Roman law. He had studied that law. He had admired the principles on which it was based, and the whole Roman process of justice at home and abroad. And neither at home nor abroad were the spirit, process, and award of the Roman tribunal more fully illustrated than at those trials in Judea at which Paul and Paul's Master were brought to its bar. Even the wicked and cruel

14

Pilate felt himself in the august presence of Roman law, as well as face to face with a sublime and innocent prisoner, when he declared to the boisterous priests, scribes, and rulers of the Jews, "I find no fault in him;" — nothing that violated or disregarded a single statute of that law. At that momentous and affecting trial he planted his feet upon it as upon a rock, and seemed for a while to beat back the surging and shouting crowd that dashed against it. It was only in the face of their fierce will that he suffered himself to be drawn from his impregnable position by a fatal compromise with justice. He sought to save the life of the innocent prisoner, not by Roman law, but through a Jewish custom. The expedient was a bitter failure; for the multitude, incited by their priests, chose a murderer instead of The Prince of Life. Then it was that the Roman governor, finding himself thus intrapped, yielded to the mob with an act and expression which will be perpetuated to the end of time in the saying, "I wash my hands" of this or that. "He took water and washed his hands before the multitude, saying, I am innocent of the blood of this just person; see ye to it." But he did not wash out of his conscience the conviction that, in yielding to the clamor of the Jews, he had set aside those sacred forms of justice he was appointed to enforce. He could not, by washing his hands before the multitude, give over an innocent man to them to be put to death without any fault amenable to Roman law. He must put up some accusation on the cross, for he dared not erect it in the face of the Roman empire as a mere sacrifice to Jewish superstition and bigotry. He therefore sought to avoid this responsibility, and to avenge himself on the priests and their mob, by implicating them in the crime they pretended to impute to Christ, when all other charges had fallen to the ground. "And Pilate wrote a title, and put it on the cross. And the writing was, JESUS OF NAZARETH, THE KING OF THE JEWS." This was not for the Jews only to read. It was an inscription to face Rome as well as Jerusalem. It was written in Hebrew, Greek, and Latin, to be read by his Roman soldiers, and all the subjects of the Roman empire dwelling in the city. This, then, was the only accusation: Christ, and not Cæsar, was the King of the Jews' choice. As such a rival and pretender he was crucified, and the Jews were made *participes criminis*. They begged of him to be released from this implication, but he held them fast to it, saying, " What I have written I have written." And he wrote it in his own defence, as well as to punish them for forcing him to swerve from the rigid rules and forms of justice he was to administer.

But, as hypocrisy is a compliment to virtue, so was Pilate's wretched expedient a testimony to that legal *régime* which, from one corner of the Roman empire to the other, made the words " *Romanus civis sum* " of such great meaning to every man entitled to utter them. And who ever uttered them more boldly and confidently than Paul before the Roman governors and captains? " When the centurion heard that, he went and told the chief captain, saying, Take heed what thou doest, for this man is a Roman. Then the chief captain came and said unto him, Tell me, art thou a Roman? He said, Yea. . . . Then straightway they departed from him which should have examined him; and the chief captain also was afraid after he knew he was a Roman, and because he had bound him." The great Apostle to the Gentiles exercised the prerogative of his citizenship sparingly, and did not abuse it. When he was in the heart of Greece, he did not avail himself of it to save himself and his companion from scourging and imprisonment in Philippi. It was after he had suffered both that he declared his citizenship. As a Roman, if he had done anything worthy of death he did not refuse to die, either at Jerusalem, Athens, or Rome; but he did refuse to die or suffer without trial at a regular tribunal of justice. Hear what he says to the magistrates of Philippi: "They have beaten us openly, uncondemned, being Romans, and have cast us into prison, and now do they thrust us out privily? Nay, verily, but let them come themselves and fetch us out." The magistrates "feared when they heard they were Romans;" that was, because they had subjected them to mob law — had beaten them openly and imprisoned them privily without trial or judicial sentence. The Grecian authorities honored Roman justice by their fear; "and they *besought* them, and brought them out, and desired them to depart out of the city." They made humble apologies to the two Jew-born Romans, and doubtless begged them to forgive their sin of ignorance in treating them in such a manner without first inquiring out their citizenship.

Cæsar and the Roman power and name were never more honored than by the eloquent Apostle before the judgment-seat of Festus, when the Jewish priests tried to inveigle him to Jerusalem to sacrifice him to their blind bigotry. "Then said Paul, I stand at Cæsar's judgment-seat, where I ought to be judged; . . . if there be none of these things whereof these accuse me, no man may deliver me unto them. I appeal unto Cæsar." Then answered Festus, "Hast thou appealed unto Cæsar? unto Cæsar shalt thou go;" and unto Cæsar he went, with "certain other prisoners," to be judged at a tribunal which could not be moved by the clamor of Jewish fanaticism.

The Roman rule was rough and stern in the countries they conquered, but it established in all of them a system of law, order, and equality, which they never knew before. Then it was a utilitarian rule everywhere. Other armies had marched over the peopled continents and subjugated nations, leaving destruction and desolation in their pathways. But the Roman legions, when they had done the work appointed them with the sword, took up the pick and spade with equal bravery and patience, and became the missionaries of a higher civilization. They left every land they occupied better than they found it; and they found none lower than Britain, and none profited more by their presence and influence. The Romans changed their systems of government as many times as did the Greeks before them; and they invented systems which even the Athenians never thought of. In looking back over past centuries, the spaces between them grow narrower as they recede, and the events that marked them more frequent. Thus the change from kings to consuls, republics or monarchies, and *vice versâ*, appear nearer to each other in this retrospect than they really were. Still those who wrought these changes by force or intrigue could say, if they loved Cæsar less it was because they loved Rome more. They had many revolutions and conspiracies, but no internecine wars like those of Greece. They who smote " the foremost man of all this world," struck for Rome. Up to the last year of the Augustan age that metropolis was to the remotest corner of the empire what Paris is to France. It was the eradiating and irradiating centre of patriotism to patrician and plebeian, tribune and dictator. Even Tarquin the Proud, impious as he was, and Coriolanus and Camillus, found and sought no Lacedemon in their voluntary or involuntary exile. It was Rome or nothing with them.

Thus, with all these sudden and violent changes of government, the Imperial " We " of Rome, at the time of Augustus Cæsar, was broader in circumference, stronger and steadier in sentiment, and more well-working in action than any national sentiment and organization ever attained before by any people or race. There is something sad in the decline and extinction of this mighty power. Its career is like the Rhine. Between the rugged mountains it is a noble river; but when its current slackens and parts into sluggish streams in the quicksands of low morality, the main channel is swallowed up and lost. One may as well seek for the true mouth of the Rhine as for the continuity of the Roman character. The sky of Italy was the same in Cæsar's day as in this. The marshes and malaria, the plagues and pestilences, were as fatal then as now. What, then, has wrought the transformation? Many students and writers of history have addressed themselves to the solution of this problem, and must have failed even to satisfy their own minds. Still, from our stand-point, we may see the grand march of the human race, and observe how these great nations had their day and its work. When the lamp of Greece was full ablaze, it shone with all the light that Assyria, Egypt, and Palestine had emitted. When she fell, she passed that lamp over to Rome, who, adding oil of her own, held it up for centuries before the world with steadier illumination. When it fell from her hands, it was lifted by another race, and set alight with a lustre that had never shone on Rome, Greece, Egypt, or Assyria. Following the sun, and, like it, westward, the star of empire takes its way by the light of that lamp, replenished with oil which neither Cæsar, nor Pericles, nor Ptolemy ever tested. It will be more gratifying to read the history of nations marching by that light.

LIFE AND DIGNITY OF THE ENGLISH LANGUAGE.

The most precious and powerful vitality of a nation's life is its language. A nation's political institutions may change from decade to decade, or from century to century; but its language is its breathing life, whose pulse the revolutions which upset thrones and dynasties cannot break nor still. The great heart of a people breathes and beats in their language. In its warm and sleepless life live, and move, and have their being, their thoughts, hopes, aspirations, patriotism, religion, and history. The words that Shakespeare puts into the mouth of one of his characters, with but slight change, have come from the lips of many a nation, great or small : " He that filches from me my own language, robs me of that which not enriches him, and makes me poor indeed." How many a people have clung to this as the immediate jewel of their soul! They have looked on, powerless and saddened, to see the political structure of their nationality rent in twain, and demolished beam by beam and stone by stone. They have seen the regalia worn by their kings pass over to the brows of foreign potentates, and the very name of their national habitation dimmed and diluted in the appellation of provinces or counties of an alien and conquering empire. But to save this immediate jewel of their soul — their language — they have dashed into the burning wreck of national entity, as a mother would into the flames and smoke of her dwelling to pluck her darling infant from its burning cradle, forgetful of all other treasures. How the Poles, Hungarians, and the Germans of Sleswig have struggled for this treasure, as if it were more precious and costly than any other that despotic power could filch from them ! With what desperate tenacity the Welsh have held to it, though gladly surrendering every other faculty of their national existence to the British empire ! Lest the surging wave of English literature and life should some day overflow their Principality and quench the light of their rude language, a Welsh colony has gone out to " Patagonia's snow-invested wilds," apparently for no other earthly object than to keep the vestal flame of their old speech burning under the cold shadow of those icy mountains.

But not all alike have nations and peoples valued, cherished, and honored their languages. Indeed, the noblest ever written or spoken has been least honored by the race that call it their own. This may be a strong assertion, but we believe it is justified by facts manifold and irrefutable. We have witnessed proofs of the truth of this statement which are its sufficient warrant. The English-speaking race for two hundred years have, as a mass, appreciated the vitality and victory of their language, the battles it has fought and won. The Normans under William the Conqueror and his successors overpowered the English Saxons, broke down their nobility, and endeavored to serf their common people. They confiscated Saxon estates, demolished Saxon institutions, and labored to Latinize the Saxon race in England. With the oppressors there was power, but not power enough to put down the old, simple, honest Saxon language. It held its own against Norman courts, customs, learning, and scholars. Its pulse was feeble at Oxford and Cambridge, and in all the cathedral cities of the realm, but quick, and warm, and sleepless in the village and rural communities of the land. It was the speech of their inner home and heart life. It was the speech of their hopes, prayers, faith, memory, and affection. It held its own and more against every burden and barrier. It worked its way upward from rank to rank of the ruling classes. It worked its way in face of fagot and fire into the Bible, and the whole realm and outside empires shook with emotion when all the holy words of Divine Revelation were translated into it.

Still, with all its power and progress, with all its unparalleled faculties for moving the mind of the world with its life-breathing literature, there is still perceptible and prevalent among the English and American writers, schools, scholars, and learning-smatterers, a kind of old Norman affectation for Latin, just as if the language of Shakespeare, Milton, Tennyson, and Macaulay, that is making the tour of the world, were still the Saxon *patois* of the rural districts of England. This affectation seems to be reviving. We see it in the titles of new books, all in English between the lids. Go into any well-stocked book-shop, and you will notice *Lyra Germanica*, *Lyra Anglicana*, *Ecce Homo*, and the like. The other day we saw a new magazine with a foot of Saxon clay and a head of Latin brass, or with the name " *The Academia.*" We have recently stood by the side of four altars on which our noble English is sacrificed to the manes of a dead language. The immolation on two of these sacrilegious shrines is heathenish enough to make the dumb victim led to the slaughter cry out with indignation. The first of the twain is erected in that Christian temple, St. Paul's, to the memory of Samuel Johnson. He was the great captain, if not the Columbus, of the English language. He erected, and crowned, and introduced it to the world as the grandest of human speeches. And all who spoke and wrote it after his day crowned him with the honor due for this mighty undertaking. He was proud, and had ample reason to be proud, of the work, for it cost him infinite toil. He had brought to it intellect-

ual energies that commanded the admiration of the whole
English-speaking world. He had compacted and beauti-
fied the structure with all the treasures of Chaucer,
Shakespeare, Milton, and other old masters; and yet,
after this long life's aspiration and work so fully accomplished, he, or his friends, knowing the bent of his mind,
made a heathen altar of his tomb, and sacrificed upon it
the great language he had elaborated and adorned to the
shades of this dead Latin tongue! His own, which he
had made so noble, and held up to the world embellished
with all its splendid jewelry, was not good enough for
his epitaph! The millions and the masses who can read
no other, may come by twos or threes to his monument
in St. Paul's, and, looking with wonder at his huge, half-
naked, gladiator-like statue, and seeing the Latin inscription beneath, may well take him for an old prize-fighter
of pagan Rome, but never for the author of the great
English Dictionary, and a Christian besides. In this
sacrifice to a dead language, the friends of the illustrious
lexicographer, it must be said in their justification, only
carried out his well-known predilection, and, perhaps,
his expressed wish.

Still, there stands another altar on which a sacrifice
more strange has been offered to "the dead past." Dr.
Johnson was a scholar, and almost pedantic in classical
reading and reputation. Doubtless his ruling passion,
if not pedantry, was strong in death, and, when approaching it, would be likely to quote Juvenal. But there is a
tall monument erected by the sea, at Great Yarmouth, to
the memory of one of England's greatest heroes. One
perhaps may say that he was to Britain's naval power

and reputation what Johnson was to the English language.
The tall monument of Horatio Nelson stands facing the
sea and all the sailors of that coast. He was one of the
greatest of sailors, as well as naval commanders. He
went to sea at twelve, and lived, fought, and died upon it.
With such small opportunity for education, it is doubtful
if he coul·l write or read a sentence in Latin to the day
of his death. But no Englishman born ever uttered ten
words of our common language which so thrilled the
British nation as his " *This day England expects every
man to do his duty !* " This was his last " good night ! "
to the country for which he fought, bled, and died. He
was proud of his nation, and it was proud of him. To
put into its hands the sceptre of the seas was the great,
burning ambition of his life. At Trafalgar he accomplished his life's ambition and work. His country recognized the consummation, and crowned his memory with
all the honors such recognition could dictate. Here on
the eastern coast of the island, where he first saw the
grand face of the sea, stands the tall, pedestaled shaft
of his monument. It is there, the beacon-light of a
great life, to kindle up in the breasts of the rough sailors
and fishermen a glow of patriotism, as well as to point
the way of humble men to the highest places in their
country's esteem and honor. All you sea-beaten men,
come hither in your yawls, smacks, and sloops ; come to
this monument of a sailor's glory. Read what he was
at the beginning and end of his life ; what he did for his
country, and what his country did for him. Read it,
indeed ! why, this is a Roman monument, erected to the
memory of Julius Cæsar's flag-captain on his invasion of

England! Look at the inscription: it is in Latin of Trajan's time. The very letters are unreadable. This is not the monument of our great English sailor. He fought and died for a country that was an empire, and an empire that had a language which all its heroes spoke with a power that awed its enemies. The most intelligent sailor that comes to Nelson's monument at Yarmouth may say all this and more, and say it with honest indignation at this sacrifice on the altar of a dead language.

But a classical scholar may say, this Latin inscription on Nelson's monument was not for sailors or common men to read. Then for whose eyes and hearts was it meant? Was it a short exercise in Latin cut in stone for a school-boy to decipher, construe, and transmute into English as a morning lesson? Is it for University men alone? We would ask the most classical of them all how he would like to see the sublime battle-word of Nelson at Trafalgar turned into Latin. Let him try himself to turn a thrilling shaft of barbed lightning into a pointless icicle. How would it read? How would it sound? Thus:—

Hodie Anglia expectat quemque
Virum daturum esse debitum suum.

Or, in the many changes that might be played on the sentiment, would this read or sound any better?—

Quid unusquisque debet hunc
Anglia hodie expectat redditurum esse.

If the Latin amateur should not succeed in giving all the stirring pulse of life in a dead language which he

would to Nelson's sublime signal words, let him try his
hand on that beautiful and affecting expression of manly
tenderness with which the hero closed his life : " *Kiss me,
Hardy !* " How would these last words breathe in Latin ?
Let us see, —

> " Oscula me, Duramens ! "
>
> Or,   " Da mihi osculum, Durumcor ! "

In another part of England we were struck with a
third and very elaborate monument to the same dead
language. It was a beautiful fountain, wrought with the
most artistic taste and skill from Devonshire stone, and
erected at the most central and conspicuous point in the
town. It was for use as well as ornament. It was for
the special and exclusive use of the toiling, thirsty
masses ; for middle-class people seldom resort to the
chained dipper or basin of a public fountain. Here the
carters, costermongers, stevedores, and sailors were to
come and quench their thirst from this pure and running
stream. It was though tby the authorities that erected
this fountain that it would be a good thing to have a
healthy, pious sentence cut into the face of the stone,
just above the mouth of the stream. It would discredit
such beautiful marble, and be too common, to carve plain
English words in it ; so they cut in these, deep and large :
" *Nomen Jehovah est turris fortissima.*" Here was something for the hodmen and coal-porters to read that would
do them good ! If they had put in plain and honest
English, " The name of the Lord is a strong tower,"
most of the drinkers at the fountain would have known
what it meant and where it came from. But this would

be vulgarizing the sentiment. If any illiterate working-man would like to know the meaning of " *turris fortissima* " and all that, let him ask some school-boy who could read Virgil.

But there is another scene of this sacrifice which we always contemplate with greater sadness. It is an ancient and amiable custom to strew flowers upon the graves of departed friends. An occasional handful is deemed an adequate token of affectionate memory. The Latin language, as a living speech, has been dead for many centuries. But the whole English-speaking world gather all the flowers and pleasant plants of the earth and strew them upon the marble tomb of this mighty dead. Walk up and down Kew, or any other great garden of plants and flowers, and you will see this, we could almost say, sacrilegious homage. All the loves, prayers, songs, dreams, and hopes of all the ages that ever got into written language have been translated into English. In it we have all the flowering thoughts of the world's poets from Sanskrit to Saxon. In it we have the master-ideas of the old monarchs of mental power. Its first great effort and feat were to give its simple and hearty words to all the Holy Scriptures that came from God in Hebrew and Greek. But these beautiful, sweet-breathing Scriptures which He has written in His own letters all over the earth, have never been permitted to be thus translated by the pedantic amateurs and worshippers of a dead language. Walk up and down these great flower-gardens or flower-shows. From the names of all the green and tinted things that bloom and breathe by these embroidered aisles, a common man from the rural districts of daisies and ferns would think that neither England nor America ever had an indigenous flower or plant of its own; that every rose, lily, and pansy, and every delicate plant seen here, comes from a foreign land. And yet the classical botanists who crush these meek, sweet flowers with ponderous Latin names, would lift up their eyes and hands in pious horror at the idea of the masses of the common people saying their prayers or singing their hymns in church or chapel in Latin. Then why should these very masses come into the temple of Nature, and be obliged to say, as it were, the litany of flowers in the same dead language? How cruel to make an honest country girl mouth *rosa rubiginosa* for the sweet-brier that perfumes her garden hedge, or *gompholobium* for a kind of the beans she plants!

We hope the day is coming, and very near, when all who speak it around the globe will feel, and let the world know, that the English language is a living power among men; that it can furnish for every thought, hope, or joy that grows out of the human heart, or for every flower or plant that grows out of the earth, a name of as few letters and of as full meaning as any other language, living or dead, can supply; and that the English name given to any flower, plant, or tree, or to any beast, bird, or creeping thing, shall stand before it, and not behind in brackets, forever and wherever our mother tongue is spoken.

SOCIAL AND ARTISTIC SCIENCE.

THE SONGS AND SONGSTERS OF LABOR.

" He giveth songs in the night."

Songs in the day, songs in the night; songs on the land, songs on the sea; songs at the plough, songs at the anvil; songs at the cradle, songs at the grave; songs of the birds, of the bees, of the breeze; songs of childhood, of manhood, of old age; harvest songs, Sabbath songs, Christmas songs; songs of hope, of love, of sympathy, of triumph, of sorrow, of faith, and fear, and joy; songs of mortals, songs of the immortals; songs in the lowest lanes of human life on earth, songs in the loftiest promenades of paradise; songs of spheres, songs of angels, songs of Moses and earlier saints by the crystal River of Life; songs of little Carrie here over the penny cradle of her doll.

It is wonderful how much singing there is, after all, in this world of trouble and sorrow! It is a marvel how much there is said of it in Revelation, how much is done for it in Nature, and by it in Humanity. We will let " the music of the spheres " go as an extravagant fiction of a poetical imagination. If they sing on their axes and in their orbits, well and good; but there is no human articulation of joy in their music if we could hear it. Nor is it a very pleasant-sounding figure of speech to our human ears, for it suggests the

monotonous noise of friction, or the great breezy whir
of revolving bodies.   Without running into these high-
sounding but rather hackneyed fancies, it is really a wonderful and most blessed thing that there is so much
singing in this world of toil, affliction, and sorrow, — veritable singing, with tongues of flesh and blood, of man,
and bird, and bee, and creeping thing, and swimming
thing, and things amphibious ; now piping in pools, now
in the tree-tops, tall and leafy : relays of singers, that
take up the song of the day musicians of the hedge, grove,
and sky, and carry it on, with sweet variations of their
own, far into the stillest hours of the night, warbling
to the listening woods, till their mottled breasts quiver
and palpitate with the ecstasy of their joy.   It is one of
the happiest things about this great earthly home of mankind.   Beautiful and blessed is this companionship !
Beautiful are the symphonies of these varied tongues of
hope, joy, and sympathy.   They are all striving to make
the music of human happiness, and give it speech to the
ear of God.

But there is a feature of this arrangement I love to
contemplate ; that is, the special and God-hearted provision of " Songs and Songsters for Labor."   Whoever
gives attentive thought to the subject must come to the
belief, I think, that the first human being taught to sing
on earth was the man of the spade and the pruning-hook,
and he was taught by the singing-birds inside or outside
of Eden.   Happy birds, of the same feather, wing, and
voice, have sung ever since over the thorns and briers,
over the mines, fields, forests, and factories, in which labor has bent to its task with bronzed brow and hands,

weary and worn. They have been the poor men's minstrels through all the dark ages of their poverty and toil. They have sung their roundelays of cheer to the supperless, and even taught hungry children to sing songs of hope and courage to silent fathers and mothers hanging their heads in the sad sense of their penury. These winged blessings of God have hovered over the homes of the poor ever since the garden-gates of Eden were closed against man, and have dropped as sweet a music upon their hard and stony paths of life as they ever made for Adam in his holiest hours. The very sweetest of " the street musicians of the heavenly city " — the very bird that, above all others of the feathered choir, might have come straight down to earth from the branches of Heaven's Tree of Life with the notes on its tongue it sung to angels there — the Skylark, has been, is now, and ever shall be, the ploughman's and the reaper's minstrel, singing over the morning furrow and the midday sheaf, and all the sweat-drops between that bead their brows, the twittering warble of its happy heart. It is on the lookout for them. The rising sun lights them to no hour of labor unblessed with the lark's song and companionship overhead. It leaves the bird singing to them still when it withdraws its last beams, as if the ministry of music should outlast the ministry of light. And it does outlast it, by many, many a cheery hour, at the poor man's hearth. With all the want and woe, the heart-sickenings, heart-achings, and heart-breakings, half hidden and half revealed in the experience of the poor, no condition of humanity has been so seasoned with song as labor. No human dwellings have been so set to music as the cottages and cabins of the men of the plough, the hammer, the pick, and the spade. Song to them has been ever the spontaneous speech of hope ; and their brave hearts would hope against hope in the darkest days of life. Even when all the years of childhood, manhood, and old age were surrounded with the iron wall of slavery, with nothing he could call his own, either wife, child, or his own being, the chattelized negro has sung in his hut by night when the birds were asleep in the trees ; ay, even in the coffle on the hot road to a new auction-block. If his earthly lot could touch his lips to no song by night or day, his heart's hope has scaled the walls of his prison-house, and climbed up into the great immortalities of the hereafter, and set the harp-strings of his soul a-going melodiously.

Go where you will, and you will see how wonderfully music and song are blended with the most laborious occupations of human life ; not only as the natural breathing of cheery thoughts and gladdening hopes, faiths, and feelings, but as giving nerve, measure, and harmony to the physical forces of men bending to the most arduous toil. We will say nothing here of the influence of martial music on the weary battalions of an army on a forced march. That illustration would not be apposite to the point we are considering. Any one who has travelled by sea and land, and visited different countries, must have been struck with the variety, the use, and universality of the songs of labor. Who that has crossed the Atlantic, and been awakened at night by the " merrily, cheerily," of that song with which the sailors hoist the great mainsail to the rising breeze, can ever forget the thrill of those

manly voices? There they stand in the darkness, with
the salt sea spray in their faces, and the tarred rope in
their hands, holding the long and ponderous yard against
the mast until their rollicking song reaches the hoisting
turn, and all their sinews are strung to the harmony of a
unison for the telling pull. Everywhere, and in all ages,
the week-day music of the world has been the songs of
labor, by men and women at their toil, and by the birds
of heaven singing to them overhead and around them.
And no ears drink in with richer relish the melodies of
these outside songsters. No home more safe and welcome does the swallow find than under the eaves of the
poor man's cottage. Go through the densest courts and
lanes of Spitalfields, and see what a companionship of
bird-life the silk-weavers maintain in their garrets, even
when the loaf is too small for their children. The papers
recently published a touching and beautiful illustration
of the fondness which working-men show for singing
birds. When the first English lark was taken to Australia by a poor widow, the stalwart, sunburnt, hard-
visaged gold-diggers would come down from their pits on
the Sabbath, to hear it sing the songs they loved to listen
to at home in their childhood. An instance still more
interesting has been noted lately in connection with one
of the large manufacturing towns in North Wales. The
men, women, and children employed in the great factories not many times a week heard the lark's song or the
music of the free birds of heaven. These loved the
bright air and the green, fresh meadows and groves too
well to sing many voluntaries in the smoky atmosphere
of the furnace and factory. Thus the cheap concerts of

these songsters cost the operatives of the mills long walks beyond the brick-and-mortar mazes of the town. But thousands come to think them cheap at that price. Well, some time ago a new and strange singer came into the neighborhood, like an invisible spirit, with the music of another world on its tongue. In the dark and stilly night, when all other birds were silent, this poured forth in distant woods a flood of music most wonderful and strange. What could it be? The like was never heard in that region before. The rumor of its voice spread among the spindles. Men in fustian, after a long day of toil in the greasy factory, walked out silently away, farther and farther across the sooty fields, to the shadow of the woods, and stood there stock still, and held their breath, and listened. Towards midnight there came the notes so strange to their ears; notes of every song-bird they ever heard, strung on one voice. They decided it all came from one tongue, though, for variation, it might have come from a dozen trained for popular concerts. It all streamed out from one point; and, besides, they knew the blackbird, thrush, lark, sparrow, and robin were all abed and asleep three hours agone. This mysterious, invisible thing sang by turns, then chirruped and whistled with notes of its own. Night after night they walked the long way to hear it, and talked of its singing at their work by day. Their wives and children wanted to hear it too; but the walk was too long and toilsome for their feet. They got a van to take them to hear the bird perform its wonderful solos in the woods. It so varied its notes night after night, they thought it sang a new song on each. The van was soon too small for the humble listeners at the concert. So the railway put on a special train to convey them to the Nightingale's Music Hall — the dark wood, lighted from above with the still stars of heaven, and curtained with the drapery of the night. Many a trip the special train made, and hundreds and thousands were the men, women, and children of the hammer, spindle, and loom, who listened with wonder and delight to the invisible bird sent to give them such songs in the night.

ALEXANDRA AND HIBERNIA.

IF one of the old Norse bards, who, a thousand years ago, wrote songs and *sagas* for the Iceland firesides lighted by Hecla, could have seen Alexandra's visit to Hibernia, he would have felt his muse touched to unusual inspiration. In his day he sang of many Norse expeditions to Ireland ; of raids and ravage on its coasts ; of battles fought ; of heroic deeds of Viking and Berserker. He sang, too, of royal ships with " silken sails and gilded masts ; " of sailor kings and sailor princesses, of their courage, faith, and beauty. How changed the scene from that to this ! How he would have sung had he seen it ! this blue-eyed daughter of the North laying the little hand that is to wield the first sceptre of the world in that of the Cinderella of the British realms ; looking with her sweet face into that of her weeping sister's, which has anon glowed hot and red behind the wettest tears ; speaking to that sister's heart soft, low words of sympathy, clothed with more power than the best utterances of a whole British Parliament, or even the most generous accents of Justice itself! No living poet could sing that scene in such a song as one of the old Norse bards of the tenth century. In no human language would it rhyme so well as in his. He would dip his torch into the fires of Hecla, and crown and zone the Norse blue-eyed queen to be and the black-eyed sister of her future realms with the most gorgeous night-lights of the polar sky. He would tell, in his softened heroics, how the mild sunlight of her little white face blanched that visage on which it shone of every darkening stain of tear and shade of grieving thought, and flooded it with the rose and lily tints of joy and love. He would bring his rainbows, like a roll of ribbons, from Thor's sky-temple, and, unreeling them under the eyes of the bystanding nations, fold them around the two islands as sisters belted in embrace. Both might well learn the language of the Icelandic sagas, to see how such a poem would look and read in its unique letters and metre. Then the name he would choose for Alexandra out of the nomenclature of Scandinavian mythology! One would need to read the whole Heimskringla to guess what he would call her. If there be a bard left who has kept aglow the old Norse fire of song, we hope this visit of Alexandra to Hibernia will set it ablaze.

THE ANTE-PRINTING POETS OF ENGLAND.

ONE may well wonder what was the largest thought of Chaucer in regard to the readers of his immortal poems. How difficult for a modern writer of celebrity to conceive the ambition or expectation of the father of English poetry in this respect! Who would read his best thoughts, and how many? How many copies would constitute the largest and last edition of his works? How many copies could a good penman write out in a year, to say nothing of illumination? Could the prince and father of English poets reasonably expect that five hundred copies would ever be made in manuscript, and be treasured in the private libraries of the nobility and gentry of his country? The printing press had not in his lifetime cast the shadow of its advent before it. No writer or reader in Europe had ever conceived of any other than quill-power in making and multiplying books. What a small disk of public mind for his ambition to play on! to reach and impress five hundred readers with the thoughts that cost him the exercise of the finest genius! Still he thought and wrote as if for a world. But what a spirit would have moved over his thoughts if he could have caught the vision of Caxton's press, set up a century after he finished his last poem! Like all the prophets, apostles, orators, the kings and princes of thought before him, he lived, wrote, and died without that sight. But the printing press has not lost sight of him, or of the apostles, prophets, poets, and writers of earlier centuries. From the dew of their intellectual life and genius, that scarce filled an acorn's bowl, it has exhaled clouds full of refreshing rains of thought to water all " the green lands of song," and the dryer lands of common life.

In the library of Lichfield Cathedral are several volumes worth each more than its weight in gold. One of these was written six hundred years before Chaucer was born, — before the English language was born. It is a copy of the four Gospels in Anglo-Saxon in manuscript, written in the eighth century. It once belonged to the Cathedral of Llandaff, and ran the gantlet of perils innumerable, passing through many hands. One record of its experience is written by one of the owners in a blank page, stating that he gave a load of hay for it. It would take the hay of several meadows to buy it now. Then by its side is another volume in manuscript, held perhaps at a higher price as a relic and treasure. It is a copy of Chaucer's poems, not only written with exquisite taste and skill, but most beautifully illuminated, the gold being as bright as if recently put upon the page. One can but approach the two books with reverence. They are twin head-springs, from each of which have welled rivers of literature and spirit-life. One is the mother of all the Holy Gospels that have gone forth in the English tongue. The other is the mother of all the epics, songs, and ballads that have been printed in that tongue since letters were typed on paper. It is fitting and proper for men of this generation, who face the future with eager expectation, to go back occasionally to these points of departure in the progression of the ages. They will find something behind, as well as before, for grateful thought.

HANDEL'S MESSIAH IN THE CRYSTAL PALACE.

OVER the intervening space of three years our thoughts go back to the Triennial Handel Festival in the Crystal Palace, in the venture to seek expression. The place, the occasion, actors and audience, made the sublimest spectacle we ever witnessed. The place — if the *Great Eastern* steamship were worth its building for the single service of laying down the Transatlantic Telegraph, the Crystal Palace were worth its erection merely as the temple in which to uplift into the bluer heaven above its roofage Handel's *Messiah.* Every Christian nation owes such a temple to that most glorious song that the listening angels ever heard arising heavenward from the earth. Listening angels? — we say it on the strength of Revelation itself. It is not for us to fathom the mysteries of their spiritual being, or to say how they hear without human ears, or sing without human lips. The shepherds heard them singing in Oriental heavens over the manger-cradle of the Messiah ; and Handel has added a bar of music to their song worthy to be sung by them and all the heavenly host that sang chorus to their anthem at the Saviour's birth. Indeed, if it be not irreverent, one might conceive it to be the continuation of that anthem, with but slight change of place and performers. The music and the words seem equally inspired, and from the same source. The great crystal temple looks like a little sky-world let down from heaven, trussed and corded with roped sunbeams, with its lofty orchestra filled with a shining host, singing to the multitudes below the story and triumph of the Messiah. Three years have passed since we saw that sight and heard that song, and even our sober second thought of to-day clings to this simile.

We repeat, every Christian nation owes to the memory and worth of Handel a Crystal Palace, as large and splendid as that of Sydenham, for the ascension of his *Messiah ;* to harmonize the edifice with the structure and spirit of that great composition. For the building should represent the heavens under which the shepherds watched, as nearly as man could make it. Then it should be large enough to hold a small nation for listening to the song. Then the orchestra should be so lofty and large, that the multitudinous chorus should represent most of the kindreds, tribes, and tongues which John heard singing in heaven from Patmos. The choristers in the highest seats should appear to send out their hallelujahs just below the fleecy clouds, and the responses to go round from kindred to kindred in the circular amplitude of the choir. And on that soft, sunny day of June, when all the larks of the district were warbling up heavenward with their sweet hallelujahs, we saw and heard all this we have thus prefigured at Sydenham ; and we repeat, it was the sublimest concert of harmonies we ever witnessed, or the long generations have produced. It was the largest human assemblage ever gathered within the circuit of one choral song. Seemingly the sweetest singers of all the earthly Israels of the Christian faith were there. It was the recitative of the ages. The voices of their seers and singers came silvery and soft through the centuries. In the choral lulls, we heard the mournful murmur of the harps hung on the willows by the rivers of Babylon, as if the winds of the strangers' land sighed in sympathy on the silent strings, and touched them to Eolian strains of grief. Then upspoke, out of the cloud of the dark experiences of Israel, the voice of the prophet, gifted with a vision that reached far over into the after kingdom of the Messiah's glory — " Comfort ye, comfort ye my people ! Speak ye comfortably unto Jerusalem ! " Isaiah himself, as well as we, might have wished that he could have given to those glorious words of cheer and hope the voice of Sims Reeves, which seemed to bring them down from the very heavens above, and drop them like rays of music into all the rapt souls of the great multitude. On and on, through the wild ages of darkness, sorrow, grief, and hope, rolled the grand song. Here and there on the way a voice quavered up out of the eddies of affliction : " I know that my Redeemer liveth." Then, from out of the plaintive experiences of the captive and sorrowing people emerged the Hope of Israel. He came to the front of their great expectations, that were diademed with brilliant ambitions of national glory. Generations on the other side of the long captivity had watched for the pole-star of the restoration descending upon the throne of David. The prophet who was gifted to see farther and deeper into the Messiah's great Gospel than his fellow-seers, caught a glimpse of the Shiloh in his humble humanity, wearing a crown of thorns instead of imperial diamonds. His eyes became a fountain of tears at the sight, and in them he saw reflected the humiliations and sufferings of the world's

Emmanuel ; and his quivering lips sent up the pathetic plaint, " He was despised and rejected of men ; a man of sorrows and acquainted with grief ! " How soft and mournful were the voices of sympathy and sorrow that told to the world these sad experiences of the Son of God on earth ! The congregated tribes of Israel, who saw the Cross arising before the throne of David's glory, bowed their heads at the revelation. A cloud, dark and heavy with tears, exhaled from the griefs of ages, passed over them for a moment. And a voice, sweet and clear, came out of the cloud, rending it clean through to the Sun of Righteousness — " But thou didst not leave his soul in hell ; nor didst thou suffer thy Holy One to see corruption ! " Then the tribes arose ; — the whole twelve of them arose and sang, like the voices of many waters, which John heard — " Lift up your heads, O ye gates, and be ye lift up, ye everlasting doors, and the King of Glory shall come in ! " The everlasting doors obeyed the summons and opened spontaneously to the mighty song of triumph ; and the great Crystal Temple seemed to lift its arched roofage to the bluer sky above on the uprising flood of hosannas.

Looking around for some salient circumstance to which to tether our memory of the day, we saw the dusky, boy-ish faces of several young Japanese princes peering out upon the scene from the royal boxes over against the orchestra. It was to us a most striking incident. There sat the young heathens, with eyes, mouths, and ears, and all the windows of their souls opening wider and wider with rapt astonishment, as the Palace vibrated with the sublime chorals. There they sat right over against the great host of singers, representing in themselves all the peoples "that walked in darkness, and them that dwell in the land of the shadow of death." And the thought was natural and pleasant, that here was the whole of Christendom singing, through its choicest singers, to the whole heathen world the great song of the Saviour's Gospel, Kingdom, and Glory on earth. They told the whole story of the difference between the two hemispheres of human being in a few words — words that the angels who sang to the shepherds could not have uttered to human ears with sweeter modulation. Who that listened will ever forget them? If voices of men and women had power to go clean around the globe without exhaustion, whose could have sent forth with more thrilling utterance than Titjens, Grisi, Patti, Dolby, and Sherrington gave to them, the words, "Unto us a child is born; unto us a son is given"? It seemed, when the chorus took up the words, and rolled them forth on the great ground-swell of the sublime harmony, as if in very deed all the Christian nations between the poles spoke the triumph in unison; and spoke it to all the benighted populations of the earth that still walk in darkness. We could not but turn our eyes at every new outburst and turn of the song to look at the copper-colored faces of the Japanese boy-princes, to see if the great light was beginning to shine into their souls. They were evidently lifted, if not lighted. When the grand Hallelujah Chorus began to ascend on its sweeping cycles of glory, like a flood of thunder mellowed to the bass, alto, and treble of human melodies, these easternmost boys of the unlighted world were carried up on the tide of sympathy that lifted the vast multitude.

16

These are some of the thoughts that hover around the Handel Festival of 1865. The intervening space, with all it has brought of varied events, has not dimmed the memory of that occasion. It was worthy of a great nation. It was worthy of a great Christendom.

THE LAW OF KINDNESS, OR THE OLD WOMAN'S RAILWAY SIGNAL.

THE most effective working force in the world in which we live is the law of kindness. For it is the only moral force that operates with the same effect upon mankind, brutekind, and birdkind. From time immemorial music has wonderfully affected all beings, reasoning or unreasoning, that have ears to hear. The prettiest idea and simile of ancient literature relate to Orpheus playing his lyre to animals listening in intoxicated silence to its strains. Well, kindness is the music of good-will to men and beasts. And both listen to it with their hearts instead of their ears; and the hearts of both are affected by it in the same way, if not to the same degree. Volumes might be written filled with beautiful illustrations of its effect upon both. The music of kindness has not only power to charm, but even to transform both the savage breast of man and beast; and on this harp the smallest fingers in the world may play Heaven's sweetest tunes on earth.

Some time ago we read of an incident in America that

will serve as a good illustration of this beautiful law. It was substantially to this effect: A poor, coarse-featured old woman lived on the line of the Baltimore and Ohio Railway, where it passed through a wild, unpeopled district in Western Virginia. She was a widow, with only one daughter living with her in a log hut, near a deep, precipitous gorge crossed by the railway bridge. Here she contrived to support herself by raising and selling poultry and eggs, adding berries in their season, and other little articles for the market. She had to make a long, weary walk of many miles to a town where she could sell her basket of produce. The railway passed by her house to this town; but the ride would cost too much of the profit of her small sales; so she trudged on generally to the market on foot. The conductor or guard came finally to notice her travelling by the side of the line or on the foot-path between the rails; and, being a good-natured, benevolent man, he would often give her a ride to and fro without charge. The engine-man and brake-men also were good to the old woman, and felt that they were not wronging the interests of the railway company by giving her these free rides. And soon an accident occurred that proved they were quite right in this view of the matter. In the wild month of March the rain descended, and the mountains sent down their rolling, roaring torrents of melted snow and ice into this gorge, near the old woman's house. The flood arose with the darkness of the night, until she heard the crash of the railway bridge, as it was swept from its abutments, and dashed its broken timbers against the craggy sides of the precipice on either side. It was nearly midnight. The rain fell in a flood, and the darkness was deep and howling. In another half hour the train would be due. There was no telegraph on the line, and the stations were separated by great distances. What could she do to warn the train against the awful destruction it was approaching? She had hardly a tallow candle in her house, and no light she could make of tallow or oil, if she had it, would live a moment in that tempest of wind and rain. Not a moment was to be lost; and her thought was equal to the moment. She cut the cords of her only bedstead, and shouldered the dry posts, head-pieces, and side-pieces. Her daughter followed her with their two wooden chairs. Up the steep embankment they climbed, and piled their all of household furniture upon the line a few rods beyond the black, awful gap, gurgling with the roaring flood. The distant rumbling of the train came upon them just as they had fired the well-dried combustibles. The pile blazed up into the night, throwing its red, swaling, booming light a long way up the line. In fifteen minutes it would begin to wane, and she could not revive it with green, wet wood. The thunder of the train grew louder. It was within five miles of the fire. Would they see it in time? They might not put on the brakes soon enough. Awful thought! She tore her red woollen gown from her in a moment, and, tying it to the end of a stick, ran up the line, waving it in both hands, while her daughter swung around her head a blazing chair-post a little before. The lives of a hundred unconscious passengers hung on the issue of the next minute. The ground trembled at the old woman's feet. The great red eye of the engine showed itself coming round a curve. Like as a huge, sharp-sighted lion coming suddenly upon a fire, it sent forth a thrilling roar, that echoed through all the wild heights and ravines around. The train was at full speed; but the brakemen wrestled at their leverage with all the strength of desperation. The wheels ground along on the heated rails slower and slower, until the engine stopped at the roaring fire. It still blazed enough to show them the beetling edge of the black abyss into which the train and all its passengers would have plunged into a death and destruction too horrible to think of, had it not been for the old woman's signal. They did not stop to thank her first for the deliverance. The conductor knelt down by the side of the engine; the engine-driver and the brakemen came and knelt down by him; all the passengers came and knelt down by them; and there, in the expiring light of the burnt-out pile, in the rain and the wind, they thanked God for the salvation of their lives. All in a line the kneelers and prayers sent up into the dark heavens such a midnight prayer and voice of thanksgiving as seldom, if ever, ascended from the earth to Him who seeth in darkness as well as in secret.

Kindness is the music of good-will to men; and on this harp the smallest fingers in the world may play Heaven's sweetest tunes on earth.

LIFE OF BENEVOLENCE IN ENGLAND.

It is probable that more money is given to benevolent objects in England than in all the other countries of the world put together. It is impossible to know the whole amount contributed by individuals to hospitals, schools, and other charitable purposes. We can only guess at this amount from the sums raised by the various religious and benevolent societies which hold their yearly meetings in London. But no one can travel through the country, with an observant eye, without being surprised at the number of associations in almost every town, all working for the poor and needy at home and abroad. In fact, one might think that nearly every man, woman, and child belonged to some one of these little societies. The whole population seems to be apprenticed to a life of benevolence. Little children are often put upon the pathway of kindly charities as soon as they can run alone. Thus a vast number of persons are early trained to thoughts and acts of good-will towards their fellow-beings. And after all they do, there are, and always will be, objects enough to engage their benevolent efforts. "The poor ye have always with you," said our Saviour to the Jews. That is true of every country, even of our own beloved land. And it is a sad thought, that as America grows richer, the number of poor people in its cities will increase, and their poverty will become more and more pinching. This will be sad for them, poor things! sad, indeed, for them, but for the nation it should work much good. Were it not that the poor were always with us; were there none for us to help, to comfort, to raise; were there none that needed our sympathy, our aid, counsel, and kindness, — what would become of benevolence? It would die out of our hearts altogether, I fear. Many persons are disposed to reproach England because she has so many poor within her borders. Perhaps it is partly her fault, as well as misfortune; but it is the fault of a thousand years. Things that happened a thousand years ago helped to make a portion of the poverty that now exists along with unbounded wealth in the land. I am inclined to think, however, that through this poverty many have become rich in good thoughts and good works; that it has created a vast wealth of benevolence, which is ever flowing, in deep and silent streams, in every direction, even into distant countries, to enlighten and uplift the benighted and down-trodden. Within the last dozen years this benevolence has been working through new and interesting societies, in town, village, and hamlet. It would be a curious sight to see a list of all these little associations. One might wonder how they found names for them all. Some of them are very singular; and many of our young readers would hardly be able to conceive what they meant, without an explanation. What, for instance, would they think that Blanket Societies, Coal Clubs, Penny Savings' Institutes, Branch Bible Societies, Twig Bible Societies, Scripture Readers' Associations, &c., were? These are only a few of the associations operating in almost every large town for the good of the needy. Some are engaged in visiting all the houses of the poor, to see that they are provided with

Bibles. Those who are destitute are supplied on the condition that they pay at least a part of the price of a copy, and this is sometimes not more than twenty-five cents of our money. But even this small sum is frequently paid in little bits, or a penny or two at a time, for the Bible visitor does not tire of calling a dozen times for a shilling, paid by the poor widow by pennies. It has been found the best way to encourage the poor to help themselves, and to pay at least a part for what they obtain. They then feel as if they had bought it out of their own little earnings, and it encourages them to try again for something they need. As the cold weather approaches, many a kind mother and wife, seated before her cheerful fire, thinks of the frosty nights in the lowly cottages of the poor ; how that many an infirm and destitute widow will shiver beneath her scanty covering of rags or straw. A Blanket Society, Club, or Association is formed for the purpose of providing these cold and cheerless homes with good warm blankets for the winter. Members of this society will go around among those likely to be destitute of these important articles, and encourage them to save a penny a week, which is deposited in the hands of the treasurer. Then, perhaps, to every shilling thus saved by the poor, benevolent persons of the town will add a shilling. Thus a nice thick blanket will be given out, about Christmas, for half its cost, to the penny subscribers. Then frequently a society for furnishing the poor with coal operates in the same way. In almost every town Savings' Institutes are opened to receive the pennies of those who earn but few daily, and who are tempted to spend them in drink. The sums thus deposited cannot be withdrawn, I think, until they reach a certain amount. In this way the wives and children even of intemperate working-men frequently have a little laid by for them to meet the day of sickness or of greater need.

Now, all these benevolent societies, scattered over the country, give plenty of work to young and old, rich and poor. Every year they deepen and widen the river of good-will to man ; and this river overflows and blesses them who give, more even than those who receive. Its little rills come trickling and singing into the lowest lanes of poverty, even into the very dens of hardened thieves. Those who think these kind thoughts and put their hands to these quiet acts of Christian sympathy, gain more and more faith and courage in their hearts to go on in their work — to go to the most unhopeful and sinful, and endeavor to recover them and bring them back to a better life. These thoughts and feelings spread a pleasant light over their faces, and their eyes beam with it, and it makes their voices gentle and kind ; and they can go by night into the corners, cellars, and garrets which the worst thieves and vicious people inhabit, and talk to them without fear or danger.

THE EMPIRE OF PUBLIC OPINION.

ITS INTELLECTUAL AND MECHANICAL POWERS.

WE know not in what age, or by what sage, that long-questioned and oft-repeated apothegm was first put forth : " Vox populi vox Dei " (" The voice of the people is the voice of God "). A thousand years after its first utterance some man of commanding eminence may have gained the credit of being its original author, merely from having repeated it impressively at some particular turn or aspect of human affairs. It may have sounded to some ears loudest and truest in the crash of the Bastile and of the throne and crown of the Bourbons in the French Revolution. Certainly *vox populi* was loud and strong in those startling emotions. But it was a clap of thunder, that shook down a demoralized dynasty, and made far-off despotism quake a little. The reverberation was wide, reaching to the extremest promontories · of Christendom. But it was but an explosion of public sentiment ; and, wide as was its projectile force, it was virtually a local earthquake. The voice of God was not in the earthquake, nor the windy tempest with such emphasis and might as in that still small voice of public opinion that does not explode in thunder, but moves day and night over the life of nations, and transforms their being, as the omnipotent spirit of the Creator moved over the black deformities of chaos, and shaped it into beauty and order. The vox populi which holds and utters vox

Dei is a vital breath, not a fitful wind, bursting forth in hail-storms here and sand-storms there. It is not the breath of one nation. It is the second, sober, settled thought of all the civilized commonwealths of mankind. It is the spontaneous utterance of the universal conscience. It is the sleepless, vital force of a universal sentiment that acts upon governments, legislation, and laws, as did the Spirit of God, in the morning of Creation, upon the face of the waters, and upon the face and form of the earth.

How little did the first author, or the first believer of that saying, "Vox populi vox Dei," see or conceive of the stupendous forces and faculties of public opinion in the later centuries of the world! How little the un-chained masses that shouted over the fall of the Bastile and the Bourbon monarchy in France dreamt of these new forces of a popular sentiment; of the enginery it would wield, and which should-ally it to the faculties of omnipotence! At that day, gunpowder and the sounding brass and tinkling cymbals of martial music made the loudest voice with which a people could speak their will, rights, and wants to the world. The printing press had not as yet begun to give daily speech to its types. The newspaper had not yet become a power in Christendom. Few, and small, and weak were its weekly sheets, and few and scattered were their readers. Steam and electricity were unborn; and MacAdam too. Four miles an hour by land or sea was the high average of locomotion for news or news-makers. All the nations of Christendom were so many hostile, jealous, concentrated *selfs*, walled in from sympathy and companionship with each other by Baby-

lonish environments of dynastic and popular antipathies
centuries old and sky high.   Until the breaking out of the
American Revolution, followed by the French, there was
no such thing as a public sentiment in a wider, nobler
sense than the local feeling of a single nation.   Even if
a people's opinion breathed freely, pure and strong, it
did not arise high enough above its natural barriers to
mingle in the air which other nations breathed.   Thus,
up to the beginning of the present century there was no
public sentiment of Christendom, or half of Christendom.
It was localized to different communities, and it acted
only on domestic institutions.   In pleading and working
for human rights, for just, righteous, and merciful laws
at home, it learned to soar with stronger beats over the
walls that had bounded and barred its outward flight.
It learned the lessons of a wider humanity ; to feel for
human wrongs beyond those walls ; to feel and speak for
the oppressed of far-off lands ; to be touched with enno-
bling sympathies with people struggling for freedom ; to
be stirred with the great and everlasting pulses of human
nature ; to see in millions groping in the valley and
shadow of pagan darkness brother beings of a common
immortality.

Just as public sentiment scaled the cramped walls of
nationality, and breathed in the outside air, just in that
proportion its mechanical faculties of utterance multiplied
in number and power.   The printing press worked with
longer leverage by night and day.   Its lengthened and
widened sheets collected and scattered the best thoughts
of the public mind among the people by a machinery
like that of the dews of heaven.   Every faculty that

could liken the voice of the people to the voice of God
was given successively to its utterance. Steam gave all
its power to it by sea and land, and abolished four fifths
of the old distances between all the communities and
capitals of the civilized world. Steam printed and pro-
pelled the thoughts of nations, and mingled them in a
common atmosphere. It required all this machinery of
thought to form a public opinion of the latter-day sense
and force of that power ; and that public opinion equally
needed some great supernational object on which to con-
centrate its unorganized energies. It found just the object
it needed in the abolition of African Slavery. This was
an outrage on universal humanity. It was the first and
only great wrong that confronted the public conscience
and sentiment of Christendom when thus organized into
a common force for common good. It was just the kind
of wrong to educate that public opinion in the struggle
for its abolition ; to elevate and strengthen it with new
perceptions and convictions of everlasting truth and right,
of what man is and owes to God and his fellow-man.
These perceptions and convictions, brought out and impressed upon the universal conscience during the agitation
against slavery, have elevated it to a higher stage of
moral sensibility, so that it feels for wrongs and sufferings to which it was cold and silent before. The census
of benevolent institutions which that sensibility has
breathed into life and action since the great anti-slavery
agitation in Great Britain, presents a list of remarkable
number and variety. The vox populi that broke the
chains of eight hundred thousand African slaves in the
West Indies was not a clap of thunder ; it was not a

sudden and sharp explosion of popular sentiment; it was not an earthquake; but if ever vox Dei spoke in human speech it did in that great act of emancipation.

We have now entered upon a new era and arena of public opinion. That opinion is becoming more and more generalized. It is coming to be internationalized, to be uttered like the chant of nations whose lips are touched simultaneously by the same live coal from the altar of human sympathy. And vox populi is becoming vox Dei in a sense sublime, startling, and almost over-awing. It has taken to itself powers of utterance which a few years ago would have been ascribed only to Omnip-otence; powers so seemingly supernatural that it almost makes one's heart and hand tremble to describe their capacity in the simplest prose of fact. Did vox populi take these powers by violence? profanely, sacrilegiously? No! Omnipotence opened its mighty hand, and gave will-ingly, fatherly, and lovingly these great gifts to man. It gave to the voice of human opinion a power of utterance which it never gave nor promised to Gabriel's lips; a power that as much outruns the speed of light as light outruns the heavy footsteps of sound around the earth. If the seer of old, who looked out from the mountain-cave with half-veiled face to see the Divine Presence pass before him, could have put his trembling fingers to the wire of the Trans-Atlantic Telegraph, — if John of Pat-mos could have felt the pulse of its message from the Old World to the New, — both would have described it in figures of speech which we may not venture to use. Surely the venerable saint might well believe that several portions of his Apocalypse had been realized; that "there was no more sea" separating continents; that "there was time no longer" separating current events from the simultaneous knowledge of all the nations.

From this new leverage-point of public opinion let us glance back into the past and forward into the future for a moment. If some classic writer of ancient Rome could say, and some French Revolutionary leader could repeat, vox populi vox Dei, what may we hopefully say and believe of the voice and power of the public sentiment of Christendom, gifted with these new and stupendous energies? If with the forces given to it by steam, railways, cheap postage, and all the other facilities invented to give it movement and momentum, it has driven Slavery out of the world, and brought down the level of other great sins and miseries, what may, what ought it not do with all these electric wires that thread the oceans, and the seas, and the wide world itself? When any event worth the world's notice may be known the very hour of its occurrence at all the capitals of Christendom; when, instead of twelve men, twelve great nations may be summoned by lightning to sit in jury upon any great act or intent of wrong; when any outrage upon human rights may thrill the palpitating nerves that connect all the Parliaments and Congresses of the two hemispheres with all the localities and realities of mankind; when the thunder of universal opinion may follow instantaneously its lightning hurled in one burning bolt against a sinning government or people in the very act and moment of the wrong; in a word, when the voice of the people is so made by Him the speech of God to mankind; when He has clothed it with such omnipotence for His glory and the good of man, — what next? What great monster of iniquity, what huge, Gorgon-headed enemy and destroyer of the peoples should fall next under the thunder and lightning of the world's opinion? What new mechanical forces wait we for, what new machinery of thought do the peoples need to sweep WAR from the face of the civilized world? What more wait they for? Let them feel the edge, the pulse, and the point of these mighty, these almost over-awing instrumentalities of omnipotence put into their hands by Almighty Power and Wisdom. Why should War stand up longer in their midst like the very abomination of desolation, bending them to the earth, battening upon the spoils of their peace and prosperity, consuming their substance, throwing the bread earned with such toil for their children to its greedy dogs? Who shall lead the van? Who shall sound the charge of the nations against the great DESTROYER?

INDUSTRIAL AND FINANCIAL
QUESTIONS.

THE WORLD'S WORKING–MEN'S STRIKE AGAINST WAR.

NATIONS, like individuals, often come to junctures in their lives where two, if not four, roads meet, and one of these they must take with all the hazards of the choice. The world has seen pretty clearly the road which all the nations of Europe have been travelling for the last quarter of a century. The world sees now what their armed-peace system has brought them to. For all this period they have been running neck and neck in this costly and perilous race of war armaments. This delusion has grown by that it fed upon. Every additional regiment on land, or iron-clad put on the sea by one, has created more suspicion in the other, and that suspicion has reproduced its kind in *defences* against the increased danger. Thus, while all these nations have been stoutly protesting against an intention to invade or injure a neighbor *offensively*, their *defences* have been steadily growing from year to year, until they have reached that point and peril of magnitude at which Disraeli has called them " bloated armaments."

This, then, is the juncture at which two roads meet on the highway thus far travelled by the nations of Europe. They are now to determine whether they will go straight forward in the old beaten track, or diverge into a new path. At this junction-point there are several finger-posts of much significance, and a mile-stone covered with deeply-engraved figures relating to the periodical totals of past experience. All these should be like warning voices before and behind them at the opening of the new road, saying, " This is the way; walk ye therein." With all these voices from before and behind them, will they take the new road? If they do, they must first hold a council at the junction. We cannot expect that one of them will be brave enough to enter it alone. They must hold a congress to agree upon taking step and keeping step in this new march in another direction.

There is no time to lose in this decision. The great, honest, toiling masses of the world have waited for them long to take this new road. These masses are beginning to feel a strength that their governments would do well to heed now, before it takes an inconvenient direction for the powers that be. They have been feeling for some time past the strength of a common sentiment, interest, and experience, and inheritance. They are beginning to get their eyes open to some of the wicked delusions that have victimized them in past generations. They begin to see whither they have been led, and how they have been cheated, by the siren lights and siren songs of a false patriotism. And while this deceptive music was still in their ears, they have shaken hands with each other across the boundaries that once made them enemies. And the hands they interfolded in friendly grasp felt very much like each other, hard and horny with their common lot. And they have compared the blisters and callous ridges made on their hands by " foreign policies." They have weighted and compared the burdens put upon them by their governments, and found and said that the most crushing of them all was the Armed-Peace System of Christendom. And their governments, at the junction of the two roads, will do well to heed now, and honestly, what these working-men, in congress assembled, feel, and say, and determine in regard to this system. Their feeling and meaning grow stronger and louder on the subject every time they meet in their international assembly ; and, doubtless, they will meet every year, and their annual parliaments will begin soon to legislate for the grand democracy of labor throughout the civilized world. And " the Great Powers," at the junction of the two roads, will do well to heed this habit of their working-men of sending their representatives, chosen at primary meetings, to these annual parliaments. It is a very significant and portentous habit in itself. And their *agenda* and *facienda* are more portentous still to the powers that be. If they work out their programme, it will upset the classic poetry of that malignant patriotism which worships silken rags covered with bestial emblems, and sacrifices to the idolatry more human blood than all the pagan altars of this wide world ever drank this side of the murder of Abel. It is very rude, very unsentimental and unpatriotic, for them to say and purpose these things when they come together in this way. It will doubtless shock the sensibilities of the whole military aristocracy of Christendom, and of all the students, professors, and amateurs of the school and history of military glory, to hear what these working-men will say in the next session of their parliament. They have said strong things before about war and its burdens upon them. But this time their representatives will have to pass to their assembly half a million of fresh graves in France and Germany, wherein lie, like buried dogs, half a million of their own fraternity of toil, taken from honest labor to mutual butchery on the field of battle. They will see a million of blackened, blasted homes on their way, and widows and orphans trying to quench the still red ashes of those homes with their own tears. They will see wan, armless or legless men, by the ten thousands, begging on crutches, by the roadside, for the bread they once earned and ate by the sweat of the brow. Now, these sights and the low, faint voices of woe they will see and hear on their way to their parliament will very sensibly affect their discussions, and give an utterance and a character to their resolutions which their governments, at the junction of the two roads, will do well to heed in advance, anticipate and supersede by their own action. Such action, honest, and effective, and immediate, is their only alternative, if they would evade or check the rising of a power too strong for their old " foreign policy."

What is asked of the Great Powers, at the junction of the two roads, is a very simple, straightforward matter. It is the step proposed to them, before these late and bloody wars, by Louis Napoleon ; to convene a Congress of Nations to agree upon a *ratio* of general and simultaneous disarmament. The idea was not original with him ; for it had been developed and propounded by eminent philosophers and philanthropists for two hundred years. But he was the first reigning sovereign in the world that ever proposed the measure to the nations. We may justly say that for him in his prison, which he would never have seen had the other Great Powers accepted his proposition. The toiling, patient masses of the great commonwealth of labor do not ask a great deal of these powers; they do not say how far in the new road they shall reach at the first step, but that they shall make one, however small. They know what a thorny crop of suspicions the armed-peace system has grown among them. Therefore they will be contented with a very short step that brings their faces and feet in the right direction. Even if they should only venture to reduce their standing armies by sending home to the plough or hammer one man in five, they would be satisfied with the instalment, knowing that it would be followed by larger reductions. Even a reduction of one fifth of the present armed-peace expenditure, to begin with, would so lighten the burden upon the masses of the people of Christendom that they would feel the relief at every meal and at every hour of their toil. Just think what that small, tentative reduction would do. In the first place, it would send back to peaceful and reproductive labor nearly a million of picked, stalwart men from the armies of Europe. See what it would do for England, who does not pretend to be a military power in the French or German sense. One fifth taken from the expense of her armed-peace establishment for 1870 would be £5,600,000. Think what taxes might be lifted from the people by that small *ratio* of reduction. But the working-men and women in France, Germany, Italy, and other continental countries would be more relieved still by this reduction, because their wages do not average, in the gross, more than half what their English brethren receive for their labor.

Now, if the press, the platform, and the pulpit of these Christian countries have any power with their governments, every consideration that should move them ought to enlist their best influence in behalf of a Congress of Nations for this one object, to begin with, whatever other measures it might subsequently accomplish. The necessity is very pressing for such a congress, to be convened before the next parliament of the working-men of Christendom. Their national organizations, represented in these parliaments, are growing more and more powerful. And when they meet next time, they will see the condition and prospects of their class in a new light, and feel them with a new sensibility. They may not strive to alter the past, but they will grasp at their future with a rough strength of heart and hand which the Great Powers, at the junction of the two roads, will do well to anticipate and avoid. Poor, patient masses! thousands and tens of thousands of them have fought, bled, and died for national territory who could not buy enough in that or their own land to make their graves in. They cannot change this new and horrible past of one year's length. This huge abomination of desolation wrought upon the late peaceful and sunny bosom of Europe will fall upon their industry and life of toil and trial with a burden they never bore before. As the yoke upon the necks of two working oxen presses upon each with equal weight, so the yoke of this great war's burden will bear with equal weight upon the raw necks of the French and German working-classes. They will have to work out the damages done to each other by this war. The yoke will gall and bend alike victors and vanquished; and the weight will tell on every plough, sickle, and spindle in Europe, and on every meal earned by these honest tools.

This is the new weight that the armed-peace system has just now added to the burdens it had before put upon the working-classes of Europe. Now, then, if the Great Powers, at the junction of the two roads, do not say to this destroying angel, begottened and winged of their madness and folly, " It is enough," its millions of patient victims, even without a Moses, may break the bondage, and find on their side and behalf the same God who led an equal number of working-men, more lightly taxed, to a better land and condition. It may appear unnatural and unseemly for an edge-tool to rebel and turn against the hand that wields it. It will doubtless spoil the romance of modern chivalry, and many martial songs of military glory, if the " food for powder " should rebel at the cannon's mouth. It may even disgust the classic predilections of the great class of hero-worshippers and hero-makers if the working-men of Christendom venture to put an end to such pretentious valuations upon their earthly possibilities as to believe they are worth more for producing food for man and beast than for feeding with their own flesh and blood the hungry maws of mortars and *mitrailleuses* on fields of human slaughter. But the Great Powers, at the junction of the two roads, must face the alternative before them. These working-men have been practising for several years on " strikes," organized to affect their condition throughout large sections of their country. They have been perfecting the machinery and the forces of these combinations for a wider field of action, and in their last parliament they decided upon the field for employing their co-operative forces ; they proposed a Strike against War, and the whole armed-peace system, when they last met. If they had motive then for this resolution what a trebled one will they have at their next session to carry out that resolution ! This, then, is the alternative : either a Congress of Nations for simultaneous and proportionate disarmament, or an organized strike of the working-men of Christendom against war, root and branch. The Great Powers, at the junction of the two roads, must choose without delay which of these two measures they will adopt.

THE MOST HIGHLY–TAXED LUXURY IN THE WORLD.

It has become an axiom of political economy, recognized by all governments, and especially popular with the industrial masses, that luxuries should bear the heaviest tax for revenue. It is a favorite and natural idea among the laboring classes, that the articles which the rich only can buy and enjoy should be taxed at such a figure that those which poor men need may go " scot free." Most governments admit and adopt this principle, apparently, in regard to some articles of comsumption. They tax silks, furs, jewelry, &c., heavily, and the rich, perhaps, buy them all the more readily for this enhancement of cost, valuing them more for the price than for the real worth of them. But governments derive their greatest revenues from the tax they levy on the appetites of the common working masses of the people. Now, in the best of countries, there are at least twenty men who work for wages against one who employs them. And these working-men have as large bodies to clothe, as hungry stomachs to feed, as their employers, or any of the rich capitalists of the land. They not only consume twenty times as much tea, coffee, and sugar as the capitalist class, but they contract the costliest appetites in the world. And these appetites of working-men yield to governments the richest sources of revenue. The stronger the appetites, the heavier tax will they bear. Thus governments have a large pecuniary interest in stimulating them, or "working" them, as people say of mines. Now, the appetite for tobacco is one of the strongest ever contracted. It bears the heaviest tax that European governments ever imposed upon any article of consumption. It has been worth more to England, as a source of direct revenue, than all the gold mines of Australia. Then, the appetite for intoxicating spirits, which is more general, is still a richer pasturage for taxation. And this, too, is the appetite of the working-classes, as much as, or more than, that of the rich. As they number twenty times the rich, they produce twenty times more drinkers, and twenty times as much revenue for their government from the consumption of spirits. Although tobacco will bear a tax in England of from three hundred to five hundred per cent., while alcohol will not bear one eighth of that impost, the latter produces quite as much revenue, from its more general use.

Thus we see that the strongest physical appetites of the masses in different countries are taxed more heavily than their desires and longings for the necessaries of life, as food, clothing, furniture, housing, and education. These appetites are the luxuries of rich and poor alike, and they are thus taxed in the articles that gratify them. I have called these rich sources of revenue to governments *physical* appetites. They are the longings or yearnings of the palate, stomach, or nervous system of man; the cry of his physical nature for something that shall give it a momentary sensation of pleasure; and perhaps this sensation is generally realized when that something is granted. To be charitable and generous, we will call it an innocent accident that the governments of Christendom find themselves in the condition to regard these unhealthy and universal appetites of their peoples as their safest, surest, and richest sources of revenue. Governments are human as well as common men, and as they need money as much, why, it is according to nature that they should regard such pecuniary resources as individuals regard an ill wind that blows a great good to them, though it destroys the lives and property of hundreds at a distance.

But what are the taxes levied on all the physical appetites in the wide world compared with the tax imposed by its foremost nations on one single appetite of the mind, which can honestly be called by no other name than Suspicion? What would become of taxes on silks, teas, coffee, spirits, and tobacco, were it not for this "aching void" in the minds of nations? Suspicion is the mother of all the custom-houses in Christendom; for what a preposterous fantasy it would be in any nation to erect custom-houses, and all the costly machinery of indirect taxation, merely to pay the cost of its *civil* government! All the taxation, all the burdens that the masses in England, France, Germany, and other countries have felt for a hundred years, have been imposed on them by Suspicion — that hungry vampire, which poisons the mind of a nation while it consumes its best attributes. All the wars that have desolated Europe for a century have been produced by Suspicion. The great Civil War that rent the American Union in twain for four years, and reddened it with its best blood, was the product of the same sentiment — a suspicion on the part of the South that the North was going to do something terrible to it when it should attain to a power equal to its disposition.

It is quite common and natural to point to England as the nation most dominated and victimized by Suspicion. She has undoubtedly exhibited more paroxysms of the sentiment than any other country. For several decades of profound peace, and without the slightest unfriendly act or word on the part of her neighbor, she has had a quartennial "French invasion panic." These periodical excitements show the nature of the sentiment very clearly. Put in frank and honest speech, and in the mouth of an individual man, it means this: " I am a polished Christian gentleman, but all my neighbors are pagans and pirates. The one nearest me is the worst of all, and I fear him the most. To be sure, I cannot say that he ever injures or insults me ; indeed, he is very polite, and professes to be very friendly to me. But I have no confidence in him ; I believe him to be a pirate at heart, and ready to waylay me, or burn my house over my head, if he should catch me off my guard, or not armed to the teeth against him. Don't tell me that because I arm myself so against him he ought to arm against me. Why, I am a Christian gentleman. Do you suppose that I am such a base buccaneer as to pounce upon him because he is unarmed? Whom do you take me to be, in suggesting such a possibility? ' Is thy servant a dog, that he should do this great thing' of crime and shame? Can you, who know me, really believe that all the rifles, revolvers, and bowie-knives that I carry with me day and night can affect my disposition or deportment towards him, or can give him any reason to fear any injury or insult from me?—from *me*, a Christian gentleman! I scorn the imputation."

Yes; England, an enlightened and noble-hearted nation, scorns the imputation. She is a good and honorable neighbor. She is actuated by the most friendly dispositions towards France, and, although she arms herself against that neighbor more than against all the other powers of the world put together, it is not from any unfriendly intention or feeling. If France should scuttle every one of her war-ships, and disband every one of her regiments, she would be as safe, so far as England is concerned, as she is to-day with all her present armaments. Of course she would be. It would be safe in us and all other nations to believe it. Yes; "they are all honorable" powers. Germany could and would say the same to France to-day, and say it honestly. It is doubtful if there is a man in civil or military life in the German empire who does not in his heart honestly believe, and would honestly say, that if France had not a single regiment or a single frigate, she would be as free from attack or insult on the part of Germany as she is to-day, or as she was five years ago. Russia could and would say the same to Sweden, Prussia, and Austria. And why should not the whole world believe that these nations were sincere and truthful in such protestations? Are there any facts in their history to disprove the truth of these professions? Glance at their history. Has any one of them for the last fifty years touched another with a finger of violence or wrong? Has any one of them perpetrated an international insult on the other? If so, when, where, how? But there have been terrible wars in Europe and America, not only between nations, but between parts of nations? To be sure. But every one of them has been a war of suspicion. Look at the Crimean war. Did Russia touch England, France, Italy, or even Turkey, with a little finger of violence before they rushed upon her with their armies? No: not one of them can say she did this. It was not an overt act on her part that precipitated or "drifted" them into the war, but a *suspected* intention. It was because if she were allowed a protectorate over the Greek Christians in Turkey, she might, in some future year, make it the pretence of going to war with that power, and thus take Constantinople, and oust the Mohammedan despotism out of Europe, and, in years still more future, march eastward, even to India.

Then there came the terrible war between Germany and France. Can any reasoning mind believe that that was not a war of suspicion? Was it not, pure and simple, a product of the old balance-of-power theory? Or

because the German states had consolidated themselves
into a compact and mighty empire, abutting upon France
for its whole length; and because, in addition to this
augmentation of power, Germany proposed to outflank
France by putting a Prussian prince on the throne of
Spain? What was there in the act alone of consolidating
the German states into such an empire, or in giving
Spain a Prussian king, that was injurious to France?
Nothing. The war was one of sheer suspicion. It was
predicated solely on the new possibility that Germany
had acquired — a possibility that might generate an intention, which might pass into an act. Take the great
civil war in America; and none ever waged was more the
offspring of suspicion. The whole outside world will
testify that the North had never, by an overt act, given
the South cause to believe that it would ever lay a finger
of force upon southern slavery, though the free states
should come to number fifty against fifteen slave states.
It was not for the past that the latter plunged headlong
into the gulf of secession. It was a future that they
feared. It was from a mere suspicion that a new possibility would beget a new intention, and a new intention would beget a new act, which would swamp the
South with the wreck of its " peculiar institution."
Thus all the great wars that have been waged in Christendom for fifty years have been wars of suspicion; and
nineteen twentieths of all the war-armaments that lie like
loads of lead upon the nations are the sole products of
that unmanly and degrading sentiment.

" How happy it is for our great Republic that we are
sundered by a wide ocean from European states under

the domination of this balance-of-power rule ! " We often hear this sentiment in different forms of congratulation. Yes ; we are free from the European balance-of-power fantasy ; but there is not a nation in the old world that so needlessly yields itself a victim to suspicion as this great country. For fifty years and more no power in Europe has touched our territory, our rights, honor, or interests with its little finger of violence, injury, or insult. Accidents have happened which have been unhappy. We have had boundary and other questions that have led to some irritation ; but all these have been peacefully settled by negotiation or arbitration. Searching the record for half a century, we cannot put our finger upon any act which indicates a sentiment of ill will or evil intent on the part of any nation towards us. But suppose such an intent did or could exist ; let us see what possibility it could achieve. Well, then, there is not a power in Europe that could send across the ocean at once a force of fifty thousand infantry and cavalry, with the arms and equipments, forage, food, and ammunition, for both. There is not a power in Europe that could land such a force on our shores in less than three days and nights, even if no one opposed them. If any naval or military reader doubts the truth of this statement, let him consult the statistics of the Crimean war. If these do not convince him of the impossibility I have assumed, let me ask him what he thinks fifty thousand men would be expected to do or become by the power that sent them to a distant continent, peopled by a nation of forty millions ! Certainly they could not come for conquest. Could they possibly come for revenge or retaliation ? For

18

what act on our part? What act in the past are we conscious of, or that any other nation remembers against us,
which could provoke such a senseless invasion? If we
have not committed such an act in the past, do we intend
to do it when we number fifty millions?

Then what is the meaning, intent, or use of these ten
new ships of war to be added to our navy? Are they to
fight the Indians on either side of the Rocky Mountains?
Why is this new and costly armament to be put upon
this tax-burdened nation? What contingency does it
anticipate? Is it to provide a new squadron for a new
Corean expedition, or the bombardment of another Grey-
town, or any other foreign hamlet or village? Is it to
escort our merchant vessels to the West or East Indies,
to China or Japan, or to protect our coasts or commerce
against pirates? If not for any of these uses, then
what one power in Europe do they refer to? for our past
experience proves that we must deal with European nations singly. . Is it England that is coming over here to
invade us, or are we going to invade her with these ten
new ships of war? For what possible cause either way?
Certainly not for any cause less aggravated than the
questions we have just settled by arbitration. Certainly
even an " Alabama question " can never be possible
again, even if we have another civil war, for the same
cause that produced the last. Here is a *tabula rasa* between the two nations. Even all their boundary questions are " off." Then what can she do to us, or we to
her, in future, that we cannot and shall not settle as easily
and satisfactorily as any difficulty we submitted to a satisfactory arbitration last year? Are these new war-ships

to affect our disposition or attitude towards her? Are we going to pounce upon Canada, and compel the Dominion to volunteer, as Patrick would say, to unite with us; or are we, with this new naval force, going to do anything to her, or any other power, which might provoke a quarrel?

These are questions which the American people should consider. Are we forever to follow in the wake of European powers; to drift in the current of this cowardly suspicion that has so long victimized them? The expenses of the Navy Department during the last fiscal year amounted to $21,249,809, or more than twice as much as it cost during the costliest year of war with Great Britain, or in 1815. Put our naval armaments in the two periods together. In the last war, for 1814 and 1815, whole amount, $15,971,291. In 1872, a year of profound peace, except the Corean glory, $21,249,809. Thus last year's naval expenses cost us $5,000,000 more than they cost during two years of war with Great Britain. But the old hungry horse-leech still cries, "Give! give!" It cries for ten new war-ships, each of which, with its armament, will cost nearly $1,000,000, and to "run" it full-manned, as much as all that Harvard or Yale receives for the education they impart. It is time for the patriotic and Christian public to give second sober thought to this unrepublican tendency of sentiment and action. We boast that we have no standing army after the European standard of force. But we conceal from ourselves, if not from foreign powers, the vast expenditures of time and money which our military system involves. There is not a state in the Union that does not pay more for the drilling and arms of its militia than for its normal school for training teachers to educate its children. And there is not a train-band in the Union that is not sustained as a contingent to the national army, and a contribution to the expense of our military system; and both army and navy are only a tax on the luxury of suspicion.

POLITICAL QUESTIONS.

ATTENUATION OF SUFFRAGE IN THE UNITED STATES.

DURING the last ten years, two very vivid impersonations have figured before the public mind — one in America, the other in England. This important personage has been called "the intelligent contraband" with us, in England he is called "the intelligent foreigner," whose name, presence, and opinions are so often quoted in Parliament, and exert such influence upon its proceedings. There is no potentate in Europe so potent in England as "the intelligent foreigner;" none whose impressions are so much respected or feared. This sentiment of deference to an observing but invisible outsider is natural and creditable. It recognizes the fact that others may see us with their own eyes instead of ours ; that the view of a country and its institutions from an outside stand-point may, and even must, be somewhat different from the view from an inside point of observation. It is therefore natural and desirable that we should like to know what "the intelligent foreigner" thinks of us.

With our stoutest faith in our republican institutions, and with all our pretended indifference to the opinion of them which European outsiders may hold, it is quite evident that we are "chips of the old block," to every straight or twisted grain. We cannot, and do not, ignore "the intelligent foreigner;" and he is an ever-present personage among us, whose supposed or possible opinion is as much thought of in this country as in England. He is the most useful personage in the world to any nation or government, and the most influential. He is a kind of supplementary conscience to both — the living and speaking impersonation of the outside world's opinion, which no autocracy or despotism can banish from its dominion. He performs a service for the best government which no loyal subject or citizen can supply. For it is difficult, if not impossible, for such a subject, with his heart full of love and pride for his country, to abstract himself from his loyalty so far as to see it and its institutions as the impartial and thoughtful outsider sees them. I will not pretend to be able to do this more approximately than the most concentrated and uncompromising patriot in the land. I will not try to erect a stand-point of observation even on the extreme verge or rim of our Republic, and to say how the inward view looks to an eye cleared by that atmosphere. One does not need to go from the centre to the circumference of our institutions, or from the present to the past or future, to see some of their tendencies and results. And some of these I would most earnestly commend to the thoughtful consideration of those who may notice these reflections.

As in the past, and in all the future they are to see and share, England and America have been, and are to be, neck and neck, hand and hand, and foot and foot, in moral and political being and progress. I associate them, and compare their footsteps on the high road of democratic development and power. We are, perhaps, the foremost among the nations in applying the derogatory term *insular* to the English mind. We speak of her *insular* views, policies, and prejudices, just as if the form and the contracted area of one island of her empire must naturally narrow and contract her mind and thought, forgetting that, by the same measure, a nation that belts almost without a break the great globe itself, with its many-tongued and populous communities, ought to have the largest views of any power in the world. But, at the worst, if England is *insular*, America is equally *continental* in mind and speech. And one is just as exaggerated as the other, ourselves being witnesses. What sentiment does the intelligent foreigner or the intelligent citizen hear in so many forms and phases of expression as, " This is a great country " ? This " great-country " impression and phraseology enter into the very life, thought, and being of the nation, and crop out in every form, and figure, and illustration. One can almost detect in them the idea that the continent itself, from ocean to ocean, is a republican institution created by an Act of Congress ; that the Mississippi and our greatest rivers, lakes, mountains, forests, and prairies are the achievements of " the smartest nation on earth," in the language of a popular boast. Now if we are not to mind what the intelligent foreigner says of us, I think every thoughtful reader must have noticed this tendency of the American mind to " rob Peter to pay Paul," or to attribute to our political institutions what we owe to nature. This habit ignores or depreciates that debt, and gives to them an honor, power, and result which the thoughtful citizen, as well as the best-minded outsider, cannot admit.

Now in this competition or comparison between the

insular and the *continental*, I will not here put the actual achievements of English legislation against the acts of the American Congress for the last eighty years. I will only compare the two peoples in the machinery and capacity of their democratic power and progress ; and I will ask the reader to examine the comparison thoughtfully, to see if it diverges from the line of fact at any stage of it. In the first place, then, let us notice the constitutional, deliberate, and well-organized arrangements to attenuate the suffrage and citizen-power of the American people ; to lessen their political value, and to bar or break the force of their opinion on the government. It would require a volume to set forth the elaborate system of checks and balances our national constitution provides thus to interpose buffers to break the force of popular opinion on the wheels of state.— to use a railroad figure. Let us first take the decennial apportionment, and see how the census literally *decimates* the working power of that opinion. We started off as the truest and completest representative government in the world, as we claimed, with the old thirteen states, and a population of less than four millions. The first Congress, in both Houses, numbered nearly three hundred members, or a representative to every fourteen thousand men, women, and children of the population. Great Britain, at the same date, had in her two Houses of Parliament about one thousand representatives for fifteen millions of the people, or one to every fifteen thousand. So our young nation was ahead of her mother in representative force in the matter of number, to say nothing of quality. But by a constitutional arrangement it was provided that the suf-

frage power of the American citizen should be diminished
at the rate of more than ten per cent. every decade. In
1810 every man, woman, and child in the United States
was the twenty-four thousandth part of a member of
Congress in a political capacity. In 1830 the " new
apportionment" axe fell upon every individual of the
country, and lopped off more than a tenth of his political valuation at the ballot-box, so that he became only
the thirty-two thousandth part of an M. C. At each
successive decade the same well-sharpened axe fell upon
him with equal effect. In 1840 he was reduced to about
the fifty thousandth part ; and now he will probably stand
at the ballot-box weighing in the scales of suffrage only
the one hundred and twenty-five thousandth part of a
member of the national Congress. Such is the sliding
scale which our republican constitution and custom provide for the attenuation of American suffrage. There is
no representative government in the world in which the
individual has so little ballot power as in ours. Counting out four hundred and fifty members of the House of
Lords, as no representatives at all of the people of the
United Kingdom, every man, woman, and child in England, Scotland, and Ireland is the 'forty thousandth part
of a member of the House of Commons ; that is, every
subject of that kingdom has three times the ballot power
of an American citizen, putting the House of Lords, or
its representation, entirely out of count.

Having thus provided for the decennial decimation of
the ballot power of the people, a very astute system of
checks and balances was adopted to *buff* off the direct
action of this diminished power on the government. One

might infer that the venerated authors of this system thought it unsafe to let in the rough breath of public opinion directly upon the nobility of the higher elective offices of the nations; that it must be softened and diluted, if not by intervening non-conductors, at least by ingenious respirators, to modify its force. In a word, no higher dignity in our Republic was to be approached broadside on, and chosen direct by the people, than that of member of the Lower House at Washington. Poor man! the constitution provides no buffer nor breakwater to break the force of the people's will, opinion, and choice in regard to him. It leaves him to the tender mercies or adroit manipulations of political rings and caucuses within the constitution he aspires to represent. From his to all superior dignities, the rough hands of the people are kept off; and fewer and softer hands are alone allowed to touch these higher honors. The people of a state may elect by direct vote the senators of their state legislature, and even their governor. To this extent they may go, for the interests and dignities involved are accounted smaller. But to elect the governor and senators of the nation by direct vote! to allow its millions to put these great officers of state, with their own ungloved hands, in their high positions! " *Procul, O procul este, profani!* " says our republican constitution at the door of the White House, or a Congress with as deep a sense of propriety as any priest of pagan Rome ever said it to the impious intruders at his temple door.

No; both the nation's governor and senators must not be allowed to come direct between the breath of public opinion and their nobility. That opinion must breathe upon these high offices gently through the artificial respirator of indirect election. The hard, rough hands of the people must not drop their stained and greasy ballots straight into the lap of these grand dignities. Only two or three hundred chosen men in three millions may vote for a national senator. Only three hundred men in thirty millions may approach the sacred urn of the presidential election and vote for the governor of the Republic. And these presidential electors may, and sometimes do, put in his chair of state and power a candidate whom more than half the population of the Union do not wish to fill it. This is another part of the machinery for attenuating American suffrage, and it is as effective to this end as the decennial decimation by "the new apportionment." Where did the venerated inventors and advocates of this indirect election machinery find their model or suggestion? Certainly not in England.

Well, let us go on to the other parts and workings of this wheel-within-wheel system. By indirect election we have a president put irremovably in power for four years, and a Senate, half for four and the other half for six years, all irremovable except by death or impeachment. It matters not how the circumstances or how public opinion may change in this space; these powers that be cannot be changed. The nation must wait patiently until their lease of authority expires, and then try to supply their place by the same machinery of indirect election. The system pretends to drop a small bone of privilege to the people within this space of time by allowing them to change, by direct vote, their representatives in the Lower House. But what does this amount to, if they cannot change the Senate, a body that stands athwart the door-way of every act of legislation? Put the force of American opinion and suffrage against the people-power of the English nation at this point of comparison. There a strong government, with a Lord Derby and a Disraeli, or a Russell and a Gladstone, may be turned out of power after a single week's holding by a vote in Parliament. Public opinion acts with instantaneous force on the government, and no American four-years'-lease can delay its fall.

Let us glance at one of the small cogs of this wheel-system provided to regulate and temper the action of public opinion in this country. True, it allows the people by direct vote to renew the Lower House once in two years, but it does not permit them to renew the Senate, even by indirect vote, once in four years. A number of six-year senators survive the presidential term, and " hold over," in order to temper the action of too complete and radical a change in the people's choice. They are held in reserve against such a change, to form a constitutional " opposition " to the incoming president and the party he represents. This is truly only a small cog of the wheel, provided to act like the brake on the railroad car, but it answers its design to check the train of public opinion.

Well, we have the president, his cabinet, and the Senate which indirect election allows us. We have seen the process by which they are put in their high places of trust and power. Let us see how near to the people these places stand. As among the highest powers of state in other countries, there is often rivalry, hostility, or open rupture, so the same conditions may exist between the same powers here. So far as the outside world is concerned, the most important and dignified prerogative of a government is the treaty-making power. Well, our senatorial barons, though dividing this power with the executive constitutionally, claim, and often exercise, the lion's share of it. They may reject any treaty which the executive makes with a foreign power after the most protracted and patient negotiation. Even if the nation suspects private or partisan pique at the bottom of this rejection, there is no help for it ; it is done in secret session. Here a transaction that involves the interests, the honor, and dignity of a great nation is consummated, and the people are powerless to prevent it. What can their own representatives in the Lower House do in the matter? Just nothing, constitutionally. Their hands bear too plainly the plebeian touch of the people to be trusted with treaties, or the powers of peace and war involved in treaty-making.

There is only one more wheel of this buffing system that we will notice at this time, though a volume would hardly suffice to describe them all. We now have the great result of indirect election in the president in the White House, and his cabinet ministers in brown and gray houses close by it. Happy beings ! how removed from contact with public opinion, even breathing through its constitutional respirator ! They never come face to face to it even in this secondary form and force. They never face the Lower House or Upper House in person, to answer any unpleasant questions as to their policy. No ; that sort of thing may do for Gladstone, Bismarck,

or Thiers. They may stand up before five hundred angry
or anxious faces, and be badgered till they are pale and
haggared with exhaustion about their measures; but it is
not for American statesmen, wearing the white kid gloves
of indirect election, to be subjected to that sort of thing;
to approach so near even to the indirect mouth-pieces of
public opinion. No; if Congress wishes to ask such
questions, let it drop a line into the post-office, or send it
by messenger to the White House, or the state secretary's house, or to some other great house in the West
End; and if it is a respectful and proper note an answer
shall come back through the same medium. I wonder
if any who may read these remarks failed to notice this
peculiar feature of our constitutional system during the
recent anxiety and excitement of the public mind in regard to the Washington Treaty and the consequential
claims. How powerless our House of Commons and the
whole nation seemed to be in the matter! Even the post-
office, that carries on the diplomatic correspondence at
Washington between the Ministry and Congress, was
silent. Not even a note in answer to the most anxious
inquiry touching " the immediate jewel " of the nation's
honor was vouchsafed to the people by the secretary of
state. And all the while, almost every morning's tele-
gram from England brought us the questions which angry
men addressed to Lord Granville and Gladstone in the
British Parliament, and their brave answers in regard to
the same subject.

Here, then, are a few of the constitutional provisions
now in force to attenuate American suffrage and opinion,
or to bar their full and immediate action on our govern-

ment. I say constitutional, for the contrivances to pervert, divert, and dilute public opinion by town caucuses, state caucuses, and national caucuses, by rings, lobbies, and " previous questions," are legion in both number and character, and I will not touch upon them here.

——◆◇◆——

THE GREATEST AND LAST OF PERSONAL EDITORS.

" A change of some importance took place, during last week, on the staff of the " Times." Mr. Mowbray Morris, who has for many years been manager of that paper, has retired, and Mr. Stephens has been appointed his successor. The new manager is taken from the parliamentary corps, and is, comparatively speaking, quite a young man."

THE foregoing announcement appeared in a London journal a few days before Horace Greeley articulated his last words on earth : " IT *is done !* " They went up in a feeble whisper to the ears that bent to hear it from those death-frosted lips. But the angel of the telegraph, whose human wings are as fleet as Gabriel's, waiting reverently for that whisper, bore it to the listening continents at the quickest speed of thought. The listening continents heard it, and felt all their multitudinous populations stirred as by an event that somehow affected the world.

But Horace Greeley was only an editor. He never won nor wielded official power. His country elevated him to no position of influence. If it had so willed, it

19

could not have added one cubit to his stature. It had
no gift sufficient even to crown or adorn its growth.
The pinnacle of his greatness was the height of his own
character. This grand structure was the spontaneous
evolution of its own innate vitalities; and these, in an
honest heart, could not but grow, for they fed at the
life of Truth, which " has the eternal years of God."
They were principles that shaped the purpose of his
life, and, without consulting with flesh and blood, even
with his own, he followed them, without shadow of
turning, to the end of his days, and to the greater end
to which they led. And, for him, the two issues were
blended in one consummation. When he whispered his
last words, " It is done ! " they had a broader meaning for the world than the mere ending of what could
die of his life on earth. They announced the greatest
fact in American history — that the principles he had
contended for, with a heroism of faith and courage that
no obloquy could daunt or dim, had become the living
forces of the nation's life and power.

When passing the eye over the salient characteristics
of Horace Greeley's life, we must recognize a new significance to certain peculiarities of thought and expression which were once attributed to an amusing
eccentricity of mind. One of these habits was to
impersonate great principles, truths, and facts, or to
raise them up to living entities by giving each, as it
were, the sceptre of a capital letter. This habit was
no affectation, nor unconscious eccentricity. It came
from his deep reverence for these principles, which
were ever a kind of divine presence to him. Truth,

Right, Freedom, Humanity, and People, he always put among the immortals; and he would as soon have written Gabriel without an initial capital as one of them. Then, from the outset to the end of his career, from the first types he set up as a printer's apprentice, to the last lines he wrote as the greatest editor of his own or any other age, he adopted one unvarying standard of valuation, by which he measured the worth and *raison d'être* of all governments, laws, institutions, political parties, and popular sentiment. MAN was the unit by which he computed their valuations — man as an abstract entity, with no government nor national stamp on him, in his pure and simple intrinsic worth, as the gold before it receives the guinea's stamp. This living and immortal unit he weighed against all governments, laws, and institutions, monarchical and republican, and if they ignored or depreciated its worth, he wrote *Mene, Mene, Tekel, Upharsin,* over against them on the wall, with a hand and a distinctness which the whole nation saw and felt.

Horace Greeley was not only the last, but the greatest, of personal editors. Never before did a writer-in-chief put so much powerful and all-absorbing individuality into a great journal. All who noticed the little army of associate and assistant writers who followed him to the grave, must have realized as they never did before the assimilating power of his master mind, that could make the Tribune his own breathing, speaking life, the very express image and embodiment of his own individuality. The best and brightest of these associate editors made no separate lustre; it was only a ray of the central light that seemed to illuminate every page. The very journal itself was apparently affected by this assimilating force, even to its type, ink, and paper. Every successive number carried to its readers the speaking portrait of Horace Greeley. The large, Germanic title-type at the head of the first page was as much a part of his personal dress to thousands on the Ohio and Mississippi as any great-coat he ever wore was to those who knew him in New York.

Who can measure the orbit of Horace Greeley's life, influence, name, and reputation? To say these were known to every man, woman, and child on this continent who can read the shortest words of our English tongue, would be to limit the area of his fame. Millions of southern slaves, whom it was a penal offence to teach a written syllable, heard his name while bending to their bondage, and it sounded to their listening ears like the distant footstep of some Greatheart that God was sending to their release. On what other continent or island, peopled by men who read in any language put in newspaper type, is his name unhonored or unknown? How few of the eighty millions who speak our own on the globe have not already seen those short words on their pathetic tour around the earth, "It is done"? What enlightened nation did not know the wide meaning of those words, as well as his own, when it bent its head and wept at his bier?

I put at the beginning of these reflections, without note or comment, a paragraph from an English journal, announcing the end of another editorial career. I was confident that the full scope and motive of the antithesis would be recognized without any suggestion. Here the

managing editor of the foremost journal of all this world
closes his career. The mighty man who wielded the
thunderbolts of Olympus descends from Jove's seat to an
unnoticed life, and does not rustle a leaf by his fall.
For twenty years or more he had directed the voice of
the great Thunderer. For all this eventful period he
had marshalled the most vigorous intellectual forces that
the education of an empire could supply. At their head,
as a compact unit, moving at the impulse of his will, he
mounted to the throne of public opinion, and launched its
utterance out upon the world. The " We " of the Thunderer was a power behind, before, and above Victoria's
throne. It issued and echoed over all the great questions
that moved the nation and the world — over Eastern and
Western Questions, the Crimean War, the Indian Mutiny,
Continental Struggles, Reform Bills, Disestablishment of
the Irish Church, National Education, the Washington
Treaty, and all Domestic and Foreign Policies. It was
a power abroad as well as at home ; and many a foreign
cabinet felt its force. Never was there such editorial
power concentrated in one utterance. But you might
as well essay to " fall a drop of water into the breaking
gulf, and take that drop unmingled thence," as to detach
any personal individuality from this great organization
of intellectual force. Its constituent atoms made but one
body, and it had but one breath and voice. Mowbray
Morris's deposition from its head made no more change in
its unity, and no more sensation without or within, than
the deposition of a single atom from the human body in
its seven-year renovation. He had been as invisible and
intangible to the great public as the Grand Lama ever

was to his subjects.   Had not Richard Cobden, incensed
at his anonymous attacks, penetrated the mystery of his
personality and disclosed his name, the readers of the
London Times would not have known who was its editor-
in-chief.   For him it may be said, " It is done."   But
what, in his case, is done?   What is the individuality
he brings away from his great position?   Why, it is
doubtful if there are twenty men in England who ever
recognized a line he wrote, or any peculiarity of sentiment, view, character, or expression that distinguished
him from the rank and file of anonymous writers.   Not
all he did, or was known to do, or be, in Jove's seat,
would probably commend him as a successful candidate
to the smallest municipal office in a country town.   After
twenty years' reign on this Olympian height of editorial
power, what a pygmy he is when measured against the
great and immortal individuality of Horace Greeley!
Measured by the sublime standard of truth and right,
the moral disparity was equally great between the two
journals they edited.   With all the unparalleled intellectual and pecuniary power the London Times could command, it never pretended nor aimed to be anything better
or more than the current *times*, or the opinion, sentiment,
and voice of the majority.   It did not seek to create or
rectify public opinion, but to represent it.   The majority,
right or wrong, was its watchword, and it never diverged
from the line of this small and shifty policy.

Now, let us see what an unknown and anonymous
atom of individuality is to succeed Mowbray Morris on
the throne of the London Times.   His accession to this
high place is not deemed worthy of an independent

paragraph, like the postscript to the foregoing announcement. See how it reads, like "the chronicle of small beer:" "And Mr. Stephens has been appointed his successor. The new manager is taken from the parliamentary corps, and is, comparatively speaking, quite a young man." This young man appears to have been the foreman of the parliamentary reporters. Undoubtedly they all know him. But, outside of their circle, it is doubtful if fifty men in England ever heard his name before, or will ever hear it again. They do not know, and never will know, whether or not he ever wrote anything else than the copy of a speech in the House of Commons. They will never be able to recognize a thought of his in the London Times. His individuality, if he ever had any perceptible, will melt away and disappear in that amalgam of intellectual being and force which constitutes the life and power of the great journal. We never more shall see his name in print until he dies, or descends from his high place. Momentous questions touching the integrity of the British empire, the reconstruction of its government, colonial independence, dissolution of church and state, and questions affecting other nations intensely, will come up in his editorial reign; but he, and all the intellectual forces marshalled under his sceptre, will be as anonymous, invisible, and "impalpable as the viewless winds."

Thus measured against the foremost journalists of Europe, every thoughtful mind must see and feel that Horace Greeley was the greatest personal editor that ever lived; that no one ever developed in his own character and influence such an intense and powerful individuality. And this is only half the admission that we must make. He was not only the greatest, but *last* of personal editors on either side of the Atlantic. Indeed, they were almost exclusively an American production in the formative years of our Republic. And here their succession ends forever, with the — "It is done!" of the most illustrious of them all. From him we may go back on the line to Raymond, Bennett, Prentice, Isaac Hill, Father Ritchie, and Duff Green. But the future is blank, and barren of all promise of editorial personality. Our great journalists have become corporations of anonymous intellect, owned by anonymous stockholders, and managed by Mowbray Morrises, or "quite young men, comparatively speaking," like young Mr. Stephens. So, in this new tomb, and in the coffin of Horace Greeley, lies buried the last year of Personal Editorship.

But was Horace Greeley a statesman? Had he the grasp of a trained intellect to comprehend and realize the written letter and the broader spirit of the American system of government? Did he, by that inspired intuition of a great heart which erudite statesmen often lack, understand the life and soul of the American Constitution, the concentric series of its relations to man as an individual, to men as a state, to states as a nation? His country, while he lived, doubted this perception and ability. It hesitated, and refused to make him an official statesman. But there is one ability and fact which it must concede to him, now that he is gone. He made the best statesmen that are to guide his country hereafter. Whoever of them drifts out of the current of his character will find himself stranded on the slimy shore of oblivion. The principles he bore to the front, and which, may be, bore him to the grave, will forevermore live and act as the shaping forces of the nation's life and destiny.

Disraeli said of Cobden, the day after his death, that he would thenceforward be an ever-present member of the House of Commons, where his wise counsels would be heard and honored over all the strife of party debates. It may be said with equal truth that Horace Greeley will forever sit in the presidential chair at Washington, with his hand on the helm of the state. Already it begins to respond to the magnetic force of the principles he endowed with such powerful vitality. Was he a statesman? If any young man who listens to this question, and would like to know what it means, will read Horace Greeley's short speeches during the last months of his life, he will feel himself listening to the father of all true American statesmen to be. In these " apples of gold in pictures of silver ; " in logic as clear and strong as Cobbett's and Cobden's combined ; in diction as chaste and beautiful as that of Burke's best perorations, he may see the living mind, soul, and spirit of the American Constitution unfolded with a breadth of view, and fullness and refinement of perception, which it would be the best training of an American statesman to study and to attain.

WOMAN SUFFRAGE AND ITS LIABILITIES.

THE Woman's Rights Question, as it is called, has passed beyond the stage of the ridiculous as a theory. We may laugh at it and pooh-pooh it with the best satire and wit that can be put in words or in caricatures ; but it cannot be put down or put back by such arguments. The foothold it has got in England as a political question, and the progress it has made in Parliament, and in other departments of public life, tend to give it an impetus here that cannot be laughed down or weakened by ridicule. So, with all the jeers and gibes of pen and pencil against it, this very question is assuming every year new and vigorous force in both countries. In England it has reached a more serious stage than in America. In the first place, it has John Stuart Mill, Jacob Bright, and many other eminent men, both in and out of Parliament, who are advocating it with all the force of their deep and honest convictions, as well as with their great ability and influence. Then it is free there from those associations and prejudices that attach to it here. It is not affected there by the aspect or odor of free-and-easy virtue, or free love, or Bloomerism, or strong-minded womanism, as it is in this country. The men and women who advocate it there are not suspected of these *isms*, and, therefore, do not have to meet the same prejudice and ridicule as in America. Then women are actually getting on the register as voters in some of the municipal elections. They are not only beginning to vote, but to be voted into very important offices. The mayor, aldermen, and councilmen of London do not have a much more responsible and important field of labor and duty devolving upon them than the new school-board of that city. This board is a governing power, clothed with an authority almost sufficient to rule an American state or a German principality. Well, on this great central school-board there are several women of high position and cultivation. Women are among the members of other boards throughout the kingdom. The great universities of Oxford, Cambridge, and London are virtually opened to them. Classes of ladies are instructed by the most eminent professors in those institutions.

Thus there is a steady advance in England of all that is embraced in the Woman's Rights Question, both in and out of Parliament. Although public opinion moves slower, it moves surer, than with us. When a movement that has the force of truth and right in it has once been set agoing, however small its beginning, it progresses slowly but certainly to its realization. When the public mind has watched it a while, and seen it reach a certain stage of progress, the belief soon becomes general that it must and will succeed in the end. This is illustrated in other public questions that have been carried. No sooner was the disestablishment of the Irish Church accomplished, in face of a powerful opposition, than the belief began to prevail that the disestablishment of the English Church would follow, although more than half the population of England belonged to that church, and were strongly attached to it.   The nation began to expect the question would be brought into Parliament even before any one proposed to do it, and it was ; and it received nearly one hundred votes at the first trial.   The whole country knows how these votes will grow from year to year, until they carry the question.   Just so with Woman Suffrage.   It has made a still more favorable beginning in Parliament, and will be as sure of the same victory. Even the most caustic, severe, and satirical paper in England, the Saturday Review, gives it up virtually, and assumes the question will be carried.   At the end of a long article denouncing the movement, it says, —

" However, what will be will be.   If it is so ordained that this uncomfortable phase of active feminine ambition has to be worked through, nothing that we or any one else can say will prevent it. But, at least, we may give one note of warning by the way, and do what we can to mitigate the absurdities resulting.   In particular, we would urge the incompatibility of the old sacredness with the new self-assertion, and the unwisdom of wincing at satire voluntarily courted.   To run with the hare and hunt with the hounds has been a feat as yet found impossible with the best will in the world.   If women are able to unite the coarse life of men with the sacredness of womanhood, they will have solved the problem in their own favor.   But, until the new phenomenon is made manifest, we must take the liberty of questioning its possibility, and of maintaining that, if the sacred sex wishes to remain the sacred sex still, it must not offer itself as a mark for public discussion on a more than questionable line of action. If it wishes to keep its head whole, it must not thrust it where blows are falling; and, if it likes clean fingers, it must not touch pitch."

These are the words of an English weekly paper distinguished for its intellectual force as well as its keen and cynical satire. They virtually concede that woman suffrage is to triumph in England, in spite of all ridicule and other opposition. And I think we must all agree that it cannot triumph there without being victorious here soon afterwards. Now, this fact brings it home to us in its most serious aspect. We must face it in this light, as a question that will have a new power here from its success in England. Indeed, I do not see what opposition is to prevent its triumph here, unless the great majority of the women of this country oppose it themselves. The same note of warning addressed by the Saturday Review to the women of England may be addressed more properly to the women of America for several reasons. One of these reasons ought to have great weight with them. It is admitted by travellers and writers of different countries who visit us, that nowhere else in the world are women treated with so much delicate homage and tender consideration as in America. In this respect there is no other country where their sex is held so sacred as in this, and it is the unanimous opinion, both at home and abroad, that in no other country do women *expect* so much homage and deference as with us. In no other country do women of the same rank assume to be so delicate, and exact so much deference from men, as in America. Setting aside the comparatively small number of strong-minded women, spiritualists, free lovers, and other visionary extremists, the great body of American women are more feminine in their deportment and sensibilities than English women of the same classes. And this, doubtless, is the very reason why they are treated with more delicate consideration, and why they even claim such consideration as a right, and not as a gracious homage on the part of men.

Now, this delicate and tender consideration that American women receive and claim above any other women in the world is the most precious, costly, and valuable right, and the most honorable dignity, that women ever did or ever can attain in any age or country. It is a right including all others, social or moral, that society can recognize. It is a right that embraces all the influences woman can exert upon any question of the day. It is a right in which she can exercise on the legislation of the country, and upon public life and morality, all the intelligence and all the graces and virtues of her own character.

Now, to use the rough figure so common in England, if woman cannot run with the hare and hunt with the hounds in that country, it is more unwise and dangerous still for her to attempt such a race here. It is impossible for her to keep at its full value the right she now has, and at the same time get and use the right that woman suffrage would give her. She cannot serve God and Mammon at the same moment. She cannot be a man and woman too at the ballot-box or in the political arena. She cannot wrap all the American sacredness of her sex about her, and go down to these places of rough concourse, and expect that no mote of their black dust will soil her robe or touch her woman's sensibilities. For there will inevitably be more of such soot and dust afloat here than in England. We all know, and the outside world knows, what political warfare means in America; what are the sharp missiles and defiling mud hurled to and fro in the conflict. Even thousands of our best educated men, of refined and honorable sensibilities, shrink from a contest where all that is sacred in private character and conscientious motive is trampled in the mire or blotched with its defilement. How can American women wish to rush in where such men dare not tread? It is true enough that they have not only received, but claimed, an homage which the women of England never expected. They are proud, or have reason above all other women in the world to be proud, of that homage — to prize and treasure it as the immediate jewel of their souls; as more than a jewel, more than any ornament or honor; as the richest source of their domestic and social happiness. This homage has never failed them in any of the common walks of life that nature has made for woman's foot. But the moment she descends into the arena of political warfare, that homage will not shield her from the missiles and mire of the conflict. Her presence there will not exclude nor blunt a single weapon known to our great party contests. On the contrary, a new set of missiles from the arsenal of satire will be brought in to hit and wound her sensibilities. There can be no discharge from this kind of war, if she voluntarily enters into it. She must encounter all its weapons and all its turmoil and rough exposure. If she will insist upon entering such a field of strife, we cannot prevent her. The women of America must decide this question for themselves. The men of America cannot withhold the right of suffrage from them, if they insist upon it. But it is for themselves to decide whether they will exchange the koh-i-noor they now possess for the brassy, lackered bauble contained in the ballot-box.

NATIONAL AND INTERNATIONAL QUESTIONS.

20   305

RUSSIA FROM A COSMOPOLITAN STAND-POINT.

IF any nation in the world is enabled and bound by its position to view the great questions that agitate Europe from a cosmopolitan stand-point, it is America. The force and value of our opinion on such questions depend upon this point of view. The moment we descend into the low arena of local interests and prejudices, we lay off the dignity of the umpire for the badge and bludgeon of the partisan. As the position of Russia is henceforth to become an exciting question to the Old World, we owe it to her, to ourselves, and to universal civilization, to form and utter our opinion from a higher level of consideration than the one assumed by the partisan powers of Europe. To ascend to this point of reflection will cost our national mind an effort in which it has never yet succeeded. The power of English opinion is so great upon us, say what we will, — so much of our knowledge and conception of European matters comes to us through the English press and literature, — that, in spite of our boasted independence of thought and action, our first views of European nations and questions become, almost mechanically, English. In watching this tendency of American opinion, one may see it in all our leading journals of both political parties. A few days ago a leader appeared in one of the most influential of them, not only urging the ability, but apparently the duty, of England to ally to herself, or subsidize, Holland, Denmark, and Sweden, and raise an army of four hundred 'thousand men to oppose Russia's growth and march ; or rather to prevent her from becoming, two or three centuries hence, as near a neighbor to England in India as she is now to France or America itself. Nothing could be more completely English than the whole argument of that article. It was perfectly English in its view of Russia, past, present, and to come. It was as full of the old balance-of-power animus and theory as any tory argument you could find in the Edinburgh Review. .

Now, the very worst thing we can do to the English people by our opinion, is to adopt and express theirs on these great questions ; to justify and increase their panics and prejudices in regard to the character, and intent, or even ability, of their neighbor nations. And if we really have an honest and loyal wish for her well-being in the world, the best we can do to promote it is to erect a fair, impartial opinion of our own, which shall serve to check her drift into these periodical fantasies of suspicion and alarm. Our opinion should be a harbor buoy, fast anchored in a firm holding, not a sham lightship, drifting with the same current that bears her towards a lee shore of disaster. The best that America can do for her, or any other European nation, is to establish such a moorage for her, and any other power driving out rudderless to the wild sea of war. But America must re-read, if she cannot stop to re-write, for herself the history and character of other peoples and governments, before she can anchor such a moorage of fair and independent opinion. She owes it to them to write their histories for herself, and from her own stand-point. This she will do some time or other; but, without waiting for that, she may read their histories as they have been written in the salient acts of their life and being.

Of all European histories the American mind has studied, not one of them, probably, has been read so completely through English spectacles as that of Russia. I think it is safe to say, that American opinion as to a foreign nation has never been so completely English as in regard to that power and people. And this identity of view and sentiment is as hurtful to England as it is unfair in us. I am conscious that this opinion is so common to both countries, and so strong in each, that an American may be charged with political heresy if he ventures to view Russia from a fair, cosmopolitan standpoint. In attempting this, I do not wish to differ without motive from the authorities which the American public has so long accepted.

It is impossible to condense within a few pages the structure of an argument which requires for its development the space of a large volume. In such contracted limits the statement of facts must be bald, and the reasoning brief. Out of this necessity, then, I think, no fair and impartial mind, that has well studied the subject, will demur to the statement, that no nation in the world ever did or suffered more for civilization in the same space of time, and with the same means, than Russia has done. In the way of suffering, certainly no intelligent reader of history will doubt the truth of that part of the statement. For several centuries she served as a breakwater against the barbarous and blasting hordes of Tartary, which else would have flooded the whole of Europe with their tyranny.   But though she broke the flood that would have beat upon Germany, France, and perhaps England, she could not save herself from the ruinous inundation.   Though it engulfed her for centuries, she absorbed it so that it did not spread farther west. In this long period of suffering for civilization — longer than the Egyptian bondage, and harder to bear — the nations of Central and Western Europe had time and means to grow to the status and stature of independent governments and peoples.   But their fairest historians have never recognized how much of their safety and growth in these centuries they owed to Russia, who braved and bore the worst dangers of them all.

But Russia has done even far more than she has suffered for the civilization of the world; and done more in the same time and with the same means, than any other nation, to that end.   It is remarkable how rarely we find an English or American writer who measures her against other countries by these standards; who seems even to recognize how little working capital she had to begin with, and what she has accomplished with it.   Indeed, she had to import into her realm the very seeds of civilization she possessed; or the few Scandinavian, German, Italian, Greek, and other foreign elements that she introduced.   If all the enlightenment they produced were put in one lustre, it is doubtful if it would have made as much light as the single town of Salem could emit when St. Petersburg was founded.   In this world's history did ever a sovereign feel and deplore so deeply the want of this working capital of civilization as did Peter the Great? How he apprenticed himself and his young nobles to common trades in foreign countries, how he, scoured those countries for teachers of every useful art and branch of instruction, is partially 'recorded in our school-books. From his time to this, no nation has been more teachable, or learned more from foreign instructors, and from the experience and example of other countries, than Russia. Then look at the heterogeneous populations out of which she had to construct her empire. Begin at the Arctic Sea and gauge them through to the Euxine, and from the Baltic through Siberia to Behring's Straits. Apply a moral standard to their races, religions, and habits, not as they are now, but as they were when she took them under her sceptre. Was there any other power in the wide world that could reach them with more of the elements or influences of civilization? On the whole, is not the world indebted greatly to her for what she has done for these barbarous populations? Consider how comparatively brief is the space of time that she has had them under her sway, and how in this period their old pagan idolatries and superstitions have been displaced for at least the nominal faith and worship of the Christian religion.

And now comes that great act and proof of advancing civilization that emancipated her millions of serfs, and which makes them the freemen of the empire, to constitute that middle class to be what the emancipated serfs or *villains* of other countries have been to them. Did any nation ever surpass Russia in this single act of civilization? It is impossible for her to stop at this step. She must take others in the same direction. She is taking them rapidly and successively in every department of enlightenment and progress — in literature, in popular education, railways, and all kinds of internal improvements. The Russia of Peter the Great is as dead as the England of the last Henry. The Russia of the next generation will not be the Russia of to-day, but a nation, if not abreast, at least not far behind, the civilization of older and more favored countries. This is a fact in the future almost as certain as any in arithmetical or geometrical progression. And in all these anxieties and preparations for incoming events, this fact must be recognized and appreciated by those who consider them from a cosmopolitan stand-point.

THE COMMERCIAL RELATIONS AND CAPACITIES OF RUSSIA.

THE geographical position and producing power of Russia qualify her for a great part to act for the benefit of the whole Eastern hemisphere. What Egypt was to Canaan and other countries in time of dearth, Russia is to Western and Southern Europe in seasons of short crops. Her granaries pour forth a steady abundance that countries under famine cannot exhaust. What her stores of grain are worth to them in such a time of need, no nation knows better by repeated experience than England. What could she have done for Ireland, even with America to draw from, if she could not have had Odessa and other grain ports of the Black Sea to go to? Now that railways and other facilities of transportation are progressing so rapidly, they will become more and more the granaries of Europe, which will supply its teeming populations with cheaper bread than they can grow at home. Every year Russia's producing power will become a more vital necessity to England and other countries of Western Europe. This she and they are coming to recognize more and more distinctly. Their vital or material interests, more truthful and reliable than their political instincts, have and feel an immense stake in all the railways and internal improvements in Russia that tend to increase this producing power, and to make it more accessible and available to them. In a word, they want to bring Russia *nearer* to them; and with one hand they are lending her money and helping her to this end, while with the other, or political hand, they are trying to push her up against the icebergs of the Frozen Ocean.

But grain is only one of the productions which Russia supplies to Western Europe. Her iron, flax, hemp, tar, and turpentine are increasing and indispensable necessities to them. In the Crimean war the Irish linen manufactories would have stopped, and Ireland would have suffered a flax famine as severe as was the cotton famine to England, if it had not been for a supply of the raw material imported at the enhancement of fifty per cent. through Prussia. Every ship in the British navy that thundered in the Black Sea or Baltic showed its sails and cordage of Russian hemp, and every rope hardened with Russian tar. In spite of all orders in council or proclamations to the contrary, England imported during the war nearly as much from Russia as in time of peace, and paid nearly twice as much for it. Indeed, she could not carry on the war without commercial help from her enemy.

But with all these vital or food-relations to the rest of Europe, with all that Russia is commercially now, and is to be, to the civilized world, it is distinguished over all other large regions of the globe by one remarkable physical characteristic. It is virtually a riverless empire. It is full of rivers great and small, but either they run to no ports of her own, or they are worthless for commerce. Those that flow into the Northern Sea are frozen up half the year, and cannot be counted. The narrow straits that connect Lakes Ladoga and Onega can hardly be called rivers. The only one really that Russia may call her own in Europe is the Dwina, with the port of Riga at its mouth ; and that is inaccessible and unavailable during the winter months. I would earnestly commend to the reader a few minutes' study of the map of that vast and important empire. Aside from the subject under notice, he must be struck with a peculiarity unparalleled in any region of the globe of equal extent. He will see that " rivers to the ocean run," is not true of Russian rivers, or seas either. Count the rivers that run into the Black Sea. They are many and large, but none of them really debouch in Russian territory. To appreciate this singular circumstance we must apply to it an easy standard of measurement. Imagine, then, a great bayou in the Mississippi, just below Vicksburg, of the dimensions of the Black Sea. Imagine all the rivers in the United

States, from Maine to Texas, to run into this salt water bayou, and that all the commerce that floats on those rivers has to pass through that short length of the river that connects the inland sea with the Gulf of Mexico. Then realize, if you can, that this short and narrow strait is called the Bosphorus, and that New Orleans is Constantinople, and that all the commerce of the United States east of the Rocky Mountains, that finds its way to the Atlantic, has to pass between the forts of a foreign nation, of a race, language, and religion as alien to us as any pagan people can be. Then in the north we have the St. Lawrence, and we can get out to the ocean that way, except in the winter, when Quebec becomes a Riga to us. It must be very difficult for an American mind to imagine our great country subjected to such conditions, not by nature, but by dynastic arrangements that are in open and incessant war with nature. But this illustrates the commercial position of Russia almost to the smallest detail of its character. Just consider this fact for a moment. With all the extent of her empire, and with all its productive power, she has not a single port of her own in Europe that is open all the year round.

While the map is in your hands, just glance at the Russian territory in Asia, and see how its rivers and seas are isolated worse still from the world's oceans. See what long rivers run northward into the Arctic Ocean, or the Obi, Yenisei, Lena, and others. But what is their commercial worth to the world? Look the other way, and see the length and course of the famous Volga and Ural. These fall into the Caspian, a warmer sea; but they might as well run into our Lake of the Woods, so far as ocean connection and commerce are concerned. Five minutes' study of the physical geography of the Russian empire will impress any fair and intelligent mind with an approximate sense of the bars and embargoes which nature has imposed upon its commerce with the rest of the world. This sense will prepare one to appreciate the bars and embargoes which a coalition of suspicious and jealous powers is endeavoring to add to those nature has imposed, or to aggravate and perpetuate them.

If England, France, or Prussia had been in Russia's place, either of those powers, a hundred years ago, would have possessed itself of the right of way to the Mediterranean, as we did to the Gulf of Mexico, and by more forcible means. Would England have tolerated such a condition a single year? Would she have suffered a Turkish Constantinople at the mouth of the Thames, and her ships to pass to and from the sea between the forts of a Mohammedan power? But this is the very condition for which she has poured out so much precious blood and treasure to fasten forever upon Russia. This is the prime object aimed at in all these leagues, coalitions, and conferences against that country. And these allies, when they wrestled her to the earth, and put their feet on her neck for her suspected attempt to break this condition, charge her with treachery for attempting or proposing again to throw it off after they had fettered it upon her anew as she lay exhausted on the ground. And, *mirabile dictu, Anglicized* American opinion sides mechanically with theirs, and approves their coercion.

What does " neutralizing " the Black Sea mean, as

stipulated in the Paris Conference, after Russia had been overpowered by the four allied powers that rushed upon her in behalf of *civilization?* It means, in plain and honest English, a perpetual blockade of the Russian navy in her frozen ports in the North Baltic. It means that none of her war-ships shall ever get into the Mediterranean or the Atlantic except by the roundabout way of the Cattegat and Skagerack. It means that they shall never be allowed to enter the Mediterranean except under the British guns at Gibraltar. And does any other nation load more ships for the world in that sea than Russia? And what is the reciprocation, or the equivalent, conceded by the allied powers for this blockade? This — that they will not send their ships of war into the Black Sea in time of peace! That is all. They might as well promise that they would not send them into Lake Ontario. The Black Sea is not on the road to any other country than Russia, any more than Lake Ontario is to any other country than ours. If they go there at all in peace, it is to menace or admonish Russia; if in war, it is to attack her.

This, then, is but a glance at the physical position and the commercial capacities and relations of Russia. It is a mere peep over that structure of fanatical suspicion and jealousy by which Western Europe is trying to bar her way to the seas they claim and use without restriction; to compress her growth; to weaken and thwart her civilizing power; to shut her away from any new points of contact with the more enlightened world. Now, it is in regard to the animus and aim of this policy that America is in duty bound to form and express a fair, dispassionate, independent opinion of her own. I would fain hope that the preceding and succeeding facts and reflections may induce at least a few intelligent and thoughtful minds to review, and perhaps correct, the impression they have hitherto entertained in regard to the " Eastern Question."

———◦◦◦———

RUSSIA AS A POLITICAL NEIGHBOR AND POWER.

WE have considered some of the aspects and characteristics of Russia as a civilizing, producing, and commercial power. These have been presented from a cosmopolitan stand-point, or that point of view which, we may hope, the American mind may be yet trained to adopt when forming an opinion on these European questions that are agitating the Old World. An American opinion, unanimous, clear, and vigorous, uttered from such a high level of reflection, is the only leverage of our moral power on the issue of these questions. And England is now, and must ever be, our *point d'appui* for this leverage. If we move the European world for its good by our opinion, it must be by its force on the public and governing mind of England. Until the tongue she and we speak shall become the universal language of Europe, she is the only nation, as it were, that leans on our bosom, puts her ear to our lips, and her fingers to the pulse of our sentiment. If it can be made to beat, and breathe, and speak as it should, it will do more than any other moral influence in the world to break the spell of those periodical fanaticisms of suspicion and alarm which have so often plunged her, and other nations with her, into aimless and calamitous wars, and which are now again threatening her and them with heavier disasters to civilization. No other living American can have greater cause or desire than myself to contribute what little influence he can to the formation of an American opinion that shall work this immeasurable good to her, and through her to the rest of the world. If any intelligent Englishman, in his own or in this country, shall happen to notice these reflections, I believe he will recognize in them a fair and generous spirit towards England, and an earnest and loyal desire to promote her well-being, even in the strongest phrases and statements of the argument.

There is no other power in the world that is now and ever will be such a close, conterminous neighbor to so many nations as Russia. Indeed, until we bought her estate in America, her empire extended through three continents, and abutted upon countries of almost every race, and language, and government on the globe. For a hundred years or more she has been almost a universal neighbor, or one to European, Asiatic, and American nations. And now I would ask any thoughtful, reading American or Englishman to bring his political theodolite and level, and take the altitude, or the right ascension or declination, of any people bordering upon Russia, and see if they have been lowered one iota by their proximity to her. Take Sweden, for example. She may be called Russia's nearest neighbor, or nearest to her right arm of power.　Has that small nation suffered in its interests or institutions by this neighborhood?　With all the blood and treasure England has poured out for Spain, and with all the protection she has extended to that country, has it lived a freer or purer political life than Sweden has done, almost encircled by the right arm of Russia?　Follow her boundary line west and south, from the mouth of the Neva to the mouth of the Amoor, and see if you can find a people that has been depressed by her near neighborhood.　Poland, who invaded and half subjugated Russia for many centuries, died of heart disease, like the republic of Venice; and all the doctors in the world could not keep her alive and whole as a nation, because she rent herself asunder in the convulsions of her malady.　And, we may say, in passing, there is more hopeful life in each of the three parts than there was in them all when a factious, discordant, and corrupted whole.　Look at Prussia, from the time she was a small duchy to this day of her mighty empire.　She has abutted upon Russia for the whole length of her eastern boundary in the most naked proximity, with not even a Rhine between them. Has she been put back in the development of her political or educational institutions by this near neighborhood? Has her political life been chilled at its pulse by the frosty breath of Russian despotism?　Look at Turkey. Have the masses of the people of that country suffered in their political, religious, or manhood rights by the neighborhood of Russia?　Suffered! they owe it to her influence if centuries ago they had not sunk under Mohammedan fanaticism to a depth of degradation and oppression that no serfs nor helots of any other country or age ever reached. *Suffered!* Why, the Jews under Roman or Assyrian rule never had greater occasion or longing for their Messiah to come for their deliverance, than have the Christian populations of Turkey for the coming of Russia to Constantinople, to break such a yoke of bondage as the Jews never wore, even in Egypt. What was Nebuchadnezzar, or Darius, or any Roman emperor, or Pharaoh himself, to the Jews, compared with what the Turkish sultans have been to the Christians of their realm, numbering two thirds of their population? Now, if never before, the universal American mind ought to have learned that golden rule of democratic arithmetic that counts in the census of a nation every human being in it, of whatever color, condition, race, or religion. We are doing that now with the millions lifted from slavery into our great and free peoplehood. Russia is doing the same with the millions of her emancipated serfs. The time, then, has come when America will sin against her own soul if she longer follows the sentiment of Western Europe, and refuses to recognize the large Christian majority of the inhabitants of Turkey as the Turkish nation. Such a sin will be doubled in guilt and shame if she sides with any European coalition that shall renew the attempt to fetter that majority with new thongs of iron to the Mohammedan rule.

Who is afraid? What civilized nation has anything to fear from Russia's possessing her Mississippi to its mouth? What has mankind to fear in case that she should have the city of the Constantines, the centre of the old Christian civilization of the world, as the fulcrum-point for the leverage of her civilizing power? Would that

21

increase the proximity of her neighborhood to Sweden, Prussia, or Austria? If she is such a dangerous foe to civilization, to her nearest neighbor, — if she has been plotting to trample upon their rights and liberties, — why need she wait until she gets to Constantinople to carry out her schemes? Would her army and navy be any nearer Sweden, Prussia, Austria, France, or England at that point than at Cronstadt? But let us come to the very head and front of the suspicion that has so long dominated England and involved her in sacrifice of blood and treasure. Would Russia be any nearer India at Constantinople than she is now? If any one thinks so, let him take the map and tell us the road by which she could reach India with an army more easily and speedily than by the road she owns and is on at this moment. Why, she is on the Caspian Sea now, with great rivers running through her territory into it. And that sea is nearer to India by thousands of miles, measured by facility of transportation, than the Mediterranean. Let any intelligent man consider the character of the country and the populations between the Caspian and India, and try to imagine the attempt of a Russian force to march upon Calcutta or Delhi. If such a force is not to go by land, and by this route, — if it is not to bore its road through the Himalayas, or cross their heights of snow and ice, — how is it to go by water from Constantinople? Just think of the attempt to pass a Russian fleet with one hundred thousand men through the Suez Canal. Let us suppose that Russia could build, borrow, or hire two hundred ships, half of which should be able to carry one thousand men each, and the other half arms, ammunition, horses and forage enough for the whole force. Think of the insanity of putting these two hundred ships and all their armaments on that canal. Fancy them, bow to stern, midway in the narrow channel when a dozen men with their picks and shovels should cut the embankment and settle the whole fleet in the mud, with a row of masts three miles long standing up like a line of dead trees in the desert. Imagine the condition of such an army in this predicament, and the folly of exposing it to such destruction.

But if a Russian force could not go to India by land through or over the Himalayas and intervening populations, nor by water *via* the Suez Canal, how would the possession of Constantinople give her any additional facility to reach England's Indian empire, either by land or sea? It is evident there would be no new, shorter, or better way by land. The only new way by sea would be *via* the Mediterranean, under the British guns at Gibraltar, and around the Cape of Good Hope ; and that would be more dangerous than from the mouth of the Neva through the Baltic. But admit the possibility which excites this baseless fear. Suppose Russia could reach India, by sea or land, with a force equal to that which she sent to the Crimea in the desperate struggle with the four allied powers. Certainly this admission must be as large as any intelligent Englishman could ask us to make. Well, what would a Russian army of one hundred thousand encounter on the frontier of India? Why, an empire containing a population three or four times as large as that of the whole Russian realm ; an army outnumbering her own force by three to one ; seaports of great capacity, full of ships ; inland cities, in Scripture simile, " walled up to heaven ; " a new and vigorous English nation in Australia, that would hear by telegraph the first footstep of a Russian soldier on the Himalayas, or on their southern slopes. To see such a nation as England subject itself to the bondage of such a fear as this, to see her pour out blood and treasure like water under the fantasy of these suspicions, ought to affect us, as her posterity, as the nakedness of Noah affected his saddened sons. All but one short century in the last thousand years of England's history is our history and our glory. We know she is brave. The red seals of her valor, like threaded brilliants, encircle the globe. Never did a nation face and fight the actual giants that offered her battle with stouter courage. Never did a nation so shake with fear before the impalpable spectres of fancy.

If England would say to us, in answer to this opinion, " Physician, heal thyself," or, " Put yourself in my place," we ought and are able to reply, " We have done both. We have never been attacked by such a fear of our neighbors. Ever since we have been a nation we have not been afraid of you, nor you of us, as to any invasion of each other's territory planned in time of peace. We have divided this continent with you from sea to sea. For hundreds of miles not a river or mountain separates us. In some cases the boundary line may run between the kitchen and parlor of the same house. The St. Lawrence is a northern Mississippi, with its immense bayous mostly on our side, while its mouth is in your territory. Your American family is one with ours in speech, religion, and more intimate affinities. It would doubtless be a great advantage to them to cast in their lot with ours, and become a happy and influential part of one great continental nation. Perhaps you think so yourself; it is quite certain you believe we think so. Nor can you for a moment doubt our ability to make this territory part of our own, if we were so disposed. Then why do you not send an army of one hundred thousand men to defend your provinces against us? For this, and no other possible reason : you have an abiding confidence in our good faith and disposition. You believe us incapable of harboring such intentions as you impute to Russia, who has shown as little disposition to trespass upon your territory as we have ever done. What can be her motive and temptation to annex India across the Himalayas compared with ours to annex your American provinces, if it could be effected honorably to all parties? Then we would earnestly exhort you, for your best good, to concede to Russia a little of that confidence you repose in us. We can say this from our own experience; for we have proved her as a neighbor."

For twenty-five years, if no more, Russia has been a nearer neighbor to us than she could be to England in India, even if she were to-day at Constantinople. The treasures of California were as rich as any she could seize in India. When they were richest they were utterly defenceless. They were farther from our navy-yard at Brooklyn or Norfolk than is Calcutta from Portsmouth or London. Two Russian frigates, each with a thousand men, from the mouth of the Amoor, might have captured San Francisco and all our Pacific settlements. We all knew that, but we never put an additional sloop of war on the

Pacific for fear of such a Russian invasion. Why not? Because we believed her not only incapable of such an act, but also of such an intention. We had faith in her honorable disposition. We carried out in our thought that golden rule which should govern the deportment and disposition of nations towards each other : we believed that Russia would not do unto us what we would not do unto her. If we could inspire England with like faith in that nation and her nearer neighbors, it would work more for her peace and safety, and honor too, than all the coalitions she could organize.

TURKEY'S VALUE TO THE WORLD.

It is a phenomenon in the moral world, which never before and never elsewhere had a parallel, that the great Christian nations, that have poured out their blood and treasure in rivers for Turkey, feel and recognize most fully her utter worthlessness to civilized humanity and to herself. An English writer, a few weeks ago, who doubtless defended the Crimean war, and would urge his country to plunge into another for the same object, complains of the heavy bill of costs that falls upon the Christian nations of Western Europe to keep that Mohammedan power on its legs, or, rather, squatting on its Turkish mat, in time of peace. He says the annuity of sustentation that England, France, and other Christian countries pay for this purpose in loans has amounted to £10,000,000, or $50,000,000, for most of the years since the war with Russia. And this writer goes on, with an honest simplicity of wonderment, to inquire what has been done with the money; where and what are the railroads it has built in Turkey; what are the public roads, internal improvements, and useful and reproductive investments that can be shown for all this borrowed capital. There is Egypt, a little slice of a country, sandwiched between two deserts, and hasped to Turkish rule by the irons forged and fastened by Christian powers. She has borrowed money, too, on her own credit, which the sultan wanted and claimed for his own purposes. But she has the Suez Canal to show as one of her assets in favor of civilization. But what great public works has Turkey to show for all the money that she has borrowed in England, France, Holland, and Germany, since the Crimean war, which was to galvanize her into the activity and progress of civilized life? To this question of the English writer let us add one more important and urgent still, and on the same line of reflection.

It is natural and right that the capitalists of the present day, and the nations to whom they belong, and whose wealth they disburse in foreign loans, should begin to inquire what Turkey has done with the money they have lent her. It is natural and proper that they should begin to look a little anxiously to see how all this hard-earned money of Christian industries and commerce has been invested; what practical, tangible securities it has produced; in a word, what assets Turkey would leave available for them if she should sink into bankruptcy under her protested paper. They know the sultan would leave a lot of palaces, seraglios, harems, and many gewgawries of Oriental luxury and dissipation; but what solid works and values could be placed in the inventory as her securities? It is pretty certain and clear what the results of an examination of the books of that country would be before taking an inventory of the available properties left to its creditors. But if they find that all their lent gold was lavished upon the fantastic fripperies of the Ottoman dynasty, they will have this fact to remember : that their loans to Turkey were perfectly voluntary; that they made these loans with their eyes wide open to the character and habits of that government. If they are not satisfied as to the reproductive results of their *voluntary* loans, what has the civilized world to say as to the results of the *forced* loans that Turkey has levied upon it? For several centuries she has set herself down on the very bosom of the Old World, and stretched her limbs over the most ancient and sacred centres of its civilization and history — upon Jerusalem, Alexandria, and Athens, upon Tyre and Sidon, and Smyrna and Damascus, as well as Constantinople, and other cities and centres of more modern times. Just feel the pulse of the moral and political life of every country and city on which one of the fingers, not to say a foot, of Turkey rests ; then say and believe, if you can, that she is anything less or else than a huge nightmare, lying right athwart the very breast of the world, chilling and stopping the circulation of blood between its head and feet. Is not the time of reckoning nearly come? Is it too early, after these sad centuries, for the Christian nations to take an inventory of Turkey's assets to humanity? to demand the results of its forced loans of so many capitals of ancient civilization? to inquire searchingly what they were when she laid her paralyzing hand upon them, and what they are now, and what they can be, under her rule? Let them do this fairly and honestly, and then see if, in face of all this history, they can unite in a new coalition to squander more precious blood and treasure to perpetuate her power and domination.

Neither the English nor American mind is ignorant or insensible as to the character of Turkey, and to the history it has made in the world. This has been taught and illustrated in the school-books of both countries, especially in this. Fifty years ago our geographies represented, in rude but graphic wood-cuts, the only activities which have distinguished Turkey above the most barbarous nations. In these homely pictures she was seen busy at her first, her old, and only work. We children saw her sawing in sunder, breaking and mutilating, the Corinthian columns of Grecian temples, as if the choicest and costliest monuments of civilization in marble were as hateful and dangerous to her bloody fanaticism as the great library of Alexandria itself. And, what is strange above all other moral phenomena of modern times, the crusades of the middle ages have been transformed by the ruling spirit of the ruling policies of Christendom. Once its thinly-peopled lands poured forth their armed hosts to rescue Jerusalem and the holy places, so precious to their religious faith, from the clutches of Mahomet or of his possession and rule. Now, after six centuries more of the history of that rule, the greatest crusades these same Christian powers can organize are in defence and perpetuation of the system ; — as it were, to rebuild the tomb of Mahomet over the sepulchre of Christ, and a Turkish harem over the holy home of His immaculate mother. The Crimean war was one of these crusades, and the four powers that waged it numbered in their realms more souls than breathed in Europe in the time of Peter the Hermit. We are now threatened with another crusade for the same object. England, our self-blinded but noble mother, with more vitality of Christian life beating in her soul than in all the nations she summons to this crusade for the rescue of the Crescent — England is making ready to lead again ; to take the hard-earned bread from her children's mouths, and throw it, soaked in their blood, to the dogs of another war for Mahomet!

Why? What is Turkey to England, or England to Turkey, that she can rush foremost, and blindmost, into another crusade to prevent the Cross from superseding the Crescent at Constantinople — that old capital of Christianity? Our Webster's grand figure about England's morning drum beating a *reveille* around all the awakening continents is more than realized in her better missionaries of civilization, that sound the *reveille* of Christ's gospel in lands and tribes that never heard her war-drum. How strange and sad the fact! — that she should summon the Cross-bearing nations to an Armageddon, lest a Christian power should remove the dead corpse that lies athwart the very highway of Christian civilization which she has labored for centuries to cast up all round the globe! Of all the discordant noises that war ever made on earth, none could so jar and drown

the hopeful harmonies of human progress, or the consistencies of Christian policy, as the voice of England's
war-trumpet sounding the charge of the Crescent against
the Cross, lest this should regain its old capital and glory
in the East.

Since this American Republic first had a being and a
voice among the nations, no juncture in the Old World
has arisen at which that being and voice could more fitly
and effectually pay their debt to universal humanity, and
to God's temporal kingdom on earth, than at this turning
crisis of civilization involved in " The Eastern Question."
It is localizing and belittling this question to call it
Eastern. It is a question of the whole world, involving
the progress and interests of all mankind. In moral
proximity, it is the nearest question of the Old World to
us of this continent. In this sense we are fast becoming
an Eastern nation, more eastern than England can ever
be. Our Pacific shore and Asia's are being brought lip
to lip. Another decade will convey the intercourse and
speech of near neighbors between them. We have more
vital than material interests in this question. We have
reason and motive to claim a right of way for our civilization westward through Asia *via* Constantinople. We
have reason to urge, in behalf of humanity, that that old
Pharos tower of Christian enlightenment, that so long
held aloft its glorious lamp over the centre of the world,
and over its middle centuries of progress, shall no longer
stand, an extinguished lighthouse, to block and blacken
the high road of Christian civilization across the hemisphere, to which it was once, and should be again, such a
central and shining light. And we can wish and say all

this without wishing ill or evil to Turkey. We have just learned, and other nations are learning, to number all the inhabitants of the national domain into the grand totality of its peoplehood, and to give the rule to its majority. The Ottoman dynasty and rule may die; it must die; and then only can Turkey begin to live; then alone can its great majority, its true peoplehood, shake off its fetters, arise to its feet, and walk erect the broad pathway of the Christian nations. In raising down-trodden millions to their feet for such a march, we have stood and wrought nearer to the side of Russia than to any other nation in the last decade. We may well rejoice, if we cannot share, with her in the uplifting of the great majority of Turkey to the political footing of other Christian peoples. And we may as heartily rejoice for, if not with, England at this consummation. No other nation could derive more good from it than she. The best service we can do her is to induce and enable her to see this with her own eyes. There is a condition from which no coalition ever can or ever will release her. She might as well hope to arrest the force and law of gravitation by " a foreign policy," as to avert that condition. Russia is now, and ever will be, her nearest civil-ized neighbor in Asia. There is a vast space yet between them. But let us admit her fear and our hope, that this rough and savage interval shall be swallowed up in time; that Russia shall abut upon her northern line for its whole length. Would not the Russians be as good, peaceful, and profitable neighbors as the Afghans, or any other tribes of similar character? Would they not buy as many of her goods, and make as much lucrative commerce with her as these uncivilized and costly customers? Would not Turkey under Russian rule, under a development that should raise the dead cities, and centres of populations, buried alive under Mohammedanism, be worth to England ten times its present value?

It is time not only for England, but for America, to prepare for our mutual relations to Russia in the Oriental world. These three nations are to form an isosceles triangle which shall include most of Eastern Asia. Russia's line already extends from Riga, at the mouth of the Dwina, across both continents, to the mouth of the Amoor. England's line starts at an acute angle with Russia's in the north-west corner of India, and diverges eastward towards Southern China; and the world will not complain if it reaches the Pacific. The base of this triangle is the Pacific coast, including commercial China and Japan. The whole length of this base is now brought broadside on to our Pacific America. In all the years to come, we shall be nearer to that base than England, or even Russia. The ceaseless and increasing activities of our commerce, civilization, and Christianity must penetrate and permeate it with a new life. Then have we not a national as well as a human motive and reason to urge England to desist from her old antagonism to Russia? no longer to kick against the pricks of a Providence that is shaping the great ends of humanity, including her own? It is not armed coalitions she needs to form, but enlightened and large-minded copartnerships in spreading her own civilization over the world. Where can she look for partners for this great work in Asia? Is it not as clear as day that Russia and America are her only possible or practicable partners on that continent? Are they not partners with her there now by preoccupation? — and is not possession nine points in the law and motive force of that civilizing power which is to transform Asia? Would that our American mind could ascend to this high level of reflection, and then raise England's to the same stand-point; that they might look off together towards the morning of their great and common destiny and duty. They would soon see a light they never beheld before — a light that would reveal the darkness of those low-ground " foreign policies" which have cost the world so much blood and treasure.

THE COST OF SMALL NATIONALITIES.

THE hyperbole of popular comparisons or measurements may exaggerate contrasts, but they make them impressive. It is common to hear even a poor man say this or that " is worth its weight in gold," sometimes even when the this or that is his bright and active boy of fifteen years, and weighing a hundred pounds avoirdupois. This simile exaggerates the relative value of the two things compared, but the estimate expressed is clear and impressive. The same simile reversed may be applied even more truthfully to entities in the political world, which have been held at a higher price then they are worth to themselves or to mankind. By the simile reversed, I mean that there are several small nationalities in Europe which cost their weight in gold, though they are worth virtually nothing to themselves as political communities, and less than nothing to the great family of nations. And this vast cost of their worthless being is not borne by themselves, but by outside powers and peoples. Their present political existence is of no more value to their own subjects than each of seven kingdoms would be to its subjects if England were again resolved into the old Saxon heptarchy, or if France were reparcelled into as many independent states.

Let us glance at the status of these small nationalities as they appear in the scale of dignity. They are the " unprotected females" in the community of European nations. They themselves no more pretend to the ability of self-standing and self-defending powers than does a lone and defenceless woman sojourning or travelling among rude and stalwart men. Her very weakness is her safety. She feels and trusts it as such. She believes it will enlist some stout and gallant champion in her defence, should she be assaulted by a ruffian. This weakness may be safety, but it is not dignity. And this weakness is not the *raison d'être*, but the *pouvoir d'être*, of these small nationalities. And it is a wonder that enlightened patriotism can see in them a reason for independent existence. Their subjects are yet as patriotic as those of the Great Powers, and as intelligent, doubtless. But with all this patriotism, they must at times see and feel how the pygmy stature of their little state dwarfs their own political status. What is their opinion, what is their political entity worth, when weighed against that of the same number of Englishmen, French, Prussians, or Russians? What is the weight of their government's opinion or ability in a great " question " that moves Christendom?

Let us glance at the reason and value of these small states in the light of the freedom, the liberal institutions, and the general " rights of man," which they procure and maintain for their subjects or citizens. Take Ireland, for example. Could any form of independent nationality, under a constitutional monarchy, or a republic, raise an Irishman one political inch above an Englishman on the sister island, or in any quality or enjoyment of freedom to think, speak, move or act in " the pursuit of happiness " ? Would the " repeal of the union," or a republic, cheapen a single acre of land, or even transfer one to a new owner without pay to somebody? Ireland elects and sends to the Imperial Parliament more representatives *pro rata* of her population than she would be allowed to send to Washington were she united to the American Republic. If independent, would she send more or better representatives to Dublin? If she could and did, could and would they be more unanimous at Dublin than in London, or make better laws for the best good of her people, than they could if equally honest and united in the British Parliament? In a word, could any form of national independence give an Irishman in Ireland a single possibility of freedom in " the pursuit of happiness " which he cannot enjoy or reach, as a subject of the United Kingdom, on the same footing as an Englishman in England?

We might go around the whole circle of would-be independent nationalities, and apply the same questions to them. Crossing the diameter of this circle, what, may we ask, can the subjects of the two Danubian Principalities be, enjoy, or hope more than they could if they were part and parcel of the Austrian empire? What possibilities of progress, freedom, political dignity, and material prosperity can the motley populations of European Turkey attain under the Mohammedan rule of Constantinople, which they could not possess under the Russian sceptre at St. Petersburg? What liberties do the few millions of Sweden enjoy, or pretend to, which the population of Denmark do not possess and use? What is the *raison d'être?* Wherein does it pay, in political privilege or status, to keep up two independent nationalities for Spain and Portugal? To use a term more familiar to the American than perhaps to any other community, these old sovereignties do not pay, in dignity, strength, and freedom, for what they expend themselves to keep up their independent existence.

But, in some cases at least, where one of these small nationalities has paid out of its own pocket a shilling for its own deceptive and fruitless independence, the "Great Powers" around it have paid a pound sterling as their annuity on this life assurance policy. If any thoughtful reader thinks this an aggravated estimate, let him just glance at the causes of all the wars in Europe for the last two hundred years, at the "wars of succession," or wars to maintain a "balance of power." Let him analyze the composition of the English national debt, and see how much the nationality of Spain has cost the English people, and how they have been paid in ingratitude and indignity for their money and their blood. Why, a few days ago the English Chancellor of the Exchequer, in answer to a question in the House of Commons, stated

22

that England's bill of costs in the Crimean war was £80,000,000 in money, not counting the blood she poured out like water in the struggle. Now $400,000,000, besides the sacrifice of precious life, was a pretty large sum to sweat out of the incomes and industries of the English people in less than two years. It was a pretty large sum for them to pay for the sham *autonomy* of two Danubian provinces, or even for the existence of Turkey itself as an independent nationality. But this sum is small compared with the cost of Belgium to England. It involved a great expense to France and other outside nations to rive that small country from Holland, one of the freest and most solidly prosperous nations in Europe ; one of the first maritime countries in the world, of which Belgium formed a part, and from which she could have derived as much advantage as any section of the Netherlands. Well, from the time this new nationality was first set upon its feet, its " protection " has cost England more than it has Belgium itself. Although three or four other Great Powers signed the guarantee papers with her, she knows that not one of them attached more obligation to the compact than to the old vitiated treaty of Vienna : that not one of them feels bound to fight for Belgium, unless its own individual interests were involved. So England has virtually assumed the whole obligation and cost of defending that small nationality. From the date of the treaty, 1839, she has apprehended an attack upon the independence of her *protégée*, and she has felt bound to prepare to resist such an attack. For thirty years or more, the invasion of Belgium has been one of the frontrank probabilities for which she has provided in her armed peace establishments. It is a moderate estimate that these preparations for the defence of Belgium have cost England £5,000,000 a year for the last thirty years. She has just now voted £2,000,000 as an extra appropriation, to provide against the increased peril of the hour. But this sum is only a small instalment of the amount involved in her military armaments in behalf of Belgium. If no outside power touches that little kingdom with its little finger, this new danger will cost England £20,000,000. But think of what would come if either Prussia or France should attack Belgium. England has just released all the other parties that signed with her the Belgian guarantee ; she has engaged, single-handed, to enter into this tremendous struggle, and fight for France or against France for the independence of Belgium. Just think, for one moment, of the illimitable peril of blood and treasure involved in this obligation, whichever horn of the dilemma England shall be obligated to take. Suppose, at some desperate crisis of this conflict, Prussia should violate the territory of Belgium, and France should call upon England to fulfil the letter of her bond, and send her iron-clad fleet to the Baltic to shell the Prussian ports, bombard Berlin, and depose and capture Victoria's eldest daughter, and destroy Potsdam and all the royal palaces. Or pursue the alternative, and suppose that England should oblige herself, by this new bond, to join Prussia in the complete subjugation of France. In either case, when all that Belgium shall have cost England, from 1839 to the end of the chapter, shall have been computed, will not the total illustrate the cost of small nationalities?

IRELAND AS AN INDEPENDENT NATION.

I HAVE tried to prove that every Irishman in Ireland is an equal heir with every Englishman in England, and every Scotchman in Scotland, to all the estate of Great Britain's greatness and glory, past, present, and to come. Now, let an intelligent and patriotic Irishman compare this sentiment, or the reason for it, with his feeling after the first emotion of independence had subsided, and left him in calm reflection upon Ireland's new present and future. He must look first at her raw materials for a republic or a self-standing nation. What are her popular elements for such a government? He must remember what Ireland was when she stood alone, and see what she is now in oneness of sentiment and interest. And he will see that the antagonisms of religion and race, which the Union has hardly been able to curb, threaten to burst forth with new fury when the connection is dissolved ; that independent Ireland will have such a North and South as never existed in America.

But let us grant that these antagonisms may be conciliated under a republic. We pass on to the next step generally taken in erecting a nationality. Is Ireland to have an army and navy for its defence? If so, for defence against whom? Great Britain or Germany? Think of a standing army of one hundred thousand and fifty iron-clads for a poor young republic of five millions to maintain ! But our Irish friend may say, We will throw ourselves into the arms of France for protection. But this would be an economy like that of one of his humbler countrymen who told his neighbor that "he had to kill his pig to save its life;" meaning that his corn was exhausted. What kind of independence can a *protected* nation enjoy? What sentiment of dignity can such a foreign *protection* inspire? What could France do for Ireland as a protector that Great Britain does not and cannot do as a partner with her in their great and common empire?

But, says our Irish patriot, we will then cast in our lot with the American Republic. We will annex ourselves to her. She will defend us. She is rich and powerful; she has ships of war, enough and to spare. We will call our counties states; or we will divide up the island into congressional districts, and send over a member for each, and half a dozen senators to Washington, who shall speak out and vote on American matters as well as our own, just as our members now do on imperial matters in the British Parliament. This is a fair-looking programme, and reads pleasantly; but let us see how it would work. If it allowed you a state legislature in Dublin, that would have to legislate under the American Constitution. It could do no more for Ireland than the legislature at Albany does for the State of New York. It would have to accept the relations of each of our states to the federal government. It would be allowed a large scope of action, but would find itself under some restrictions. It could not enact and enforce *post-facto* laws to affect life or confiscate private property, even if such property were held only by right of possession. There are some other things that our several states cannot do, and which Ireland could not do if she became part and parcel of our Union. She could not enter into any political relations with France, Great Britain, or other countries, any more than Ohio. The American Constitution would cover every acre, and every man, woman, and child on the island, politically, economically, and financially. Even if England consented to the connection at first, the liability of trouble with her on account of it would augment our " peace establishment," and Ireland would be expected to pay her share of the general expense. Then what could we possibly do for her that Great Britain does not or is unwilling to do? Let us look at the advantage in this light. We could give no greater political right to her people than universal suffrage. That they have, or may have, now. We could not give them freer or cheaper use of the right of public meeting, or of freedom of opinion, speech, or of the press, than they now enjoy, or may enjoy. We could not give them more than one member of Congress at Washington to one hundred thousand of their population, because our home people would complain bitterly if the Irish were put on a more favored footing than themselves in this respect. Well, this ratio would give Ireland only about fifty members, or not half as many as she now has in the British House of Commons. We could not give her half the number of seats in our Senate that she now has in the House of Lords. We could not insure that the fifty members she sent to our Congress would be better men for her interests than the hundred and more she now sends to Parliament.

Then there is another contingency to the union of Ire-

land with the American Republic which both parties
would have to conform to. There is a page of restrictions and duties over against the list of advantages anticipated. Our Congress would feel bound to insure a
republican form of government in Ireland when she had
espoused it of her own free will. We should have to
do just what England has done in one respect for a
century and more. We could not allow old feuds and
religious antagonisms to break out into bloody riots or
revolutions. We could no more allow Ku-Klux burnings
and massacres in Ulster or Connaught than in South
Carolina or Georgia. If the Irish legislature at Dublin
did not and could not suppress such doings with a native
force, American soldiers would have to be sent over to
do the work. While covering Ireland with its protection,
the American Constitution would impose its obligations
upon her, as much as upon Maine or Texas. It could
not allow her to dispossess the present proprietors of their
landed estates by force or without equitable compensation.
If the connection worked in any degree for the prosperity
of the country, then it would inevitably *increase* the price
of land ; and, if wages increased in the same proportion,
the laborer could buy no more of it than he can now.
We, as a consolidated republic, could not do so much for
him in this respect as the British government is offering
and actually doing at this moment. We could not pass
an act to take money out of our national treasury to buy
up estates in Ireland, cut them up in small holdings, and
sell them to small farmers, who should own them outright
by paying six or even seven per cent. annually for twenty-
one or twenty-two years. We could not buy and lease lands

to them at that rate, even if the farms should continue to be national property at the expiration of that period. In a word, we could pass no such Land Bill at Washington as the British Parliament in London has enacted, even if there were a hundred Irish members to speak and vote in our Congress.

It would require a volume's space to balance the gains and losses involved in the secession of Ireland from Great Britain, and in its erection into a *protected* nationality, or a part of the American Republic. The few considerations adduced may suggest to thoughtful minds many more of equal weight. There is one, not yet referred to, which ought to commend itself to every patriotic Irishman. In seceding from Great Britain, Ireland must tear out all the brilliant threads she has contributed to the warp and woof of the history of the British empire — the most splendid textile ever woven out of human characters and events. A "repeal of the union" must sever Ireland from her part and lot in all this glorious past. She must relinquish it all to her two sister kingdoms of the other island, and start out in the world only with the poor capital of her own annals before the union. And what are they? Ask the best educated men in America to say offhand what Ireland was and did for herself and for the world when she stood alone ; what history she made worth a better record or appreciation than it has received. Look at the experience of other secessionists. Does the outside world credit to Belgium any part of the glory she contributed to Dutch history? Suppose our Southern States had succeeded in their attempt, and established themselves as an independent nation, with the help of England or

France. Would they have celebrated thereafter the Fourth of July? Would they not have severed themselves from all the American history that preceded and followed that event up to another Fourth of July of their own making?

There is another consideration which should weigh more still with the patriotic and intelligent Irishman. The union he has so long hated and denounced is already repealed. The England of Elizabeth, of the Charleses and Georges, is dead and buried beyond the reach of resurrection. A new England is arising, ready, and willing, and working to right all the wrongs of by-gone centuries. It is an England that in less than ten years will have and exercise a democratic force equal to the people power of any republic on earth; a force which, unlike ours, may be brought to bear upon the helm of the government in twenty-four hours after the telegraphic signal is given; a force that can change the pilot and the helmsman in a month or week, if need be, after they take the ship's wheel. This young, new democratic England has suffered bitterly and long from the same rule that oppressed Ireland in the past. It hates that rule and its memories as heartily as the Irish can do. But it has entered upon a new present with a great heart and eye of hope upon a near and glorious future. It is ready, willing, and working to put every Irishman in Ireland upon the same political footing, and in the same capacity of freedom in the pursuit of happiness as every Englishman in England or as every Scotchman in Scotland. If there still remains any difference to the disadvantage of the Irishman, say what it is, and you will find English and Scotch ready to rectify it. There are a few things which neither the Imperial Parliament in London nor a Republican Congress at Dublin or Washington can do. Neither nor all can change the Irish climate, nor transmute nor transpose metals or minerals. They cannot transfer the coal mines, and iron mines, copper, tin, and lead mines of England to Ireland. - They cannot transform the hereditary characteristics of the Irish people, nor extinguish the antagonisms of their religious faiths. We have never been able to extinguish these here, right under the sunlight of our best institutions, much less could we do it in Ireland.

These reflections lead to this conclusion : The best we can advise or wish the Irish people is to be content with what the English and Scotch are contented with, or are able to attain ; or to come to America, and be contented with what they can enjoy here. If there is now or shall hereafter be the slightest difference to his disadvantage, before the law, between an Irishman in Ireland and an Englishman in England, agitate until the two conditions are perfectly equalized. You will find plenty of noble-minded men in the two other kingdoms to help you in this or any other practical advantage to Ireland. But be *contented* there or here. A man cannot serve two masters. He cannot love two countries with equal loyalty. Patriotism, like conjugal love, cannot divide itself between two rivals. If American citizenship is worth to our Irish citizens all that draws them hither, then it is worth their undivided patriotism, as much as that of native Americans. We have a right to claim that patriotism from them. There is no land the sun shines on that has done more or paid more for the loyalty of a one-hearted people than America. And this we should have as fully as France or Germany, if our Irish citizens would, forsaking all other, keep themselves only unto this Republic so long as they both shall live.

In a word, it is high time that Irishmen in Ireland or other regions shall take to their hearts some country which they will serve, love, honor, and keep, in sickness and in health. They have two of the best countries and governments in the world to choose between. Either merits their best patriotism. If an Irishman prefers to be a republican in America to being a democrat in the new Ireland to be, if he chooses to be in political valuation the hundred thousandth part of a member of our Congress rather than to be the fifty thousandth part of a member of the House of Commons, let him come here. We have plenty of room in America for every Irishman in the world who wishes to be a republican. But, in the name of all loyal patriotism, let us have peace, let us have content in one country or the other. In the name of all that is pure and of good report in conjugal love and fidelity, away with these *morganatic* marriages in the political relations of subjects or citizens to the countries of their birth or adoption.

BIRTHPLACE OF THE REFORMATION.

TAKE it for what it was and is to the most vital life
of the Anglo-Saxon race, and of all peoples that have
wrestled up to the high levels of civil and religious liberty, there is no square foot of space in England, or in
Europe, upon which an Englishman or an American
should set his foot more reverentially than upon the iron-
hard, thin-worn floor of Wycliffe's pulpit in the old church
of Lutterworth. So we believed and felt when we made
that venture with a little of the deep veneration which
the place should inspire in a thoughtful man. We say,
inspire, which expresses a faculty that one does not often
ascribe to wood, stone, or any inanimate thing. A poet
of respected genius has versified " Sermons in Stones,"
which mean audible or intelligible speech. There are no
stones put one upon another in the walls of any English
or European church so full of instructive speech, and
inward and outward breathing, as these that enclose Wycliffe's oaken pulpit. If there be a point of space and a
point of time in conjunction where and when a devoutly-
read man in history might feel the impulse on him to take
off his shoes and stand softly on his naked feet upon a
given spot, it might well be in his first silent minute on
this thin floor, on which the first apostle of the English
tongue and of the Reformed faith of Christendom preached
the truth of the great Gospel as he saw and felt it five
hundred years ago. Stand reverently on these worn and
narrow boards, and listen with attentive faculties to the

preaching of these time-eaten walls. Some of their loosened stones have fallen inward upon the paved floor. But they preach their silent sermons as they lie crumbling in the half-demolished pews. Who has not read of Archimedes and his lever? of his bold boast that if he could make it long enough and find an outside fulcrum-point, he could raise the solid globe with it? Mind your standing, because the breath of centuries has thinned and weakened it. What Archimedes sought Wycliffe found just where you stand — a fulcrum-point and a lever that lifted a greater weight than the Grecian Samson of mathematics promised to raise. Here he found and worked a leverage that made the Vatican and the Papal cathedrals of Christendom rock and vibrate as if an earthquake were shaking their foundations.

How wonderful are these moral forces that move the world of mind, transform the life and structure of nations, and regenerate the cycles of human history! Here in this quiet, rural village in Leicestershire, in the midst of tree-bound and level farms, threaded and illumined by a branch stream of the gentle Avon, Wycliffe set in motion a force that moved the world; and while the world was moving on the ground-swell of mental emotion, little Lutterworth was perhaps as quiet and still as to-day. He has been called "the morning-star of the Reformation." But the light and warmth of stars do not equal or express the vitality which he infused into the great movement. His life was more than a light to it. It gave to it virtually its first pulse of action; and the beats of the onward movement, though sometimes slow and faint, were felt through the two centuries that intervened between him and Luther. This he did, and did it here in this rural village; he first put the Gospel of Jesus Christ into the homely, honest English tongue of the common people; for there were no English people nor Englsih language in Alfred's day; and a small portion of the English nation in Wycliffe's could read what Alfred wrote or speak what he spoke. The pope at Rome, and his legates, cardinals, and bishops in England, and all through Christendom, were not much moved with fear at Wycliffe's Latin disputations with the monks at Oxford. He might overmaster them in argument, without breaking or bending a beam in the great structure of their system. But when he took Christ's Gospel out of the iron coffin of the coldest of all dead tongues, in which they had shut it from the masses of Europe for centuries, and put it in the living vernacular of the English people, fearfulness surprised them, as if they saw the same handwriting on the walls of papal dominion that Belshazzar saw on his. No Reformation in England, or France, or Germany, could have been produced or begun while the New Testament was shut up in Latin. None knew this better than the Roman hierarchy; and they regarded it as the most pernicious and guilty high treason to their system for any one to put the pure and simple truths of the Gospel before the masses in their own native tongue. This Wycliffe did, and did it here in quiet little Lutterworth, whither he had been driven by a persecution that would have drunk his blood had it not been for stout John of Gaunt and a crown more jealous of the political than the spiritual domination or doctrines of the pope. Here he translated the New Testament verse by verse, feeling that in each he was putting out a lamp into the darkness which no tempest of papal persecution nor night-damps of ignorance could ever extinguish. A modern painting represents him here sending forth apostolic couples of converted monks with copies of his manuscript Gospels. Another equally impressive might be painted representing his copiers at work upon the text written with his own hand, showing two or three shaven polls clustering over the manuscripts; for some of his missionary monks doubtless transcribed those Gospel words which they carried forth to the people. What faith! what labor! to lighten a great land of darkness through a few gimlet-holes! to revolutionize a people's creed and customs with manuscript books! What a mighty belief uplifted his soul, that, put in those quaint, hearty words of the common people's speech, the Spirit of God would clothe them with tongues of fire! One of his Testaments must have spoken to Chaucer in this way, for he was one of Wycliffe's earliest converts. He was but two or three years the junior of the great Reformer, and was a special favorite at court and in aristocratic circles. He lacked the bold heart and strong convictions of his master. He ran well for a time, and bore much obliquy and persecution. But the strain was too great for his endurance. He succumbed, recanted, and betrayed his associates of the new faith, and in other defections made work for bitter and healthy repentance in later years, as his "Testament of Love" fully proves. It was only one of the truth-rays that radiated outward from Wycliffe's life that alighted upon Chaucer's opening mind. It lit up within him that light and glow of thought which made him as much the father of English poetry as his teacher was the father of the English Reformation. Wycliffe's Testament, very likely, was the first book that Chaucer ever saw written in the English language, as it existed after the Norman conquest; and had the poet not seen what expression and working power it gave to the words of the Gospel, he might have penned his immortal verse in Latin or Norman-French.

Who that has read the very hornbook of English history can stand in Wycliffe's pulpit, and look around upon the dilapidated walls of the old Lutterworth church without being stirred with these impressive reminiscences? Here he stood for years and put forth those brave utterances that made the principalities and powers of the papal empire writhe with rage. When their long arms of persecution had well nigh reached him, a stronger than theirs rescued him from their grasp. In the middle of a sermon which their persecution threatened to arrest, he fell dead in this his pulpit. He looked, and spoke, and breathed his last within these walls. Now, what house built with men's hands on the island of Great Britain should be held more sacred by the whole English-speaking race in both hemispheres than this old Lutterworth church, in which Wycliffe preached and died? In what English edifice should all the offspring states of the mother country feel a more precious and costly ownership? Why, Wycliffe was not only the father of the great Reformation, and of all it begot of religious and civil life, but his Bible was the mother of all English literature. He stands in the same relation to Shakespeare as Lutterworth, on one of the head streams of the Avon, stands to Stratford. The river of the bard at the place of his birth and burial does not drink more of the little Swift of the Leicestershire village, than did his genius drink from the fountain-head of Wycliffe's thoughts. How affecting is the incidental connection between the burial-place of the one and the birthplace of the other! A century and a half before Shakespeare was born, the ashes of the great Reformer, thrown into the stream at Lutterworth, and floating down the Avon, may have lodged their sacred sediment upon the green rim of the poet's river, which his baby feet pressed in his first walk in Stratford church-yard. Shakespeare has had his ter-centenary. Why should not Wycliffe have his quinque-centenary, in which the whole English-speaking race should join to commemorate what they owe to his great life's work for all that is precious and everlasting in civil and religious freedom and vitality? It is now just five hundred years since he sent forth the first copies of his English Gospels from Lutterworth. Nothing could be more graceful and appropriate than for those who value his memory to mark the anniversary with some useful and lasting token of their gratitude for his life. And no such token would be more appropriate or appreciated than the restoration of the church in which he preached and died. It is now sadly dilapidated. From the pulpit one may see fragments of wall and cornice lying at the broken feet of the pillars. The villagers are making a strenuous effort to raise the means for renovating and perpetuating the edifice. The people of our American Boston felt moved by a kind of proud as well as filial affection to contribute to the restoration of the grand old mother church of Eng-

23

land's Boston. We earnestly believe that thousands from Maine to California would contribute as gladly and as gratefully to the restoration of Wycliffe's church in Lutterworth, if they knew its state and need, and the pleasure with which their gifts would be received by those now about to put their hands to the work. Lutterworth is a small, secluded market-town, with no large sources of manufacturing or commercial wealth. Consequently a large share of the requisite sum must come from abroad. We earnestly hope that many American hands will join in the work of rebuilding the broken walls of this village church, consecrated by so many precious memories. The medium for the transmission of their free-will offerings may be easily and quickly instituted, and a new centre of interest established in the mother country for all who inherit and value the vigorous vitalities of Christian faith and civil freedom which it has begotten and bequeathed to the world.

THE THREE GRAND ARMIES OF CIVILI-ZATION.

An "Eastern Question," of a compass and issue the foremost men in the political and diplomatic world have not comprehended, is about to surprise and agitate the nations. The slow and almost imperceptible processes by which Divine Providence shapes their being, progress, and destiny, are now bringing them face to face with a fact that will astonish them. For nearly two thousand years the grand march of Christian civilization was westward. It is now changing front and movement; and its great armies are bearing down upon the vast continent of its birth in a triangular advance, already inclosing its whole arena. And, what is rather interesting, but not at all uncommon to these slow movements, the three armies are not only unconscious of the direction and issue of their movement, but are averse from both. Providence has made them involuntary allies; but they can no more loose themselves from the alliance than they can "loose the bands of Orion." Two of these hosts are as antagonistic to each other as possible, and threaten to fight each other on the way to the great victory for mankind for which the three have been chosen and put in the field. It is for this reason that the third should, at this stage of the movement, apprehend more fully and fairly the great result to be accomplished by the alliance.

It must be clear to all thoughtful minds that have

watched the tendencies of this movement for the last few years, that England, Russia, and America are the three great powers of the world selected, prepared, and put in unconscious and involuntary alliance for the reduction of the whole continent of Asia to the rule and *rôle* of Christian civilization. To two of these powers — England and Russia — this alliance is not only unrecognized, but very repugnant. It is for America, then, being free from this prejudice, to recognize this calling of Providence, and to induce her two allies to be " obedient to the heavenly vision " of this great duty to mankind. It is impossible for one or the other to withdraw from this alliance, or pause in the march. Why should one of them try or wish to do it? There is no possible alternative for one or two of the three. They cannot change places ; they cannot change partners ; they cannot change the direction of their march.

What other power in this world could be substituted for Russia in the northern half of Asia? Is it not as clear as day that the world must make the best of her as a civilizing power? Does she lack the possible capacity of doing her share of this great work? What is the work? Remember, it is not to enlighten Western Europe. It is not to add her lamp-light or star-light to the sun's, in those bright latitudes of civilization. It is to carry its growing illumination into the darkest lands of paganism, which she only can reach. Has she not done something already towards the enlightenment of millions of different race and tongue, who would have been in utter darkness to-day had it not been for her? Has she not walked with her small lamp, lighted at divine revelation, over steppes, mountains, and thinly peopled deserts of snow, from the Baltic to the Pacific, revealing to the benighted some of the fundamental facts and principles of the Christian religion? Why, one of her queens, Catharine II., put these central verities into more languages in her time than all the churches of England had done up to that date. These single or central truths must be impressed upon the minds of heathen populations before they can be raised to higher levels of Christian faith and life. And it is inevitable that Russia alone must do this work for the northern half of Asia.

Certainly, every mind well read in modern history, must concede that no nation in Christendom ever *suffered* so much for civilization as Russia. For several centu-'ries she barred with her lacerated and prostrate body the flood of Tartar barbarism which threatened to break over the whole of Western Europe. The intelligent and honest mind that can concede this fact, must also admit, that she has *done* as much for civilization as any nation in the world in the same space of time and with the same means. Every unprejudiced man, disposed to be fair and just in his mind towards her, must admit this as a fact. He must concede that she is the youngest nation in Europe; that she entered upon her political existence, as such, with a smaller capital of civilization than any other nation ever started with; that she was pushed up against the North Pole, and to this day owns no port open all the year round to the sea; that it has been the policy of suspicious and unfriendly powers to keep her as far as possible from contact with the great illuminating points of civilization; that she was obliged to construct her

nationality out of the ignorant, degraded, and heterogeneous populations between the Gulf of Bothnia and Bher-
ing's Straits. In a word, it is doubtful if Peter the Great
had as much of the working force of civilization to start
with, as the single town of Salem possessed, when he
founded St. Petersburgh. Now, it is not fair to expect
of her as much work for civilization as France or England has performed, each with the heritage of a thousand
years of enlightenment. It is not fair to demand proof
that she has done as much with the benighted and scattered
races of Northern Asia, as England has done with the
most civilized peoples south of the Himalayas. It is the
question of the future, of her progressive capacity to do
the part devolving on her as a copartner with England
and America.

To perform her part of this joint work for Asia, the
world must be willing to see Russia close down upon the
northern line of England in India. On this great triangular march, the right and left wings of the two armies
are deploying towards each other. They must, ere
long, meet, and they should meet in peace. Whatever
America can do to promote such a meeting, she owes it
to her own part and position to do. In the language of
the old stirring song, she " is marching on." She must
march, she will march, from the Asiatic coast of the
Pacific on and on westward into the heart of the continent, till she meets the two hosts of her allies marching
eastward, each on its line of the triangle. " There is no
discharge from the war" of civilization for one or the
other. They must march on, even if they fight by the
way with each other. Why should they turn their arms,

or hatred, or jealousy towards each other? Is it any more dangerous for England to have Russia her nearest neighbor in India, than it has been for Prussia or Sweden to have her in closer proximity to the centre of her power? In the long run, has she been a bad neighbor to them? Have they not enjoyed as much solid freedom, and made as much solid progress, as any other continental nations, while abutting upon her empire? Certainly we may say that she has been a good neighbor to us. She has been far nearer to us, *via* the Pacific, than she has been to England in India, *via* the Himalayas. There was a time when, with a single frigate from the mouth of the Amoor, she might have captured the whole of California and its gold mines.

It then behooves America to say to her two allies in the field, " Fall not out by the way. March on in parallel columns, and I will meet you midway with mine. I am planting all my civilizing forces on the Pacific coast of the continent. I am marching on westward to meet you. We are training thousands and tens of thousands of Chinese and Japanese to act as guides and interpreters of our institutions, our literature, religion, and political life. We are marching on with our school-houses, school-books, and school-teachers; with our railway engines, sewing-machines, and sowing, mowing, and reaping machines, with all the best interests of our mechanical and agricultural industry and progress. Here is Japan — an empire born in a day. She strikes her old glory to our irresistible civilization. She is the first great victory it has won. She offers herself as a new base for our march from conquering to conquer. Press on, and we will meet you;

and when the great conquest is accomplished, we allies will share its glory with all the rest of the wide world."

One can only touch the fringe of this great question, which will agitate the world, in the space of a few pages. The American mind cannot be made up and expressed too soon on the subject. Its opinion should be so clear, fair, dispassionate, and outspoken, as to produce a salutary impression on the two great nations with which we are allied on this great triangular march of civilization.